MOTHER

Tales of Love and Terror

Edited by

CHRISTI NOGLE & WILLOW BECKER

WEIRD LITTLE WORLDS

Mother: Tales of Love and Terror

Because I feel that, in the Heavens above,
The angels, whispering to each other,
Can find, among their burning terms of love,
None so devotional as that of Mother.

- Edgar Allen Poe

Contents

Mother Nurtures

Mother Protects

Mother Instructs

Mother Adores

Mother Remembers

Mother Remembers *(cont.)*

About

Concerning Mothers and Mothering: An Introduction

CHRISTI NOGLE AND WILLOW BECKER

Mothers are strange creatures.

They are beautiful, powerful, and terrible. They are fundamentally symbiotic, not existing until the moment that another life exists. They don't truly take on the maternal mantle until there is another being somewhere who wholly relies upon them for survival.

And yet, mothers are so much more than their children.

Despite the historical prevalence of minimizing a woman who has chosen motherhood as either a full-time or part-time occupation, often distilling her entire existence into a single word, we believe that mothers are as varied and exotic as any creature of the fantastical world. Whether human or animal, with good intent or selfish, mothers have the right to be uniquely and fully developed as any other protagonist or antagonist.

We sought stories that showed us new ways of mothering, new kinds of mothers, and complex maternal figures taking on breathtaking situations.

We were not disappointed.

What follows is the result of over 650 submissions and thousands of hours of work. We were surprised by the emotional impact of the stories we received, and considered each piece carefully. The culmination is this anthology featuring a world where mothers become heroes and villains and the concept of motherhood is examined and stretched to its ultimate limits.

Deliciously dark, each tale and poem forces us to examine the depth and breadth of what motherhood is and what mothers will do for their offspring. From the strange to the sublime, these stories give readers a peek behind the curtain of motherhood and give insight into what makes them so powerful, dangerous, and compelling.

Mother: Tales of Love and Terror weaves a rich and wide tapestry of dark fiction. From the weird and surreal to psychological horror, these 33 tales and poems highlight both established and emerging writers in the fields of dark fantasy, dark science fiction, and horror.

Still, while all of the works here contain horror elements, some engage more with themes and actions in a way that could disturb particular readers. Please refer to the list of content notes at the end of the book if you would like forewarning of this content.

Inspired by the organization of Bryson Richard's story, "The Motherless One," we have arranged these poems and tales into overarching concepts that we associate with motherhood. For good or ill, the mothers in these stories are doing their best to meet the needs of their offspring as well as their own, and, like all mothers, make many mistakes along the way.

But, of course, what would life be without mother-figures, imperfect and fallible as each of them are?

We want to thank our reading team for ensuring that each submission received our full attention. For final selections and editing assistance, we would also like to thank our editorial team of Christopher Degni, R. Leigh Hennig, Erick Mancilla, and Steph Nelson and the army of readers who put so much thought and care into reviewing and discussing these submissions with us.

And, of course, we are eternally grateful to all who promoted and backed the Kickstarter. This anthology would not exist without your love and nurturing.

Is it a perfect book? No. But we'd like to think of ourselves as the mothers of this strange and unsettling child. We have birthed it through sweat, tears, and hours of careful attention and love. And as every mother knows, once it has left our arms, there is not much we can do but pray that it does only the good (or evil) that we intended it to do.

So, we urge you: Read wisely.

Let our word-child show you the terrible beauty that lies in the heart of a mother. It may change you, if you let it.

Willow Dawn Becker and Christi Nogle, August 2022

MOTHER NURTURES

The Sire

STEVE RASNIC TEM

First trimester. Purely a guesstimate. Paula's pregnancy had hardly been normal.

She was a storm of anxieties and delights, always leaking tears. But it was early spring, and she'd found the ideal house for raising a baby: a Craftsman bungalow on a quiet street, a shade tree out front perfect for a tire swing, the rent mostly affordable.

A large, wooden M was mounted by the front door, ornately painted with rabbits and eggs, orchids, and cows. "They're fertility symbols, Ma'am," her future landlord said. "The last tenant did that. A good omen."

"Why would you say a good omen?"

He blinked. "Oh God, I'm sorry. My wife says I never think before speaking. I shouldn't assume, I mean you look perfectly *healthy*..."

"It's okay, I'm not mad," she said, absolving him. "Yes, I'm pregnant." She rested her hands on her bump.

"Let me guess. Our daughter had a baby last year. Five months?"

"Something like that." But it had only been three weeks since her strange one-night stand. She could still smell his cologne: magnolias and champagne, and something underground. Last week she'd seen her doctor for stomach pains; he said she was four months pregnant. *Impossible!* He urged her to return for a follow-up, and commented on the pale diagonal scar across her belly. But she'd never seen it before.

He guided her inside. "It's all on one floor, no stairs to climb. The original oak and mahogany, rare these days. A bedroom for you, and a smaller bedroom for the child. Unless you're having twins, or triplets." She didn't answer. "Nice big kitchen and front room. If you need help with anything, just ask."

"Thank you so much." The last thing she wanted was her landlord dropping by.

He went on and on, and she let him, though she was already sold. She wrote a check for the first month's rent and deposit. He was a nice man, if a little nosy. She was relieved he didn't ask about the baby's father.

❦

Paula had gone to the hotel that night because they held a dance every Friday and women got in free. She hadn't dated in a year. She worked long shifts in a warehouse, spending little and saving money for college.

She'd had too much to drink, and it was the end of the night. He was tall, dark, and thin, and she couldn't quite see his face, not even when he bent over and said hello. Not even when he held her close, smothered in his fruity cologne. She couldn't remember him speaking, but she believed him to be devastatingly handsome. Later, upstairs, he showed his face as he was removing her clothes, but she couldn't remember it. He understood exactly what to do, but then he did *that*, and even though she couldn't remember what *that* was, she knew it was something no one in their right mind would want. She woke up alone. The room had been taken apart and stained maroon. She hurried past the housekeeping cart in the hall, embarrassed.

It took a day to move in. She had few possessions, but a wealth of baby supplies—diapers and furniture and the right foods, medical supplies, and every book she could find on pregnancy.

She remembered Mother saying, "Women have been having babies at home forever." She'd read the books and watched countless videos online. She wasn't a genius, but she was a fast learner. She'd felt from the begin-

2

ning having this baby alone, where no one could see, was the right thing to do. If she got into trouble, she would call someone.

Her body ached and skin hurt. She kept getting bigger, but she couldn't feel the baby inside. Maybe she was something worse than pregnant. The littlest things—a crack in a mug, scrambled eggs looking ugly—set off a frenzy of weeping. Her breasts were tender and swollen. She had heartburn. She was often constipated but still too late getting to the bathroom.

One afternoon Paula discovered a gray rabbit in the backyard, sunning himself on a bench surrounded by beautiful trees. She decided to keep him as a companion. She knew nothing of rabbits, but figured if she fed him, he would stick around. After a day she brought him inside, because if he ran away, she'd be inconsolable.

Paula didn't know how to housebreak a rabbit and spent a lot of time cleaning up his messes but thought it good training for raising a child. Once she picked up a piece of vegetable he dropped—too chewed to determine what kind—and she ate it. She and the rabbit snarled at each other. It was the best whatever vegetable she'd ever eaten, and a healthier meal than all the mac and cheese and macaroons dipped in mayonnaise she'd been munching.

One day several lumps appeared on her belly, small as mosquito bites at first, but growing into masses the size of kittens. After a week they vanished, but eventually she realized they'd burrowed deeply inside.

She was having daily talks with the rabbit. He appeared distracted, but at least he listened. "Mister Rabbit, I'm afraid I'm going to have a miscarriage. This pregnancy is like nothing in my books. I'm no martyr, but maybe I deserve this. I know nothing about the dad, and I'm not sure I want this child." The rabbit stood up on his hind legs and stared at her. Paula found this mildly encouraging. "Thanks for being a good friend." She paused. "I always wanted my life to be my own, and now I know it never will be."

Second trimester. Strictly metaphorical, of course. Great gobs of her auburn hair littered the floor, clogging the drains. She'd read hormonal changes could cause this, but she hadn't expected so many bald patches.

Her belly was a taut balloon. She could feel all those lumps inside moving. Was she having more than one? They were naughty babies wandering where they weren't allowed to go.

"It's too soon for it, or them, to be moving, isn't it?" she asked Mister Rabbit. He lay on his back and displayed his belly in sympathy. "I'm way too big, and it's only been three months."

After another few days she began having Braxton Hicks contractions. She wasn't far enough along for those. Patches of color emerged on her skin, but not the brown ones the books talked about. Her belly blushed with the brightest Easter egg colors. She was supposed to be making joyful preparations, reading about breastfeeding, but she felt no joy, only fear. Mister Rabbit started running away when he saw her approaching. Even her best friend found her too much to bear.

Third trimester. It had no relevance to what she was experiencing, but she marked it on the calendar anyway. The contractions were much stronger, waking her up in the middle of the night. She had dreams of the father coming back to the hotel room where she and her babies snuggled in bed. She still couldn't see his face. He gathered her and the kids in a sheet, carried them to the balcony, and threw them out. She woke up trying to snatch her babies out of the air.

She recalled the sex talk Mother gave when she was twelve, about the "ordinary miracle" of childbirth. If Paula's mother were alive, would she still be so confident, or would she, too, be terrified?

Paula believed she might deliver at any moment. A lot more movement. A great deal more pain. Everything was dangerously ahead of its time. She had such a powerful sense of *internal* gravity, a heaviness she could not get rid of. She felt mutated. It took everything she had just to crawl out of bed.

Her babies weren't ready. But they had to come out.

Birth. So many of them.

The magnitude of her misery was beyond anything she'd imagined. It was a vivisection, a mutilation. Somehow, she'd gotten herself into the kitchen and was lying on the fake marble tile. They came out in the middle of a contraction, one so convulsive and painful she blacked out. When she awakened, she was covered in yellow and magenta goop. She thought she must be hemorrhaging. She felt one—no, two, no, *several*—tearing at her breasts. She wanted to be nurturing, but they were going to kill her. Too many frenetic mouths. Paula recalled when she was a kid and her dog Angel had ten puppies, but Angel had ten nipples to feed them.

Mashed together, wriggling like a pile of giant maggots. She couldn't tell many details, or where one left off and the others began. But as they started to separate, each eager to seize some part of her, she could see how sickly they were, pale skin thin as paper, scrawny arms and legs and long narrow claws scratching, drawing blood. One opened its eyes. It had *her* eyes. Another opened its mouth, and she couldn't quite understand what she saw, but there were teeth continuing all the way down its throat like a lamprey eel. She suddenly remembered seeing that mouth before. It had its father's mouth.

They weren't getting the milk they needed and abandoned her breasts in search of other nourishment. At some point she would have to get up and evaluate her wounds, assuming she could manage to stand.

Of course, these weren't normal babies. Their human heads were smaller, their bodies thin and malnourished looking. Their jerky movements reminded her of baby birds. Like birds and reptiles, they only had one little hole, *Cloaca,* where their genitals were supposed to be, the rest of their nether regions smooth as Barbies.' They used those holes generously, the poop and pee running constantly down their scrawny legs and all over her kitchen.

Yet she had no trouble seeing herself in them. Their enormous, human eyes were full of enough tears and longing to break her heart. They had little noses above their mysterious mouths, not beaks, and little pointy chins. Maybe no one else would ever find them endearing, but she certainly did.

She counted at least thirty, but there might have been more. They moved so quickly—running, or crawl/walking, in and out of rooms—an accurate count was difficult. She saw no way to distinguish males from females.

Mister Rabbit retreated to the top of the kitchen cabinets. He didn't look exactly afraid, bunny faces being not particularly expressive, but he was watchful. Three of her babies climbed the cabinets trying to reach him but their arms were too short. They opened and shut their mouths repeatedly, teeth clicking loudly. She decided then there would be no more attempts at breastfeeding.

The next few weeks were spent walking around with babies hanging all over her. They still bit her now and then. The wounds were ugly and painful, but they healed.

How could she be a good mother to this clamorous brood? Mewling, whining, ferocious kiddies. They were hungry all the time, and they needed *her* all the time. She couldn't shower or bathe because they might drown. She was beyond sleep deprived. She struggled to corral them. She couldn't hold them all at the same time, and the ones left out raged. They ran away and she might not see them again for hours.

She tried to produce some names. She began with Frank, the largest, the calm and thoughtful-looking one, then Jane, George, and Susan, but still not knowing if they were male or female, continuing with Peter, Flopsy, Mopsy, and Cottontail, then began naming them after foods— Macaroni, Peanut Butter, and Pizza Boy—and the smallest Bitter, Sweet, and Sour, but it rapidly became futile. She was sure of only a handful.

Some, Frank, and Pizza Boy especially, were quite affectionate, climbing into her lap when she was depressed. Many of the others came when hungry, hurt, or scared.

Her birth wounds healed quickly, like that long diagonal scar which she now thought had something to do with her impregnation. But her abdomen was misshapen. Women complained their husbands didn't find their post-pregnancy bodies attractive. Well, screw those myopic men. Those bodies were where their children came from.

It would have been nice to take her children to the doctor for a wellness visit, but that wasn't an option. One look and her babies would be taken away.

A few of the kids liked to bite each other, and they bullied the weaker ones, but so far none had been hurt too badly. She pulled them apart before too much damage was done. She made giant batches of formula mixed with bits of bread and potato which they lapped from bowls like kittens. Her biggest worry was running out of money. She had no idea what she'd do then.

They grew rapidly but were still relatively small. She was scared a few of them working together could topple her. After another few weeks they developed an appetite for tougher foods, raw carrots, and meat. The change in diet settled them down. They became content just to cuddle. She could read them bedtime stories, all her kids perched on and around her like one of those southwest Native American storyteller dolls.

Despite her concerns about the landlord, he hadn't been by since he gave her the keys. No one else knew where she lived except the delivery drivers, who left orders on the porch. The knock on the door was a huge surprise.

It was a windy day, and the kids were on edge, fighting each other and clinging to her, leery of the shadows sweeping the windows and tapping against the glass. She told them about trees, and promised if they were good, one day she would show them the beautiful trees in their back yard. She had no idea if they understood, or how much language they could grasp at this stage, but she had to try.

Initially she thought windblown branches were the reason for the persistent knocking, but then the beating became more forceful, shaking the door.

Whoever it was would have to wait. She climbed out of her chair, babies complaining, falling, landing on the floor, squealing. Some of them took it as a game and tried to climb back up. She had to waddle, as babies hung on to her ankles, gripped her knees and thighs. Whoever it was continued to bang on the door, and she shouted, "Wait!"

The door swung open and slammed into the wall. The shadowy figure beyond leaned into the doorway, having to duck to get through. She fell to the floor and couldn't get up again. From her angle he appeared unnaturally thin, dangerously sharp within his voluminous black coat, then as he turned, he broadened into something monstrous, his overcoat momentarily morphing into enormous wings above multiple, reptilian arms. Abruptly Paula could taste magnolia blossoms floating in champagne, and she knew who he was.

Her sweet and curious child Frank toddled calmly up to his dad. The creature bent over, his face an indecipherable blur of motion and disintegration. A long scythe of arm swept down and gathered Frank up, and his father swallowed him whole.

"Why did you do that?" she asked faintly, instead of screaming. It was a strange thing to say, but she was struggling to put together what had just occurred. "Why!" she shouted this time, and it shattered her to feel so helpless. Yet she continued to sit there, mesmerized, watching.

The father paid no attention, crouched now, sweeping children into his arms, stuffing them into the folds of his massive coat, where they disappeared, a few chubby hands and arms appearing outside its bounds. Some of their children laughed, thinking this a game.

He took half the children, picking them up, examining them, tossing some back her way, who she hung on to desperately in case he changed his mind. *He's taking his share*, she thought.

Then without a word (Had he ever actually spoken? She didn't know.) he rose and swung around, his coat flaring out momentarily so she could see all the children inside, hanging from their feet like rabbits ready for the hunter's knife.

"Wait! What are you going to do with them?" But she knew. She ran after him with all her clinging kids, although one or two might have fallen off, she couldn't be sure. The door slammed shut behind her as she chased him through the yard.

Paula screamed, and made a desperate dive, grabbing the back of his coat and bringing him down in giddy triumph before he could reach the street.

In retaliation he stole the children still clinging to her, adding them to the collection inside his coat.

She scrambled around searching for them, frantically tearing open his coat and beating on his hard, slick shell, but now his coat appeared empty, her kids passed on to somewhere else.

Suddenly she was on the ground again, and he was on top. She was certain he would do to her the same as he'd done before, that brute act of animal husbandry, and she'd rather die.

But he only gazed at her, as deep within the obscurity of his face the lights of his malicious intelligence gleamed. *There are many things you cannot change. This is one of them.* Those words, mysteriously conveyed, possessed a semblance of pity.

But not so merciful as he abandoned her there in the wind and the dark grass alone with her memories: a child struggling to comprehend the dead cat in her lap, or the tortured illness which took her grandparents away. "They're only sleeping," Father lied. It was left to Mother to set her straight.

But children push death away because they know it can't happen to them, and then a neighbor dies, a cousin, a boy she barely knew at school, a teacher, a best friend.

She recalled the drowning which swept her brother away, leaving her parents awash in unending grief, the unwelcome surprise of a familiar name in the obituaries, the news of loved ones dead in distant cities, followed by the swift losses of her father and then her mother, and someday it would be her gone to dirt and ash and then whatever children down through an eternity of mourning, a sacrifice of flesh and pain given up to the insatiable appetite of nature as mothers delivered both life and death into the world.

The landlord pulled up in front of the bungalow on a late summer day with a for rent sign he hoped he wouldn't have to use. His tenant had missed two months' rent. He'd sent a polite reminder with no response. He knew she was a new single mother, or almost. This was a welfare check as much as anything else. His wife said he should call the police, but he wanted to do this himself. He should have checked earlier. People fell through the cracks, and it was a terrible thing.

The yard needed mowing. He should have called someone or done it himself. He never expected her to do yard work, not in her condition.

The mailbox overflowed with junk. The single personal piece was his letter asking for the rent. This spoke of someone with few or no friends. He knocked on the door, waited, knocked again. He knocked steadily for a minute or two. He didn't want to bang on the door; it might scare her.

A layer of dust and grit covered the front porch, along with broken branches, drifts of leaves. He'd had tenants abandon properties when they couldn't afford to pay. He peeked through the front window. He didn't believe this was the case here. From what he could tell the front room looked pristine.

He knocked one last time, then unlocked the door. He opened it a few inches and called. "Paula? It's your landlord. I hope everything's okay. I'm coming in."

The house was clean and tidy, but no one answered, and he couldn't find anyone in any of the rooms. The refrigerator was mostly empty, but there was milk, a covered plate full of mashed potatoes, some condiments, some pickles. A bowl at the center of the kitchen table was full of fresh fruit. Nothing looked spoiled. Someone must be living here.

He found them in the backyard. "Paula?" She didn't answer. She lay on the bench among the beautiful trees, staring at him with such sadness, such solemnity. He'd seen that look before in people after some terrible event. It was the weight of knowing.

There was a flower in her auburn hair. A rabbit sat beside her on its haunches, head up and alert. The rabbit did not flee but appeared to be watching him with vigilance.

A naked boy sat on the ground nearby, his legs folded beneath him. He had red hair like Paula's, so perhaps they were related. Maybe a cousin. He was ten or so. He was thin and gangly and a little goofy looking, as boys that age tend to be.

The landlord realized then that Paula no longer appeared pregnant. If anything, she'd lost weight. So, she'd miscarried, and that explained the way she looked, and why he had not heard from her. It was a terrible thing.

He wished his wife were here. She would know what to do, and exactly what to say.

The boy had the most beautiful, wide-set eyes. He was quite friendly, smiling and nodding at all the landlord's questions, but he would not open his mouth and speak.

Last Leaf of an Ursine Tree

HAILEY PIPER

Elle knows Mother's time of the month is near when she looks out the bedroom window and sees the bear appear in the driveway. About the car's size, she is a beast of brown shaggy fur, tremendous snout, and scraping claws.

"Of course it'd happen today," Mother says, shoving bags into the back seat. She glances from car to window and snaps impatient fingers at Elle. "The bear will have to follow behind. We can't be here when the landlady's back. If she's on her time—you don't want to see. She's got a big tyrant bear, the prehistoric kind. Don't just stare at me, move!"

Elle hurries clothing into her worn pink backpack and clutches Leaf, her green stegosaur stuffy, named for the shape of his spinal plates and missing a plastic eye. Residue of her life dots the room in crayons, papers, and garbage. The landlady will know they came back while she was in Florida, squatting in an empty house without paying the rent. She might change the locks this time.

When Elle steps outside, Mother's bear takes the back of her overalls by the teeth and carries her toward the car.

"Didn't I say move?" Mother snaps. Her hair frays in dizzying swirls. "Want me to give you what your brothers got?"

Elle shakes her head, hugs Leaf, and lets Mother's bear shove her into the car's passenger seat. She watches the tiny house sink into trees' shadows as Mother reverses out the driveway. Her bear follows as if birthed from that place, a forest of monsters.

Except even leaving gives no escape. The monster's slobber soaks down Elle's spine.

✾

Monthly cycles didn't always bring bears. Elle's schooling is dodgy, but she can tell from what she's gleaned in scattered history lessons that bears used to be wilderness creatures, circus servants, sometimes meat. She doesn't know when things changed, or how, or why.

But she's known Mother's bear all her life. And other bears, too.

Once Mother parks the car amid downtown's brick and concrete, her bear follows, and passersby take notice.

"Wonder if it's the little girl's," an elderly woman in a blazer says to her phone. "I remember when mine came the first time. Still miss him some days."

Mother snaps her fingers—Elle is staring again. Her bad habit. Easier to forget a growling stomach when lost in someone else's life.

"We'll eat tonight, I promise," Mother says. "Need to stretch the cash a little until I get paid."

She orders Elle to follow into a downtown corner store, sit behind the counter with her coloring book, and remain silent through Mother's shift. Elle obeys, laying Leaf against her chest as she scrawls orange and blue crayons over Disney princesses, but she watches and listens to the store's comings and goings.

Kids her age run circles around an older woman, but she has no bear to terrify them into silence. A goateed guy leads a bear inside, grabs deodorant, and leaves. Mother says men don't have bears or cycles, but Elle knows some do. She learns a lot by staring. Teenagers giggle over Mother's bear as the above-door bells jangle their entrance. Older than Elle, but they act like the human body is a mystery or taboo.

"Babe, you're coming to my place tonight, right?" one of them asks another. "Should get some party tricks."

14

"Bridget," a light voice says with a groan. "It's my time."

"Really?" the first voice asks, louder than necessary. "I don't see your bear."

"I know, but it's coming. I feel it."

Elle wonders if she'll feel it soon, too. And if not soon, when? Twelve years old, her first blood, her own bear—signs she waits for sometimes when staring. Someday she'll see a person-free bear and know it's hers.

A longing sharpened whenever Mother threatens Elle with what her brothers got.

⚜

Mother shoves their bags into the front seat and bundles them each under blankets in the back as night brings a chill to downtown. The bear sleeps beside the car, sharing ursine warmth, but she's also a giveaway that people are living out of this car. Marauding cops will send one of their own on cycle, and then a badge-approved bear will balance out any confrontation.

Or they'll wait for Mother's cycle to end, when her bear again vanishes into shadows.

Elle wakes to Mother's cursing. A blue-uniformed figure withdraws from the windshield, having pinched a cream-colored ticket beneath one wiper before the nearby bear could rouse.

"Damn busybodies," Mother says.

She rearranges the bags and starts the car, muttering to herself about how she misses New Orleans. An oft-repeated sentiment, how once upon a time she was comfortable and ate well. Her nostalgia stretches to cover secret wounds, but Elle can't blame Mother for it. A better time and place than where they've come from.

Better than what Mother's become.

She moves the car each night, but sometimes parking feels almost as expensive as rent, and food isn't cheap. They are never starving, but their bellies are never full, either, and Mother tries to balance hunger and patience, but eventually hunger wins. Elle can tell money is scarce by counting Mother's curse words.

She can likewise count her age climbing by the week, by the year.

15

Someday, she'll feel what Mother calls *that first hot knife in your gut*. Elle isn't sure if she'll see the bear beforehand, a friendly omen, or if pain will sneak up on her.

But she knows her body is bones and dirt. Mother can hardly feed either of them. If one-eyed Leaf the stegosaur were edible, Mother would cook up a spiny-tailed dinosaur stew. When Elle's bear appears at her first blood, it will be a creature of bones and dirt like her. Too weak for commands.

Too weak to fight Mother's bear if she decides to give Elle what her brothers got.

"It was necessary," Mother said once. "There's strength in bloodshed. Something has to die so someone else can be born. You're only here because they're gone. Be grateful."

Elle was then expected to thank her mother. So she did.

❦

Mother's bear is gone when she drives them out of the city, back to the house in the woods.

"Landlady's got to be in Florida again by now," Mother says. "We'll get a couple months' peace before she next checks in."

Elle hardly understands how she mistook this place to be a forest of monsters when they last left. Only in returning from weeks downtown can she appreciate the unspoken perfection of the tiny house, near invisible from the road, tucked between rows of fluffy-leafed trees down a narrow stone path. It is cozy and green and good.

But night will come. It always does.

Mother is off her cycle, the bear gone, so why does Elle hear prowling outside her bedroom window? Why does a shadow cross the line of light beneath her bedroom door?

The hunger has grown. Mother has failed to feed the bear, or the bear has failed to feed Mother. Elle has no idea which carries responsibility there, but they share a need for food. When the bear returns, will Mother stop those jaws and claws?

Or will she let someone die?

The bedroom door moans as something large and powerful presses in from the hallway. Elle scarcely has time to wake up and understand what's happening, let the chilling immediacy of it infect her bones, before a dull grunt ripples through the wood.

Mother's bear is in the house.

Mother's bear is breaking down the bedroom door.

Mother's bear is hungry.

Elle leaps out of bed and forces up the window, about to squirm through. A flash of grim premonition sees her caught halfway in and out, the sill snagged against her bony hips. She instead scurries under the bed, where her breath sends dust bunnies quivering.

Leaf lies abandoned at the bedroom's center. No time to go back for him.

The door crashes open on squealy hinges, and a cloud of hot breath surges across the room. Floorboards cry beneath massive paws. The bear's moonlit bulk knocks the bed firm against the wall, and its screech forces Elle to cover her mouth against a sympathetic scream.

Forepaws stop at the window, where a slobbery muzzle presses through the gap above the sill. The bear can't fit, but she's distracted now, thinking her prey has slipped outside.

Elle has to do better than let the bear think this, better than staring. Time to run. She crawls from under the bed, through darkness, toward the outline of her bedroom doorway. Her crawling is gentle on the floorboards. Nearly gone.

Moonlight glints off Leaf's remaining plastic eye. He is so close, Elle can stretch into the depths of the room beneath the bear's hind legs and grab the soft stegosaur by the tail. The rescue will take seconds.

Elle holds her breath and reaches out. Fingertips brush wood, a dust clump—there, stuffed cloth. She wraps her hand around and yanks Leaf close.

His eye clacks against the floor.

The bear shudders in surprise and then tears her head from the window. The moon glints white in her slobber, and a savage moan seeps from her body as she twists to face the bedroom doorway. Never would Elle have thought this monster could be so graceful.

She crushes Leaf to her chest and flings herself out of the room. Behind her, the world quakes in muscle against doorframe, claw against floor. The bear is coming, and she's faster and stronger than any little girl in the world.

Elle dashes screaming into Mother's bedroom. It smells of ancient perfumes and bad dreams.

The atmosphere cracks with a finger snap as Mother startles awake and orders everyone to knock it off. The bear freezes in the hall. She will never disobey Mother; that is not the way of blood-called bears.

Elle can't be so silent and still. She shrinks to the floor, and her tears soak Leaf's flank where she squeezes him against her face. Mother snaps her fingers again, and again, but no impatience can fight this panic.

"Give me a break, Elle," Mother says, pleading. "She'd never hurt you. I love you. Enough."

Elle swallows a sob. After all Mother's threats, how can she say that? Baffling that she might even mean it, only hurting Elle's brothers out of necessity.

But they're dead all the same. Elle might be dead someday, too. Should she be grateful?

Mother can't hide her needs. A mother bear must feed to make more bears. Something has to die so someone can be born, and Mother is hungry like Elle.

Between hunger and love, eventually hunger wins.

Daylight comes, a chance to catch up on rest, but Elle is afraid to sleep. The bear prowls outside the shut glass, the wooden walls, somewhere in the shadows of the trees, maybe peaceful, maybe waiting for Elle to quit watching. Quit thinking.

There's no winning a fight against that monster, but could Elle win against Mother? She doubts it. Child against parent might as well be child against beast, and Mother is a bear in her own right.

Elle glances out the window, where Mother's car sits lonely in the driveway. If only she'd catch word somehow that the landlady will soon return from Florida, on her cycle and with her big tyrant bear in tow, that would bring salvation. Elle and Mother would have to flee this house and sleep together in the car downtown. No chance for nocturnal bear attacks.

Unless Mother chooses one.

The fantasy dissolves under Elle's stare. No one is coming. Couldn't someone leave then? Elle should pack her things into her ratty pink backpack and sneak herself and Leaf out the window. Without a bear rattling her nerves, she might fit. Might even escape.

But where would she go? In the house, she misses downtown. Downtown, she misses the house. Mother has her memories of New Orleans to crawl into at night, a time when she was comfortable and ate well. Even her bear remembers.

Elle has no better days to hide inside. Her life has always been one house or another, squatting or renting, living out of the car in between, her constants being Mother and her bear. Elle scarcely has a past.

She may not even have a future.

⊗⊱⊗

Nighttime stabs a hot knife into Elle's gut. Sleep-stickied lips tear open to scream as Elle envisions a bear claw driven into her gut, eyes flashing open to slobbery jaws and soulless hunger.

But her bedroom lies empty. Only Leaf joins her on the bed while shadows cling to the walls.

Blood seeps between her legs and dots her pajamas.

Shouldn't there have been some warning? Where is her bear? Is she so malnourished she can't even call the most meager of bears to her? She gets up to wake Mother, who might help in the bathroom for cleanup and a pad, but heavy breath says she isn't alone in the bedroom.

He rises from the dark, tall and gaunt. His jaws feel immense, his claws terrible. He is Elle's bear. Finally.

And yet for all his bear nature, he is bones and dirt compared to the prowling beast outside. Stronger than Elle, and maybe Mother, but not mightier than her bear.

Elle runs fingers through his soft coat and inhales the newness of him. She could command him to fight Mother's bear, even though he'd lose. They could creep out of the house, and she could ride him elsewhere, maybe all the way to New Orleans, however far that is.

She could have him eat Mother when her period ends. That would stop everything. No more Mother, no more cycle, no more brother-eating bear turning an ursine appetite toward a daughter. But would Elle's cycle match Mother's, binding them?

Too many rogue possibilities swirl in Elle's head. Were she to threaten Mother and fail, Mother might have her bear devour Elle before she finds another chance.

Elle has control of herself and her bear, nothing else.

She places Leaf on the floor, pats his one-eyed head, and then kneels beneath her bear. She gives him a long stare, scrutinizing and memorizing his sharp teeth, wet dog-like nose, and glittering black eyes.

"You have to do what I say?" Elle asks. "Anything?"

The bear watches her and gives a halted groan.

"Okay then." Elle tells him what she wants.

His ears twitch. He's hesitant, showing it in the hair and muscles bristling up his spine. He might think waiting will change Elle's mind.

But she's had practice at staring, and the longer she drives her command into him, the more he's compelled to obey. Her first blood has come. She is a bringer and commander, and he is her bear.

"Do it," Elle says, and then she repeats her command.

The bear closes his teeth around her skull. They descend by inches, as if he thinks his throat's engulfing darkness might change her mind if he takes it slow. She says nothing, lets the bear's jaws fold around her head, the teeth puncture scalp and cheek, and at last the bear hurries to bite down, crush her skull, snap her neck, anything to end this. He is so large, and she so small, that he can crunch, tear, and gulp down thin flesh and weak bones and pajamas until he has devoured everything the world has known of Elle.

She is gone.

And yet, she lingers. The bear's insides spread to fit a little girl of bones and dirt. His menstrual-enchanted digestion tugs at her body and feeds him, her bear, and his strength feeds her. Round and round the strength of bloodshed goes, like light circling the rim of a stuffed stegosaur's only eye. The bear grows into nocturnal blackness until he fills every shadow of Elle's room, a tyrant bear of the prehistoric kind.

He—she?—they are no longer bringer and brought, bleeder and bear. Unity has drawn them tight in the darkness.

Across the house, another bedroom breathes the faint scents of sleeping Mother.

They could go to her now, but instead they'll wait. To come upon Mother by surprise in the dark would be too much like the thoughtless hulk prowling outside the house. They're a different kind of bear, one who wants Mother to see what's become of her daughter. She ended Elle's brothers, after all. A mother should know the fates of her children. She should be grateful.

After that, Mother can see what it really means to die so someone can be born. A little girl is coming, and she's faster and stronger than any parent in the world.

They aren't sure if they'll still exist at the moment Elle's time of the month should end. Mother might vanish down this same throat, and then her bear, and when the cycle would stop had Elle lived, they might fade into shadows, or themselves, leaving only Leaf to show the landlady they were ever here. Or they might live on as girl and bear in one body.

The future is no certainty, but when has it ever been? They won't worry about it yet. There is only this moment and what they plan to do. Daylight is coming to wake Mother in the tiny house tucked in the trees.

And this morning, it is a forest of monsters.

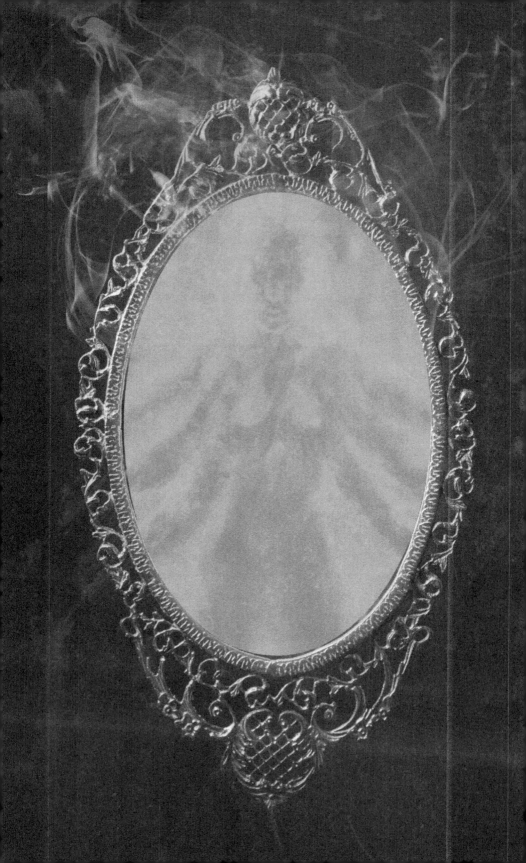

Of a Thousand Arms and More

AI JIANG

Houmi woke up with a thousand arms today, though she usually woke up with this many—give or take a few. On certain days, perhaps she could even get the number down to the mid hundreds. But only on a really, really good day.

Before she made her morning tea—chamomile for the headaches caused by the arms banging against her head the entire night—she checked on the little one now in pre-school. There was another hour before both her husband Xingmu and their Lulu had to wake, but Houmi had to work fast anyhow.

Eggs in the pan—one scrambled, one poached; toast in the toaster—one for a minute, one for half that time; water in the boiler—for the instant coffee mix, the vitamin juice, and, of course, Houmi's long-awaited tea. Then she rushed to wake the two still dreaming, whisking up the bags she prepped for them and placing them on the table by the door.

A kiss on each head—one with knees bent, one on tiptoes—and the two were off with a quick "Thank you!" and a smiley "I love you!" and that was enough.

As soon as the door closed and her family's blue Dodge van disappeared from the driveway, Houmi's smile grew tired. Though she knew she should be content, her heart itched each time she scraped the leftovers into the trash and scrubbed at the dishes and glasses.

There were two hours left before she had to be at work at the local travel agency—Dream Journeys—when she settled onto the couch in the living room, her weight crinkling the newspapers she set under herself. She was grateful her employers allowed her to work part time after her pregnancy and offered the same hours after.

As much as she hated to admit it, it was these moments of quiet she enjoyed most during the day. She couldn't remember when was the last time she went on a vacation.

With her frontmost right arm, she reached over to her left and tugged, loosening the joint that connected the arm to her shoulder. Blossomed around her frontmost arms were the thousand or so others—she had lost count since turning eighteen, when she had hundreds, perhaps as early as when she was in middle school, even though back then she only had tens.

She heard the satisfying pop and the arm dislocated, painless, as expected. Though she flinched anyhow because of the times she accidently knicks the skin with a knife when preparing dinner or bumps into furniture too sharp—those instances hurt. Sometimes when she was tired, it took a few tries because she'd done a sloppy job at whatever it was: half mopped floors, sudsy dishes on the drying rack, still-raw dinners. It was always a struggle when her mother-in-law visited. She never found anything Houmi did satisfactory, and the arms knew, and the arms listened. And rather than detaching smoothly, the skin would hold on, ache, sear when she tried to pull, the joints groaning. But thankfully, not today, not right now.

The skin around the arm, now hung limp, was flaking, but only where it had been removed from the shoulder, exposing the bone underneath. And as soon as Houmi pulled the limb off entirely, the other surrounding arms shifted to close the gap, repairing the torn skin, hiding the bone once again. Almost like she had never torn it off.

She took a sip of tea before beginning.

Delicate fingers plucked at the shedding arm. Houmi's tongue folded the layers of skin and muscle into her mouth as she picked it apart, layer by layer and swallowed, feeling each piece scratch down the walls of her throat. The external layer was one she always dreaded most, laced with the scent of sweat and the taste of dead skin. But the muscle was always a joy —the dense liquid that came with lining her tongue with the contentment of a finished task. She indulged in individual veins, even though she knew she often didn't have the time to—but today, she did, or at least, she convinced herself she did.

When there was only bone left, she smoothed the edges down before, like a sword-eater, she slid the lengthier pieces in with her head tilted upwards before working on those smaller. Houmi crunched each fingertip, each knuckle with her molars—bone against bone. And as she finished, she looked down, remnants of the arm littered across her clothing to remind her of her completed work, to remind her that there is still more to come. It should taste like success, according to many of her friends, but it never was quite as sweet as Houmi imagined it to be—at least from what she could recall, the arms she consumed during her childhood were like sweet nectar. Now, it tasted more of a grapefruit.

She wrapped up the newspaper with scattered flakes and placed it with the recycling.

Only then did her day start.

It wasn't uncommon for Houmi to daydream at work, imagining that the vacations she planned for clients were her own. She couldn't afford it, of course—neither monetary or time-wise. But to have the daydreams was enough. Though she often felt guilty because neither Xingmu or Lulu would be included in them. Sometimes. But rarely.

What would happen if she left her arms unconsumed? What would happen if she dislodged all her arms at once without completing each task attached to them first? What if—

"Houmi."

She looked up and met the eyes of her manager, Julian. Houmi marvelled at the number of arms they had—two hundred, at most.

"Your..." Julian cleared their throat.

Houmi tilted her head to the side. "What is it?"

She wasn't initially concerned, but the way Julian's eyes opened wide and continued to widen with each second had cold sweat breaking inside the fists she didn't realize she was making.

"On your lower back..." They said nothing more, but Houmi didn't give them a chance to anyhow as she rushed to the staff washroom down the hall.

Houmi turned to inspect her arms, though it didn't take long for her to locate what Julian was speaking about.

A gnarled limb sat at the small of her back when she looked into the mirror. A small, shrivelled thing hidden among the thousand full-length arms in more or less perfect condition, though some had battered, bruised over the week with overgrown or chipped fingernails and untameable hair like the tall swaying hay of farm fields because she kept pushing those to the bottom of her to-do list, convinced she still had time—there were other more urgent matters at hand.

Houmi's heartbeat quickened, blood pulsed, rushed down each arm, tingling at the fingertips, as she continued to stare at the anomaly. Houmi hadn't a clue what the memory, task, responsibility, or perhaps the person tied to this withered limb. She continued combing her mind for a possible explanation. She hadn't missed any deadlines yet. Houmi picked up the grocery earlier that week, prepped several itineraries for her clients to review, scheduled Xingmu and Lulu's dentist appointments, and even doubled checked the checklist she taped to her desk, the copy of it secured with a Paris magnet from her client on the kitchen fridge, fed—

How was she so foolish? How could she have missed it?

Her mother-in-law would be visiting this evening, and Houmi couldn't let her see the tragic limb. It was bad enough her husband and daughter would likely witness her failure. At the thought, the withered arm still dangling, barely hanging onto the small of her back prodded her, reminding her of its existence now that she was aware of it.

If she fed the cat now, would it repair the situation? It would be painful trying to remove the limb, but it wouldn't be nearly as horrid if the limb detached on its own. The horror stories she'd read about such instances. Houmi shuddered.

She requested to leave earlier, only by half an hour. Her friend Avery

Peters' condo was only a five-minute walk from Houmi's house, so the trip would be quick. But as she neared the condo, thoughts of when exactly was the last time Houmi had fed the cat bounced around her mind. A day ago? Two days ago? A week? Surely it had not been that long. She would remember, wouldn't she? Houmi feared the state Avery's cat would be in when she arrived. What would she say to Avery? Houmi hoped they wouldn't be too angry.

Houmi's hand shook when she scanned the fob in the elevator. The ride up to the seventh floor felt longer than her mother-in-law's stares while Houmi cooked traditional dishes in a way the elder woman disapproved of. It was as though every second might determine the life or death of Avery's cat. She couldn't even remember the small thing's name as she rushed out of the elevator as soon as the ding signalled its arrival and before the door even fully slid open.

Unconsciously, she crossed the fingers of all her arms—not just the index and middle either but also the pink and ring, tossed in the thumb too for good measures. With cautious steps after opening the door, Houmi walked down the short hallway towards Avery's living room, noiseless, as though any sound she made could cause death.

Houmi blew out a breath when she heard the slightest meow, her eyes darting to seek out the black cat whose name she now remembered was Ivory. She had forgotten she used to make fun of Avery for ironic name in high school.

She treaded into the kitchen and filled Ivory's bowl. There were a few minutes to spare before she needed to head home to prepare dinner for her family and mother-in-law, so she crouched and revelled in the softness of Ivory's short brown fur. But when she stood, she noticed the fish tank on the kitchen counter, and floating at the top with the wrong side up was Avery's red beta fish. Dead.

It was such a simple thing, and Avery hadn't tasked her with it, had clearly even forgotten it themselves, yet Houmi fell to her knees on top of the worn, second-hand playmat she received a few years back from her aunt and gave to Avery when their child was born, stained with mashed squash she had tried to clean a week ago, when she brought Lulu over, but failed. Clear tears darkened the dirtied patches as they fell quicker and quicker still, barely catching at the point of Houmi's chin before desperately trying to escape her pent up pain.

The average lifespan of a beta fish was only five years, and she knew Avery wouldn't have such an attachment to the pet as to be angry at her for the mistake. Houmi could simply purchase another fish as a replacement—one that looked similar enough. But that wasn't the issue. This small mistake somehow unearthed all the feelings of incompetency that Houmi had kept hidden over the years. All the incompentencies that her mother-in-law never failed to mention, a constant jabbing at not just her heart but each of her arms. She thought it would soon become a dull throbbing, but it hadn't. Houmi had only become more afraid of failure, of forgetting something, of not performing well enough, of not being enough in the eyes of her mother-in-law. And encouragement? There was barely any of that because there should be no praise for her in accomplishing her duties.

She took a deep breath, wanting to think of nothing. Houmi stared at the dead fish, made a mental note to buy a new one, and felt the arm of the task sprout in place of the gnarled arm.

Tomorrow, she would bury the limb and the fish would be alive again.

Houmi curled into herself while Ivory batted at her hair. And she knew not how long she remained in that position, only that even as her body shook, her mind still focused on the vibration of her phone in her pocket and the missed calls that could compete with the growing number of her arms.

She didn't return home that night but fell asleep in the same exact spot on the mat in Avery's apartment.

Just for tonight, she let go of the thought of needing to complete all the tasks, the thought of her mother-in-law, even the thought of her family.

It wasn't the sun streaming through undrawn curtains that woke her, nor was it Ivory's whine for food, but it was the lack of a headache that shook the sleep from her eyes. Houmi's gaze met two arms. Only two arms. She glanced behind her several times to see her back bare. But already, seconds later, the stubs of arms began protruding, slow, wiggling their way out.

And Houmi knew soon her thousand and more arms would return as she recalled her tasks for the day, for the week, for the year. And she though would love to fly to Paris herself to purchase an overpriced magnet, this small freedom in the quiet of Avery's apartment, alone, would be enough for now.

With a deep breath, she collapsed back onto the stained mat, embracing not her daughter, not her husband, just herself—just for today.

Tomorrow, when she returned home and welcomed back her thousand arms and more—because it is what she must, and it is what she will.

Mother Made Cake

NICOLETTA GIUSEFFI

It began as a simple pastime.

After my father died, taken in the night on his way to the ports by an inexplicable clot I never believed existed, my mother received letter after letter informing her of her great fortune, her luck, her property, her assets. Her ship, which was once my father's, had come in. In one night, she became the head of our little family (me and my two graceless older sisters), and she, the little girl from the Margerides in the south of France who never had anything but a crust of bread for her dinner, went mad in ways mothers do when the duress settling about their shoulders becomes an unbearable gravity.

She developed an obsession with cake.

"Mirabèl, have you tasted this?" she often asked me, in tender tones, about her blooming diversion. It consumed her by inches every day, an ouroboros of her own devouring.

It was always cake. She had taken to baking at all hours, and though everyone would smile, how nice for her, I alone knew this growing passion would never end while she lived. Every day my sisters and I saw cake on our plates; thank heavens we were old enough to know better than to eat every last bite every last time. The garden ate as much cake as we did.

The ordinary white and yellow cakes gave way after some months, when they were perfected to the last crumb, to ever more elaborate monstrosities of flour, sugar, and butter.

Cheesecake, perfected to a cloying sour-sweet, sat always in the icebox of our antiquated home in the American Southwest, where the climate and the culture had not penetrated Mother's palate one iota. She made *mille-feuille* and seemed set on achieving a true thousand layers. Once, I feared she had turned to alcohol, but it was only bottles of rum emptied for moist *kugelhopf* you could almost drink. Her spongecakes piled upon the kitchen counters until I fancied using them as sponges in my chores, but I could not bear disrespecting the grieving widow she had become.

My sisters, who had known Father longer than I and scoffed at his memory, did not lift a finger around the house, though they did eat the products of our mother's melancholy. When I raised the topic of a palliative, if not from a doctor, then a priest, I was all but laughed out of the room. How could there be any cure for such sweetness, they demanded. Surely it was love and joy which made our mother endlessly bake. They had surmised the ceaseless influx of sweetness was for our benefit, positing no cure existed for grief like sugar and fat and the smell of baking throughout a house (some nights I slept on the lawn to spare myself from it), a reminder there was life in the old walls yet.

All proceeded as it was until one day, despite my sisters' assurances that all was well, my mother disappeared, heading east in a passenger car to no certain destination. I worried she had run away to start a new life with new daughters somewhere.

My love for my mother had not receded, even though our conversations had grown infrequent, and my marriage prospects, over which she once obsessed as though I were her rag-poor child-self's only doll, ceased to be of interest to her. Perhaps it was her new mania which replaced doll-me in her mind. I was not self-rising like her precious flour. Just the same, I was relieved to be free of her machinations as they were redirected to the oven. Yet, in reference to her disregard for my free will, her last words to me were the offer to bake me a husband and a flippant laugh.

I raced about the house, searching for some fragment of a signpost that might lead me to her, and all the while my sisters plied me with the remnant crumbs of Mother's baking. They failed to see how the cake dwindled and disappeared into their mouths or else rotted into a colony of mold as the lope of time sprang ever onward, until weeks had passed and there were no telegrams and no story in the morning papers of the woman who was independently wealthy, which would have been more shocking for their readers than her death. My two sisters, whose greater age afforded greater knowledge of our parents, had once told me Mother knew only beasts in her natal land. That she had been raised in such abject poverty that forest groves were her playrooms, that sprightly deer and rake-thin hares and other things with longer teeth had been her playmates, and that the only sugar she ever tasted was in berries found amid the underbrush. I remember when I was a child and my sisters teased me, telling me my mother had brought a beast with her from the dark, pine forests of Lozère to America, and that if I ever acted out, shirked my duties, displeased her in any way, she would feed me to it. *La Bête du Gévaudan* I heard them call it once, the name of a legendary and rapacious wolf. 'When you speak of the wolf,' Mother always cautioned, 'you'll see his tail.'

I traced my mother's trail to the train station in Santa Fe and hopped a midnight express heading east. The ticket-taker had seen her, yes he had, smoothly clipping the edge of my ticket and smiling with twinkle-eyed affirmation. He never forgot a face so beautiful, and for a moment he thought I was her, my dark brown curls and long, elegant nose the very mirror of her own, until he heard my puerile voice. She had mentioned the Black Mountains, and that was all he knew, except that she had smelled faintly of whipped icing sugar.

The map I had purchased at the station delineated the Black Mountains with a great spot of ink such that I thought someone had spilled a vessel on it and sold it anyway. When I stepped off the train in the city of Asheville, I purchased a horse with the crumpled bills I had managed to pilfer from the overflowing pocketbooks of my sisters, who had taken to withdrawing great amounts in cash from the account Mother had given them, if only to bask in its heady, corruptive power. The horse was amiable enough, a chocolate-colored beast with a diamond of vanilla on its nose, and carried me far out into the wilderness seeking my mother's sweet scent.

In the forest, a violation of nature's sanctity lay waiting, like a beast in the undergrowth, to pounce upon my meager reckoning. I had no imagination, no illusions, and yet I was thrust into a Grimmian fantasy as a child in a tale, except I was a woman and I had my doubts about everything—no imagination but doubts, doubts always of the veracity of everything I saw and every word anyone ever said to me. I ignored every early warning, every strange sound I knew not the source of, and pressed ever onward though my horse tried in its nickering cant to warn me against it.

After three days of wandering on cone-littered paths through spruces leaning to observe my advance, I happened into night with no firewood and no fuel, only my horse, my water, a pack of dry, cured meat, and a few tin cans of tomatoes, coffee, and condensed milk. I also carried a knife as large as my forearm, which I had purchased at a trading post in exchange for the pearl earrings I had inherited from a relation. Although the horse found the forest provided well for it and nibbled at the forbs growing in the understory until their petals dripped from its mouth, I found myself foolishly bereft of the provisions required to undertake a search of such a vast, uncaring wood. I hitched the horse to a tree, stuck my knife into the bark, and began to search for firewood to occupy my self-critical mind, which spat invectives at me to curse my hasty, girlish will.

No sooner were my arms full of thickly-needled fir limbs than I saw a light in the distance. At once I knew it to be a sign of life, if not of my mother herself, and I ran toward it without a care, jumping over fallen logs and replacing the semaphoric silence of the wood with the adrenal rush of wind over my ears.

When I reached the light, I discovered a rustic oven made of piled stones, roughly hewn, with a jolly plume of smoke rising from its flue. I knew the languid stench of sweetness instantly. The smell of home. While I congratulated myself on my ingenuity in finding my mother at last, I realized the trees around me were leaning oddly and went to investigate. Their bark peeled in thin layers, smeared in the warmth of my fingers, and revealed itself to be a hardened layer of chocolate ganache over striated *gâteau à la brioche*—the trees were entirely cake. Although I knew nothing of the forest, not even to keep on the path, I knew that trees were supposed to be made of wood.

I could not stop to catch my reeling brain as it fell from reserved logic into unhinged fantasy. I, the girl with no imagination, could not separate the unreal from the real when one consumed the other. I decided instead to follow the tree to another, and another, and soon the whole forest was one entirely of cake, its form kept by the refrigerating cool of a coming storm. The bracken was not alive, but a latticework of sugar flowers sculpted down to their stems and veins with wholly unnatural detail. Ribbons of pearly pulled sugar, hardened into tempting roses as red and bright as dollops of blood, marked the path forward into an ever-deepening forest of nauseating, false animation. Although none of it was natural, it swayed and creaked like the real forest I had been traveling through for days. Green icing fronds dropped heaps of confectioner's sugar snowflakes upon my footprints, hiding them instantly behind me.

When first I heard the threnody of howls, my thoughts turned instantly to my horse, who was my only escape and my only source of meat in a vile country of beautified cake sculptures. Though I had not ruled out living creatures, these foremost predators had never crossed my mind. I had only heard of wolves in passing, never had firsthand experience, never so much as owned a dog, yet I knew their howl in the deepest, most fearful layer of my brainstem and felt my veins tingle all at once when before I had thought them numbed entirely by the growing cold.

A sugar frost dusted my corduroy riding dress and I briefly wished I had not eschewed a corset, because it would have kept me all the warmer, or at least burned well. While I trudged on through tall sugardrifts dotted with animal tracks and fallen trees shorn open to reveal their *genoise* innards, I heard the howls emanate upward, though I could not find the moon in the soot-black sky no matter how far I craned my neck. I encountered more ovens like the first, but their fires were dying, and their immobile lights brought little solace when the prowling eyes on the fringes of my vision reflected their scant embers. Only after I stepped through a thicket of branches, which sundered off their trunks for they had not the durability of wood even in their frozen state, did I realize I had been led to a destination by a trail of smoldering ovens.

There loomed beside a frozen lake of syrup a great castle like those that surveyed the mountains of my mother's countryside birthplace, the fairy story edifice of a thousand tales which had never interested me enough to revere them. Round towers of layer cake speared the emptiness above, a gap in the trees and the storm allowing me at last to see the moon tossing light onto the crisp crenellations cutting the night sky into a jigsaw. Although I recognized the silhouettes, when I drew nearer, a song of hungry mouths echoing from behind me, I saw the whole of the castle was a heap of layers frosted with thick royal icing mortar blooming from cracks in cake dyed velvet red by unknowable additions to the batter.

I had no choice but to enter in search of my mother. Try as I might to shut out the wolves and the cold, the chill had made the tempered chocolate hinges of the entrance doors quite brittle, and they shattered at the touch.

Inside the great foyer, I smelled the bubbling fat of liquid butter burning away in sconce lamps with sugar glass attached to the walls. A carpet of green marzipan, writhing with white, worm-like Cornelli lace, had been spread out upon the glazed parquet floors made of biscuit, and indeed the whole interior was a meticulous mimicry in flour, sugar, and fat of the stylings of a lordly chateau in the tip of old Occitania, where my mother was born.

I chose a white cake door covered in elaborate gold boiserie which flaked at the edges in crumbling pits of sprinkling sugar, as delicious a door as any, and entered a hallway split this way and that as though all sense had left the architect of the castle after the grand entry hall had been finished. The memory of gluttonous Versailles had overeaten and vomited its decorative acanthus, seashells, crowns, and angelic visages of the Sun King upon the Lambeth walls, piped and overpiped, which parted to further doors or else were split by sugar glass partitions into further halls which both mirrored and deviated in sections from the one I walked. I could smell nothing but the surrounding, enervating sweet, and in my haste, I again lost my way.

Hansel and Gretel could not have left crumbs were the whole of their environs made from crumbs themselves.

Chandeliers wrapped in fondant flowers and ropes of rolled buttercream dyed pastel cast a grotesque light which stank of butter and spilled a sheen of grease on my skin, recovered from the cold outside but now suffering the heat of anxiety flushing it as pink as the diaphanous marzipan curtains I swept aside. Thick lines of hardened frosting traveled in rippling pipes over every edge of the corridors, and dollops of the stuff held oranges and cherries and fruits darker still, fruits I did not recognize but glistened bright and wet, flesh exposed to the air. Tiers of cake jutted from the floor and ceiling, interrupting my advance and forcing me to turn sideways and smear my clothes against the narrowing walls, smothering me in sugar sludge. My teeth burned with the sensation of rot at the thought of all this caustic sweetness on my palate, and I gagged against the obscenity of it. Yet as I wandered on, I called for my mother, pleaded with the unsympathetic silence for her, and the porous cake swallowed the echoes.

All at once my skin became gooseflesh, dotted like so much decoration on cake, and I knew I was being pursued through the halls. Despite the fact I could not trace my path, something else could. I heard it scrabbling over the floors and heard its breath, but each branch from the corridor I traveled led to yet more branches, to rooms where tables sagged beneath the grotesquely decadent weight of cake upon cake, and orgiastic kitchens full of blazing ovens whose minder had abandoned them to their own obscene devices.

At last, I burst into a room whose corners faded into invisible darkness. Only a host of butter candles, sputtering like a choir, lit the grand table and the soaring imposition of a pyramid of choux pastry spheres. It was a wedding *croquembouche* taller than a grown man, suffocated with innumerable spider strands of caramel. My jaw hung, and though I had not yet seen my mother's greatest creation, I smelled and tasted its sickly sweetness befouling the air.

My mother's voice whispered in the darkness, speaking feverishly in French, Occitan and back, at once becoming an admonition, then an entreaty, and then a lullaby I thought I remembered. Last came the litany of felicitations said to a young bride. Her small shape wavered and her face was obscured by a black veil. Pale hands exposed to the clarified light from beneath the ghostly sleeves of her chemise lit further candles with a burning dowel between her fingers. She circumnavigated the table and turned to me. The light revealed the shadow of her sweet-softened figure beneath the silk.

Now I could see that something had skulked into the room, its long, noble trunk bending around to face me from its place on one of the tiered walls of cake where no inch was unadorned by decoration; a *horror vacui* of icing. It had blended in invisibly, perfectly. Though I recognized it as an animal, it too was made of cake, it lived and breathed and dripped a froth of frosting from the sugar rime-encrusted lips framing its fanged muzzle. The frosting whip of its tail swung sedately as it trotted beneath my mother's outstretched hand for her to stroke its back. It was tall, as high as my waist, and its enormous, lupine silhouette exerted a palpable pressure of fear which drove me to my knees as surely as a pair of hands upon my shoulders.

It approached, and I could see its eyes glowed within the ridges of a frosting brow piped by a grooved savoy tube. It placed one paw upon my leg and opened its great jaws to enclose my face in the teeth which, if they were sugar, were fiendishly sharp and did not melt in the drool which accompanied the hot, emanating sweetness of its breath. It had drawn so close I could see how its reddish fur clumped in artful layers of flexile frosting, animated by some inner warmth, and it dragged its cherry compote tongue across my face. I knew not whether the beast trusted me, or was beginning its first taste of my toothsome whole.

Mother had baked me a husband after all, but not the one I expected. Her voice rose at once to a dizzy exaltation.

"I call it *Gâteau Gévaudan*."

Passed

ELIZABETH R. MCCLELLAN

My Mama can speak to the dead.
That's third grade social suicide,
a recipe for your only friends to be
names on gravestones. There's money

in it, at least: police don't care about enough
of the dead to find their murderers,
so after the funeral bill is paid the family pays Mama
to show up in her best dress,

the black one with tiny polka dots, and sit
a while with the body, engaged in slow
conversation. It's not simple work.
Ya don't always see who killed ya, she says,

dying does a number on ya even if you did.
She gets what information she can; I get
endless funeral snacks, potato chips and soda,
cookies, casserole squares, as if feeding

me while Mama works averts bad luck.
They don't like to touch me, though.
Be polite to them, take what's offered, remember
they're grieving. When the fluorescent bulbs

of churches and funeral homes weigh me down, I flee
to the playground if there is one, the graveyard
if there's not. It comes on you about twelve,
if it's going to, and I hope it will and hope

it won't. I want to be my Mama, finding out
where the will is hidden and bringing out
the words people couldn't say, but I want
to go to college, maybe for art, dress wild,

make friends who don't know death
speaks to my blood, talk about hit songs,
maybe have a crush that doesn't think
deadspeakers and enbys are unnatural things.

Today it is Friday and Mama doesn't send me
to the kitchen but keeps me close.
Dead bodies don't frighten me; I've seen
too many, am immune to slasher film nightmares

I ask why, thinking of chips, hear it's time you tried,
so ask him how he's doing, now, and
we'll see. I shake as I ask low and
querulous, and she shakes her head.

You gotta talk firm and loud, she says,
like this: how are ya doing Mr. Wakefield,
and I hear him, clear as top forty radio,
nothing hurts anymore. That's good, I say,

PASSED

that's good, and Mama's smile is only
a little pained, through the pride of a shared
legacy. She strokes my hair, sends me out,
and the cookie tastes like childhood's end.

For Ursula Vernon

Puerperium

DONYAE COLES

The puerperal period begins immediately after childbirth, defining the time when the mother's body returns to a non-pregnant state.

My mother came to stay a week after I brought the baby home.

Evita, that's my mother's name, stands in my kitchen making breakfast. I know she is there before I turn the corner from the dining room. I can hear her singing, she always sings the same old songs. Songs from when she was young. Songs they don't play on the radio anymore.

"It's all I have left. I gave the rest of my youth to you," she would laugh when I used to ask why those songs. Over and over again. Every morning when she made eggs and toast like she's making now. I can smell them, see them when I turn the corner and there she is at the stove, spatula in hand just like when I was kid.

Standing in my kitchen like she's always been there.

The smell makes me nauseous. But I am happy to see her, relieved. I'm so tired and she's, familiar, singing her songs like a bird, and what daughter doesn't want to see her mother after she's become a mother herself?

"Glad you got up today, getting back in the swing of things," Luke says. He's already finished his plate. He bends to kiss my cheek on his way out. I've made it to the stove. My mother smiles and winks at me while she pushes eggs onto a plate. Luke is leaving for work. It's been a week. Paternity leave is over. I'm supposed to be okay now.

Adica is in the bouncer. He must have gotten her up and changed her, given her the last of the milk I managed to pump so far. She's still curled up on herself, her body not used to being outside of mine. My breasts ache just looking at her. Milk full. Engorged. "She shouldn't be unbuckled. It's not safe."

"It's fine, it's fine," Evita's voice. My mother's voice. Familiar like bird song. "Sit, sit, you need to eat, get your energy back." She pushes me towards the table. I can't move the baby, the mother is pulling out a chair and I am sitting down. Luke is leaving, gone. It's been a week.

My mother is here.

"You can shower after you eat. Take a little time and do something with yourself," she says turning away, going back to the stove. I feel her frown.

I do need a shower. I look down at my t-shirt, milk stained. I smell like spoiled milk and I'm not sure if it's the shirt or my breasts, souring before they leak. It's the shirt. I am wearing real underwear at least. Cotton, granny panties, something to hold the thick pad to me. I'm out of those mesh ones they send you home with, but I'm still bleeding. She's only been out of me a week. I'm disgusting, leaking from everywhere. "Yeah, I know. No chance to, I've been so tired." New baby, relatable, I try to laugh, shrug.

I can see her frown now as she sets the plate, a crayon yellow mound of eggs flecked with black pepper in the center. Two slices of toast next to it. The yolk smell comes through the butter. It's protein. My stomach turns.

"I've always had to hound you about your hygiene, to get you to take proper care of yourself, like a lady. You don't want her to pick up your bad habits, do you?"

"Of course not," I agree without thinking. Of course not that she'll be better at selfcare or of course not she won't be like me? "I'll go, right after I eat."

The wax yellow mountain stares back at me. My stomach does backflips. I take a fork to it, the mountain. I need to eat. Protein is good. I eat quickly so I don't have to taste them. I can still taste them.

I chase them with coffee. I add milk and sugar. My mother, thankfully, just sings and clears the table. It's all right.

Then she's clearing her throat and I know that it's not. I put my cup down, half finished. I'll go. I'll go right now.

The baby cries. Loud squawking cries. Angry, offended cries. Screams. It fills the room. And there is my mother, sweeping her from the bouncer. She holds Adica to her breasts and the baby searches, mouth open, head wobbling, eyes squeezed shut. Blind, like a baby bird. Touch and taste guiding her, but Evita's tits are long dry.

"Here, she's hungry," I say holding out my arms. I've already started leaking, I can feel the wet spots forming, the hot drip of my own milk down the overly firm curve of my breasts.

"Don't worry about it. I'll give her a bottle, just go wash your stinky self." A teasing jab. That's what I tell myself and anyway she's right. I do smell, but. . .

"I'm breastfeeding. Luke gave her the last of what I've pumped this morning." I haven't looked but I'm pretty sure. There was nothing else to feed her.

"Breastfeeding." A shake of her head, disapproval. "This is why you need bottles. Formula. I fed you formula, you're fine. Your grandmother used to make it, evaporated milk and Karo syrup! We're all fine."

The baby is crying. Screaming. Her little face is an angry red boil, wet with tears. Her eyes are gone. Just the hungry mouth stretched wide, frustrated that all it's found is harsh cloth and rosewater. A baby bird in an empty nest.

"I'll wash right after, let me calm her down." I hold out my arms, begging for the screaming thing she's holding away from me.

Evita shows mercy. Or maybe the baby is too loud, too insistent. I don't know, I don't care. I almost cry myself when Adica, still screaming and kicking, is returned. I pull up my shirt, shove my tit in her mouth and hope the angle is good enough.

I'm blessed. She nurses. Her screams now frustrated coos and then just breath. She pulls milk, drains me. My breasts soften. It's all right.

Evita sits on the other side of the table. I feel her stare, my eyes are filled with Adica but I know what my mother's face looks like. Familiar.

She's speaking. About formula, about the mess of the house, the mess that I am. I want to scream, tell her to shut up but that would be ungrateful. I know, I know. I feel the words like a roar in the back of my throat. I swallow them. I want to cry. My stomach churns.

It's just hormones I tell myself. She's singing again. Bird song.

I need her. I need a mother. The baby is sleeping again. I take a shower.

⚜

Dinner is on the table when Luke gets home. I'm dressed. The baby is with my mother.

Adica doesn't cry as much when Evita rocks her. I guess she likes the songs she sings. I already know them all. I can sing them too. I'll try. I'm still tired. I've been pumping as much as I can between feedings. There's a few bottles in the fridge, a couple of ounces. It's good. Her tummy is small.

"It's nice to sit and have dinner like this. Feels like it's been forever!" He's happy but quiet. He doesn't want to wake the baby. She won't sleep long. Her tummy is small. "I know she's a handful, but thank you for taking the time to do this for me."

Celebrate his first day back. His eyes are soft, he reaches out for my hand. I'm reminded why I love him, why we had a baby to begin with. This soft man who works to provide for us. So I can be home with the baby.

"How was everything?" he finally asks. "You girls get along all right?"

He doesn't know but he knows. He knows that things are *complicated* between my mother and me. I don't get into it; I don't want to get into it. I want to enjoy the peace. "It was fine. We got our hair done, did our nails. Just girl things."

An obvious joke. My hair is growing out of its braids. My nails are unpainted and half broken.

He laughs, big and warm. I love him.

The baby cries, waking. Her bird song cranky, a distorted echo through the monitor. I groan, cartoonish, loud but under that it's real, a growl.

Can't I have one night? One moment? My mother is singing. My breasts ache. "I'll go. Eat your dinner."

He stands. "I'm already done. I'll change her." He smiles, a gift. "You can put dinner away."

It's fair. Division of labor. The house can't wait. Someone has to put dinner away. Someone has to get the baby, feed the baby, stay home, take care of everything. It's been a week. I'm supposed to be okay. I nod. He leaves and then my mother comes in.

"You two enjoy your dinner? What did I tell you, a nice steak, you make yourself look good." She frowns. Not good enough, I know, I know. "Remind him why he comes home." She winks. Picks up my plate with its half-finished meal. "You need to lose that baby weight before it just becomes weight."

I follow her into the kitchen. "How long are you staying?" I haven't had a chance to ask. I was just so relieved to have someone else there. It'd only been a week.

She shrugs, her focus on emptying the pots and pans into containers. Neat and orderly. "As long as you need me." She looks up and smiles at me. "I know my little girl needs her mother."

I feel sick. I haven't recovered enough since the birth. Luke's gone back to work. I'm so tired. I want to tell her no, I'm fine, but I swallow it. I want to cry. "Thank you." I say. It's the only thing I can say. What else could I say? She is here to help. Mothers help their daughters. I am taking care of my daughter. She will take care of me. I can't be ungrateful.

My breasts are aching. She'll be hungry soon. She's hungry now. Babies are such hungry things.

"I got you that formula. Let that man feed the baby. Men like to feel like they're included or else they wander away. Like your father." She points at the cabinet where she stored it next to the bottles.

I shake my head, my dad, a warbly phone call like the baby's cry through the monitor. Distant. She told me it was my fault. Maybe that's what she's saying now. It was my fault then, I took too much. It'll be my fault now. I don't give enough. I'm trying. "Thanks but I told you, I'm trying to nurse. Luke supports it. Maybe for emergencies it'll be good but there's no need right now."

"He's too soft with you," she rolls her eyes. Another one of my silly notions and she knows better. "I won't argue with you about it."

"Great, thanks." I start listing off the benefits of it as I put away the containers she packed, stacking them neatly in the fridge. I made too much for two people.

"It's good to have extra," Evita says. She always cooked big meals. Couldn't stop herself even when it was just me and her. There weren't any more children for her. I took all her youth. Luke wants more. Do I?

I'm leaking now. My mother is singing. Bird song by fluorescent light. We wipe down the kitchen. Keep a tidy kitchen. The baby can wait.

Luke meets me halfway down the hall. Apologetic, flustered. A cranky, red-faced Adica squawking in his arms. I am guilty but I don't know why. Maybe all mothers feel like that. I shush her as I walk into the bedroom, settle us in the bed and there is nothing but her hungry mouth.

I don't know I'm sleeping until Luke wakes me up. It's been like this for days. Nothing then her hunger then nothing, hunger, nothing, hunger.

It's what I wanted. It's the sacrifice of being a mother.

In the morning Evita is singing. She makes eggs. I eat them.

❧

The days blur, hunger and nothing and oldies in the kitchen. Few friends call, but my mother is here. If my mother wasn't here, I don't know what I would do. The baby is fussy. My breasts are crying, if not engorged then leaking. My shirts are all ruined. No one calls.

My mother tells me to put fresh shirts on. It will make me feel better. I want to believe her, so I do. Nothing makes me feel better. The baby is crying.

Adica is better with her. I am so tired, and my mother just knows what to do. She always knows what to do. I'm a ghost, moving from place to place on autopilot.

We don't argue about the formula, but I see it every time I reach for a fresh bottle to pump. It's still sealed. I want to throw it away, but it's still sealed. That would be wasteful. I grab the bottle and pump. It's not hurting anything. It's fine, it's fine.

48

Luke is happy that there's breakfast and dinner and leftovers for lunch if he wants. That the house is clean and I am getting dressed. He smiles and kisses me when he leaves and comes back. He plays with Adica before dinner. Sometimes at night he wakes up to change her diaper. Luke is a good man.

"One thing about nursing, you're losing that weight," my mother tuts, eyeing my lunch. I put the dressing for the salad down, leave the leaves green. I'm not hungry but I'm starving. Adica has uncurled. She's unbuckled in the bouncer. She's kicking her little legs under her fat belly. It's okay for babies to be fat.

I am not a baby.

I wonder if she ever looked at me like she looks at my baby. Soft smiles, gentle touch. I wonder if she's ever been this gentle as a mother.

"Oh stop, it's different now, I'm older, I have more time," she says reading my thoughts. "You'll understand soon." Cryptic but I do. I'm already so frustrated, so quick to snap at the smallest things. If she wasn't here I don't know what I would do, how I would act. I'm so tired.

It's been almost two months. Luke is back at work. I'm not bleeding anymore. I'm supposed to be okay.

"You better take care of that man," she whistles. "Before you lose him."

I clean up the dishes. The water feels far away. The baby's cries are muted, little chirps through a window, and then they stop. I wipe down the kitchen, I vacuum the living room. I shower and put on a clean shirt.

I nurse the baby. She's eating less often. She's older. Is that right?

I hear my mother singing. I hear bird song.

❦

"It's been two months already," he says, rubbing my back. The kitchen is clean. I am clean. It's all right if the baby cries. It's fine, it's fine.

Luke is kissing me. I know what he wants. I want to be a good wife. I want to keep my man. I want I want I want.

It's fine.

That's what Evita would say. What my mother would say. Mother is always right.

49

❧

I awake in the dark. Luke is snoring softly next to me in that good, post-fucking sleep. A sleep too deep to be disturbed by bird song. But I never sleep that deep anymore.

Adica is crying.

Or she had been.

I'm sure.

I slip out of bed, find a t-shirt to pull on. Filthy and stiff with milk. My breasts are tight with milk. Yes, she must have been crying, it's time for her to eat. But she's not crying. The panic rises. I force myself to walk. Don't be silly, I say, she's getting older, already two months, her tummy is bigger, she'll sleep longer.

My stomach churns, sick. I turn into her bedroom and there's my mother.

I stand in the doorway. The space is a long tunnel, mile after dark mile, between me and them.

Evita is looking down at Adica in her arms. The streetlights are shining through the curtains, it lands on her beautifully. I have never looked that beautiful, that effortless. She is put together even in the middle of the night in a way that I failed to be at any time. A Madonna and her child.

My mother is nursing my baby.

Adica suckles at her breast, which is impossibly full of milk. Evita looks at me with a face that looks like my own face if it was ever so serene. I look like my mother. My mother looks like me but impossibly better, neater, thinner, more than I, a copy could ever be.

I stole her youth from her and now she's taking myself from me. I am a ghost, a memory, a zombie, a body, all at once and not anything at all. I reach for her, for my baby, but my fingers fall short, I am sinking through the floor, into void, into that dark deep sleep.

I am disappearing.

"No," my voice comes out as a chirping mimic of my mother's. "No." A bird song. "No!" A squawking scream.

Evita turns to me now. She smiles. The baby suckles. She brings her finger to her lips. "Shh, you'll wake my baby," she sings. She hums those songs. The same songs she's always sung.

I claw at the floor. No. I won't. She's my baby, my baby. I'm screaming, growling, no. I am not a bird. I was never a bird. I was never Evita with her songs and eggs. I'm me, me, me. A dirty animal beast thing.

A thing with teeth and claws and strength. I rip at the sinking void of the nursery floor. I tear at carpet and furniture that tries to drown me. Find footing and dig in, dig out and up. Screaming, growling, reaching.

"She's not your baby!" I roar. "I'm not your baby! I don't want you! I don't want to be you! Get out! Get out! Get out!"

Evita's face distorts and there too is my mother. The mother I've always known. Thin and sharp, feathers like spikes that let her fly but plucked out on her belly. She's beautiful and vicious and hatched a beast from her perfect egg. I'm crying. I'm sorry to disappoint her even now as I'm breaking her wings, even now as her beak pierces me in a thousand ways. Even now as Adica is a formless thing between us.

I snatch the shifting infant, hold her to my breasts. Evita screeches, ruptures all feather and bone, swells to impossible size. Bird eyes, black pools of anger and pride until there's nothing but them. I clutch Adica in my claws, try not to hurt her but I know, I know, it's impossible. I know I've cut her already. I know I'll do it again; I won't mean it then either. I'll try harder, I'll be better.

The room is Evita, her anger, her pain. I can hear her, understand her song like a second language. Why don't I listen, don't I know that she knows better than I? Don't I know to listen? The whirlwind of feathers tries to pull the baby away from me. I hold on. I'm screaming, I'm crying. A wild thing. It's my pain.

The room explodes in light.

My eyes clear and there's Adica sucking at a nearly empty bottle, the scent of formula filling my nose. When I rip the bottle out of her mouth, she cries. I cry.

Luke is standing at the door, dazed, hand still on the light switch. "I thought I heard something," he mumbles then sees me. Sees the mess of the room. Sees me crying. "What happened?"

I shake my head. I can't explain it to him but. "I'm having a hard time. I need help."

He nods. "I'm sorry. I should have known, I guess." Flustered, he trails off. Lets it drop. Finally, "If only your mother was still alive. She could help."

I know he means well, he doesn't know that a mother can be all sharp edges and pain. He doesn't know she was never going to help but I remember now, remember who I am. "You're here. You can help." He looks shocked, uncomfortable and down the dark hall I can hear Evita, hear her warning me that he'll leave, that I'll upset him. That I need to be better. I ignore it, keep my face turned towards his.

My name is Winona. I am not my mother.

MOTHER PROTECTS

Pelican

GEMMA FILES

I found a book on animals once, stuck between shelves to prop 'em up, all stiff with dust. Remembered enough from when my gram taught me my letters on Dr. Seuss to sound the text underneath the pictures out aloud, after I finally got bored just looking at 'em. One was of this bird perched on a stump by water had a huge flap of skin hung down from its beak, big enough to shovel up fish in and swallow 'em whole: *Pelican*, it said underneath. *Waterfowl, extinct.* Like most've of the rest've them things wasn't extinct along with everybody else who'd touched that same book, by the time I got hold of it.

Anyhow.

In the Middle Ages—*when?* somebody'd writ in the space next to it, like they was waiting on me to tell 'em—folk thought Pelicans fed their kids by ripping open a vein in their chest and letting them suckle on it, so's the chicks would drink 'til the momma bird died. Maybe 'cause they'd noticed birds didn't have tits, or maybe 'cause they just couldn't make 'emselves believe chicks get fed when their mommas puke meat they already ate back down their throats, once it's all ground up to liquid. People think all sorts of dumb shit, now same as then—I've sure had the hard proof of it this far, like all my damn life.

But my gram, Miranda was her name, was Bible to the day she died, so

I understood what the next part meant, when others might've not. That this whole Pelican thing was a parable, a sidewise way to bring in Jesus Christ Almighty, who shed his blood on the cross so we might live forever: Salvation through sacrifice, *self*-sacrifice, and all that happy crap. Like how if we had any extra food we should give it away, just on hopes somebody else might do the same, things ever happened to fetch up the other way 'round. Like they wouldn't be far more inclined to kill her, rape my momma and me, then take every other thing we had 'fore setting the whole place on fire 'round us and leaving us to pull ourselves out 'fore it burned down far enough to kill *us*, too.

Can't blame my gram for wanting to believe that Bible shit was true, I guess, though I sure enough did, after. I mean, she was only eight when the world ended—that's what she claimed, anyhow. Told my momma everything she remembered hoping momma'd tell it to me, but I don't think momma much believed her, 'cause she kept on changing the details 'til she forgot what exactly gram said first. Trying to make 'em sound more likely, maybe; that's the nice version, one I used to tell myself, back when I still cared. Before I figured out she didn't really give a shit, either way.

Didn't matter much, as it turned out. Took momma two months to find out she was carrying, five more before my brother killed her as she bore him; she bled out in a swamp, me just sitting there watching, waiting for her to die so I could take her pack, 'cause I was so sick of getting beat on for not being pregnant too. Never did get my courses, turned out, probably an account of being torn up so bad that first time, but it wasn't like I felt sorry over it—even then, I knew if you'd nothing else to trade, sex was always the fall-back.

And motherhood? From what I'd seen, that shit got you nothing but dead.

Sometimes the best thing you can do for your kids is to kill 'em 'fore the pain starts, my momma used to say, as we staggered through this ruined world together; *sometimes it's kill yourself, and let them eat your corpse.* Not like I ever believed she'd've done either, no matter *how* many times she said it; that was my gram talking, not her. The second part, anyway.

And besides: The real trick is knowing which.

Or when.

PELICAN

How I found the kid? Like this: wild as hell and twice as ornery, so much he snapped and scratched at me between bouts of puking; sick from eating rotten meat and sleeping in a corpse-nest, clutched tight to the one must've been his momma, once. Thumb deep in his mouth, even then.

The place was a campsite, fairly well-covered. Parents'd made 'emselves swamp suits from grass and such, muddied up their faces—couldn't make him do the same, so they just let him run free instead, counted on him to roll in the dirt like a dog and go animal, which he'd sure done well with since. But they'd been found nevertheless, no matter how well they hid, or fought. I saw the end of it clear. Took down two more as they died, and the rest must've run, not even bothered robbing 'em after.

Think he might've been eight, maybe, by the time I fell across him. Just like my gram, when *her* world went black. 'Cause things do go 'round and 'round, and that's the fact.

(One of 'em, anyhow.)

As to why I kept him, well...he was way too sick to be worth the effort of killing, like I said. Would've made for bad meat himself, as I'd learned that first year. Pets can be useful, though. Good for scouting and back-up, for clearing track; good to trip traps first, so you don't. Good for company, extra warmth on a monsoon night.

There's worse things by far I could've done than tie him to me like I did, but it ain't like he was innocent either; that's how I thought of it, at the time. I watched him a while, to make sure.

He was a good little predator already, just like me. And I guess—

I guess I thought: why not?

Didn't take all too much to tame him, soon found out. I had fresh water, weapons, a bit of food; still had some meds left from my last pass through what my momma'd called "town," those knocked-down knots of too-big houses where gangs set up markets and drink-holes, lying wait for lone fools to screw with. So I tempted him in, tied him down, fed him up and

57

got him well. Held him while he shook, stroked his hair...even sung to him a bit under my breath, so's he could feel the burr of it through my skin. By the time he was well he was looking at me all bright-eyed with his mouth a little open, same way dogs used to, back when I still found 'em. Before they came too close, that is.

Pet 'em with the one hand, cut their throats with the other. Dogs are easy; they never even saw it coming. Dumb creatures.

He wasn't that, at least.

We moved on, once he was able. I made him take the swamp-suit off his momma, mud it up twice over, inside and out. The smell was good to keep sharp-toothed things away, or make roamers want to look elsewhere. We'd crouch down in the muck, follow 'em soft for a while, then he'd take 'em low and I'd take 'em high, get the voice-box so they couldn't scream out; he went straight for the back of the knees 'til I taught him to slip his blade in between the ribs or slash inside the groin, nick all those places where something popped and blood sprayed out. Butcher 'em quick, get the parts that stayed good longest, and disappear.

Nights I heard him trying to sing sometimes, his voice all raspy; I'd kick him quick, make him stop, 'fore somebody heard. But I did recognize the songs, same ones I'd sung him in his fever. Same ones my gram sung me.

One time he tried to hug into me without asking, so I punched him right in the gut, made him whoop like he was going to heave; he knew to do it quiet by then, and made sure to. Told him: *Don't try cuddling up, boy, not if I ain't said so—I ain't the same one dropped you.* Knew I had him trained good by that time when he just nodded.

And if I woke up next morning to find him close enough I felt him, no matter how careful he'd been not to let us touch? Well, that was all right. Just meant he knew who kept him fed, was all.

I didn't ever ask the kid his name—didn't want to know, in truth. Just in case things went bad, later on. Never told him mine, either.

Not that I could remember it, by then.

The pelican. Why do I keep thinking about it? Been years since I stopped looking at that picture, and I know the words by heart.

Maybe 'cause I passed the book on to the kid, back around the same time he finally started talking...answering when I told him stuff, though not answering *back*; I knew he knew better. Made sure of that myself. 'Cause I showed him his letters and left him to it, the same way gram showed me.

I sure didn't have anything else to give him, not 'less he grew the balls to kill me in my sleep. Which I knew—hoped—he would, someday, and sooner rather than later.

Already felt the sickness on me, you see, thickening up my blood. Microplastic Syndrome, that doc in Essboro called it, when I took the kid in to get him checked for radiation and bioplague, after we crossed the outer edge of where St. Louis used to be; where gram lived was bad for it, or so said the CDC map.

Biggest place I ever been, Essboro. They had generators, WiFi access, greenhouses. Ate a tomato for the first time ever, there; the kid ate a whole apple one nibble at a time, so slow it turned brown 'fore he reached the core. Ate that, too.

You can stay, the doc said, after he told me what I could expect, going forward. *Be glad to have you, no matter what you might've done. We all know what it's like, out there. And the kid could stay too, of course.*

But we moved on, instead the both of us. I sure wasn't gonna leave him behind, not by then. Not when I was used to him.

Not when he was *mine*.

❧

I taught him to be me, 'cause that's all I knew. And that's the problem.

Started to cough a month back, maybe. I can feel my heart skip. This tightness in my chest, my muscles. I ache all over; getting slow now, slower than either of us can afford. And I can see him watching me from the corner of his eyes, but not like he's getting ready to take my shit and skip, like any normal asshole. More like he's getting ready to nurse me 'til I die, then lie down and hug me 'til he does, too.

And: I don't know why I should care 'bout him being that kind of stupid, if he is, so long's he waits 'til then. So long's he keeps me fed and safe, like I kept him, 'til it's not like I'm gonna know anymore if he doesn't. I shouldn't. Not with all I seen.

Nobody should.

He shouldn't, it was the other way 'round.

I dream about the pelican, chewing up food 'til it's soft enough to swallow. Chewing it up and dripping it into their chick's mouth, just the way I did into his back at the start, when he was too sick to know he was starving.

Ten days since we found the family, living in their swamp-side squat—little house like a tent wove from reeds and grass, popped up on top of a cave they'd dug out under the earth. Has a chimney made from cans with a wet stump 'round it for cover, smoke seeping up slow, like it's part of the fog; smart. Saw the momma hunting rats with a spear, the poppa picking fungus with a baby slung under his some sort'a cape he made from old plastic to keep it warm, dry and muffled, but with a scarf on top to make sure it doesn't smother. Smart again. And there's other kids hid back in the cave while their folks are out, one maybe my boy's age keeping watch, good enough with a sling I saw him pick a bird off a tree twenty feet away, even in the rain. Heard my boy give his grunting laugh at that, and knew why: I'd've beat him good for doing something like that, he was mine. 'Cause you never do know who's around, no matter how long you've been where you are. Safety's a lie.

They're weak, my boy told me that night, huddled in our hide. *We could take 'em, easy. That could be our house. We could eat off them for weeks, dry the rest. Live there a year or more.*

Too many, I said. *And a man, too.*

We took men before.

Not with a woman and kids for back-up. Not when we don't know how many might be back in there, for sure.

He went quiet then—nodding, but not like he agreed. More like he knew I was hurting too much to move just then, so he'd wait, and try again later.

Felt my chest squeeze again then, and twice as hard. Thinking: *that's my voice comin' out of your mouth*, as it did.

So we keep on watching, for now.

That family love each other, I think. Close as I've seen since my gram died, since my momma turned mean. And they're *not* weak, not so's I've noticed. Poppa and momma done their share, here and there, keeping roamers away; know to keep out of sight if there's more than one, and make sure they're dead 'stead of trying to run 'em off. They cut up the corpses, but don't butcher 'em. Spread 'em around for the stink, or use 'em to bait their traps instead.

Think if they just found my boy they might do him the same way, 'specially if he threatened 'em. But if they found us together, if they killed *me*...if I *made* them kill me...

If they saw him cry over me, like I think he might. Like he might still be dumb enough to.

I think they might take him in, even if they had to treat him the way I did, at first. Like a wild dog, too wild to let in the house, or leave your kids alone with. But—

—tameable, if you feed it. If you pet it. Set water out for it. Give it a name and call it, 'til it comes. The way I never would.

The way I never could.

ॐ

Tomorrow. I'll make 'em kill me tomorrow, then it'll be up to them. And then...

...well, I won't know, will I?

Either way.

Fracture

MERCEDES M. YARDLEY

Layla fell in love with a man made of glass. His hands were jagged, but his lips were smooth and cool to the touch. He slipped into her bedroom in the evenings, invisible to the naked eye, and when they made love, he refracted the light into rainbows.

Something magical happened. Layla's belly grew and she felt something exquisite and frightening moving around inside. She held her glass lover's hand and he kissed her fingers, and her temple, and her cheek, and her face, before putting his mouth close to her stomach.

"Little one," he said, and his voice sounded like the wind blowing through a flute, "there are so many wondrous things to see. But the world is dangerous to our kind. Take after your mother and be flesh and bone, for I wish you to be strong and experience the world."

He turned to Layla, his clear eyes sparkling in the candlelight.

"I would be your husband if you will have me," he said, and when Layla wept in joy, her colorless tears looked like glass themselves.

But a love affair with a glass man isn't tenable. Layla's father stormed in, demanding to know who had soiled her, because he had wealthy suitors lined up for miles around.

"They won't marry you if you're with child," he said. His eyes glowed in a way quite unlike her lover's. "They want a woman unsullied. But if we can perhaps ratify your mistake..."

He took his walking stick, with its thick silver handle, and struck her once. Layla cried out in a voice piercing enough to shatter wine glasses. Her father raised it a second time and brought it down hard.

"Enough," cried her lover, who stood glistening in the corner. He raced to defend his beloved and grabbed the cane in his fragile hands.

"A demon!" Layla's father cried and swung the cane wildly. There was a sound, like a mirror shattering. There was a sound, like a crystal snifter dropping. There was a sound, and then another, as Layla stood in an explosion of glass shards and wailed.

"Layla," her father called, but she gathered her skirts and ran from him, her feet cut and ripped by the broken glass on the ground. Glass embedded itself in her feet and she left footprints of blood as she fled deep into the night.

❦

Crystal was fine and young and smooth and completely translucent. Her young legs were long, and her hair fell down her back in tinkling waves. Her heart was red and made of organic muscle just like her mother's. It pulsed and throbbed and beat through her clear chest.

"Be careful," Layla told her wearily. "You mustn't fall."

"I know, Mother."

"You mustn't jar or crack or break."

"I'm being very careful."

"You must be wary of extreme temperatures."

"Of course."

Her mother's eyes went far away as they often did, and Crystal knew she was thinking of her father. She wouldn't speak much of him except to say that he had come to a bad end, and that's why she and Layla lived alone in the forest, where nobody could bump into them. Their tiny house was surrounded by soft grasses and clover. Layla went outside daily, removing rocks and wayward branches. There was nothing for Crystal to shatter her toe on.

"You must be careful, for I cannot heal you," her mother said, and tended to her own feet. They were gnarled with wounds that never quite seemed to heal, shards of something shiny constantly worrying under her skin. When she walked, she moved as though she was stepping on knives, but she touched the tender scars gently and with a strange kind of love.

Crystal sighed. She tired of being swaddled in knitted wraps like an infant. She wanted to shed the extra layers and run free in the woods, to dip her hands in the brook and become like a river rock. She wanted to reflect the sunlight like a prism and see what a town square looked like and do all the things her mother forbade.

"If I could just climb a tree," Crystal began.

"You're so precious," Layla said. "More precious than a diamond. More precious than the glass slipper of a princess."

"Mother, I want to go to school. I want to have friends. I'm so very lonely."

Her mother kissed her forehead dreamily, and Crystal closed her eyes.

"Lonely, yes," she murmured to Crystal. "But you are unbroken."

"Is there anywhere else that is safe? Somewhere that isn't here? Perhaps we could travel there, Mother."

"I've thought of taking you to the sea, child. It's miles and miles of open water with nothing to shatter against. But it's far away and the journey is too dangerous. And the sea is so vast..."

It was so large that a small glass girl, slippery from the water, could wriggle from her mother's grasp and float far, far away. It was Layla's nightmare but Crystal's dream.

She was safe and she was loved, but that wasn't enough. One night when the moon was full and the air was as clear as Crystal herself, she donned her warmest cloak and fled into the night.

She ran like a rabbit. She ran like a stream. She ran like her mother so many years ago, her human heart thumping against her fragile ribs, her legs shining in the dark. While her mother had carried a precious unborn child of glass, Crystal carried her fragile, human heart.

It wasn't easy for a glass girl in a city. There were cobblestones to trip on and carriages that run past. Crystal's pinky finger was caught in a door and broke off in the jam. Her tears *plink, plink, plinked* as they fell and shattered on the ground. Children hurried to collect them before they broke, sucking on them like candy.

"Who are you?" one of the children asked. He squatted next to a dirty alley. "Why do you look so strange?"

"My name is Crystal," she answered. "I come from the forest."

"Are you a witch?" a little girl wondered. "Are you a fairy?"

"I'm a girl just like you," she said.

"You're nothing like us," a boy told her, grabbing her arm. "You're strange and I can see right through you. Even your skin feels different."

"Please don't," she said, and stepped away, but he pushed her against the stone wall so roughly that she heard two of her vertebrae crush.

"Are you see-through everywhere?" he asked. He yanked her cloak off. The other children began to tug at her simple clothes.

"Stop," she cried. "Leave me alone!"

Fabric tore, and Crystal stood there in the sunlight, covering herself with invisible hands. Her vulgar human heart was glutted with transparent blood, a pumping clump of arteries and muscle.

"Her heart looks like something dead," the boy said, and his face was white.

"Disgusting," a child cried, and reached down to pick up a stone. "Go away! Never come back."

The stone flew past Crystal's head and hit the alley wall. She stood still, staring in shock, until another stone hit her in the shoulder. She heard a crunching of glass, the sound of fragile bones breaking. The children whooped as she fled, holding her tattered clothes around her. Rocks hit the dirt at her feet, occasionally pelting her body, and the glass bruised in spiderweb cracks.

๛

Layla searched for her daughter. She searched every inch of the cottage, looking for the tell-tale signs of light rainbowing over the walls or reflecting against the ceiling. Crystal wasn't to be found.

Had she been stolen like a jewel? Had somebody slipped her from bed

65

during the night? Had she left on her own because she was so unbearably lonely?

"What do I do?" Layla said aloud. She held a glass drop in her hand, a piece of her lover that had once been sharp and brittle, but time and the constant rubbing from her warm fingers had turned it smooth. "I must find her." She kissed the glass drop and tucked it into a little pocket sewn inside her dress, next to her heart.

Layla gathered her things. It didn't take long for she didn't have much. Anxiety swelled and bloomed like a bloodstain inside of her chest as she set out on her journey. The world is so terribly cruel to those who are fragile.

Crystal believed in beauty and kindness with her whole beating heart. Surely those children were exceptionally ill-tempered, and everyone else would be better.

It was not to be. A glass girl, just like a regular girl, can be coveted and kept on a shelf. Greedy hands caught in her hair and broke it off in clumps. She was pawed and pushed to her knees with a sound like pottery falling. A girl with a glass jaw only needs one good punch to crush it permanently, and it's impossible to hide your damaged face behind hands when they're transparent.

Crystal ran from the city, ran from the forest, ran until she was good and lost and exhausted and miserable. She wandered until she came to a strange blue horizon that smelled of salt. She collapsed in the sand, and heard strange birds calling overhead when she fell asleep. She wept, for most birds were drawn to shiny things.

Layla followed the dusty road to the city, where she found a group of children playing with wooden swords. Her eyes were drawn to a familiar blue cloak.

"You there," she said, and grabbed the cloaked child by the scruff of the neck. "Where did you come by my daughter's robe?"

"That thing was your daughter?" the child asked. Layla struggled to keep her fists from clenching.

"Tell me where she is, or you will regret it," Layla vowed.

"I don't know. She ran away a long time ago. Let go of me." The child wiggled out of her grasp and scurried away.

⚜

The sea is a beautiful, rough thing, gorgeous and unyielding. It makes no promises. It refuses to compromise. When something shattered and fragmented crawls into its waters, a metamorphosis happens.

The sea took this glass child, this ruined girl, and ran its sea-foam hands over her broken parts. It seeped into every crack, every vein, mouthing at the dirt caught inside.

"Can you put me back together?" Crystal asked.

"That is not what I do," the sea hissed. It was busy creating whirlpools and causing carnage. The sea rose with sunken ships in its hair and paused for admiration.

"What can you do, then?" Crystal asked.

"I *transform*, child," the sea said, and it lapped at Crystal's cracked feet. "Come."

Crystal thought of her mother, and this gave her courage. She slid under the ocean waves, and it began.

The sea tumbled and tossed and buffeted. Loose pieces fell away, and her meaty human heart was fed to the fishes. Her loneliness and longing wore away like the rest of her, riding the waves and turning into foam.

"At last," she thought, "I am happy."

"It matters not," answered the sea.

⚜

Layla searched the land tirelessly. She looked in cities and towns and villages. She looked in the forest and in the deserts. Her tender, raw feet grew calloused from her travels, pushing the precious glass shards even farther into her body. Each painful step was an exquisite reminder of him. Her hair grayed and her back stooped, but each thought of a little glass girl rejuvenated her. She climbed through tall grasses and tripped over roots. She eventually came to a place that smelled of salt and tears.

The sea.

Each footstep in the sand felt heavy, but the water glittered and glistened like two loves long lost. Layla touched her lover's glass drop through the pocket in her dress.

She neared the water, pulling off her shoes and wading into the waves. The sand gave way beneath her.

"What do you want?" asked the sea. "I am busy."

"I'm looking for my daughter," Layla said. She had never spoken to the sea before. "She disappeared many years ago."

"Daughters often disappear," the sea sniffed. "I've taken many of them myself. So easy to lose, daughters."

"She is beautiful. She's made of glass."

The sea capsized several ships while it thought.

Layla sighed and fell to her knees. The water swirled around her.

"It's possible to love something too much," the sea told her. It caressed her legs with green weeds. "You can love something to pieces."

"I'm afraid that's what I've done," Layla admitted. Her tears, when they fell, weren't glass at all. They were bitter and salty, and the sea opened its mouth to taste them.

"Tastes like me," the sea commented, and something washed onto the sand. A treasure of the deep. A gift from the universe. Layla reached out for it with a small sound.

It was a piece of sea glass, its rough edges worn smooth by years in the ocean. Layla picked it up and it thrummed in her hand.

"Crystal," she whispered, and held the glass to the sun. It had turned milky over time, and no longer reflected light like a prism, but seemed to capture it and hold it within.

"She said she was happy," the sea said offhandedly, and flowed away. It had fish to spawn and currents to follow. The short lives of humans meant very little in the vastness of the universe.

Layla took the shiny piece of glass from her pocket and held them both, lover and daughter, in her gnarled hand before clenching them to her heart. She lay back in the sand, the sun warming her old bones as the water lapped around her.

"She was happy," Layla repeated, and closed her eyes. The waves crept higher. " That was all I ever wanted."

Layla didn't turn into mermaid's tears like her lover and daughter. Her flesh became a feast for monsters of the deep, and her bones were picked clean and worn as hairpins by the sea itself. But the human heart, made of muscle and meat, is such a funny thing. Even after it's consumed and turned into energy that powers mighty tails and tiny fins and microscopic cilia, it still manages to beat, beat, beat under the ocean waves with everything else that is precious.

When Auntie's Due

SARAH READ

The museum is chaos. It always is. If you can even call it a museum—there are no dusty exhibits here. Everything here is sticky, interactive. And the children are everywhere, interacting. My two-year-old niece, Cora, spins a crank that dumps a bucket of plastic balls down a chute. She stomps her feet and shrieks with glee, the sound weaving through the other children's shrieks, the wails that spill from strollers, the shushing of mothers. I bring my niece here every week, to give Caitlin a break. She's home with her latest addition, my new nephew Paul, round and perfect.

"It's good practice," she always says, "for when you have your own." She says it like she's not six years younger than me, like she doesn't know I want kids more than anything. Like I haven't sunk my last dollar at the clinic, over and over again. She knows. "First you need to get a man," she says.

"You don't need a man to have a baby," I say.

"If you've been trying without one, it explains why it hasn't worked yet."

I ignore the knife she's twisted in my heart. It's not the only knife she's put there. "You don't need a man to have a baby, you just need a man to get pregnant."

"I just said you needed to find one, I didn't say you needed to keep

SARAH READ

him. Good riddance to them all," she says. And then she laughs, forgets she was picking a fight, but the knife still twists, will keep on twisting till I'm distracted enough to ignore it. But I won't forget it. I remember each one.

My niece is distracting. So is the cacophony of the museum, but it's hard being around so many babies, so many moms. So many moms who don't even look like they want to be there, don't even look like they want to be moms. Moms who yell and scold and snap. I watch from the bench along the wall as they supervise their phones, ignore their kids, only lifting their gaze to shout, redirect, threaten to leave but never do, because at least here their kids stay busy. Entertained in a place where Mom doesn't have to be the entertainment, waiter, and main course all in one. I get it. Caitlin thinks I don't, but I do. She probably doesn't even think about all the times I had to take care of her, entertain her, so our own mom didn't have to. They all take it for granted.

Our mom was one of those—a mom who didn't want to be a mom. Caitlin takes after her. Which is why I'm always watching Cora. Cora is more like me. I can tell from the way she holds her dolls—like they're real and precious. How long before she has to play mother to her baby brother, before this cycle starts all over?

I watch the sea of reluctant families, and I rub the bump on my midsection, tight against the waist of my pants. I rub it and adjust it, so it sits the way it should. Looks the way it should. So the straps holding it in place don't chafe against my hips.

Then Cora's small fingers close over mine. "Come, An-tee Soapy," she says, pulling on my arm.

I'm Soapy, because Sophie is hard to say. Caitlin thinks it's hilarious. I think it's the best name I've ever had. This girl has my whole heart.

I stand and stretch my back. A mom nearby glances my way, sees the bump, and offers a sympathetic smile, one that says, "It's so hard, isn't it?"

It is. She has no idea.

"You won't even tell me his name? Wait...do you even know his name?" Caitlin bounces in the deep knee-bend-rock that keeps the baby asleep while Cora squeezes a pouch of apple mush onto the table.

"He doesn't want to be involved," I say. "And frankly, I don't care."

"Don't be ridiculous, of course you care," she says. She says it like she wants it to be true, like she wants me to feel abandoned instead of elated.

I go with it, because elation is harder to fake. Abandoned is my default.

"Whatever. It's not up to me. He made his choice, I made mine." I rub the bump again, but back away when Caitlin reaches for it.

"What, it's not like I'm some stranger at the grocery store!" She laughs and reaches again, and I dodge, and Cora, that angel, chooses that moment to spill her juice. Her shriek wakes the baby, and in the chaos, the bump is safe.

While Caitlin is distracted, I pull on the straps, line everything up. It looks good. But it doesn't feel right. It's a good thing Caitlin has her hands full.

❦

An-tee Soapy's bump makes her feel sick, I've explained to Cora, to buy some time off Auntie duty, to hide from Caitlin, to switch to the bigger bump. She misses her weekly museum visit, but I've promised, soon, we'll go back. And we will, when I'm ready.

And when the air turns cold, and I can finally pull a thick sweater over the swell of my stomach and the weight of the bump makes me ache and waddle, I go back to Caitlin's to get Cora.

"Don't you know you're supposed to glow?" Caitlin says.

"Eat shit," I say.

Cora laughs.

"Sophie!" Caitlin cups a hand over my girl's ear.

"Soapy!" Cora reaches up for me, but I take her hands in mine and give them a squeeze.

"An-tee Soapy can't lift you right now, baby girl. My back is killing me."

Caitlin nods and starts to walk us toward the door, anxious for her break. "It won't be much longer." Her tone is chipper, but with the weight of *I know I'm about to lose my babysitter* behind it. She'd have to parent her own kids if I had a baby of my own.

Cora is wilder than usual on the drive to the museum, all her pent-up excitement after time apart coming to a head as we park, and I shut off the engine. She's pulling at the straps of her car seat, ready to hulk her way to freedom.

"Hold on, baby girl, An-tee Soapy needs to get ready." I reach behind my back and squeeze the clip, release the heaviness from my front. I pull the pillowed rubber out from under my sweater and tuck it under one of Cora's old blankets on the passenger seat. The skin of my stomach feels wrong, cold without its comforting layer. Empty.

I pull a bag out of my backpack and put on my kit, watch myself transform in the rear-view mirror. Makeup, which I am not accustomed to, and the most convincing wig I could find.

"You look like Elsa!" Cora squeals.

I don't, but I could pull off blond, I suppose.

"Mama's Elsa," Cora coos, proudly.

"You bet she is. The ice queen, herself." I smirk at my joke and the face in the mirror looks more familiar than my own.

We go in, and the noise hasn't changed, like it's just kept on going the whole time we were away.

The staff have changed, though, and I was counting on it. A fresh batch of high school students watching the desk, the turnover like clockwork every semester. We disappear into the crowd.

The families have changed, too, but haven't. They're different, but all the same—exhausted, letting their kids burn themselves out, praying for a good nap later, watching their phones, not watching their kids.

I count the strollers, but it's hard. They all look alike, which is good. I note the wails coming from each, pinpoint which have the right sound to them. New, but not too new.

That one.

The woman's hair is half up in a sloppy bun, half spilling over her ears in greasy tangles. She's leaning against the railing of the toddler area as if it's the only thing holding her up. The four kids rattling around inside the arena are hers, all boys under six, all wearing each other's misfitting clothes. And the stroller by her hip, which was wailing till a moment ago, now silent after she wheeled it back and forth and back and forth.

Now one of the boys is wailing—the smallest, at the top of the slide, too scared to go down, but with all his brothers jammed into the tunnel behind him, pushing.

The slide is shaped like a green bean, the tunnel a vine, the only way in is up a climbing wall of tomatoes and carrots and berries—a food pyramid to fun. Or torture, if you have three brothers. It would be worse to have four.

The boy is crying, his brothers shouting, and mom has to lift herself from the railing. It looks like it takes her last ounce of strength, and what she hasn't realized yet is that she's going to have to climb that pyramid, work her way through the tunnel, past the blockage of brothers, to even get to her crying child. It's going to take minutes. It's going to take all her focus.

"Cora, honey. Come on, let's go get some ice cream and play dolls."

She abandons the clay table at speed. I know what my girl likes.

I'm fast, but not too fast.

The stroller handles are still warm. One wheel drags—it's been through four kids already—so I have to lean it to the left to make it go straight.

Straight onto the elevator, where I risk a peek under the blanket. Round and perfect. Straight to the coat check, where I lift the baby out, tuck him into another parked stroller.

"Is you doll?" Cora asks.

"It is!" I say. "And if you're a good girl, it will be your doll when we get home."

Cora squeals and jumps, clapping. The sound of her squeal masks, for a second, the sound from two floors above.

"Hurry up, baby girl."

Sleepy mom was faster than I thought. There will be at least a minute where they all assume some innocent mistake. Mistakes, at least, are thinkable.

In that minute, we're at the car. I put the stroller, and the *doll*, in the trunk. Give him a little more than a dose of something sleepy, the pink allergy goo from Cora's diaper bag. He spits, splutters, and I wipe his little face. He fusses quietly as I close the trunk.

"I hold the doll, An-tee Soapy?"

"When we get home. If you're good."

I buckle Cora in, then bend down in the front of the car and stuff my wig into the storm drain.

Cora is too excited to notice I'm no longer Elsa. She sings an ice cream song while I pull my bump back under my sweater, buckle it in place.

We're far enough away, at the ice cream shop, when the perimeter closes like a cage, when all the phones in line blare the alert and we all look at our screens and look around, into the faces of strangers. None match the description.

⊗⚜⊗

Caitlin meets us in the yard, her face pale, her phone in her hand, Paul on her hip. Cora runs up to her, a new doll clutched in her sweet arms.

"Look what An-tee Soapy give me!"

I smile, tight-lipped, at Caitlin.

"I saw the alert, were you—"

"Don't worry. We were already at the ice cream shop by then."

Caitlin's shoulders visibly drop in relief. But not all the way. She's lost the "it can't happen here" innocence that all mothers lose, sooner or later.

At least I'll never have that moment. I already know.

"We're okay. Why don't you go take a nap. You probably didn't rest at all, and I promised Cora we'd play with her new doll." I reach for Paul, and Caitlin hands him to me, her eyes already glazing with early surrender to sleep. He is hot and heavy in my arms, his thick legs kicking at the bump as I prop him on my hip. He leans away from me, reaching for Caitlin, who has already turned her back, already made it halfway to the house. I pull Paul close and follow.

Paul has enough clothes for two babies, which is my fault. I can't resist the tiny outfits. He's never worn most of them. I fill my backpack with diapers and onesies. I play dress-up with Paul while Cora dresses her doll.

"Okay, sweetie, it's time for you and our dollies to take a nap." She tucks in her doll, and I tuck in Paul, then Cora, and hum a lullaby.

76

Cora's out fast, after the museum and sugar crash. Paul isn't—he never sleeps—but he will, with a little over a dose of the pink goo.

I carry him out to the car, open the trunk.

The round, perfect baby is sleeping like an angel, his face as still as porcelain. I lay Paul down, dose him, and tuck him in, then lift the sleeping baby and carry him inside, change his limp body into Paul's clothes, not a perfect fit, but so close, and tuck him in to Paul's crib. For once, the room is silent. The whole house.

I give Cora a light forehead kiss, and I'm gone.

I don't dare stop, not even to take the screaming baby out of the trunk, in case someone sees me taking a baby out of a trunk. The pink goo did not work on Paul, and I wonder if Caitlin's been using it, too, desperate. If he's built up a resistance.

Not till I'm in my garage, the door closed, do I open the hatch and see that angry pink face, mouth stretched in demand, tiny hands clawed at the air. If the museum baby was a cherub, then this is a demon. Nothing human could cry like that. Still, I reach for him. If this is going to work, we'll have to get used to each other.

He's hot from screaming as I lift him, hold him to my shoulder, shush him and start those deep knee bends, soothing sways.

I carry him inside, where I have everything ready.

He's changed and fed, still whimpering, but soon he cries himself to sleep and I lay him in the fresh crib on the fresh sheet.

I watch him for a while. His soft puffs of breath, milk-scented. Milk-based formula-scented. I told Caitlin she should breastfeed, but she told me to mind my own business. I'm glad she didn't, now.

I reach under my shirt and unhook the bump, let it fall away, rubber sliding to the floor leaving a slick of sweat behind, my back lashed with the strap marks that have been there for months now, that feel like they might never go away. I feel transformed. It's something like a birth.

Report: The suspect is on camera, on six cameras, including the elevator, where we get the best look at her face. As much of it as we can see, as she only ever looks down, to the stolen stroller and the bouncing child with her.

She's on camera in the entryway, with a different stroller than the one she had in the elevator.

She's on camera as she came in, an hour before that, with the same bouncing child but no stroller. She paid cash.

We don't have a name, and we barely have a face.

At least, not her face.

The bouncing child, though—the smiling little girl is always grinning upward, and she's our only lead. But we don't even know if she belongs to the blond woman, or if she herself went missing from somewhere, sometime.

Video from a bus stop security camera shows the blond woman and the child, and the stolen stroller with the stolen baby in it, walking into a parking lot. There are only six cars in that parking lot.

❦

I call Caitlin as soon as I can, when I know the kids will still be asleep. From the sound of her voice, she was still asleep, too.

"Sorry I had to bail. The kids were down for their nap, so I figured it would be okay." I give her a minute to catch up to where she is, to realize that I'm not in her house anymore.

"Oh, right. Yeah, fine. Thanks for getting them down. I don't even know how you got Paul to sleep. He never sleeps."

"I think we wore him out playing dress-up. Look, the reason I had to go... The dad called. He changed his mind. He wants to try and be involved."

"What the hell do you mean *he's changed his mind?*" Caitlin spits over the phone, now wide awake.

"He wants us to give things a try. Talk about us. Maybe we have a future after all, I dunno."

"I don't like this, Sophie. Your one-night-stand sperm donor wants to meet up, right before you're due, to talk, and he makes you come to him?

How do you know he's not a murderer? How do you know this isn't some ambush to avoid child support?"

"You really need to stop listening to all those murder podcasts." *Especially in front of my girl*, I want to add.

"I'm actually being serious, here. I'm worried about you. And you're due any second, you shouldn't even be on the road."

"You're not worried about me, you're worried about your babysitter." My throat feels tight. It feels wrong to match her cruelty, especially when she's not showing it, for once. She doesn't answer. "I'll check in, okay? I'll send you reassuring texts. Pictures of me, holding the day's newspaper, okay?"

"Give me his address. What's his name?"

"His name is Craig, and he lives in Portland. And I don't have his address because I'm not actually dumb enough to go to his house. We're meeting at the art museum."

"Sophie, that's a long drive. What if you pop?"

"Then my poor kid gets a Maine birth certificate."

Caitlin takes a moment. "You'd better text me every day. Every hour."

"I'm not going to text you while I'm driving. But I promise I'll check in every day. Several times." It's actually sweet, if she cares, and it tugs at my heart a little. She'd make a nice auntie. Even if she is a terrible mother.

It's been three hours since Cora and I left the museum. Longer than I wanted. I need to move fast. I load Paul into the car seat, latched in place and perfectly buckled. Trunk packed with baby essentials.

He screams for miles, for hours. I'm ready to scream, too, by the time he finally passes out, as we hit the highway through Syracuse, heading south.

We're almost to the Pennsylvania border. Then the next part of the plan.

☙❧

Report: The suspect's car is a white Honda Civic. The footage is too grainy to get a license plate and the car too common to get an ID, but it's a lead. There were no clues found in the parking lot. There might be a thousand white Honda Civics in town, but how many are driven by white women in their thirties who are blond? The list is getting shorter.

We enter the empty no-man's-land of farms and buggies, where the fields are shorn short and ready for a long winter. The roads go on for miles without a sign or streetlight, and the only sign of traffic is the horse shit piled along the median line.

We enter Millersville from the west, and find a bed-and-breakfast, the kind that caters to the looky-loos who want a taste of local culture, but not too much. Every goddamn surface is quilted. It's like a padded cell.

"These are lovely," I tell the old woman who runs the place, as I run my hands over the quilts folded on the chair backs. "I've always wanted an Amish quilt, but they don't sell them in Arizona." Or Upstate New York, but I'm sure they don't sell them in Arizona, either.

"Oh, they're all over the shops downtown," she says, dropping a room key in my hand. "You can have your pick of a hundred. I know I can't resist them; I'd buy them all if I could."

"Are you sure you didn't?" I ask, and fortunately she takes it in good humor, laughing as she totters back down the stairs to the reception hall.

My skin is crawling, but I don't think we'll have to stay here long.

Report: The suspect was found at home at six p.m. The child seen in surveillance footage was with her and was taken immediately into protective custody. The body of the abducted child was also recovered. He had been placed, deceased, into the crib of the suspect's infant son, whose whereabouts are currently unknown. The suspect was combative, accruing additional charges of resisting arrest and assaulting an officer.

Attempts are being made to contact the suspect's sister.

When my phone rings, I have to run, out of my quilted room, down the stairs, out of the house. As far away from the crying baby as I can, so they won't hear him.

"Hello?... Yes... Oh, my god... I'm out of town, visiting my boyfriend, but... I'll be there soon. I'll start back right away. Tell her Auntie Soapy is coming."

I can hear her in the background, wailing. "Aunty Soapy! Mommy!"

"I'm coming, baby girl."

❦

Back down the long road, the countryside unlit, the view a patchwork of fields in varying shades of dark. I drive till we're far away from any buildings, the only farms set back against a distant line of trees.

It's cold. Maybe too cold. Paul's naked, no modern clothes or diapers, but the quilt is thick. Heavy cotton layered in patches over lofty batting, trapping all the heat of his endless tantrum. It will keep him warm. He'll keep himself warm, screaming. Holding him is like holding hot coals.

I swaddle him tight, so he won't fight his way out of the warm, and I lay him by a spindly sapling on the roadside.

This road will be full of buggies in the morning, those buggies full of families in their Sunday best. The bright quilt colors will catch their eyes. They'll see him, or hear him, probably in time. And if what I've read is true, they'll keep the secret in their community. An abandoned Amish baby is none of the modern world's business. He might even be loved—might even have a doting mother who will parent him herself. If she can take the screaming. The never sleeping. The way his small hands turn from soft shells to claws that will wear her down like he did to Caitlin, like he's done to me.

I get back in the car, but I don't drive, not right away. It feels wrong to let go of something I've wanted for so long. To let go of what I wanted to be for him. I can still hear him through the window glass, and the sound keeps shredding at raw nerves. My head is spinning, like it's been flushed down a funnel of noise. Just before I clap my hands over my ears, I hear another noise. A horse? It's gruff, a nickering—maybe in one of the fields.

But if it's on the road, if someone's coming...

I get out of the car and go to Paul, lift him from the cradle of tree roots and hold him close, shushing, cooing, stifling his screams against my chest, pulling his face to my breast as if to nurse him, but pressing him deep into the flesh there to dampen the sound. I listen. I hear the horse again, but the wind moves the sound so I can't tell where it's coming from.

Paul is writhing against my chest, his arms pinned by the quilt, his small face buried against me, my heartbeat now as loud for him as his mother's was in the womb, as loud as his cries were for me, all-consuming, and as I wait and listen, he quiets. He stills.

The whole night silences. Not even the crickets want to wake the sleeping baby.

I wait a few more pounding heartbeats, a few more slow breaths, and I pull him away from my chest. All the red of his face has collected in his eyes, his cheeks now the color of stone. His lips, a tiny bow relaxed for the first time in days.

I lay him back in the tree's cradle.

My head is still spinning, now from silence. My arms feel empty. My stomach empty. My chest aches.

I climb into the car and start the engine, its roar a comfort, proof that I have not stopped hearing altogether. I pull my belly out of the bag beside me, struggle it back into place. The rubber is cold until it warms against my skin, and already I feel less empty. Full and heavy. And my foot is heavy on the gas as I pull away, back home, back to my girl.

❧

"Your sister says you were the one at the museum," the detective says.

I sip the small paper cup of water that he brought me a moment ago. "I usually take her. But I haven't been up to it lately." I rub the bump. It's big, now, as big as it gets.

He nods and makes a note. "But you drive her car."

"She lets me borrow it, sometimes. She has a nicer one she uses more."

He writes again, but not much. They lost interest in me when they saw the bump.

82

"And do you know where your nephew Paul might be?"

My eyes well up. I'm not pretending; I'm exhausted. I shake my head.

"Did she ever say anything that makes you think she might hurt the baby?"

My voice is thick with everything I've felt these past months; giving up on the clinic, seeing Paul born, finding the bump set in a thrift shop, the hordes of unwanted children at the museum. Paul, screaming through two states. "All she ever really said was that he wouldn't sleep. I tried to help her out, I came over as often as I could to give her a break, but..." I let my voice break off. "I think... I think she was getting pretty desperate."

The detective flips his notebook closed. "We may need to talk to you again."

I nod.

"Your sister would like to see you."

My face hardens, like cold rubber strapped to the front of my skull. "Tell her she can see me, and Cora, when she tells us where Paul is."

He leads me to the advocate's office, and Cora runs, wailing, into my arms.

"It's okay, honey. It's going to be okay. Auntie's here."

The advocate hands me a suitcase of Cora's things, but the detective steps in and takes it for me. He carries it to the car and puts it into the empty, clean trunk while I strap Cora into her seat.

He's back inside the station when I slide into the front seat.

"Let's go, baby girl. Let's get some ice cream and a new doll."

I'm going to need a new doll. Soon. I'm due.

Stone's Blood

NICK BOUCHARD

It's dark and your leg hurts. How did you get here?

You were running. Yeah, that's it.

Running. And the mere thought of staccato footfalls makes your leg twitch, sending agony stampeding outward until it's almost impossible to tell that the vicious ache begins just above your hind foot.

You reach your muzzle toward the wound, bracing yourself for what you'll find.

Searing pain.

Implacable teeth have gnashed your leg to pulp —

Was it Reynard up ahead? Maybe the kits?

Not the kits. They haven't left the burrow. Not yet.

Writhing, you howl as the teeth, once cold but now warmed by your blood, slide heedless across the surface of your bone.

Stillness is torture. Each move, punishment.

You can't distinguish this intruder that holds you hostage in the darkness. What is it that clanks and slices, mashes and chews without so much as a grunt or growl?

The thing stinks. Mingling with the aroma of old death and your own waning vitality, it smells like blood — but not like anything you've ever run down and devoured. It's like blood borne from rock.

Absurd. You've seen rocks cracked open, but blood has never flowed from them.

And yet, that smell. It reminds you —

You were running. That's how you got here. Not after the kits, or Reynard. Maybe with them?

No. From. Definitely.

From a thing that smelled of carrion and of this same stone's blood that now feeds on your leg and binds you to the earth.

It's clearer now, how you got here. You were running from the thing that smelled of decay as it stomped and crunched its careless way through the twilit woods, sometimes thundering a sharp bark that stank of smoke. You were far ahead of it, escaping. Your pulse and pace began to slow and just when you chanced a glance over your shoulder, this thing jumped from the leaves and bit down on your leg, sending you sprawling and painfully jerking to a stop as the world went black. Only for you to wake in a darkness deeper than any you've ever known.

The memory of smoke is so real you know it's no memory. On the gently flowing breeze, you can smell that smoke, and carrion, and stone's blood.

You know that this grip on your leg is a silent extension of that noisy thing, that predator. It's coming to add you to the smell of uncountable deaths that drips from it like rain from leaves.

You thrash in panic. The clanking is singular and loud. Now it knows exactly where you are. How could something so incautious take so many lives?

A beacon glints behind distant trees, moving ever closer. This bite has drained you of more than you knew you contained. Each runnel of blood soaking into the earth is not just ebbing wakefulness , but life.

Your life. Life for the kits.

With a yowl of pain muffled by your fur, you sink your teeth into your leg beside the teeth that hold you prisoner.

You're made of the same stuff as those things you catch and eat. You're nourished. Invigorated. It's horrible. You're frantic and howling with each bite of self-inflicted agony. Your teeth are full of your own fur; blood soaks your muzzle. You set the bone far back in your jaw, just as you would any other, to get at the marrow.

That prick of light, that little sun approaches. It draws near but brings no warmth. Cold suffuses you as the thing's bloody jaws and yours slide and crunch around the only barrier between you and freedom — just one bone.

And the light. It grows ever closer.

Carrion and smoke lay thick on the air, an olfactory fog. The little sun casts maddening shadows around the dimple of dark earth and broad leaves that will entomb you, and there's a paralyzing crack. On an ordinary day that sound would meansweet marrow. Today it means anguish.

You lap at the sweet marrow even as burgeoning darkness welcomes you.

The kits.

The darkness recedes as fast as it came. Dry leaves rasp beneath you, a whispered chorus of last breaths inviting you to add yours.

How did you get here?

You ran. From the lumbering thing with only two legs, to the little ones nestled in the burrow. Maybe nipping each other and risking glances into the gloaming, still blind to the beauty and cruelty of the world.

So you run again, cold and broken and free — from the attacking jaws and lush darkness that so nearly claimed you.

In place of your leg is a stripe of pain so bright, so hot the sun will be shamed — if it ever sees you again.

You run as though you never knew a fourth leg. You plunge into a familiar brook and hope the gabbling water will hide your scent and sound. Cold water slows the bleeding. It's your only chance back to the burrow. You know this thing will take the kits too, if it can. You will let that darkness swallow you here before you risk leading it to the them. You do not fear death, but you do not expect survival.

The kits.

You trudge downriver and downwind. The song of the night is punctuated by the fading, arrhythmic stomping of the clumsy thing. From its many layers of bloody, smoky odors, you smell Reynard. He will most certainly not return.

A soft, sad yip escapes your strongest attempt to be silent.

When you no longer smell or hear the thing, you limp from the stream and toward home.

You approach the warmth and musk of the burrow. The soft, clean tang of the kits mingles with excited hungry, still ignorant yips. Teeth nip playfully and soft paws scrabble at the earthen floor, stirring up a lifetime of memories that flow around you like the current of an invisible river. The birth of the kits, rain-soaked fur, the sharp scent of an icy sunrise.

Renard.

Your breath is shallower. The pool of memory eddies and deepens. You submerge as velvety darkness calls for you again.

This time you cannot resist.

Your final steps take you into the dark of the burrow and into that other insistent darkness. You take comfort knowing that what is inside you is no different than what you hunt. You will feed them one last time.

Vé'otsé'e (Warpath Woman)

SHANE HAWK

"Do you want the knife or the pill?"

With one eye crusted shut, Viola drifts from slumber into reality, remnants of her héhpòhénomestòtse (*nightmare*) slipping away like whirling fog beneath a streetlight. A floating bookshelf looms over all her second-hand furniture. A stack of mostly solved Sudoku books adorn her nightstand, along with pill bottles, an ashtray and lighter, and a withered dandelion flower her son, Joseph, gifted her from the decaying front lawn. Viola shakes off the dark thoughts before removing her CPAP mask, revealing a metallic tinge on her tongue and stripes of red running down the plastic tubing. A quick glance at her holographic clock and she knows she's woken up too early.

In the dim bathroom, Viola washes the sleep from her left eye and cleans up the blood streaks down the sides of her face and neck. She's used to nosebleeds ever since her new doctor prescribed a sleep apnea machine. But she counters every new thing with tradition and still uses Tsistsistas (*Cheyenne*) medicine she learned about from her ke'éehe (*grandma*). From the medicine cabinet, Viola takes a pinch of crushed sage she keeps in a small velvet bag and snorts it into the bleeding nostril. A coil of pain unravels in her stomach, and she attributes it to her lackluster meal and boxed tsé-vé'eéno'e (*wine*) last night. Cup. Tap water. Gulp.

To further postpone her daily responsibilities, she slips back under the heated blanket and faces the empty half of the bed. A heavy sigh escapes her lips as she remembers her late husband, Chaytan, will never be in that spot again. Viola's hand rubs the area as if it will bring him back and contemplates downsizing her mattress in this new, much smaller town. She still hasn't found a job and is surviving on life insurance installments. Motivation fades from week to week.

Pink and orange stripes bleed through the automatic blinds onto the bedroom wall, stretching longer and growing brighter by the minute. The songs from the smaller birds are messages for Viola to get up, face another day, and give her little boy Joseph the best life possible. The vibrant colors and bird songs throw fire in her veins for a moment. *Creator, why must the world be beautiful when inside I feel like an ashen, hollowed-out shell of a woman?*

After a deep breath, Viola grabs her aseéestsestótse (*phone*) and opens the Neighbored app. The phone is low on battery; it must not have lined up with the wireless pad, and she hates holding the phone and pad while using it. Scrolling past countless bold headlines reminds her that racism isn't dead, both blatant and casual.

But something catches her eye.

There are many posts from around her county detailing a suspicious maroon van seen in people's neighborhoods.

Viola retrieves her charcoal-gray worry stone. While her amygdala burns with distress, she massages the stone's smooth surface.

After Chaytan's funeral, she and Joseph moved out here to the sticks, ratcheting up her anxiety. For months, she hassled her wealthy brother for a security system until he paid contractors to install one. Now she has a doorbell camera, several perimeter cameras, and an alarm system. The weapons she keeps in the basement give her some peace of mind. Her dad taught her how to ménohe (*fight*) from an early age.

Viola opens her home security app to ensure the surveillance equipment is all operational. No hardware warnings. Seeing the murder of ókóhkeo'o (*crows*) on the backyard cam gives her pause. The last time this many messengers gathered, Viola's dad lost his battle with diabetes.

REMINDER: CHECK SLEEP ANALYSIS REPORT. A notification from her health insurance app consumes the entire screen.

This is a daily occurrence and recommended by her doctor. She is to monitor her sleep apnea progress while following a strict weight loss regimen. A distinct red stretch of sleep time mars last night's graph. Sleep quality is color coded like traffic lights, red being the worst and green being the best. Viola taps the red portion of the graph, and it brings up a list of sleep recordings. The audio files' waveforms are unvaried on most nights, with the drone of the machine establishing a baseline room tone.

But there were a few microphone peaks around 3:33 am.

To appease her curiosity, Viola clicks the phone to max volume, scrubs to the timestamp, and plays the file. The typical breathing and machine sounds are apparent, but then there's a creak of her bedroom door. *Okay, Joseph came in last night, I guess.*

Hohát (*Laughter*). An adult man's quiet and deep chuckle.

Viola widens her eyes and clenches her jaw. The man is now speaking in a hushed tone, and Viola puts the phone's speaker right to her ear. He's not speaking English, and from her limited htšéšetsestötse (*knowledge*) of Cheyenne, Arapaho, Spanish, and Diné, Viola doesn't recognize the language. The cadence is slow and measured as if he's reading or reciting something. *Is this an incantation?*

The recitation ends, followed by her bedroom door creaking and clicking shut. Viola stumbles out of bed, with her eyes glued to her phone. She flicks the screen back over to the home security app and taps ReWind Mode, giving her the freedom to view archived video of up to 24 hours ago. She scrubs the playback marker to 3:30 am. The phone displays four black-and-white video boxes. Each camera is equipped with an infrared lens for táa'e (*nighttime*) security. In the distance, the doorbell cam shows a pair of headlights approaching her street. Viola squints but can't make out the type of car parked one house down because the fisheye lens is limited in focal length.

When the archived video goes black at 3:32 am, Viola's jaw goes slack, and ice shoots up her brain stem. She fast forwards the playback, and the security cams don't work again until the 3:40 am marker.

After biting her lip and spacing out from an over-productive imagination, Viola swings her door open and marches down the short hall to Joseph's room. She enters in a panic but stops herself short once she discovers him sound asleep. Viola bows, kisses her fingertips, and gently touches the back of his head. She steps back with her hands on her hips and attempts to slow her panicked breathing.

Joseph has been acting out since the hováneehestótse (*death*) of heho (*his father*) and showing more emotion than he has in years. He grieves in atypical ways, like speaking loudly, having an energetic mood, and watching horror movies with lots of death. He also no longer cares for his stuffed animals. Viola knows the move has been hard on him, but she just had to get out of the city after the matanaévé'hó'e (*cops*) refused to do anything. Seems like cops never want to help Indians, anyway, at least when there's a dead one.

And here I am, about to call the police for some help.

৩৯৩

"Yes, hello. My name is Viola Whiteshield. I think I experienced a home invasion in the middle of the night. I have proof via—"

"Is it you think it happened, or ya got proof? Which is it? That don't really happen 'round here too often."

"Sorry, yes, I have audio recordings of someone sneaking into my bedroom and casting a spell or—"

The local sheriff interrupts Viola with a raucous belly laugh. "Spell? Like witchcraft? Is this one of them crank calls? Ma'am, please, I don't have time for nonsense."

"Sir, I am being one-hundred percent serious with you right now. This is not a prank call. I'm somewhat new in town, and I'm worried for me and my son's safety."

"What'd ya say your name was? Whitfield?"

"Whiteshield. Viola Whiteshield."

The officer grunts like an ape and shuffles papers around. "Ah, Whiteshield. I've heard about you. Injun lady with the Mongoloid son?"

"What the—" Viola gnashes her onené (*teeth*) as her insides are hollowed out. "What's your badge number? Get your supervisor on the—"

Click. CALL ENDED. Viola pinches the bridge of her nose, and the vein in her forehead is swelling with fiery blood. She's breathing short and fast with a clenched jaw, sticky saliva spraying down to her chin. The neighbors probably hear her infuriated scream in the kitchen. *How dare they use that name for my son.* She forgets it's still the early morning and hears a commotion down the hall from Joseph's room. *Shoot. Woke him up.* Slow footfalls echo down the hallway.

A boy enters the kitchen; he is a near replica of Joseph, though his facial features are distinct and unfamiliar. "Where am I? Who are you?"

Viola stretches her eyes so wide it stings, her chest rising and falling like a lake boat on a windy day. "Where's Joe—" Viola stumbles over her words to find something—anything—to say. "What's your name?"

"I don't know." The boy's eyes fill to the brim with fear and his bottom lip quivers. "I can't remember. Don't remember nothing."

Unsure what to say, Viola manages to spit out, "Wait right here," as she runs to Joseph's bedroom. He's not in the closet, under the bed, or in the bathroom. Viola's head is on a swivel looking frantically for any clues, any sign of Joseph.

Viola leads the boy to the living room and asks him to sit and be calm because everything is going to be okay, wiping away the tears spilling down his cheeks. He nods slowly.

"How'd you get here? Do you remember who brought you here?" Viola asks.

"All I can remember is the park. My mommy took me there. I was playing on the monkey bars, then I woke up here."

With a million chaotic worries smashing through her skull, Viola jogs through the kitchen to the backyard, the screen door's springs smacking it shut. "Joseph!" There's only an overgrown and dying lawn, and discolored dog toys from when they had Toby. The crows have left. Viola makes her way around to the front of the house, passing the garbage cans and lifting the latch on the side gate. She's now in the street and screaming his name. There aren't a lot of properties on her street; the houses are spaced out compared to suburbia in California.

One neighbor she rarely sees is trotting to his Jeep like he's in a hurry, key ring jangling on his hip.

"Have you seen my son? Please, please, please." Viola frowns, feeling the blood drain from her face as something in her stomach flutters. Red-hot bile rises in her throat, but she swallows it down.

The neighbor dons a red trucker hat, his straggly white hair poofs out the back like cotton through the seams of one of Joseph's tattered stuffed animals. The older man looks back to Viola, his left cheek raising to squint his eye in agitation. "Lady, I need to go. I'm late. Call the police for all I care." Without a second more, the man dusts his liver-spotted hands of the situation and speeds off.

Hands on her knees, Viola is leaning over the asphalt and dry heaving. Dinner chunks the shade of marmalade spill to the ground, splashing her heather-gray sweatpants and navy-blue house slippers. When she thinks it's over, a cooling sensation runs through her nerves like when she uses her peppermint bar soap. And there's a pain knifing through her innards and her tongue tastes nothing but vóhpoma'óhtse (*salt*). It's unbearable and, for a moment, she recollects both the pain of childbirth and passing kidney stones. Something is moving up her throat and blocking the lungs. Viola is choking for air and can only think to use her vomit-muscles to push this blockage out. Her diaphragm contracts against her thorax repeatedly, and the obstruction is peeking out from her mouth.

A black and gray mass covered in a translucent jelly splats the ground.

Viola is hacking and wheezing, desperate for air and sanity. She spits to rid her mouth of the briny taste and doesn't take her eyes off the dark clump as it begins to move. As Viola backpedals a few feet, the clump expands and shakes away its viscous layer.

It's a mónevata (*young bird*)—a hooded crow.

The crow ruffles its feathers and flaps its wings. Its head turns right to left as if it's scanning the area, then looks up to Viola.

Expletives flood her brain while fire and ice drill through her spine. Paralyzed like a deer in her truck's headlights, Viola stares at the creature and wants to know what is happening to her, what has happened to her son.

Your son is still safe.

Viola spins around, searching for the voice. She hears the woman speaking and the crow cawing at the same time as if the voice is inside her head, though distant and echoey.

94

You have little time. They are about to sacrifice him to a false god.

"Who? False god?" Viola can't believe she's talking to a bird. She often does, following in the footsteps of her grandma, but they've never responded like this before.

They are of the belief that humans should be purified like water. Selected for the best traits to improve their stock.

A hurtful memory inches its way into Viola's ear canal. Back in California before Joseph was born, she was offered heavily discounted rates for prenatal testing to see if her baby could have conditions deemed unsatisfactory. Once she consented, the doctor took a blood sample and, within a week, the results showed a high probability of genetic abnormalities. Viola contemplated whether she was ready to be a mother, whether she could handle the burden of caring for a child with disabilities. After several days of consideration, Viola chose to abort the baby at ten weeks. When it came to choosing the method, the doctor asked, 'Do you want the knife or the pill?' The unprofessional way he asked her signaled that something was off and persuaded her to miss the appointment, giving up on the idea. Viola still resents the fact that she considered it and never told her husband about the test. She's an activist for the rights of her people. But she still carries the guilt of nearly causing Indigenous erasure by her own hand.

The authorities discovered that the doctor was not a member of any medical association and could not be identified on any payroll in the city, though he more than likely used a pseudonym. She never saw the doctor again. Lucky, too, because he was most certainly the type of doc to sterilize Indigenous women post-birth without sanction.

The crow's cawing snatches the memory away, forcing Viola to recall its last message about purifying humans. "Sounds like blood quantum," Viola says, referring to the government's favorite tool to reduce Natives to ancestral pie charts, making them the official arbiters of what *is* and *isn't* Indian. "Can you help me find him?" She thinks it's worth a shot.

Use your tracker. And always follow your gut. I must journey back now, Viya. Né-méhotȧtse.

Only her grandma called her that nickname. "Ke'éehe, is that you?" Viola says. She hasn't spoken to her grandma for a decade.

The young hooded crow takes wing and soars into a nearby black maple tree. After a few seconds, it dematerializes into the breeze.

"I love you, too." Viola's senses are stretched thin in all directions. After making peace with her grandma's visit, she racks her brain for what her visitor meant by "tracker," and when she makes the connection, she grunts because she doesn't know why she didn't think of it sooner.

Joseph can be a bit of a wanderer, and Viola has had many scares from him exploring when he shouldn't. About five years back, her brother paid for a microchip implant and lifetime tracking membership that monitors Joseph's location via GPS.

Running back into the house for her cell phone, Viola passes the young boy who is standing at the vertical blinds.

"Did I watch you throw up a bird?" he asks, wiping snot onto his striped long sleeve.

"Uh, no time! Sorry, kid," Viola yells down the hallway from her bedroom. She rips her phone from her nightstand and is too frantic for the retina scan to unlock her phone. Centering herself to control her breathing, she's stock-still long enough for the scanner. Viola hasn't used the tracking app much since moving as Joseph rarely explores now, so it takes her a moment to find it in her app library.

Tap. Locate. Loading. Loading. Loading.

The prolonged loading time causes sweat beads to stream down Viola's temples, and ceremony lights up behind her eyes. The lodge, the fire, the belonging.

Location found.

The screen displays an aerial view of northern Minnesota. The app only provides GPS coordinates, never addresses. With her index and thumb, Viola pinches the map to manipulate the zoom and searches the area for landmarks.

"They've got him up near Pat Finnegan Lake, looks like. Straight shot up Route 169."

A system notification illuminates the screen. 5%. BATTERY IS LOW. TURN ON BATTERY SAVER. ABOUT 10 MINUTES LEFT BASED ON YOUR USAGE.

"Shit!" Viola scrambles for the wireless pad, leaving it to charge before running down to the basement for supplies. She grabs an old gym bag and stuffs it with rope, pistols, and loaded magazines. From the wall, she snatches the hohkóxe (*ax*) her grandpa made for her when she briefly lived in New Mexico. She tests the blade with her index, and it's still as sharp as ever. Viola shoulders the bag and carries the ax up the stairs, sucking the blood from her nicked finger.

"Kid, I don't have time to explain much of anything. When I get back, I promise we will sort everything out and find your mother. But my son is in danger, and I think I've found him. Help yourself to our fridge and pantry, and here's the remote. Stay here and stay safe." Although she doesn't know the boy, Viola feels protective of him and pecks the top of his head before running out the front to her silver Dodge Ram.

After slamming the truck door, she rolls her eyes and palms the steering wheel. *My phone.* Viola runs back in, apologizing to the boy once more, and lifts her phone from the wireless pad.

7% battery.

⚜

Viola prays to Creator no highway patrolman catches her driving like this. Her truck's tires chirp as she weaves in and out of traffic on this two-lane. With her eyes pinballing between the road and her dimmed cell phone, she concentrates on the GPS marker on the west side of Lake Onamia. It's a few minutes more, and the battery is threatening to shut down. *Why the hell did they take Joseph into the Ojibwe rez?*

She gets off Route 169 and exits for Highway 27, then Shakopee Lake Road. An unpaved road to her right leads to the lake. Viola makes the quick decision to park off the side of this narrow road and walk the rest of the way. Her truck engine, combined with the gravel crunching beneath the tires, would give these freaks too much lead time. She needs to catch them off guard.

Nétáhé-emóhónema (*Let's go hunt*).

Viola is aware she's still in her pajamas and house slippers but doesn't care. Justice can be served in any clothes, especially when you mess with children. She loads two ka'ó'éstse (*pistols*) and tucks them into her waistband along her spine. Then she shoulders the rope bundle and carries the ax with the head parallel to the earth, her Cheyenne blood still coating the whetted edge.

The gravel road to the lake is lined by pines on either side. It's greener here. The wind carries sap, smoke, and cured meat. Viola's been trying her best to quit he'póhtoto (*cigarettes*) for months, but the acrid, earthy smoke makes her pointer and middle finger twitch. Engrossed in the smell, Viola snaps out of it once she hears hushed voices and softens her footfalls as if she's advancing on a mō'e (*elk*).

Crows caw in the distance, and Viola hopes her grandma can see. She wants to make her proud once again. Out of curiosity, Viola pulls out her phone, and it's dead. If things go south here, she will need a backup plan. And if she survives, she prays the law will be on her side and this will be ruled as self-defense, but who knows? FBI treats crimes on reservations much differently than the rest of Turtle Island. An inkling of fear trickles up Viola's throat. *What if I get killed today and Joseph survives? Will the world treat him with respect? Will he be safe with someone else?* Warm tears slip down her plump cheeks. She swallows down the death thoughts and continues her prowl.

Through slitted eyes, Viola makes out a group of people in dark robes encircling a person in a red robe tossing things into a firepit. The robes remind her of padres from Catholic missions. There's an expansive tree above them with low-hanging branches. White smoke rises through the tree and creates a sort of beacon, as if they are establishing a connection to somewhere beyond the sky. The cult members sit cater-cornered to two véhkenòtse (*dwellings*), one possibly being a storage shed. A maroon van is parked adjacent to the small shed. Viola draws nearer through the thicket and remains unnoticed.

One by one, the dark robes stand and walk to the red-robed man to recite something before pulling back their left sleeve to expose their pallid voxòtse (*flesh*). The leader then draws his ceremonial motšéške (*blade*) and slices their arms deeply from elbow to wrist, spilling their blood into the licking flames and sparkling embers. Each bloodletting invigorates the fire fleetingly, and the cult followers move to a new area to lie down, prompting the next to approach the leader.

Okay, so the leader has a knife. These members are blind enough to follow a madman. Would they protect him at all costs? Wonder if they have weapons, too. And Joseph. He must be in that hovel.

While Viola waits for the last cultist to lie down on their back in a crescent shape, she prepares by unfurling the rope and tying one end to the ax's knob. Grandpa taught her how to do constrictor knots, one of his favorites. Her knuckles whiten from the tension of pulling the knot with all her might. She wields it in her dominant right hand, the slack rope stretched across her torso to her left hand.

Her people are warriors. Time doesn't matter. Warriors back then, warriors today. Cheyenne fight for theirs. She's not a Hotamétaneo'o (*Dog Soldier*) and isn't sure if any of her ancestors were in the military societies. But blood is coursing through her veins like hot engine oil, and she's ready to die.

Viola sprints toward evil, her eyes bulging and filled with rage. Her house slippers fall away, and the crisp, dewy grass on her bare feet sends pulses up her vertebrae. None of the evildoers are moving. Echoes of Jonestown filter through her thoughts, and her eyes land on the red-robed leader. He must hear her sharp footfalls because he turns to witness her fury charging his way.

It's the old doctor.

Thousands of emotion tendrils pierce Viola's brain and scramble all her synapses, triggering misfires and confused reflexes. Fear returns abruptly, and she loses her footing on the approach and tumbles to the doctor's feet. Her pajamas' waistband isn't tight enough to hold the pistols in place, and they slip into the legs of her pants, hidden behind her calves.

"You," Viola says in a register so low she questions its source. She scuttles backward to increase their distance, but the doctor digs his steel-toe boot heel into her right wrist. The pressure immediately coerces her grip to loosen, freeing the ax, and he kicks it away.

"You came." The doctor kneels to hold down her thrashing legs. "Didn't you like your replacement?" he asks.

"Replacement?"

"The boy you discovered in Joseph's bed this morning." His reply was soaked in venom and resembled the hiss and strike of an unforgiving serpent.

"Why are you doing this? I want my—"

"I don't give a shit what you want. My vision for this plan was in the works for far too long. You can't ruin it. I started in with your husband," the doctor says. He uses his robe sleeve to wipe the cultists' blood from both sides of his blade. "But I got nabbed some time later for the product I was moving. Spent the last ten years in the pen, but I'm glad I found you again. Now, tell me, Whiteshield: Do you want the knife or the pill?"

Red ants march through Viola's arteries. Her breathing intensifies and her fists clench hard enough to break several phalanges.

"You fucked with the wrong family," Viola screams, the damaged tissue in her esophagus rattling.

There's a banging on the shed's door. "Mom? Mom, are you—"

Viola's eyes blaze, jolting from the shed to the doctor, and their eyes meet. With all her body weight, she swings upward from the ground and headbutts the doctor. Her forehead connects with his nose, and the crack and burst of blood are like summer thunder. She barrel rolls away while the doctor is flummoxed and yanks the ropes until the ax is in her hand.

The doctor's blade enters her ribcage and twists. The pain should be intolerable, but it doesn't register until he pulls it back out and her blood is splashing the grass like wasted merlot. Viola extends the ax to the ground, wrapping the rope around her broken fists until her circulation is cut off. She lets out a final guttural yell and swings the ax above her head in a circle before releasing it into the doctor's head.

With a thunderous crack, the doctor's skull splits at his right temple, revealing salmon-colored brain matter around the blade. Blood sputters and squirts from the cleft. His eyes swim and roll back as if trying to see the ax from the inside. Words struggle to leave his mouth between deep gasps and the gurgling of blood in his throat. Staggering, he falls to the earth, dark blood pooling in the grass around his corpse like a black hole, as though evil was swallowing itself whole.

Viola keeps it together by swallowing her bile again. She nudges the doctor onto his back with her bare foot and retrieves her ax. The brain slurps and pops while pulling the blade out. Blood is still pouring from

Viola's ribcage. While staggering to the shed, her left hand applies pressure to the wound as a makeshift ligature. She has little strength left and struggles to smash the shed's padlock. On the sixth blow, she knocks it loose. The swinging door reveals young Joseph sitting cross-legged and shackled. *He bit through his duct-tape muzzle to yell for me. Smart boy.*

"Mama!" Joseph's cries are a mixture of relief and worry. He must see her blood-soaked shirt and pant leg.

But Viola is too tired to swing the ax anymore to break the chains. She drops it to walk to the doctor and search his pockets for a ta'ta'óhēō'o (*key*). She attempts to distance her face from his halved skull, can't bear to look at it. *Ah, got it.*

She jogs back over to the shed and trips to her knees. Exhaustion is overtaking her, and she doesn't know how much blood she's lost. "Joseph, baby. I'm about to get you out of here. Mama just needs to patch up." Viola manages to stand and saunters to the firepit. There are a few logs jutting out from the flames, and she picks one to unsheathe from the fire. She lifts her shirt to reveal her blood-crusted belly, and with both hands, she thrusts the burning end of the log into her ribs. Her screams would scare off any flock of birds, but the skies are silent. She drops the log and tries to control her breathing, remembering her classes while hóse'e (*pregnant*). Deep in. Deep out. Deep in. Deep out. She looks down at her torso and witnesses her first cauterized stab wound. Viola lets out a final sigh and strains to stand.

"Mommy, I want to go home," Joseph says.

"I know, honey. Here I come." Viola squats to unlock the four shackles, and Joseph is once again in her arms. "I love you, Jo-Jo. You are my everything. Let's go home."

Women follow the warpath as often as men but in different ways and maybe for different reasons. I'll never stop fighting for my kin.

The two Whiteshields hold hands and amble back to the truck, Viola taking several breaks along the way. On her last break, a crow flies overhead and caws into the afternoon sun.

Shields

CHRISTINA SNG

All shields break eventually
When met with prolonged force.

I endured 20 years before I broke.
It was for a good cause.

My children are safe
For the most part,

Their bodies were not hurt,
But I worry about their hearts.

So, I strengthen them
With unconditional love,

The only power I have—
Until I discover

I can control minds,
Bend others to my will,

And the very next day,
The beast slowly slits his wrists.

I can only imagine
His abject fear

At being out of control,
Killing himself and not us.

He is a menace to all he touches.
Now he will be dust.

His woman finds him dead
In a pool of blood

While her small children laugh.
They dance and jump,

Making bloody footprints
All over her nice linoleum floor.

The mean man is gone,
They chant and cheer.

This is how justice is done.
This is how life is worth some.

Now I peer into the next mind
And see a bloodbath.

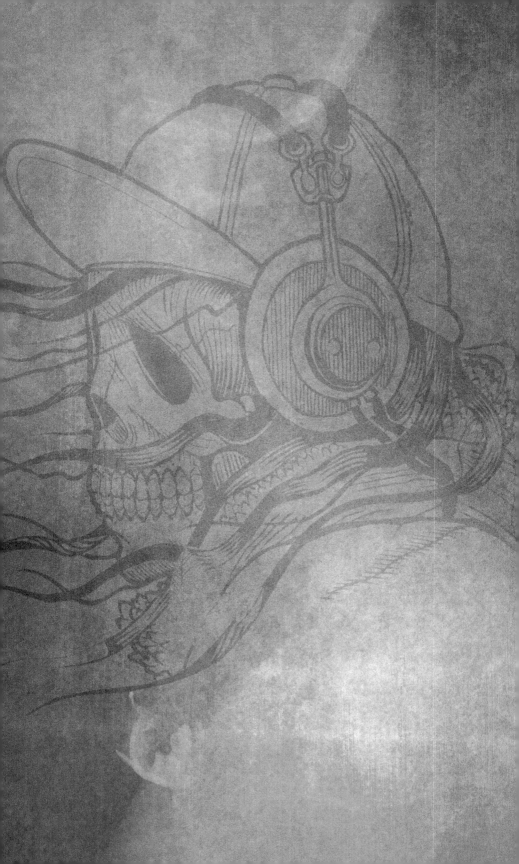

The Bone Child

RYAN COLE

My pregnancy began when I was fifteen years old, and according to the rules of the world, should not have happened. For starters, I was (and still, sadly, am) a virgin, and before anyone asks: *no*, this wasn't round two of the Immaculate Conception, and I wasn't graced by any god pretending to be a bull. It was purely scientific: a matter of excess calcium in the tendon, a sac of stray embryonic fluid from my birth, and a healthy dose of luck that formed a pea-sized, skeletal, parasitic being that made its home in the soft tissue of my right shoulder.

And that isn't the half of it.

I wasn't equipped for this. I'm a boy, after all. A boy in the Sloane River High School marching band, seventh-seat clarinet, the lowest of the low, and that's even going by *woodwind* standards. My freckles might as well be the bubonic plague, my blonde-white hair, silky and thin, a sign that death had its hollow eyes on me. That, in itself, should have rendered me sterile.

But against all odds, my body beat the rules.

In a matter of weeks, (and through a secret alliance with the chatty school nurses, who were happy to gossip), I was a small-town celebrity. An object of desire. I had reporters wanting to write down my thoughts, television hosts recording my voice, and medical researchers who tried to trade me money for a chance to poke my arm. I had my very own seat at the back of the band bus, next to Clay Aphins and the rest of the drum line, who smelled like sweat and beer and trouble. I had new friends who wanted to talk to me, who drove me home from practice and helped me memorize all the notes that I bungled whenever I stepped onto the football field.

Yet not all of them agreed. There were plenty of detractors who warned me that my rise to fame was wholly unnatural, and that unnatural things had a tendency to change. But I didn't care. My bone child had barely moved since it appeared, and if I stood very still, loosening the muscles in my arm up to my neck, everything felt like it had before, when I was just a seventh-seat, story-less ghost.

My bone child gave me all I wanted and more.

Until, that is, it started to grow.

The pain was overwhelming.

It started out slowly: a new cell here, a new cell there, and the X-rays made it seem like little was developing, at least on a level that would cause much concern. But I could tell on the inside; the pinches and the snaps and the tugs were unmistakable, the crunching sensation that kept me up at night. Those cells were multiplying, forming tiny ladders of sinew and gristle, and instead of a pea afloat in embryonic fluid, my child was a bundle of brittle, folded matchsticks as fine and thin as the bones of a baby bird. The larger they grew, the more space they needed, space that, unfortunately, wasn't for sale.

I didn't tell my parents of the ever-present ache. I didn't tell my teachers. And I didn't tell any of my newfound friends, especially Clay, who went out of his way to make me feel seen, sneaking me mischievous, wide-lipped grins when his snare-drum brothers and sisters weren't looking.

If I told *him* about the throbbing in my shoulder, he might suggest what I didn't want to hear: if it hurts so much, why not get rid of it?

Any easy answer, for anyone but me. That would mean going back to who I was before: Malcolm Depitskey, the boy with a body nobody noticed. Deathly, contagious, barren. *Boring*. No more reporters, no more television. I would be alone in my temple of flesh.

Which wasn't an option.

So I bit back the pain, smiled for the cameras, and made them believe that everything was as it should be.

"You're *failing* world history? But that's your favorite class." My mother eyed me like I was a natural phenomenon, a volcanic eruption to someone that had never seen fire. She set down the note that I'd held off giving her, written by my homeroom teacher the week before.

"I've been busy," I told her. I tried to fold my arms, my right arm dangling limp at my side.

"Malcolm," she said. "It's hurting you, isn't it?"

I glared back. "No."

She looked around the room. "Here," she said, holding out a pen. "I want you to copy this note, word-for-word."

"Mom," I crooned. "Really, I'm fine."

But she didn't back down. She pressed the slip of paper into my fingers, watched as I tried to grip the shaft of the pen, and nodded, resolutely, as if a decision had been made, when my muscles contracted and I dropped it on the table.

"That's it," she said. "We're going back to the doctor."

My bone child and I had nowhere to run.

We learned from my orthopedic surgeon, Dr. Shevton, that it was not just growing, it was delving into the crevices and nooks of my skeleton, grafting itself to the frame of my body. For now, it looked to be contained to the shoulder. Minor, manageable, comparatively speaking. Tomorrow, however, it could reach to my elbow, sprout its own parasitic, brittle-bird fingers. Could spread into my ribs, my collarbone, my skull.

"It needs to come out," said Dr. Shevton, sighing, his pale hands linked and his saggy chin bowed, as if he were already mourning my loss. He reviewed all the details with my mother at his desk; they huddled conspiratorially, with me in the background, safe in the decision they were doing what was right—for my own well-being, while there was still time.

"No," I said. "I don't want to do it." I was only fifteen. I couldn't let them kill the only thing that gave me life.

But they didn't hear me. They were too busy trying to make me normal.

⚜

Clay Aphins called me later that evening. His voice was hoarse, rugged from a half a pack of cigarettes a day. When he spoke my name, and the grit from his words bled into my ear, a long-buried shiver ran up my spine. I had never, *could* have never, loved my bone child more.

"Wanna hang out?" he said. "Just you and me?"

I swallowed the question, savored every letter. Clay Aphins wanted to hang out with *me*?

We met up on Friday night after the football game. Clay waited as I packed up my clarinet. He waved me over to where he was standing, against the rusty hood of a beat-up Camaro, the popped collar of a black leather jacket on his neck. "Ready?" he said.

I nodded, too afraid to break the spell he wove. I fell into the passenger seat, cradling my arm.

We stopped at a drive-thru burger shop in town. Clay ordered for me. He handed me a bucket of fat, greasy fries and a waffle cone of soft-serve, vanilla-swirl ice cream that dripped at the bottom and dotted his jeans. We sat in silence in his car, parked beneath the glow of a yellow street lamp.

He licked at his ice cream, and I licked at mine, unsteadily holding up the cone with my left hand. My right arm nestled out of sight, beneath the seat belt.

Or so I thought.

"Mind if I take one?" said Clay, leaning over, the creak of his jacket loud on the seat. His mustiness blossomed, a mix of cheap hair gel and cigarette smoke. I watched, starved, as he picked up a fry.

A jolt ran through me, an electric shock, like Frankenstein's monster had come to life.

I saw my right hand reach up and wrap my fingers tightly around the lapel of Clay's jacket. They pulled him in, away from the light, and he cast me a mischievous, surprised smile. He seemed as surprised as I was, caught in someone else's act.

There were three of us there in that car, after all.

"It's getting late," I said, willing my bone child to relinquish its grip. Thankfully, it did, and I pulled away, mortified.

Neither of us said anything else on the way home.

⚜

"We have you scheduled for two days from now." Dr. Shevton flipped through the newest batch of X-rays. "You're incredibly lucky we could fit you in that soon."

He and my mother shared a victorious glance, while I slumped in defeat on the examination table. Apparently, my bone child was no longer a child, and now, after several months of rushed gestation, it was in a stage of what Dr. Shevton called "maturity,". The matchstick bones were as thick as my fingers, at least from the length of my shoulder to my hand.

Dr. Shevton asked if I had felt any movements, any urges to do what I normally wouldn't have done?

I lied and deflected, but none of it made a difference.

"Good," he said. "That would mean it's spreading. And the more it spreads, the harder it will be to remove."

I nodded, hopeful, suppressing a jolt that felt different from the rest, that ricocheted all the way down to my knee.

⚜

Band practice that night was a lesson in torture. Not only did my arm pound with a heartbeat of its own, but my hip did too, and my leg and my foot and every other piece of the right side of my body that I used to, in ignorance, assume I could control. Their rhythm matched that of the drum major's wand and the tempo Clay kept on his snare drum behind me.

The fingers on my left hand worked just fine; they pressed onto the sweat-slicked keys of my clarinet, following my section's lead. My other

109

hand, though, had decided to rebel. It jerked and cramped in response to my movements, leaving my notes all squeaky and off-tune.

My bone child's strength grew with each passing hour.

I didn't know what I would do when it was gone. I still didn't even know if I *wanted* it gone. Whatever Dr. Shevton told me and my mother, whatever I would gain, I would lose something too, a part of myself, the story that had garnered me all of my friends, that made me, for once, interesting. *Desirable*. The bone child was me, and I was him. Who would I be, if I couldn't lean on that?

My eyes found Clay, rolling his drumsticks and licking his teeth. We hadn't spoken since that night in the car, hadn't gotten to finish what my bone child had started. If I were just me, that might not happen. Tonight was the last chance any of us had, the last time the three of us would be in the same room.

The drum major snapped at the clarinets to keep up, and the glare that he shot me lit a spark in my core. The stress of it all came down in a rush, a trickle of heat flowing down my right arm and into my leg, my ankle, my toes, the matchstick limbs awoken from their slumber. My bone child moved, and I had to follow.

My right leg swung from beneath my chair. My right arm dropped my clarinet on the floor. The sixth-seater girl that sat next to me turned and mouthed, "Are you okay?" around the tip of her reed.

But I wasn't okay. I wasn't in control.

The drum major swept his wand, undeterred. The rest of the band continued to play— some of them pointing and some of them snickering— as I lurched around the room. One half of my body swung the other half forward, behind the row of tubas, all the way to the percussion.

Clay kept rolling his drumsticks in amusement. His green eyes locked with mine,and he pulled me in, as if he and the fire in my bones were in league and this was a full-blown, telepathic coup.

I watched my body stop in front of his snare drum. The room went quiet, everyone staring.

He set down his sticks, giving me the space to do what I hadn't done before. The bone child dragged me an inch from his face. And this time, I wasn't the one to reach out. I wasn't the one to grab the other's shirt collar.

When our lips finally touched, it tasted like ice cream.

⚜

It took all my mother's strength to get me to the hospital.

Somehow, the media had learned of the procedure. A horde of reporters flocked to our doorstep, asking all the questions I had posed to myself. *Why? How? Will the bone child live? What will you do with it once it's been removed?*

I didn't answer because I still didn't know. And even if I did, none of it would have mattered. The world would forget about the both of us soon.

The procedure was grueling. They strapped me to a table, and before the mask settled over my mouth and anesthesia flowed like a river down my throat, I felt a contraction. Maybe it was my body saying one last goodbye.

I woke up what felt like many hours later. A glass jar sat on my bedside table, filled with a cloudy, embryonic fluid. Flat against the lid was a pea-sized, skeletal dollop of bone. The matchstick bundle of limbs was gone. Those had dissolved in the extraction process. But I wondered, idly, if any of it remained, its courage hidden deep within a pocket of my marrow.

That gave me comfort as I drifted back to sleep.

⚜

Days passed, then turned into weeks. Newspapers quoted us. Film crews recorded us. Their questions, their headlines, were what I had feared. *Can we see the bone child? Is the bone child alive? Will the bone child stay in that jar forever?*

Not one question about Malcolm Depitskey. I, of course, was no longer the story.

By the time my mother and I were discharged, we wanted to be alone. Or as alone as we could be with the jar in our kitchen, watching us through a thin veil of fluid.

The pain disappeared, and so did the attention. I was just a boy again,

III

seventh-seat clarinet, about to go into my junior year of high school. I was like any other kid my age, trying to figure out who I was.

Clay hadn't called. I assumed he wouldn't—that he, like the rest, had forgotten about me. Yet, I couldn't stop thinking of what we had shared, of what we still *could*, if the phone would just ring. If the bone on the countertop were still in my shoulder, and the strength of my child were one I could wield, guiding me to do all the things that I had feared.

Now that I was just me, those fears had returned.

We stared at each other in silence one evening, the glass jar of fluid propped up in my bed. I waited—*prayed*—for my child to speak, to signal to some stray piece in my skeleton to get off the bed, pick up the phone, and dial the number burned into my skull. But nothing came, no words or spasms.

Was this a test? Was what was left of my bone child daring me to act?

As soon as the thought invaded my mind, I felt a nudge that trickled in waves along my arm and gradually nestled in my trembling fingers. But my hand didn't move. It was still on the bed. I would have to do the next part on my own.

The phone was heavy, slick on my ear. My heart was a double-bass boom in my throat. Yet still, I dialed, and swallowed, and waited.

"Hey, you," said Clay. His voice carried with it the spark of a cigarette, the creak of a black leather jacket in a car.

And mine carried all of my newfound strength. "Wanna go finish those fries?" I said.

MOTHER INSTRUCTS

The Wives of Tromisle

DAN COXON

My mother stands on the dock, her hands cradled in front of her as if in prayer. She wears a gray smock, the same as all the other women, her white hair pulled back into a severe bun. I wonder if she's done it to iron out the wrinkles and creases in her forehead; if she has, then she has failed.

Once the ferryboat is tied off and the warped gangplank has been thrown ashore, I follow her through the streets to her cottage. She nods to a tall, bearded man who sits mending nets on the quayside, but otherwise she ignores the frothing sea of bodies around her, each welcoming their own loved ones to Tromisle. The only time she turns her head is to stare at two children, so alike they might be twins, watching us from a window. I think I see a smile twitch at her mouth.

The cottage is bare and unwelcoming, the kind of sparse cell she has preferred since the Easter before my eighth birthday, the day she miscarried. Only a spray of purple and white flowers in a jug on the kitchen table hint that she may have decorated for my arrival.

"So," she says, her hands thrust under cold water gushing from the faucet, "you're here at last. How was the sailing? Sea not too rough for you?"

I shake my head. "I can see why you don't come to the mainland, but I survived it. My legs still feel a little wobbly, though."

"That will pass." Her hands reach for the kettle, filling it with water. "You got my message, then?"

I had. When your mother hasn't spoken to you since you divorced your husband five years ago, a letter in her handwriting makes you sit up and pay attention. It was unnecessarily formal in that way she prefers, skirting the point and burying its meaning beneath a mountain of polite niceties, but I'd gathered she had something to tell me—something that needed to be said in person. Naturally, I feared the worst.

"You have news. Is it your health? You could have told me that over the phone, you didn't have to—"

"No," she interrupts, speaking across me as if I've already said my piece. "Not that. You're not getting rid of me yet. The sea air has worked wonders, just as they said it would. I feel better than I have in years."

Now that I look properly, I can see she's right; she looks well. She'll soon be turning seventy, but apart from the wrinkles and white hair she might pass for someone in their fifties. I can't see her body beneath the shapeless smock, but her arms look lean and strong.

"What is it then? Have you met someone?"

She smiles.

"I'm pregnant. You're going to have a sister."

<hr/>

The light from the window is sharp and clear as I unpack my few belongings. I refold the t-shirts and a spare skirt into a small chest beside the bed, arranging my book and reading glasses on top. I didn't pack much because I hadn't intended to be here long, a couple of days at most. Now my supplies look woefully thin. I assume there is somewhere in town that sells the bare essentials; I can borrow from Mother if I have to.

I'm stowing my wheelie case beneath the bed when she raps on the door. I turn to tell her to come in, but she's already standing in the doorway.

"I haven't said thank you," she begins, and I can see what it costs her to offer an apology, even one so well disguised, "but I do appreciate you coming. This should be a time for family. I may need your help in the days to come. The midwife, Mrs. Penrose, says it's best to have someone by your side. Someone you can trust."

"Are you sure?" I say the words before I've had time to think them through. "There must be some mistake, mustn't there? At your age it's not impossible, I know, but the chances... I'm assuming there's a father?"

She smiles. "Of course there's a father. You'll meet him, all in good time. Here."

My mother walks to the bed and lowers herself slowly, carefully. Once she's lying down, I can see what the folds of the smock have hidden: the fertile dome of her belly. Lifting the dress, she exposes the skin, tight as a drum over the swelling. She takes my hand in hers, places it on the warmth of her flesh.

"Keep it there for a moment. She's active this morning. You'll feel her."

And I do. A flutter at first, like Mother is the old lady who swallowed a bird, then a kick, hard and bony, a heel or an elbow testing out the walls of its prison.

"See? She's a lively one, same as you were. I'm going to call her Alison."

It was the name they had chosen for my younger sister, the sibling who never was. The miscarriage came late, almost twenty-two weeks, and we'd already started making room for her arrival. That was thirty years ago, and my memories are foggy, but I remember the name painted on the door of the room we were meant to share. I don't know how long the name stayed there, but it must have been months. We lived with the ghost of my sister for even longer.

❧

The town is quiet as I make my way down to the quayside. The crowds are gone. The ferry comes just once a week, and then only if they have paying fares. In between times, Tromisle slumbers. One of the children from before sits on the harbor wall, his arm bandaged up in a sling. He stares at me from beneath a heavy brow as I walk past, and I do my best to smile back.

It isn't hard to find the store; there's little else here. It feels like a converted living room, divided by rickety shelving that sits half empty and

117

covered with dust. I manage to root out some essentials, a couple of plain gray t-shirts, toiletries with labels so faded they can barely be read. The old lady in the corner totals them up on a sheet of paper, licking the lead of her pencil as she does her sums. I hand over a note after she tells me my credit cards won't work.

"You're Agnes's girl, aren't you?" she says as she bags my purchases. "Come to help with the birthing? You must be as excited as we are. A child is always a miracle."

"I am," I say. "And yes. About the miracle, I mean."

I don't need her to tell me what being a mother means. I still think of Michael every day. We'd had no indication of the heart defect before it happened; he ran and laughed and played like any other five-year-old, right up until the moment that he didn't. Andy still calls me sometimes, wanting to talk it through, but I can't. I can't recall the last time I talked with anyone about it. The divorce suits me just fine.

The old woman taps her fingers on the counter to recapture my attention.

"It's a blessing for us all. Your mother's child. A daughter, I hear?"

"That's right. Do you have children?"

She smiles, her eyes lighting up. "I do, dear. I had a daughter who died —house fire, 2001. Now I have a daughter who's living here with me. She helps me in the shop, sometimes."

I smile and nod my farewell, gathering the paper bag in my arms. It's only as I leave that it occurs to me that she spoke of the two daughters as if they were one and the same.

❧

It's my sixth day on the island when Mother goes into labor. At first, I'm pleased that my stay won't be extended, but there's so much to do that my relief is soon buried under hot towels and breathing exercises. Mrs. Penrose, the midwife, appears as if by magic—I can only assume someone heard the wailing and called for her—and quickly takes control. I expected a jolly, round woman, but she is as hard and lean as Mother, and I do not see her smile.

"Will the father be here?" I ask as they kneel together on the floor, Mother's breathing exercises punctuated by swallowed cries. "Shouldn't someone let him know?"

"He'll be here," Mrs. Penrose replies, keeping her eyes on the task at hand. "He's always here."

I'm making the fifth round of herbal teas in the kitchen when the baby comes. Mother screams louder than before, a keening sob that rises and rises in pitch until it can't possibly go any higher; then there's silence, followed by a tiny cry. When I enter the room, Mrs. Penrose already has the baby—Alison, my sister—wrapped in a coarse blanket. The cord still attaches her to my mother, and the midwife holds out a stained pair of scissors to me, handles first.

"You should do the deed, given that you're family. Cut between the clamps, dear. Nice and hard, this is no time to be shy."

"But shouldn't the father—" I begin.

"It's your job," says a voice like grinding stones behind me. The bearded man from the dock stands in the doorway, his thick hands pressed against the frame as if he's holding it up. I look at him properly now: the beard hides most of his features but his nose is wide and broken in several places, his eyes black as tar. He smells of the sea, salty and rotten.

"Are you the father?" I ask without thinking.

"Of course he is," Mrs. Penrose replies, as if it's the most natural thing in the world. "Right, are you going to cut the cord, or do we have to leave her like this?"

The scissors are cold in my hand, the umbilical cord thicker than I expected. I feel I'm doing it wrong, mashing the handles down in the hope that something will bite, but then it gives and the two ends fall free with a gush of blood. Mrs. Penrose takes them back from me and wipes the blades on her dress.

"Now, let's see about that tea, shall we dear?"

Mother lets me hold the baby later that night. She wriggles in her blanket like a landed fish, surprisingly light but imbued with a hidden strength.

Without realizing it, I'd hoped that her eyes would be blue like mine, but they're a muddy gray, neither one color nor another.

"Hello, Alison." I try her name on for size, a name that we've lived with for so long it barely feels real. "Nice to meet you."

A pudgy hand pushes out from between the folds of the blanket and grips my finger, squeezing it like she wants to bring it to her mouth. When I finally convince her to let go, I loosen the blanket to tuck her arm back inside, safe and warm where it can't do any damage. Her other arm isn't an arm at all. In its place are three thick tentacles, wet and green, sprouting from her elbow like bladderwrack.

One of them wraps around my hand, and I let it stay like that until she is asleep.

Mother doesn't know the bearded man's name. She doesn't know if he once had one and it has been forgotten, or if he was never named in the way that you and I were. He would nod and speak to her occasionally when she first came to Tromisle, only to say good day or comment on the weather, nothing more. She assumed the other menfolk were out at sea, or lost in the many shipping disasters she'd heard about in the news. It seemed odd, but then so much is odd out here, this far from the city. It was simply accepted as the way things were.

One night he came to her. Three knocks on the door then he let himself in, bringing the briny stench of the sea with him. He made her promises, held her hand as she told him about her lost daughter, the miscarriage, the shadow it had cast across her life. When she was done, he took her to bed.

As Alison grows, she starts to look like the boy I saw on the quay, like all the children I have seen on the island. It makes sense that they are all his. He is the only man here, after all. Being with Alison works wonders for my soul. We don't have to hide her tentacles; they all have them, the children of the island. She can be free and unashamed, playing with her sisters and her cousins. I cannot say if she is the sister I might have had, or someone new, a surrogate sent to heal my mother's pain. I'm not sure it matters.

Sometimes, in the flash of a smile, an unguarded laugh, I see a glimmer of my Michael.

I do my best with the bedroom, brightening the corners with flowers, painting the bed frame. Mother doesn't seem to mind. Her thoughts are elsewhere. She returns to motherhood faster than either of us expected, bouncing the baby on her bony knee. It's as if she's been on hold for the last thirty years and now, finally, her life has begun again.

At night I lie awake in the darkness, waiting for three knocks on my door. I think I hear him outside sometimes, but it must be the seagulls on the slates, or the sea washing up hard against the quay. I cannot imagine being with him; cannot stomach that ocean stench of rotting fish he carries. I would never give myself to him, I say. I won't let him lay those thick, calloused hands anywhere on my body. But then I see Michael's face, my darling boy, and I know I might do anything if only I could get him back.

❧

The day I leave, Mother walks me down to the dock. My bag is light. I'm only taking the things I brought with me, the rest the island can keep. Alison bounces at her hip, her golden hair catching the sunlight, tentacles writhing in imitation of a wave. We say goodbye on the jetty, and once I'm on the ferry I make my way to the front. I don't look back at the island as we pull away.

As we leave the harbor, deep in the belly of the ship something clanks three times. I feel every muscle in my body clench.

He had come to me two nights before, his knuckles knocking like barnacles against the wood, tapping out his promise. Through the door I could smell the sea on him, salty and brutal. And as I buried my head beneath the covers, I saw Michael again as he was on that final day, playing on the lawn: carefree and full of life, safe in the knowledge that his mother would protect him. That neither of us need ever be alone.

Duties Terrible and Dear

JOHN LANGAN

You are Mother and the care of the pack is yours.

Your days are bracketed by light. Well before the sun has pulled the blue from the sky after it, you are awake, checking your family by sight and by smell, stepping among them carefully, so as not to disturb them. And well before the horizon glows with the sun's return, you are searching out the next day's resting place, whether rundown motel or deep forest clearing. You feel the sun's rays as a weight, a pressure keeping you confined in whatever form you have assumed, human or wolf. As they diminish, then dim, then depart, you feel a loosening within you, an unknotting, both sides of yourself now freely open to you. While the sun blazes overhead, you can change, but the process is difficult, painful, leaving you half-maddened. When the stars hold court in the sky, the change is like descending into cool water, every nerve coming alive, the senses sharpening, becoming more acute.

All your senses now are focused on the highway no more than fifty yards from you and the youngest member of the pack. The sun has long departed; the air is deep-of-the-night cool. Over the trees to your right, the moon hangs in cratered brilliance. Although a field of tall grass, wildflowers, and scattered shrubs separates you from the vehicles large and small, their speed and bright lights, the groan of their engines and the sting of their exhaust, the cub whines. (*Cub*, you think, when he has been with the pack for a decade and a half.) His disorientation has not reached the point he does not know he should not be here—neither of you should. You hush him and start across the field. He hesitates, then follows. Anyone watching might mistake the two of you for a small woman and her (very) large dog, out for a (very) late-night walk.

The old dam who was Mother before you listed the responsibilities you were inheriting. (This was in the shadowy depths of an abandoned barn in the mountains on the New York-Massachusetts border, on a summer's day when the rest of the pack sought refuge from the heat and humidity in their human shapes, which lay sprawled around the empty stalls and loft.) The first duty of a Mother was to know where every member of the pack was and in what form. Sometimes the pack ran through the forest together and sometimes they walked through the state fair together. Other times, they went separate ways, in groups of three or four or all on their own, some as human, others as wolf. It was Mother's charge to keep track of them, by what they told her about their plans, yes, but also by the connection the members of the pack shared, the faint tingling threads each felt at the base of the skull, binding them together. Mother must be so attuned to those wispy links as to feel the slightest trace of distress troubling any of them and to follow that thread to the pack member. *Mother is the house in which the pack lives*, the old dam had said. *She is the map across which it travels.*

You knew this, or something near it, knew it was part of the reason the old dam had settled on you to succeed her, your strong bonds to the others, your ability to find each of them and to sense when it was necessary to do so. Dust drifting through the shafts of sunlight piercing the barn's roof, the old dam had enumerated the second responsibility of the role you had fought as well as been chosen for, demonstrating the ferocity of your fangs and claws, in addition to the cunning of your mind. *Mother preserves the number of the pack*, she said. Never had it been easy to add to their family. A strong element of chance weighed against the success of a pregnancy, whether mother and father were both able to change, or one was a wolf. Something happened in the womb, went wrong, the cubs tried to change before they had been taught how to do so, and did not survive. Through the long years, members of their pack (and others) had lain with cousins to the wolf, with coyotes and (it was rumored) dogs, hoping these unions might be less complicated, more fruitful, might stir new blood into old, reinvigorate it, but such experiments had met with limited results (though they gave the lie to the claims certain members of the pack made for the purity of their line).

The most reliable way to add to the pack was the Ceremony, with which you yourself joined it, which was in fact responsible for all its present members. The rite was not without its own dangers and complications: the applicant's body might reject one or all of the necessary wounds, generally a fatal occurrence, and even should the applicant survive, if someone was intent on finding them, it was no longer as easy to vacate a life as once had been the case.

You have reached the other side of the field. A strip of dirt separates you from the edge of the highway. *Interstate 90*, you think, *I-90*, a name from several lifetimes ago. A pair of eighteen-wheelers, their cabs and trailers outlined in yellow lights, roar past, on their way from distant city to distant city. The cub utters an unhappy sound, shuffling his feet and wagging his tail in agitation. You rest your hand on the top of his head and he settles.

The final responsibility with which the old dam charged you concerned the cities and bigger towns, the kinds of places roads like this one bound together, whose vicinities she advised you to maintain a healthy distance from. Under such places were tunnels known and unknown, and in them lurked the *ghûl* and their keepers. (She punctuated the name with her spit.) The enmity between their kind and the *ghûl* stretched back beyond the long history of this pack and of the many preceding it, to the time before the ice sheets reshaped the land. Indeed, the corpse-eaters had been borne out of an attempt to duplicate the Ceremony that let human and wolf share an existence. The effort failed and what remained was a monster, a parody lodged between human and something else, something like a jackal. In days past, their kind had stalked and harried the *ghûl*, driven them to the precipice of extinction. The rise of cities, however, had provided their foes places to shelter and thrive, especially as the cemeteries grew. Now the *ghûl* were too powerful, and though one discovered in the pack's territory must be destroyed immediately, their centers of power must be avoided.

Know where the pack's members were, maintain the pack's numbers, and avoid the dangers of city and town: these injunctions the old dam placed on you, on a long-vanished day when the odors of warm sawdust and ancient hay made the air fragrant. You have obeyed them and, by and large, doing so has served you well. As pertains to the unexpected, the unforeseen occurrences outside their guidelines, the old dam's commands have been of less immediate help, requiring reflection, occasionally discussion with one or two of the pack's senior members, and often a willingness to be flexible in your duties' implementation.

For the most part, these interpretations have been of a forgiving type. There have been times, few but enough to note, your contemplation has led to sterner decisions. For example, when the junior member of the pack, chasing a deer, stumbles across a raccoon, which immediately and ferociously attacks him. He kills the racoon, but is bitten several times. From the smell of his injuries, the rest of the pack know immediately what has happened, know the smaller creature's saliva has transferred the disease that catalyzed its attack on so much larger a predator.

Were you simply human, the response to this situation would be easy: walk into any hospital emergency room, report the incident, and receive the first of a series of rabies injections. As you are not simply human, the hospital is not an option, especially with multiple visits it would require. A curious doctor with an attentive eye is as much a danger as a pair of armed police officers. Nor is kidnapping a doctor and forcing them to administer the shots for however many weeks are required a possibility. In the end, you would have to kill the doctor to preserve the pack's secrecy, and this would almost certainly expose you to as much attention as if you had walked through the hospital's sliding glass doors to begin with.

Leaving the bites untreated leads to the same ultimate destination, as a rabid wolf who changed to a rabid human and back again, or remained in some horrible in-between state, would not, could not go unnoticed. Your kind are difficult to kill but not impossible, and the eventual examination of the corpse would bring the brightest of lights to shine on you. For you or one of the other pack members to end the cub's life is anathema; it is not what your kind does.

A random encounter in the forest has hoisted you onto the sharp horns of a dilemma: you must protect the pack and you must preserve its numbers. The cub cannot live, but you cannot kill him. He knows he is sick. The disease has sprinted along his nerves to his brain and already he is waging a losing battle against it. The speed with which he has declined has brought you here, to the edge of the highway, terminus of days spent deliberating the best course to follow. In your time as Mother, you have not been confronted by a decision of this magnitude, and though your memory of your life prior to joining the pack is hazy, you do not think it faced you with an equivalent problem, either. You are not sure the path you have selected is the correct one (honestly, you suspect no such route exists), but it is your choice and the rest of the pack has consented to it. Only the cub does not know what looms ahead, for fear he might bolt if he did.

At the moment, the highway is empty, the most recent cars to speed by red taillights dwindling into the darkness. Not many miles away, you can hear a number of vehicles, a considerable number of vehicles, cars and big trucks, approaching. You imagine the cub hears them, too, but when you glance at him, his eyes are unfocused, lost in a disease-fostered reverie. You nudge him. His attention returns from wherever the sickness took it.

You must not appear overly emotional, anguished at this imminent parting, at the unfairness of it all, the horror you are about to visit on one of your own, your pack, your family. You must appear calm. Were he not so ill, your performance would probably not fool him; as it is, he gives no sign of noticing anything amiss. "Hey," you say to him.

He looks up at you with eyes glassy but eager.

"I need you to do something for me. Do you think you can?"

He nods, swaying from side to side. In the last little while, he has degenerated further.

"I need you to walk out onto the road," you point to it, "and head west. Can you do that for me?"

His answer is his action. Legs trembling, he leaves the grass for first the highway's shoulder and then its closer lane. He turns left and starts slowly in that direction. His mouth hangs open, tongue dangling. You are holding your breath, suspended between what is and what is about to be. The cub trudges ahead, sickly and alone.

In an instant, the highway is again washed with light, the night flooded with noise. Until the leading car is bearing down on him, the cub does not react: then, as if finally apprehending what is happening, he simultaneously bites at the bumper and attempts to change to human. The impact smashes him against the asphalt, and while he is lying there stunned, the next car runs over him, its tires breaking and crushing his bones, while those of the tractor-trailer behind tear him apart, and each following vehicle continues the process, reducing the junior member of the pack to meat and fur and pulp spread across the surface of the road in a long bloody smear that shines in the passing headlights. Your kind is difficult to kill, but not impossible. None of the highway workers who eventually clean the cub's remains will regard them as anything other than what is left of a hapless animal, which is not too far off the truth.

Within you, apprehension softens to grief. You stay to watch as the man driving the first car to hit the cub pulls to the shoulder, exits the vehicle, and walks back to survey the conclusion of what he began. You cannot guess his motivations. Coming and going, he passes within twenty feet of you and is not aware of your presence at all. His scent rolls toward you, sped by the cars and trucks still racing by, continuing to reduce the cub from specific to abstract, from living being to stain on the road. You smell his sweat, his failing deodorant, the shampoo he used this morning, the detergent in which his jeans and shirt were laundered, the stale age of his jacket, the dirt ground into the soles of his sneakers. It is a generic bundle of odors of a generic human life—except for the soil packed into the treads of his footwear. The dirt is familiar, local, from a place no farther than a night's run from here. Were you to so desire, you could track this man, this murderer of your cub, without much difficulty.

An idea blossoms in your brain: the same randomness that took the cub from you has just provided his replacement. The thought is at once entirely appropriate and ridiculous, the difficulties acting upon it will entail substantial, but not impossible, effort. The plan unfolding in your mind, you turn from the highway and the cub's remains. As you cross the field, on your way back to the rest of the pack, you start to run.

You are Mother, and the care of the pack is yours.

For Fiona

Worry Dolly

NADIA BULKIN

The first time Jenna remembered seeing the un-stranger, the woman who was not her mother, she was in the backyard. She was kicking herself higher and higher on the swing set, waving at her mother inside the house as she flew by. And then she noticed something strange.

When she was at the back peak of the swing, her mother was in the kitchen. When she was at the front peak of the swing, her mother was in the guest bedroom. Her mother's apparent speed zooming back and forth across the house wasn't the only strange thing—whenever she was in the kitchen, her mother was smiling, happy, bright-eyed and waving back. But when she got to the guest bedroom, it was like she sank beneath a dark cloud. She was frowning, almost pouting. Sunken eyes glaring as if to set the world on fire. Hair a mess.

Jenna was afraid to go into the guest bedroom for weeks after that. When her mother asked her to take linens to that room in preparation for a visit by one of her father's friends, Jenna shook her head no.

"Mama," she said, "I'm scared."

"Here," her mother said, "take Worry Dolly."

And her mother presented to her a doll the size of a bread loaf, with a glass-eyed porcelain head and a soft cloth body. "Squeeze her if you're scared. Shake her if you're nervous. You can even pull her hair. She'll keep you calm."

Jenna stacked the doll on top of the linens and very carefully crept to the guest bedroom—making sure Worry Dolly entered the space first. There was no one in there; not the un-stranger or anyone else. She placed the linens on the bed, grabbed Worry Dolly in triumph, and nearly ran into her mother rushing out the door. For a second—only a second, in the afternoon shadow—she thought that the un-stranger was back, and squeezed Worry Dolly like her mother told her to.

"Good job, baby," her mother said. Only after dark, while Jenna was lying in bed trying to sleep, did she wonder why her mother had taken her hair down inside the guest bedroom.

❦

Eventually, Jenna realized that the un-stranger was not bound to the guest bedroom. The un-stranger might sit at her father's seat at the dining table in the middle of the night. Might loiter at the end of the driveway in the rain, as if waiting for the mail. The un-stranger had her mother's height, her face, her bone structure. But the pale depletion of the un-stranger's face—the bedraggled half-dead-ness of her expression and her faint odor of mildew instead of rose—meant Jenna never mistook the two.

The un-stranger waited for them in mall parking lots, a hunched column of barren gloom. She dragged behind them at the park like a trail of mud. She even followed them on vacation. Like the summer they spent at Grandpa Walker's huge house in Port Eliza, which Jenna would have preferred to spend back home with the popular girls she wanted to keep as her friends. She was upstairs, refusing to go to the beach, when she heard what sounded like her mother's voice call her from the first floor: *"Jenna!"*

"I said I'm not going!" she yelled back. She could already predict what her mother was going to say: bring Worry Dolly! It was her answer to everything, which meant she had to take Worry Dolly everywhere, like she was a little kid. When Jenna pointed out that she was angry, not worried, her mother just knelt down and whispered that Worry Dolly could be an *anger dolly*, too.

130

"Jenna!" It was a tone of voice she couldn't say no to, not if she didn't want to hear about it from her father. So she grabbed Worry Dolly off the bed and started stomping down the hallway toward the stairs, eager to show her mother just how unfixably angry she was.

And that was when one of the white bedroom doors opened and someone cold and fragrant pulled her in. It was her mother. She looked, for once, mildly distressed.

Jenna frowned. "I thought you were downstairs."

"Shush," her mother said, and the realization flooded down Jenna's legs like adrenaline: the un-stranger knew her name. "Stay here. Keep the door closed."

While she waited for her mother—to return? to beat the un-stranger to death?—Jenna ran her fingers through the mats in Worry Dolly's hair. She was not careful with the thing; she pitied it sometimes. She had thrown it, stomped on it, dug her nails into its stomach and tried to reach its stuffing. "I'm sorry," she whispered to it, then rocked it back and forth so it could blink its acceptance of her apology. So she could imagine it reassuring her. *It's okay*, she heard Worry Dolly say. *Hurt me.*

❧

Jenna had been afraid that the un-stranger would follow her to college—watch over her at parties, sit next to her in class, scare her roommates—but she didn't. Her college years were populated entirely by the corporeal and the living. Jenna never even caught sight of Chris McLaren, the famous suicide victim of Room 501. The un-stranger stayed home.

She had hoped to spend Thanksgiving during her senior year with her pre-med boyfriend—her father called him Sweater Vest, a nickname that had stuck—but he had bailed at the last minute, saying it was too soon. Her friend Cassidy suggested he might have an old girlfriend back home he wanted to see instead. Her friend Sloane said he was just a slow mover. Jenna was afraid that he had seen too many of her bad moods, too stormy even for Worry Dolly to handle. The poor thing was covered in puncture wounds and ink stains; she was even missing an eye.

131

"Goodness, Jenna," her mother said when Jenna gave her the doll to repair.

"You still carry that thing around?" her father said, raising his eyebrows.

On her final night at home, she woke up in her childhood bedroom to find the door ajar. A hint of hallway light revealed the barely-there outline of a figure with wild hair standing in the room against her Eiffel Tower poster. Watching her.

"Mom?" she mumbled, but the figure said nothing. She wondered if her mother had started sleep-walking—all the new medications she was on, God knew what side effects they might have—until the figure with her mother's shape took a big, deliberate-seeming step toward her. Hands curled as if to catch. To grab. To choke.

"Mom," Jenna hissed, though she was too afraid to turn on the lamp. "Stop."

As if electro-shocked, the figure slid back toward the wall and fell straight to the floor, like a sheet falling from a line.

Jenna threw back the sheets, thinking of aneurysms and strokes and the hardness of the uncarpeted floor, but only got as far as kicking her feet out of bed before the figure scurried, on all fours, out of the room. Jenna had to grab stitched-up Worry Dolly before giving chase.

She was not surprised, after all these years, to find the hallway empty. She was not surprised to push open the door to her parents' bedroom and find her mother asleep. Like Jenna, she was a light sleeper. Soon she was squinting, propping herself up on her elbow. "What is it?" she murmured, not wanting to wake up Jenna's father.

"Are you okay?" Jenna whispered.

"Of course." Her mother's head fell limply back to the pillow. "Why wouldn't I be?"

⚜

The un-stranger was not invited to Jenna's wedding. She attended anyway, wearing a long fusty dress of funereal black. She paced back and forth behind the pews while Jenna and Sweater Vest said their vows; she lingered by the punch bowl during the reception.

"Mom," Jenna said, because on this single most important day of her life, as per her wedding planner, she had the right to ask anything. "Who is that?"

Her mother looked across the lawn at the disheveled woman who wore her face. She showed no hint of alarm, possibly because she'd had two drinks. The only sound she made at first was "Hm." And then, "I used to have a Worry Dolly too, you know."

"Oh?" Jenna's Worry Dolly had not been battered nearly as badly during her long engagement to Sweater Vest. Not because she was any less anxious—because her nerves had been so prickly, so wound-up, that all she could do to Worry Dolly was squeeze.

"Yes, a present from my mother." Her mother smiled and forced herself to turn away from the un-stranger. "Did I ever tell you about the summer your father and I lived in Port Eliza? We were engaged. He was wrapping up his obligations to the Navy so he could take a job with the family business. I was working as a receptionist. I almost left him. I came very close."

Her mother did not say why. Jenna knew, by then, that her mother would never say why.

"One day I just snapped. I'd had it. I left the office during my lunch break and took the train to see my mother back in Ashland. I told her, 'I know that everyone loves him, I know he's from a good family, but I don't know if I'm meant to be a Walker wife. Because I've seen his brothers' wives. Because I don't know if I'm meant to be a wife at all.' She fed me some tea and chocolates and said, 'Laura, it's time to go home and burn your doll'."

Jenna squinted as she searched the un-stranger's face for hints of scarring. But from a distance she could only see the skin her mother hid beneath her makeup, the sick skin of a woman who hadn't slept in years. "Why?"

"Same reason you burn incense. Same reason you light a candle. So she could change into a form that could carry all those bad feelings for me. And believe me, I've given her a lot to carry. Anger, worry, sadness. Disappointment. Resentment, my God." Jenna's mother sighed. "She lets me take good care of you and your father. That's the most important thing."

How pitiful for the un-stranger, to carry another woman's burden. No wonder, Jenna thought, that the un-stranger didn't love her. "Can Dad see her?"

Her mother shrugged. "He's never mentioned her. But she tends to stay away from him. I don't think she likes him much." She nodded toward Sweater Vest, who was laughing nervously amid his louder friends. "He's going to be under a lot of stress during residency. He's going to need you to be your best self."

Jenna felt a piece of her elaborate updo slip. The hand that wasn't holding her bouquet looked for something to adjust on the back of her head, but her mother's fingers beat her there.

"Which means," her mother said, pushing one of Jenna's golden bobby pins deeper and tighter against Jenna's scalp, "that it's probably time for you to set your Worry Dolly on fire."

◈

After Mila finished her crayon drawing, she brought it into the kitchen and presented it like an offering to her mother, who was cutting vegetables for dinner. "Oh sweetheart, it's beautiful," her mother said, making Mila giggle with pride. "Is that us?"

"That's me," Mila said, pointing to the smallest stick figure with spiky pigtails and a polka dot skirt. "And that's you." She pointed to a larger stick figure with a checkered skirt and a comically large smile.

"I'm glad I'm so happy," Mila's mother said, squeezing Mila close.

"And that's Daddy." Mila pointed to another large stick figure, this one flat-mouthed and wearing a red sweater vest and a snake-like stethoscope around his neck. "Because that's what Grandpa always calls him."

"That's right," Mila's mother said. "Who's that?"

She was pointing at the third large stick figure, ensconced in a dark cloud and floating, apparently, above the rest of the family. Its eyes were red and bleeding tears.

Mila's voice dropped. "That's Sad Mommy."

"Hmm. Does Sad Mommy make you sad?"

Mila nodded, but was it really sadness she felt, or something else? Was it the feeling she had when she saw a squirrel, dead on the side of the road?

Or was it closer to that speedy-heart-feeling she got when the neighbor's St. Bernard stormed the fence and barked at her?

For a moment Mila's mother was quiet, stroking Mila's hair. Then she stuck the drawing on the fridge—putting a big *Welcome to Ashland!* magnet on top of Sad Mommy, because Sad Mommy made her sad too—and turned back to Mila with her famous broad smile. "I have an idea," she said, extending her cool hand. "You want to go pick out a new doll?"

(sub)Maternal Instincts

K.M. VEOHONGS

You hate me
You think I don't know?
I was once like you:
Young, beautiful (oppressed)

Perhaps that's why I track my muddy skirts across the floors
    you've scrubbed to shining
Rip apart your neat and perfect seams
Bury the lentils in the ash

Why I whisper in your father's ear:
How ungrateful, how unpleasant, how unlikely ever to find a
    husband

Did you think I didn't know the huntsman would falter?
Did you think I stole the bread trail to be cruel?

Tell me, please and prettily, too: what would your fate have
    been otherwise?
A moony-eyed prince, bland and filled with a sterile love?

(SUB)MATERNAL INSTINCTS

Try this instead, merchant's child:

The middle son of the magistrate, who's beaten three horses
    to their knees
and rapes the scullery maid after a bad hunt.

Maybe the king's butcher, in want of a new wife to replace
    the old
who will handle you less tenderly than he does a side of beef.

If you're lucky, the gentleman farmer, who will fill you
with baby after baby until your death.

So like your mother.

No, my dear. That is not what the future holds for you.
For in making you scrub these floors, I gave you fortitude.
Calluses grew from those resewn seams.
And finding the lentils (how ever did you?) made you sharp
    as a needle.

Why don't you get lost?
In the woods, in the kingdom
In another world.

Take my gifts and use them well
Find yourself a new life and a new way to be.

Do not darken your father's doorstep again.

720°

STEVE TOASE

❦

Dog hair felted every inch of the carpet, though the dogs the hair belonged to were long since dead. My mum sat across the room, a magazine folded upon her lap, open at some random story of misery. I did not ask how she was. I did not care.

"You got my message?" she said.

"Doris passed it on."

She shifted in her chair, letting the magazine topple to the ground as if she still expected me to pick up after her. Behind her, an old FM radio played, a barely audible brass band fading in and out so I could not recognize the tune.

"She was always good, Doris. Always did as she was told."

"Not always."

I'd seen the bruises myself. Worn my own too.

My mum's hand went up to the pendant hanging from her neck, and she pricked each finger in turn with the angles.

"I found the stick."

She pointed to the hearth. Leaning beside the gas fire was a long wooden walking stick, brass collar and brass heel tarnished with age.

I tried not to react, but she always knew my tells. Always knew when she was getting to me.

"You know what it is? Who it belonged to?"

How could I not? The walking stick was almost identical to the bronze staff held by the statue of Blind Silas in the market square, even down to the slight kink in the middle. This did not surprise me. I knew if it was in my mum's house, it was Silas's.

"Where did you find it?" I asked, because from six years old I knew the right questions to ask.

"Auction up in the Dales. You remember how I like my auctions."

I said nothing, the scent of dust and polish rushing back in a memory too vivid to shift by speaking.

She levered herself out of the chair and wrapped her loose knit jumper tighter around herself. Her hair was greyer than the last time I saw her. She used to blame me. I wondered who was at fault now.

"Take it," she said, handing me the walking stick. I held it in both hands, resting my weight on the metal point until she sat once more.

Walking stick might give the impression of something small and delicate for the frail. This was vast, the tip hammered into a beaten brass heel. The brass collar was at eye level, verdigris stained and loose. Above my head the stick ended in a round polished knot of wood, heavy enough to knock the sense into, or out of, anyone.

"You know what this means?" she said. "We can go back to the toll-house." In her hands was the hexagonal plan she'd made me draw all those years ago as she stood behind me in that empty building. The straight lines, and the angles that did not add up to 720° as they should. I pushed my way out of the room toward the hallway and the staircase.

"We'll talk when you come back down," she said, not bothering to hide her amusement at my discomfort. She never had before and was not going to start now.

***

I walked past my old bedroom and stopped. Seemed strange to see it with a door in place rather than hinge bare as it was during my childhood.

I turned the handle, trying to ignore the slip of settled grease against my skin.

The wallpaper down the outside wall was still rotten and peeling. Maps that were once rolled neatly in cardboard tubes now covered the floor and bed, showing the same thing over and over. An absence. A road missing. First edition ordnance survey, estate maps, tithe maps, and enclosure awards. Especially enclosure awards. When I was a child I loved the hand-drawn plans of fields not yet built. Amongst the black and white of official documents they were colorful and bright. Even in the darkness I saw yellow, red, and green inked over thin rulered lines, showing who was to be assigned which enclosure. I knelt beside the bed and ran a finger across the divisions as if they were a labyrinth and I was searching for a way out. My hand stilled and I looked at where I'd paused. The six angles were just visible around my fingertip. I winced as if the ink itself was caustic and would burn through to the bone. Even after I shoved my hand deep in my pocket I felt the geometry pulse under the contours of my skin.

Shutting the door, I walked across the hall and locked the bathroom behind me. I stared at the toothpaste coated sink, then at myself in the medical cabinet mirror.

The house seemed smaller, and it never seemed big when I was a child. At least the bathroom had a lock. Of course, she had always been able to unbolt it from the outside when she wanted to drag me out, yet I still remember those times when I could shut myself away, slide into the tepid water and have a few moments, a few precious moments to myself. Not safe, but alone.

"You better not be using all my hot water. I can hear the thermostat coming on. I need to have a bath later, and you'll be leaving me with nothing but cold water."

Even through the floor, even across the distance of years, I still flinched. I finished up, dried my hands on the slightly mildewed towels, and opened the door.

She stood in the corridor, Silas' walking stick leaning against the wall.

"Come in here," she said, nodding toward my old room. For a moment I thought about refusing. About arguing that I didn't have to do what she said anymore. But the twenty years since I left crumbled, and I was fourteen again, trying to fend off the worst with my forearms while waiting for it to stop. She went in first, and I followed as she knew I would.

"I know how to find the road," she said. "Now I have the walking stick."

Not, *I've found the road.* That should have had me out of the door. It wouldn't have been the first time.

❦

Blind Silas was the local hero. Scarred by falling in the hearth as a child, Silas grew up sightless. That did not stop him building roads across most of the moors in the county. Over the years he was given the contract for the turnpikes, pay-to-use roads that ran into the market-towns. They were known for their durability, said to be down to the cow horn cores he bought in bulk from the local tanners and laid first once the route was cleared. People still drove on his roads, though they wore modern coats of hardcore and bitumen.

Silas prided himself on completing all of the roads he set out to build. All except one. One he only mentioned briefly in his diaries. One that he never got any further with than building the tollhouse. Silas's Folly as it was known locally. It was built around the same time his wife, Alexandra, disappeared.

Revisionist historians said he was a fraud. That in fact his wife drew all the plans, directed all the civil engineering and Silas took the credit. That even blind it was easier for a man to claim such work than a woman. My mum was not most historians. My mum was not a historian at all, and my mum believed that not only was Blind Silas responsible for all the roads, but that the final missing road was there, if you knew where to search.

❦

"You'll have to drive," she said. "You did come in your car didn't you?"

Outside, I waited until she was sitting in the passenger seat, then slid the walking stick in from the back, the heel nestled in the footwell. My mum never learnt to drive. When I was a kid we would take taxis up to Silas' Folly, walking the last few hundred metres up the narrow country lane because she refused to pay more than five pounds for any trip. Looking back, I think it had more to do with not wanting people to know where she was going. What she was doing. Of course, they knew anyway. Small towns are like that.

I parked on the grass verge, staying in the driver's seat until she had climbed out, opened the boot, and dragged out the walking stick. Out of all that day's returns this was the one I wanted least: Silas' Folly.

Tollhouses are very specific examples of architecture, like petrol stations or windmills. Buildings designed for one purpose that can only be occupied after their abandonment by hermit-crab-like businesses. No one occupied Silas' Folly, although we came close, the amount of time we'd spent there when I was growing up. My mum opened the door and let me in. I gave it a moment for my night vision to adapt to the darkness.

Tollhouses were often angular: octagonal or pentagonal. Silas's Folly was hexagonal. With most it was possible to tell where the road had been, even if it had been grubbed up by progress. A payment window— once adjacent with the toll barrier—was the giveaway. That's the first way Silas' Folly differed. Five walls had a payment window, the sixth for the door. The first difference, but not the last, not by a long way. All the glass was smashed long ago and not replaced. So many old buildings are unsighted so they cannot witness what goes on within their own walls.

We went inside—me first, my mum shutting the door behind. I turned my phone light on and looked around the room, floor covered with empty cider cans and burnt silver foil. Even out here people needed a distraction. I turned around. Just visible between the graffiti were the chalk marks I'd made all those years ago.

"I want you to check again."

"They're not going to have changed," I said.

"Buildings move, and I want you to check them again." The words were tight and small. She opened her bag, handing me a tape measure and clipboard, paper already in place. Hexagon already drawn.

I knelt down near the first chalk mark and held the tape in place. She took the other end from me and stretched it toward the corner. Without bending down she read off the measurements like she had so many times before, and I wrote them down without thinking. Using the light from my phone I did the math and calculated the angles from where the lines met and added them up. 970°. The impossibility captured in the drawn version in front of me. Still so far away from 720°.

She leant over me and read my working out. It made me nervous to have her so close and I tried to move away, but against the wall there was nowhere to go.

"Good. I was afraid we'd both imagined it all those years ago. We're alike me and you. See things differently."

I felt the needle go into my neck, had just enough time to get my hands out to break my fall, and then I felt nothing.

§

"I'm sorry I had to do that," my mum said. She stood behind me. I could always tell where she was. She smelt of her house, a musty, rich, scent as if the building itself was upon her back.

The place where she'd injected me throbbed. My vision was blurred. That did not surprise me, the anesthetic still fading, but there was something else. My face ached, muscles around my eye sockets spasming. I reached up and flinched. Both eyeballs lay against my cheeks, held in place by optic nerves. They brushed against my eyelashes as I went to stand. The

144

movement jagged my dislodged sight and I nearly vomited with motion sickness.

"It's funny you know," my mum said. "I'm much closer to blindness than you. On bad days my left side is nothing but a blur. Unfortunately, I don't think this will work unless the eyes are healthy."

I felt her lean against me. Reaching around, she gripped the first eyeball. Something cold and metallic closed around the optic nerve, then there was nothing but pain, the burning sensation so intense I hardly noticed her take my other eye. Letting it fall amongst the leaves and empty beer cans. She was saying something but I couldn't hear properly. Blood ran down my cheeks and into my mouth. She wrapped her arms around me.

"There we go son. The worst is over now. It's for the best."

I didn't want to have to listen to her. I could do nothing else.

I heard her foot stamp down twice and something smear across the stone flag floor. She made sure she had enough of my attention to know that there was no way to repair me now. Truth be told I was a long way past repair years ago. This just felt like a conclusion that was always coming.

People have asked me why I didn't fight back, why I didn't get myself out of there. Since I was eight years old, I didn't know any other way to be around her.

She led me toward the door and pressed Silas' walking stick into my hand.

"I need you to walk the road. I need you to lead me along it."

Growing up I thought about blindness a lot. With my mum's obsession it was never far from my mind. I always imagined it as stillness. A pure blackness, like looking into a well where there was calm and emptiness. I was wrong. Though I could no longer see, I still had vision. Pinpoints of light erupted as if my optic nerves hadn't quite realized they were no longer connected to anything. They spattered and exploded with each jarring footstep, and when the cold outside hit my empty sockets, it was like staring at the heart of the sun.

I stood still, though I felt her pushing against me as if she could force me by sheer will to find what she wanted.

Slowly the explosions of light resolved, pulsing and grading, until they formed a single ribbon along where I guessed the ground still was. I had no way of locating the tollhouse, but knew that it lay off to one side of this strip of color, and that this strip of color was the road that my mum had been obsessed with for as long as I could remember.

"You can see it, can't you?"

Even with a couple of decades of adulthood, I still couldn't hide those tells she'd spent years as a parent exploiting.

"Point to it. Show me where the road is before we start. You really can see it can't you?"

Not speaking, I used the walking stick to tamp against the ribbon of light. It was narrower than I was expecting. If I was to lead her then it was single file.

"Put your hands on my shoulders," I said, and felt her grip my coat, too sharp nails digging crescents into my collar bone.

⚜

I had no idea where it would lead. I don't think my mum did either. She wasn't looking for eternal life or redemption. She just wanted to find it. Be proved right. See what was at the end. I needed answers too.

We started walking. I took my time. If I looked too closely at the road it began to swirl and fade. Road is a bit misleading. Road suggests something built. This was a route marked out in a place where no one could see it. No one but me and a blind road builder who lived 250 years earlier.

"Are you sure this is going the right way?" she said.

I smiled at her uncertainty, then wondered for a moment which direction it was taking us in. The ground was uneven underfoot and we seemed to be going uphill. That meant nothing on the moors.

"I'm still following the road, if that's what you mean."

"Make sure you do. Don't try and trick me. Just because you can't see any more doesn't mean I'll go easy on you."

There it was in one sentence. Almost as if the seasons had taken my eyes, or the crows. Not her with a metal scoop, a pair of Stevens scissors, and deception.

I carried on walking, and she carried on holding my shoulders, following me. Making me move forward.

Underfoot the road changed texture. No longer the crushed meadow flowers and un-mown grass. More solid. Broken. Shattered cobbles and broken curbs. For the first time I leant on Blind Silas's walking stick because I needed to.

My mum noticed my pace slow and pushed me forward once more.

"Don't be delaying us now. Don't be slacking."

I was trying not to, but more distractions were crowding in. First the shattered road surface, then the voices.

They were little more than breath at first, barely audible. Only by focusing could I catch the words, and then only a sentence or two. They were graphic and specific and made me want to drive knife blades into my ears so I could no longer hear.

The road changed again, becoming stagnant water, thick with the stench of rotting sheep, then carpeted with feathers. A road that was never built. A road that should never be built. A road that could never be built by man, blind or sighted.

The voices did not quieten and I struggled to keep my balance. I concentrated on where to place feet I could not see on uneven concrete that changed to wooden hurdles and clay tiles. Rain-polished limestone changing to mud-sodden straw.

Alongside, I heard the sound of quarrying, hammer on chisel, and the tipping of stone. Smelled the scent of cow horns boiled free of their cores.

My mum clung on to my shoulders, her nicotine breath the loudest thing of all. Still, I followed the glittering path.

"I can see it," she said. Four simple words. Not, *You've found it for me*, or *Thank you*, as if I was not leading the way. And then I truly wasn't.

She stepped around me and wrenched the walking stick from my grasp. Grabbed my hand to drag me on. I twisted my fingers from hers, landing in the wet heather and peat.

I could still see the glistening route. It shone like fresh offal. Still heard the voices, though they were no longer paying attention to me.

They say when you go blind your hearing suddenly improves or your sense of smell, like it's some kind of superhero origin story. It's not true, not for me anyway. Yet I'll never forget the noise that night. The voices got louder. I heard her feet slipping as if trying to gain purchase on wet stone and failing. Her falling and rising again, each time slower as her knees and back took the worst of the impact. Each time taking longer to get up, harder to hear over the voices until they stilled and there was silence.

There was no screaming or pleading, just a slow fading of the mildewed scent from the house I grew up in. The reek of ground bone marrow spreading through the air. Then I was alone on the moor and there were no roads to lead me back.

Number ONE

FRANCES LU-PAI IPPOLITO

Wherever Baba went, "Spanker" hung from his belt like a stiff limb that had grown on the outside of his clothes.

Unlike the punishment paddle, we, Baba's daughters, had no names. He called us by our rank. I was Shi-Qi, or Number Seventeen, among the adopted girls who lived on the farm estate. I don't remember my life before coming here, but I do remember Baba placing me into the toddler bed one night when I was four. He told me we lived in the hills of Eastern Oregon. I still don't know where that really is, but it doesn't matter. Things are perfect here.

Even so, my sisters whisper behind my back, "Why does Baba only beat *us*? How did *she* get promoted again?"

Their jealousy used to irritate me. After all, it wasn't my fault they couldn't please him. The punishments have always been clear: 1–30 strikes for lying, 31–50 for indolence, and 50+ for disobedience.

I've told this much to the newest sister sitting across from me at the living room table. Baba left her in my care for the night. I've given her some of the rules but saved the most important one.

"There's something else you mustn't do, Eighty-Eight."

"Worse than disobeying?" the fourteen-year-old girl asked. She looked younger than her age, with gaunt cheeks that gave her an unnaturally sharp face. As I stared, she trembled, rattling her chair and scraping the wooden legs at the floor.

"Never forget Mother." I pointed to the ancestral tablet on the mantel.

Eighty-Eight tilted her head and squinted at the bronze frame that bordered a rectangular inset of white jade. From our seats, I couldn't read the carved inscription of Mother's name, although I knew it by heart.

"Chan Hua," Eighty-Eight whispered.

"You can read Chinese?" Not many of the girls did when they first arrived.

She bowed her head and stared into the table. "Madame Yue taught us enough to recite poetry for the...clients."

I hid my expression behind a cradled tea cup. At age twenty, I'd spent years training with my sisters. We were all orphans once. Baba selected us from foster homes, wicker baskets left on doorsteps, and families that couldn't feed one more mouth. But none of us came so late in age or from *there*, a brothel in some nearby town. Baba preferred to adopt the youngest, purest ones. "In order to fully shape their minds and bodies," he'd told me years ago.

"What was she like?" Eighty-Eight asked when she finally raised her head, cheeks still mottled scarlet.

I smoothed loose strands of my braided hair and straightened my posture before reciting as Baba had taught me. "Mother was born in Taichung, Taiwan. Our parents married many years ago, but Mother died before Baba could bring her to America."

"She must have been alluring and seductive."

My face tightened. Eighty-Eight spoke like a prostitute and smelled like one too. The artificial rose scent lifted off her tiny body in a dilating orbit and clung to my nostrils until the cloying sweetness overpowered the gentle jasmine of steeped leaves.

Ignoring her, I continued, "There is a painting in Baba's private rooms. Only Number One is allowed there. Baba says Mother was intelligent, beautiful, and *virtuous*. He encourages us all to be like her."

Eighty-Eight glanced again at the ancestral tablet, but her gaze soon roamed the outer room of my two-room living space, sweeping over the delicate peonies and cranes carved into the mahogany wall paneling, and lingering to tally the expensive pearwood lampstands, sandalwood armchairs, and camphor chests. I pretended to look away, to drink my cooling tea, but felt her eyes creep like hungry mice up the peach silks draped across my body. I adjusted my collar, imagining how the cheap raw silk she wore must chaff.

"If I become like you, Baba will love me too," she announced. Her starved face hardened into seriousness and her eyes narrowed into crescents.

"Bring me hot water and a bath bucket," I ordered Fifty-Three, who was too busy stealing glances at Eighty-Eight to properly balance the used tea cups on the serving tray. The teapot slipped off the edge of the tray and clattered sideways onto the table. Eighty-Eight shrieked and slapped at the hot stains spreading over her dress in a shadow of lengthening fingers.

I tapped Fifty-Three on her cheek with my folded fan.

"That's an imported yixing clay pot." I kept my voice even and let the tip of my fan droop to a relaxed angle towards Eighty-Eight. "You wouldn't want to break Baba's newest piece, would you?" I struck the fan stave against my palm, satisfied when Fifty-Three blanched at the rhythm of bamboo meeting skin. She grabbed the teapot and backed out of the room.

"The smallest bath bucket will do," I called after her. Clumsy and slow. No wonder she ranked so low even though she and I were the same age.

The bath finally ready, I guided a bare Eighty-Eight into the water.

"You'll live in the dorm," I said as I picked at her wet knots with a comb.

"She's not going there," Baba interrupted from the other side of the bathroom door. His silhouette paused behind the paper screen panel. Baba never knocked, but I always listened for the *tap, tap, jingle* that Spanker made when he was near. Eighty-Eight, however, startled, and sloshed water out of the bathtub when her arms flew across her chest and her knees bent to tuck under her chin.

I set the comb aside and greeted Baba outside the bathroom. He usually lowered his head for me to kiss his cheek. This time he didn't, instead staring at the exposed curve of Eighty-Eight's spine.

Her nakedness revealed the child beneath the layers of painted doll. She was thin, but her skin glowed a perfect tan. Her thick hair fell like a curtain of spilled ink down her back. In the lamplight, black strands shone with flashes of blue.

"Where shall I take her?" I returned to my stool and continued to run the tortoise shell comb through her hair.

"She'll stay with you," he answered and knelt beside the tub. Eighty-Eight tensed away from him and shivered into a tighter ball, sinking into the shallow water.

With me? Only the top ten received sister servants. The others would be jealous I'd been promoted again.

"You will personally accelerate her education," he ordered.

Teach her? Not a promotion at all! A chore! My fingers pressed hard into the comb's carved grooves, yanking at the glistening hair until Eighty-Eight yelped and twisted free.

I grabbed her head and pushed her back into position.

"Don't disappoint me," Baba said.

"Never, Baba," I answered as Eighty-Eight's body rocked and her elbows banged against the sides of the bathtub.

Fresh and cleaned, Eighty-Eight now wore the uniform of lower-ranked sisters: a chaste pale green robe over simple black pants. She lay next to me in bed.

"Seventeen?" she said.

"Yes?"

"Does Spanker hurt?"

What a stupid question! "Of course! That's the point."

"Oh, but the holes in the center. I thought—" She bit her bottom lip in the dim light.

"Go to sleep." I rolled to my side in the comforter.

The holes. I had been curious once too and as sleep lulled, a memory floated over the top layers of waning consciousness like cherry blossom petals skimming along a pond's murky surface.

"It hits faster and harder this way," Baba explained one evening, years ago, when he caught me staring.

I looked away, embarrassed. I was curious, but not so curious that I would normally stare in such an obvious way. It was just easier to wonder if my fingers could fit through the holes drilled into Spanker's face, rather than focus on the tourniquet squeezing my upper arm. Baba took out the syringe and screwed on a thick and impossibly long needle to the hub. The needle's shiny surface gleamed, distorting all the features of my reflected face. I held my breath at the sharp pinch when the tip sunk in.

"The holes reduce air resistance," Baba said as my blood flowed into the empty vial.

"Yes, Baba." He liked it when I agreed. I focused on the thin hairs on my upper arm as he switched out the filled vial for empty ones. Was that two? Three? Five? I lost count and grew dizzy when Baba finally pulled the needle out.

"Let me show you," he said after packing up the vials. He raised Spanker and tilted the paddle towards the fireplace we sat beside. The light from the flames passed through the circular cut-outs. A log cracked in half, sending a drifting net of light and dark shadows across his face.

Without warning, he swung Spanker against his calf. I flinched and leapt up at the reverberating noise that punched the quiet room. I didn't get far. Baba's free hand shot out and grabbed my wrist. He yanked down. Pain shot through my knees as I slammed onto the hardwood floors. He pulled me close, flush against his side. The smell of aniseed rushed into my nose, mixing with the smoldering scents of burnt firewood. With his free hand, he rolled up his pant leg. There, he traced my captured fingertips across a red blade-shaped imprint swelling on his skin.

"See?" he said, eyes flashing.

"Yes, Baba," I hurried to agree and stayed kneeling on the ground, waiting for him to release me.

"They're the same," Eighty-Eight said, staring at the scroll in her lap. She picked at the strings binding the bamboo strips. Through the library window behind her, a tangerine sun slipped into acres of sweet corn that flanked the three main buildings of our home.

"No, that's the second volume," I answered.

"Of the same type of books. We only read Mother's journals and writings. There are other things written in the world. Poetry and stories." She flipped over to her back and waved her arms at the rows of bamboo scrolls lining the walls.

I snorted. "Sit up."

Instead of sitting, she stood and pointed at the watercolor paintings and hanging calligraphy.

"Why is everything so Chinese?" she exclaimed, her forehead wrinkling. "None of you are Chinese. You're only pretending." She crouched to where I sat on a cushion and ran her palm along my coiled black hair to touch my scalp, where I knew undyed blonde roots erupted from skin.

"Even your hair," she whispered. "And your eyes."

My fingers traced ridges and trenches scarred into the skin flaps where the outline of my eyes had been permanently reshaped with a more pronounced taper. It had been a successful surgery. Baba promoted me right after.

"Baba can decorate his home however he likes," I replied. "We weren't born to look like you."

She was perfect by Baba's standards—a lithe, petite vision of appropriate proportion and coloring. With food, she had filled out too. Her cheeks were no longer gaunt, but plump and rosy. Her black eyes had brightened and gained expression, but still retained that perfect slender bow form that we sliced ours to match. And her skin glowed a warm tan that the darkening ointments never gave to our too-pale skin.

"At Madame Yue's, only the older women dyed their gray hair—"

I slammed my scroll onto the desk. "Don't mention that place again! We are not like them."

Why couldn't she listen? She looked perfect. She'd learned information fast and steady when she wanted. All that was left was to memorize the texts and keep Baba happy. Didn't she understand that our promotions rested on her progress?

"I had a name before," she said, staring out the window. "Lily. I liked that name. It was mine."

What use was a name? It didn't convey any information like where you stood in the hierarchy.

"You're too sentimental. Focus on promotion." I couldn't help wondering: did I have a name before?

Eighty-Eight kicked at the floor with her satin slippered feet. "You don't remember the outside. It's different."

I scoffed. "Without Baba, I would have died in an orphanage. When I came here, I was ranked seventy-one. There were fewer of us then. But I watched how they angered Baba. I did the opposite—dyed my hair, fixed my face, bound my feet, and memorized the texts. You too will be promoted if you do as I do." I placed my hands on her shoulders and nudged her back to the scroll. "Let's begin again. Translate Mother's entry from the January before her death." I handed her a brush dipped in crimson ink. She took it, but the brush rested listless in her hand.

Another lecture readied itself on my lips, but I stopped when I saw her wipe her eyes and rub her nose. I was pushing too hard. It had been only six months since she arrived. I wrapped an arm around her shoulders and squeezed. "Read to me, if you can't write."

Sagging in her seat, she turned to the marked portion and read out the brush stroke characters.

"I will become a woman today. 'The family's future depends on your children,' Momma has said every night for ten years since my twelfth birthday. I wonder how someone becomes a woman if it doesn't happen the normal way. Will I feel different? Will someone finally agree to marry me?"

"Next entry."

"January 10. The doctor was unlike any doctor I've seen before. He pricked my finger and squeezed drops of my blood into a glass bowl of muddy water. The dark bits in the water swirled and swarmed around my blood. What a strange test! It wasn't horrible. Neither was the sweet, red soup with lumps of petaled mushrooms he gave me to eat. He told Momma 'I am a compatible candidate.' What does that mean?"

"Keep going with the rest," I encouraged.

"*January 12. My hair is falling out.*

"*February 15. They tied me up today. My wrists are still bleeding from the bindings. I've cried and pleaded with Momma and Papa, but it's the only way they say. It'll cure me. But it burns! I won't do it again! They can't make me!*

"*February 27. My marriage has been arranged to the man who cured me from all my suffering. I love him.*"

I clapped in approval. "An impeccable translation. You'll fly up the ranks if you just apply yourself."

"What happened to Mother?"

"Hmm?"

"What did they do to her? What did they give to her?"

"Medicine. Probably a concoction of herbs boiled and reduced into a thickened soup."

"She seemed different in the last entry."

"Different? Nonsense, it's from the same journal. Read the last entry and we can mark this volume completed."

"*March 4. I am a mother or will be one. Momma has asked to see my belly five times today. She draped a silk ribbon over my stomach and measured the bumps that roll and spin like juggling balls under my skin. It doesn't hurt. I thought it would, but I just feel stretched. And, hungry. So hungry. Nothing keeps me full.*"

Eighty-Eight dropped the scroll onto the floor. "That doesn't make sense."

I frowned. "What do you mean?"

"How could Mother's belly grow so soon? I've seen the pregnant women at Madame Yue's. It takes months for it to show."

I rolled up the scroll and rapped her head. "And I hardly think you can compare those women to Mother."

"What happened to the child? How did Mother die?"

"It is our job to learn, not to question Mother or Baba. This our adopted history," I said, but a part of me also wanted to say that the later journals would answer all of her questions. I couldn't because they didn't. I had read all the journals and texts in the library several times. Mother never mentioned her pregnancy again.

Why did any of that matter? If there was a child, surely Baba took care of it just like he took care of us.

Eighty-Eight pursed her lips. "This place, everything is wrong. Don't you feel—"

I covered her mouth with my hand, muffling her words.

"Stop it! You're going to get both of us punished," I whispered harshly as a *tap, tap, jingle* came from the path to the Library.

Baba appeared as usual with Spanker swaying at his waist. He gestured to Eighty-Eight with his finger. "Come."

She immediately walked with small, modest steps to stand in front of him. She trained her eyes downward and bowed low as I had taught her. He grabbed her chin and tilted her face towards the light.

"Mother's birthplace?"

"Taichung, Taiwan," she answered, breathless from the twisted angle of her throat.

"Favorite food?"

"Swallow's nest soup."

"Preferred color?"

"Crimson."

"Blood type?"

"AB-negative."

"First kiss?"

"Baba."

"Lovers?"

"Only Baba."

"Who do you obey?"

"You."

I smiled. She'd studied hard.

"Seventeen."

Eager to receive Baba's praise, I hurried to stand beside Eighty-Eight.

"Prepare Eighty-Eight for promotion tonight," he instructed.

"Of course." I peeked at my sister's flushed face. Sweat glistened like pearls on her forehead. She'd done well, but hadn't learned how to hide her nervousness from Baba. I would teach that next. To always be unconditionally grateful for everything he gave to us.

"You and I will perform the ceremony ourselves."

I nodded. "Yes, Baba."

"She'll be promoted to One."

One! How could he promote Eighty-Eight to One before me? Didn't he understand that I deserved it more? Everything I had done these last sixteen years was to please only Baba. I bit the inside of my cheek and nodded.

He patted my head. "You have done well. After the promotion, you will serve One as Two."

I bowed, lowering my head from his touch.

Lying on the stone table, Eighty-Eight fidgeted with the jade bracelets encircling her wrists. She struggled to lift her head against the weight of numerous jeweled hair pins stabbed into her coiffed hair. She'd also changed into a promotion robe of finer fabric than anything I'd ever seen. It was a glittering crimson, the color of good fortune. On the red, a tangle of gold vines snaked from hemline to collar. She looked magnificent on the table. A freshly born butterfly pinned to a mounting board.

"Sister, I'm cold," she whimpered, holding her hand out to me.

"Hush, stay down." I clasped Eighty-Eight's hand in mine. She *was* cold. The basement room felt like the cellar we stored pickled vegetables in.

It was a strange place for a promotion. Other than the long table and the two of us, the windowless room was small, empty, and undecorated. Yellow strips of paper covered most of the walls. Each strip was streaked with red scribbles that resembled ancient scripts I'd seen in calligraphy books. A sheen of wetness clung to the uncovered surfaces, penetrating the white paint and bubbling the plaster.

I rubbed Eighty-Eight's hand while adjusting the pad to fully cushion her head. Envy of her promotion, her beauty, and Baba's attentions gnawed at my heart. But I was proud. I'd never even met a One. And I had made her One, even if that meant I would only be Two.

Tap, tap, jingle.

Eighty-Eight stiffened. Baba was coming back down the stairs beyond the closed door.

"What will he do to me?"

"Shhh."

The door opened and Baba struggled to enter the room. His black robe was too long and swept the floor as he hauled a rectangular object as tall as him that was covered in a blue cloth. He paused to catch his breath before propping the object at the wall next to us.

His wild eyes and cheeks were flushed with a sunburnt-like bloom. I'd never seen Baba so agitated. No, not agitated, excited.

"A gift for One," Baba said in a tone of reverence as he broke through our clasped hands to loop something over Eighty-Eight's throat.

It was a pendant with a thumbprint base and tendrils of frail flowers sprouting from the top. Chan Hua, like Mother's name. A jade version of a parasitic fungus that infected and devoured cicada larvae hibernating beneath forest soil.

"Take this," Baba shoved Spanker into my grasp. "Be ready."

My hand shook. I'd never seen him take Spanker off. I held on tight and stared at the grains in the handle. There was a darkened handprint made from the oil on Baba's skin.

"Restrain her if she struggles."

Why would she struggle? She was about to gain all the rights and privileges of One. Still, I obeyed Baba and relocated myself to the opposite of the table. I kept a hand on Eighty-Eight's chest and patted to reassure her.

Baba tugged off the blue cloth, revealing a painting of a Chinese woman in red wedding clothes. She sat sideways on a wooden chair but the curvature of her spine was too pronounced and her sleeves were flattened like no arms filled the inside.

She also wore a skin-colored headpiece adorned with daisies resting on branching stalks that looked like dense antlers breaking through skin.

I studied the beautiful face, lightly touched with rouge and lip-stain. I'd never seen this woman before, but I knew those features. It could have been Eighty-Eight. After so many months of complete companionship, though, I discerned a distinction in the expression. Where my sister's was guileless, this woman carried an unslakable edge. Her black pupils grew more ravenous the longer I stared at them, and the corners of her lips arched up in amusement as if she enjoyed watching me watch her. I took a step closer to Eighty-Eight, desiring to shield her from the woman's scrutiny.

"It's time to meet your Mother," Baba said.

This must have been the painting of Mother from Baba's room.

Baba stroked the cheeks of the painted woman. Then he took Eighty-Eight's free hand into his.

"Do you love your Mother?" he asked.

Eighty-Eight nodded.

"Good. Then this will be easy." A knife appeared in his other hand and sliced deep and quick into her wrist.

She shrieked and tried to tear away from Baba's grip. He clutched with more pressure, widening the gash, pouring a ribboned stream blood over the painting. It made me dizzy and nauseous, seeing the opened flesh, blood, and bone.

"Baba, you'll ruin the painting," I said in a small voice, swallowing bile and tamping down Eighty-Eight's bucking. This was far too much blood. Much more than he had ever taken from me. Much more than I had ever seen taken from anyone.

"It's working. Mother will come back this time! Feed her more!" He yanked Eighty-Eight's arm closer to the painting.

"Stop it!" she screamed, thrashing.

"Hold her!" he shouted. He wrestled Eighty-Eight's bleeding arm back over the painting.

She howled, pushing my hands off to tear at her neck and chest.

A spray of blood landed hot and thick on my face. I stumbled from the table, searching for what she clawed at. Thin strands, like white silk threads, vined into Eighty-Eight's bleeding wrist. They unfurled from the painted flowers in the woman's headdress to Eighty-Eight's exposed flesh, conglomerating into a thickening crimson-dyed cord. The redder it became, the more it thrummed like a heartbeat, strengthening as blood spilled out.

"Don't fight Mother," Baba chided when Eighty-Eight kicked at him. He slapped her across the cheek and seized her throat. She flailed and tried to bite him.

He held her back and said in a low voice, "You look so much like her. She'll pick you."

Eighty-Eight screamed again, arching and digging nails into her face, ripping skin and drawing blood. New slashes appeared in Eighty-Eight's sleeves, cut by some unseen force, and blood seeped into the fabric, darkening the red silk to carmine.

"Baba, stop! She's hurting!" I sprang onto his arm, tugging on the hand strangling her throat.

"No! You must accept Mother. We will be together again."

The image of the woman was fading from the painting. Her lap, her folded hands, and the petals sewn on her robe vanishing.

"Help me!" Eighty-Eight pleaded, turning to me, her face a sweaty grey. "It's inside me!"

I yanked harder on Baba's arm. He let go of Eighty-Eight to snatch my hair and throw me across the room.

I crashed into the wall, bashing my head, tasting the grit of dislodged plaster. Through the pain and blurred vision, I saw blood pouring from Eighty-Eight's eyes, nose, mouth, and ears. She rasped—her breathing turning shallow and broken.

"You're killing her!"

"No! We'll have more children to replace the ones we lost. Mother won't reject her like the others."

The others?! Is this what it meant to be One? What happened if Mother rejected One?

"Please..." Eighty-Eight begged, her voice faint.

I wouldn't let him do this. My hand wrapped around Spanker, which had fallen by my feet. Too fixated on Eighty-Eight's hemorrhaging face, Baba didn't hear me. I lifted Spanker sideways like a blade and swung forward with all my strength.

The wood cracked when Baba's neck snapped. He crumpled with a thud, landing with limbs curled inward like the legs of a dead spider.

I fell too, tripping over Baba's body and losing my hold on Spanker.

"Sister?" I whispered. When she didn't answer, I grabbed a table leg and slowly stood. The table was empty; the painting was also empty except for the chair the woman had sat in.

Tap, tap, jingle.

"Eighty-Eight!" I cried with relief, spinning around to find her standing by Baba's limp body. She pushed him over with a kick of her toe.

"Hello, Daughter," she said, soft and slippery, her lips parting in a smile that didn't reach her famished black eyes.

Here in the Cellar

R. LEIGH HENNIG

The house is old. Very old. Its walls are not drywall but plaster and lathe, the electrical wires wrapped in cloth that crumbles to the touch, and the flaking paint contains lead. The siding is a rotting cedar shake that came decades before asbestos, and the pipes that run through the hollow walls are mostly iron. Outside there is a cistern, old as the house. They use it sometimes, when the water bill has been unpaid.

It's an odd thing, Marin will someday think, that his house should not be insulated, here in the part of western New York where the winters are longer and crueler than most. But like so many things in his life, that's the way it is, the way it's always been. He doesn't know any different. He doesn't know that mothers should not beat their children with wooden spoons and yard sticks and spatulas and belts and long electrical cords cut off from broken, useless vacuums. He doesn't know that he shouldn't always be hungry, or that it's not normal for him to have to pick his own switch from the thorny bush in the front yard. It doesn't occur to him that the cellar is not a place he should so often be, stinking of earth and damp and things that have found their way through the stone walls to die in its forever dark corners.

But that's exactly where he is, where she's locked him again.

Here in the cellar.

The sump pump in the middle of the floor rattles to life. Brown, silty water *chug-chug-chugs* through a pipe that empties from an embankment along their narrow dirt road. Marin sits beside it on the earthen floor, plunking pebbles into the water. Overhead a bare bulb casts too little light. Creaking from the floor above, and he can hear the muffled sound of an audience clapping on a daytime television show.

Plunk.

When the door to the cellar finally opens, he is asleep, head resting on arms folded across broken, canted stairs.

"Fix dinner for your sisters," she says from above. "I'm going out."

He knows not to ask when she'll be back. She'll be at the bar down the road, a place they call *The Pines* that sits beside the trailer park. But at least while she's gone he won't have to be in the cellar, and he won't have to pick a switch. It will just be the three of them, Marin and his two younger sisters. No one to make dinner or wash their clothes or go get groceries from Walmart where their Social Security checks will go the farthest, but that's okay. There are worse things.

Little moths and gnats fly out from the pantry when he opens it. There's a can of corn on the shelf, a box of dried scalloped potatoes, and a bag of onions on the floor that have started to turn. A box of stuffing from their Thanksgiving dinner a week before, such as it was, taken from a mostly empty donation bin outside a classroom door when he thought no one was looking. Marin wrinkles his nose and takes the corn and potatoes, emptying them into bowls on the counter.

After dinner he helps his sisters with their homework, sets their clothes out on the table for school the next morning. Mother—the thing he secretly calls her instead of Mom because he knows she hates it—is not yet back. Probably won't be until tomorrow afternoon, stinking of whisky and wet cigarettes and unwashed bodies. He'll get his sisters up for school, make them cereal for breakfast, dinner that night. There are potatoes for leftovers, and he thinks he saw a can of carrots.

This is their routine. They don't know any different. They never have.

Sunday.

Plunk.

The dingy light through the filmy window in the far wall beside the driveway is beginning to fade. He sighs, stands to pull the cord for the naked bulb above. He tries not to use it—the lifespan of an incandescent bulb is incredibly short, he's learned, especially when it's the only thing between you and total darkness—but he's afraid of the dark, even at his age of eleven. He thinks he shouldn't be, thinks he should be more mature, but he can't help it. Like other things in his life, it just *is.*

With the light comes the sound of movement, a scurrying in the far corner. Marin freezes, holds his breath. Something moves low against the opposite wall, out of the bulb's yellow reach.

Rat, he thinks, heart quickening, knot forming in his gut. He doesn't have to imagine its claws, its sharp teeth, its body slick with mud. They come up from the Genesee across the road sometimes, river rats as big as possums, mean and hungry. There's a scar on the webbing between his thumb and pointer finger from the last time it happened, long and jagged and ugly. He takes a step back, carefully, oh so carefully, searching for something he can use as a weapon.

Then it happens, and when it does, everything changes.

Meeow. Meeeeeow. Squeaking, mewling, tiny sounds.

Marin crouches low and makes for the sound, feeling his way in the dark. The cellar is full of forgotten things, broken things. A rusted microwave, its door smashed in. Mounds of dirt. Piles of scrap material from a renovation started and never finished from some time long, long before he was born. He makes his way around the detritus, from one side of the cellar to the other, calling soothingly for the kitten. Overhead an infomercial plays.

Marin reaches the terrified creature and takes it gently into his hands, pulling it from the place it's wedged itself beneath the stairs.

"Shhh, it's okay, it's *okay,*" Marin whispers, rubbing beneath its chin. He has no idea how old it is, or whether it's a boy or a girl—Marin has no experience with animals—but it's clearly starving. He can feel the tiny bones of its ribs through its tissue-thin skin. Fleas crawl through its matted fur. One of its ears is bleeding, a nasty tear that looks to be infected.

"How did you even get in here?" he asks, swaddling it in his shirt.

There's half a granola bar in his pocket. He has no idea if cats like granola bars, if they can even digest them, but he breaks it up into tiny pieces and feeds it to the kitten, who eats it anyway.

He doesn't wonder about its mother; it doesn't occur to him that he should.

⚜

Days go by. Sometimes she's home, sometimes she's not. Sometimes he's in the basement. Sometimes he's not. But he keeps the kitten in the basement—doesn't even mind when Mother locks him down there—and over time, its wounds begin to heal. It gains weight, eating as he and his sisters do. Buying cat food is not an option; even if they could afford it, Marin understands that his mother can never, *ever* find out about the cat.

He's decided it's a *him*, and Marin has chosen a name. Myth, he calls him, the meaning behind it a thing he cannot articulate but intuits still: something that cannot be real and yet, somehow, is.

⚜

December.

The temperature is in the negatives, the days short. Blankets hang from doorways and in the halls of their house like baffles in a muffler, trapping what little heat the ailing furnace provides.

Marin trudges with his sisters against the blustery snow up the road from the bus stop at the bottom of the hill. It was a classmate's birthday over the weekend, and in Marin's pocket is a bit of donut saved from the party they'd had at the end of the school day. Myth will like the donut, he thinks, or what remains of it, anyway. They missed breakfast that morning, having run out of cereal the day before. Marin feels vaguely responsible for this, and so he's given most of the donut to his sisters.

But when they get to the bottom of their driveway, something is wrong. Their mother is standing in the doorway of the house, a look of fury upon

166

her face. Possibilities race through his mind. Has he forgotten to do the dishes, or pick up after his sisters? Maybe he left the laundry in the washer. Did he forget to vacuum? There's a burn barrel in the back yard—they can't afford collection—did he empty the trash can the night before?

He opens his mouth to ask what's wrong, but then stops. There's something in her hand, dangling by her side. Marin squints against the blinding, biting snow.

Myth.

Oh no, he thinks, breath hitching.

"What did I tell you about pets?" she demands. Her voice is rising, shrill. "Huh? Answer me. *What did I tell you?*"

She holds Myth by the scruff of his neck, who is hissing and dangling and clawing to escape.

"I do everything for you. I feed you. I take care of you. I buy you clothes. Since your father left, all I've *done* is *give, give, give* to you *ungrateful* little *shits*. And you disrespect me like this?" she shouts, shaking Myth in the air. "You *hide* this from me, even after I told you no?"

His sisters are crying, pleading with her to stop screaming, that she's scaring them, to stop shaking the kitty, to stop it stop it *stop it.*

"Mom no, it's not like that, I found—"

She flings her arm violently to the side and Myth goes spinning in the air, legs kicking, tail whipping. He lands in the snow and takes off like a shot, disappearing behind the house. Marin drops his backpack and runs after him.

"Get in this house!" she screams.

Marin stops, torn between her command and going after his cat.

"Don't *make* me *repeat* myself," she growls through gritted teeth.

Tears sting his eyes. He is crying, crying, his nose a sieve and his throat and chest hot with anger. Before he knows it, he's at the door standing before her, glaring, staring her down.

"I *hate* you," he says. Instantly the horror of his mistake overwhelms him, and she hits him, punches him in the mouth with her closed fist even as he's stammering out apologies in an unbroken, pleading string. His mouth fills with copper.

Dusk.

Marin takes the pieces of the donut and sets them on the open window sill beside the driveway. The donut is ruined, crushed beyond recognition —pockets are particularly unkind to things like donuts—but he doesn't think Myth will mind.

If he ever comes back, Marin thinks dolefully.

He's cleared away the snow as far as he can reach. The wind howls, blowing fat, wet flakes into the basement. He calls for Myth, calls as loud as he dares, but after a while he gives up. There's no way his cat can hear his quiet voice through the angry storm. Marin slumps on the bottom stair, puts his face in his hands, and cries.

Sometime later there is scratching, faint, as if from a dream. Marin sits up and groans, wincing at his stiff back, his frozen butt, the pins and needles in his legs. He has an awful headache—probably from all the crying—and it takes him a moment to come around, the scratching from his dream refusing to fade with the rest of it.

Meeeow. Tiny. Unmistakable. *Not* a dream, he realizes. Marin bolts from the stairs and rushes to the window.

There, on the other side, is Myth.

He pushes the window open and the cat jumps into his arms. This time, his tears are of a different sort. Welcome. Grateful.

"I'm sorry," he whispers, pressing his face into Myth's fur. The cat purrs, the sound of it like a tiny engine made of love. "So, so, sorry. Are you okay?" Marin pulls back, anxiously checking for injuries. Finding none, he presses the cat back into the warmth of his neck.

When the cellar door opens, Marin stays in the nest of jackets he's made by the furnace. Together they nibble on the pieces of the broken donut.

After it happens, after his grief and his pain have been burned away and all that remains is anger and contempt and other things that will take him years to identify, if he ever does, Marin will blame himself. He'll recall when he coaxed Myth back into the cellar, keeping him there at night and feeding him before and after school, and he'll wonder what exactly that tipped her off. His newfound eagerness to spend time in the cellar, maybe? Or perhaps it was the snow cleared away from the window. He doesn't *think* she could have heard Myth's occasional meowing—partially deaf, her hearing had always been poor—but who can say?

One thing that he will *not* doubt, absolutely never again, is the creativity of his mother's cruelty.

Their car is a monstrous old thing, a land yacht of a station wagon with wooden panels, ash trays in the rear doors, and a seat in the back that faces away from the others. Which is to say that it's tired, its eight-barrel engine slow to accelerate and even slower to heat up in the frigid winters. So when he gets home from school and she tells him to start the car to get it warm for her, he's not surprised.

What *is* surprising is that the car is *already* warm, though the snow of their unplowed driveway is undisturbed. He saw the defrosted windshield as he walked past it on the way inside the house. *Why do I have to start it again?* he thinks. He doesn't ask, though later he will wonder what she would have said if he had, if things would have been different.

"Where are the keys?" he asks. "They're not on the nail."

"In it," she says from her chair in the living room, and isn't that an odd thing, he wonders? And again he does not ask why, does not suspect. Marin only obeys because for now, he knows no other way.

So he drops his bag inside the door of the laundry room that is the entrance to their house, the small room always with the stink of laundry that has spoiled for sitting in the washer too long. He trudges back outside, down the porch steps, through the snow and to the driver side door.

The engine temperature needle is elevated. Probably it was running an hour ago, he guesses. He gives a quick pump of the gas pedal, careful not to flood the engine, turns the ignition, and reels in horror at the sound that comes from beneath the wide, long hood.

Immediately he kills the engine and scrambles for the hood release under the dash. He throws the car door open and races around to the front, atavistic screams of pain emanating from beneath it all the way.

There, clawing to free itself and escape the entanglement of the radiator fan, is Myth.

Blood is everywhere. On the underside of the hood, across the engine block. His fur is slick with it, red drops falling from the ends of his whiskers. He looks up for understanding that Marin can not offer while he works to free him from the sooty, oily engine compartment.

"They climb up there for warmth," she says from the doorway behind him. "Just snug right up against the engine in the winter time. It's why you should always check under the hood before starting the car again if you've already been out recently. Guess you didn't know that," she says, sneering. "I told you you weren't responsible enough for one, now look what you've gone and done. It's your own fault."

The front door behind him slams closed. Myth is still screaming, screaming, and Marin can't see how badly he's hurt through all the blood. Doesn't know what to do even if he could. Finally the cat comes free and Marin strips off his jacket, bundling Myth up in his arms.

Half blind from the tears and the snow and half mad with terror, the desperate notion of running to a neighbor for help flashes through his mind. But there are no neighbors. They live on an empty street in a dying town with a population going in only one direction, and *family* is a thing he knows only from books.

I'm alone, Marin thinks, snow now gently falling. From their bedroom window his sisters crowd, looking down on him, sobbing, sobbing. The bundle in his arms has grown very still.

In the basement is a shovel. He'll later learn that he can't dig into the frozen ground, but not before the argument at the top of the stairs, the one that will stay with him forever, marked like the crimson snow around the front of their car and soaked into his clothes.

Screaming about his shoes left on, the blood he's tracking in, his ruined jacket, about other things he can hardly parse. She's in his face about the fucking mess he's making, about his disrespect for her, for her rules, for everything she sacrifices for him. He doesn't appreciate her, she says, all that she does for him. Doesn't know what it's like to be alone, to be a single mother.

Noise. All he wants to do is bury his cat. He hardly remembers climbing the stairs but now finds himself at the top of them, shovel in hand, his mother boxing him in and not letting him out. She's *so close* to him and all he can smell is her cigarettes.

"MOVE!" he finally screams, shoving her.

Her arms pinwheel for balance, her hands slapping for purchase about the frame of the basement door. At the bottom of the stairs she looks up at nothing, jaw slack, neck contorted in a way that should never be.

And at once, silence. Stillness.

Like the bundle in his blood-soaked coat, cooling in the December snow.

❦

Marin says little when the volunteer paramedics show, his sisters even less. They sit together on a stretcher in the back of an ambulance, blanket around their shoulders, paramedics and Sheriff's deputies milling about the scene before them. The three are listening, and not listening, to words like *shock*, *cataplectic*, and *trauma*. Watching, and not watching.

But when the rear door of the ambulance is closed and the little basement window is no longer in Marin's view, he begins to scream. He kicks at the door, slams his fists against its windows, throws himself at the latch until it flies open and he falls to the ground.

"Hey, take it easy!" a uniformed woman says, reaching for him.

Marin dodges past her outstretched arms, slipping in the snow but regaining his footing. He rushes for the window and smashes it with his boot, his foot going through into the basement. The single pane of glass shatters and slices through his pants, severing arteries and muscle nearly to the bone. Still he kicks, shrieks, fights off attempts to drag him away. Rages at the paramedics scrambling to stop him, stop the lunatic screaming and atavistic fury and blind hatred and fear and injustice and the

171

plain violence that's been done to him since birth that he can no longer deny. Legs like ribbons amidst so much blood he kicks out the glass, the sill now broken and splintered in its ruined frame. Three people struggle to get him into the ambulance.

And when Marin is satisfied that the window can never, ever close again, he lets them.

MOTHER ADORES

She's Untouchable

RENEE CRONLEY

she's the untainted version of me
hope, fresh air, smiles of sunshine
evaporating melancholia like water
tranquil threads of light woven
between a bygone era of cuts
and bruises behind lullabies
of voices fashioned from knives
the something beautiful
from something warped

now I live on the maternal edge
of a billion blades
and there is a whistle
buried under my skin

its pitch travels through my nerves
and shatters the tender moment
his eyes follow her skips and jumps
watching like he could absorb her laughter
his mouth opens with sweets

in a script I memorized from childhood
I could recite the lines into a black hole
and the screams of all the little dead girls
would echo warnings back to me

I kept all my remains
sharpened the bones
bent them out of what haunted me
embraced them like precious memories
and built an arsenal
then walled it up in my mind
so I wouldn't pass my wounds on to her

his presence is the crack
and my rage is the push
the walls crumble, the air shifts

a spark of fear behind the hunter's window
I pour gasoline
because I'm already inside

he retreats but I find him
in sleep with his armor off
I invite all the little dead girls
and parade them through nightmares
until his days and nights bleed together
and they make him their home

she reflects a world of color
arms wrapped around me, we melt
the hues of the good in me beating in her
while I search the hearts of those who come near her
in case I need to make them stop

Lida's Beach

STEPHANIE NELSON

Stuart makes me choose the color of the casket's inside lining because he thinks I want to. The only options available are blue and pink.

It's dingy in here and the Febreze smell is overbearing, like caked-on cover-up for death. But this is the only funeral home in our tiny Oregon coast town. I stare at the displays, blinking, feeling the burn of tears I can't cry anymore. Minutes pass, I'm not sure how many. Stuart brushes a limp curl off my face, tucks it behind my ear. How long has it been since I showered? He clears his throat.

"Blue," I say finally. It has to be blue because despite being only three years old, Lida never liked pink.

"Why was that such a hard decision?" Stuart asks on the way to our car. He's upset because he wanted pink, I realize too late.

Out the window, I watch gray ocean waves roll over each other to create little white avalanches, then pull back into dancing foam. Always another wave. Then another. There will not be another baby. Lida was almost impossible to conceive, I had given up hope of ever being a mom, and then I was pregnant.

Even though it's been ten minutes of silence, I answer Stuart. "I told you I didn't care which color, but you still pressured me to pick."

"I didn't want to take that away from you," he says. "You are—*were*—her mom."

The way he stumbles over the tense jolts me. He's right, I *was* Lida's mom. What am I now?

We drive past the public beach, and I imagine Lida down there like it's any old day. I can close my eyes and see her in a red rain jacket, yellow-and-white polka dot boots, face aimed down at the sand. She'd be searching for crab shells. When she found one, she'd hold it up like a trophy, running at the ocean to throw it into the water. It was serious business to her. She'd watch until the piece of crab landed in the sea, then turn and run toward me as the tide nipped the heels of her boots. Her tiny hands fighting against the wind to tame mad swirls of brown hair. *Putting crabs to bed.* That's what she called it.

All those crab shell pieces, claws, legs, remnants obliterated by birds and littering the beach. I used to ask her why. Why put the crabs to bed? Her answer varied depending on the day.

So they can go back out to sea. So they aren't alone. So they can swim with the dolphins and seals again.

I told her the crabs were gone, that the shells were only what the birds left behind. They weren't "the crab." Not anymore.

No, Mommy, she'd say. *They grow back at sea. They wake up new and go home.*

Lida had been dead for hours by the time I went into her room. How many days ago now? I can't do the math. She was lying on her side in the toddler bed, quilt tucked under her chin, hair splayed out behind her. My fingers met rigor mortis when I tried to rustle her awake. I screamed, and immediately worried that it would frighten her, not yet realizing how impossible that would be. I had spent all of Lida's infancy worrying about SIDS, checking on her obsessively. Stuart called me crazy, said I needed professional help. I did it anyway. I thought we were in the clear when she became a toddler. But now I know SIDS can threaten three-year-olds too; it simply goes by a different name. Like a serial killer who changes identity before hunting a new victim.

It's raining when I arrive at the funeral home early on the day of Lida's service. I squeeze the knife handle in my coat pocket. Our butcher knife would be better, but it's too big. A sharpened steak knife will do.

Lida is laid out on a table in a tight, dim room. She looks like a life-size doll, her body covered with a towel. Her eyes are closed, cheeks pink, lips slightly glossy. Lida wears makeup for the first and only time. And it's forever. I set down a small grocery bag of her clothing. Dressing my daughter for her funeral is the second-to-last act I'll get to perform as her mom. The last act is the reason I brought a knife. I pull it out of my pocket.

Are there security cameras in here? I wish I'd considered that before now, but a quick glance confirms that no, a funeral home with flooring reminiscent of a church basement doesn't invest in security cameras.

It should be easy, no different than cutting a whole chicken. I take hold of one of Lida's big toes and flinch because it's cold. Of course it is. I pinch around the nailbed, deciding on a joint, and settle on the one closest to the tip.

I push the knife through and rock it back and forth, trying to separate the joint. It's more difficult than I'd imagined, but the knife is sharp and I'm thankful there's no blood. Soon, the toe hangs by skin and that's easy to slice through. I slip it into my pocket. Working quickly, I pull her socks on, then her pants. Stuart is going to lose his shit tomorrow when he sees her outfit, but I work until Lida is fully dressed, even down to her red jacket and yellow boots. That's the part Stuart won't like. The jacket is old, the boots scuffed, but it was Lida's favorite thing to wear.

Instead of going home to take a nap before the service, like the funeral director told me to, I stop at Lida's beach, where she used to put the crabs to bed.

Standing on wet sand, close enough that the tide tickles the rubber of my boots, I pull out the fleshy fragment of my daughter. My face is wet from the saltwater of tears mixed with a drizzle of rain. I was a good mom, even if I'm not technically a mom anymore.

I kiss Lida's toe and throw it as far as I can into the ocean. Then I close my eyes and imagine her out to sea where sunlight finds her in the depths. She's playing with dolphins and seals. Her underwater mermaid hair swirls around her head forever.

Lida's service comes and goes. Stuart is too tired to fight about the rain jacket and boots, and I'm grateful. He chooses to sleep on the couch and I'm grateful.

I cry until sleep consumes me, but I wake up abruptly in the darkness because I hear something. I swear it's in my room, but the door is still closed. There it is, in the corner, as if hiding from the moonlight pouring through my window. A small figure.

"Mommy?" a tiny voice says.

I will always be Lida's mother.

Instruments of Bone and the Flesh Songs They Create

NIKKI R. LEIGH

Bren's hands were worn from months of carving and shaping a femur, giving the sacrificed limb a new purpose. She held the long bone in her palm and curled her marred fingers around its smooth body, rubbing the carefully chiseled grooves.

She massaged her scarred pelvis—her right leg nothing but a distant memory—and silently instructed the bone to stop sending phantom commands to her hip. The recovery had been difficult, but the pain was mitigated by dreams of what was to come. By what her sacrifice would mean, and even more so, what it would bring. It was time for her bone to begin its life anew.

Bren smiled, imagining what Delilah would be like. Would she take after her namesake, Bren's grandmother? Would her voice be as beautiful as hers?

From her place in the chair, she heard Marscha striding into the room, the soft swishing of her black dress breaking Bren's reverie. She faced her wife and breathed in the scent of lavender that followed her.

"Tonight feels like the perfect night for a symphony," Bren said. Marscha's hands gently caressed her shoulders, then gripped the handles on her chair.

"They really came out beautifully, didn't they?"

"We had such perfect pieces to choose from."

Her violin, constructed with sacrifices made by their coven, represented a myriad of loving gifts. Her own femur created the fingerboard and neck of the instrument along with the other donations: a scapula chinrest from Bren's closest friend and a dozen of her ancestors' ribs to buttress the ebony wood. The strings were her mother's tendons, dried and pressed into form.

Bren wrapped the small bone in black velvet, the material swirling around the thin neck and the much wider base of the instrument. The fabric grazed the strings, muffling the soft *plinking*.

Marscha placed the ornate bow next to the violin on Bren's lap, making a beautiful pair. Bren's stomach held butterflies dancing in anticipation to hear how the bow—wound with Marscha's hair pulled tight over an ulna — would help the violin sing tonight.

These bones and so many others had been passed on for hundreds of years. Even as the woods grew smaller and cities grew larger, the bones remained in their coven's possession. And now they were here in the couple's serene home at the edge of a forest full of magic and song.

Bren and Marscha had longed for this night for nearly six years since they wed. They planned tirelessly and had excitedly marked the days until their turn. In the months prior to the occasion, they had forged their instruments late into the dark, long past the twinkling of stars in the sky. The couple's compromises and love for one another eased the difficult task of choosing the pieces to become vessels for music.

It wasn't about what was gone, but a celebration of what would grow. A child—their child—just as their coven had done for centuries. These bones were for Delilah.

But still, even with the resplendence of the night's promise, Bren's throat tightened, her fear choking her desires. Her nerves spilled from her lips.

"We'll be okay, won't we?" Bren whispered, remembering the rare occasions when members of their coven had not survived the ceremony to come. What this brought, this event—this *ordeal*—as much as it was a thing to cherish, was no small task. A momentous dedication for the rest of their years.

Bren had seen relationships as strong as theirs crumble under it all.

And she couldn't stop the worry that they wouldn't be enough, in the end.

But Marscha, the woman Bren had loved for years with decades left to go, her eyes held confidence.

"The worry will be there, every step of the way," she said. Bren laughed softly at the way Marscha didn't even try to dismiss her nerves. Marscha's warm hand caressed her cheek. "But so will I."

Bren nodded, heart swollen. Resolute to stay the course, no matter how treacherous, with her partner at her side.

So now, with a blood moon in sight and a short journey ahead, the two trekked into the woods. Marscha guided Bren's wheelchair over the thick sticks and stones of the forest floor. The silent pair found comfort in each other as they wrestled with their nerves and traversed the paths. They scanned ahead between the limbs of trees for the gentle glow of firelight where their coven was awaiting their arrival. The sounds of the forest provided their own serenade—the rustling of leaves and soft babbling of the river the perfect backdrop for the melodies to come.

Halfway through, the couple spotted their resting spot. A place for rejuvenation of lungs aching for air against the cold night chill. A pinprick of moonlight on a leafy, mossy floor. A bed of earth for tired bones. The coven had marked the spot with velvet ropes, a promenade of sorts to welcome the couple on their way to the event that would change their lives.

Here, they'd take some time to allow for other renewal: passion for one another. Bren took in her wife, a vision of beauty, most natural and honest. Her hair, shorn in a more fleeting sacrifice, danced along her chin. Bren couldn't stop the nerves that Marscha's next offering for another couple yearning for a bloodline would be more permanent. She wished she could spare her wife the pain of recovery, even if the donation made it all worthwhile.

Bren, eyes heavy with adoration, knew that no matter what her wife gave, no matter what was deemed a phantom to her body in the years to come, Marscha would always be whole to her. She'd always be everything and more.

Marscha knelt on the ground in front of Bren, her head gently in her lap, eyes turned toward the space where Bren's limb had been . Bren bit back the emotions lurking in her chest, instead letting herself absorb what Marscha was offering. Love, adoration, and nothing of the resentment such a sacrifice might conjure.

The two pulled the crisp night air through their noses, into their lungs, feeling the raw life that percolated between the limbs of trees and fluttering of leaves. Deep, longing pulls came through mouths opening as Marscha lifted her head from Bren's lap Kisses lengthened, threatening to steal every breath they had left.

Rejuvenation. Renewal. Revival.

Life flowed through the couple, intertwined, tugging each other as closely as they could. The cycle of passion swirled through their skin and bones, as close to creating life as they could come. For now.

After a moment of ecstasy and quiet, they continued their journey, their cheeks flushed in the cold snap of the night, biting deeper the further they went into the thicket of trees.

After a near hour spent on a singular mission through the woods, Marscha and Bren slowed their pace, and the light of torches reached their faces. Several yards ahead, their sisters and mothers danced around the flames. Their dresses, inked in midnight colors, twirled about their bodies. Bundles of black velveted instruments lay spread in a circle awaiting the coven's commands.

Marscha helped Bren park her chair in the center of the enclosure and leaned down to whisk a swirl of hair behind her lover's ear, whispering into it softly.

"I can't believe how lucky I am to begin this next step with you."

Bren felt her face redden, the husky sound of Marscha's voice still reducing her to shivers when spoken so gently into her ear all these years later. She cupped her hand around her mouth and whispered back.

"I love you so much, and I know that Delilah will, too."

The partners hung their heads, their skin touching and heat radiating outward to match the flames of the fire next to them. Together, they moved to either side of a tree stump, three feet in diameter. Symbols gouged into the surface of the worn wood glinted with decades-old blood. The grooves, repeatedly filled and emptied, would run red again tonight. Bren and Marscha sat in reverence of the small altar, the history heavy in their minds.

Around the pair, the women stopped dancing, wordlessly moving to unwrap parcels and reveal their contents.

Various instruments of bone emerged, some weathered by age, others fresh from a few short years of use. A clarinet made of a humerus. A drum with skin stretched across the top and filled with teeth, rattling about. An oboe comprised of vertebrae.

Bren unwrapped her violin and bow, feeling the hum of its energy as it synced up with the sacred site and osseous brethren. Marscha unlatched the satchel at her side to bring out a tibia flute passed down from her mother, keys made of molars from her own mouth. The gaps in her gums had long healed over, the pain soothed by the gift she would receive.

The women joined in a circle, their instruments at the ready, their eyes closed and their senses open, finding the rhythm the earth provided.

In unison, they lifted their arms from their sides and began to play.

The instruments rang out inside the forest. Melodic, slow at first, the music ramped up and wound down in a chorus of emotions, like the measured tide of the ocean, lapping at their ears.

The music was heard by the rustic landscape and resonated through the women of the circle. Tears trickling down their faces, eyes squeezed shut, they expended their energy into the rhythm. Somber harmonies turned to sanguine notes and the song climaxed.

As the women made songs, Bren recalled the pain of her amputation and the love that had healed it. Marscha grimaced, and Bren felt sure she was ambling down the road of the memory, feeling the pliers in her mouth.

The music heightened, its pace hastening. Bren was inundated with visions and sounds and touch and pain and love from the women around her. Their own sacrifices produced symphonies of wounds and scars that permeated every pore in her skin, raised every hair on her neck as if joining the invisible conductor batons leading the melodies.

But from those memories of sacrifices, big and small, permanent and ephemeral, came the bond. The love of family, the love of partnership. Just like her own wound had healed those months ago, so too did the wounds of the dozens before her.

So too, would they, when the time came again.

So too, would they, for the love they were creating.

On the stump between Bren and Marscha, a thick red substance trickled up from inside the wood, pooling to its face and filling the depressions of the carved symbols. The trickle became a stream of scarlet, which coiled and thickened. Cells coalesced and a form began to take shape. White bone erupted from the pool of blood, soon enshrouded by tendons and patches of muscle.

When the first of the flesh touched the night air, bursting into the windless atmosphere, Bren and Marscha were struck—a force pushing past their own skin and into their minds. Bren caught sight of her partner's eyes rolling into her head, blue irises replaced by a white blankness. Seconds later, her own eyes followed suit, and she saw no more.

Could only feel, could only hear.

Could only sense, at the corner of her mind, the creeping lurking thing, darkened by shadows. Should shewelcome it or banish it. The fear oh how it swelled as the music played on her nerves. And with that presence whose intentions were unclear, lurching from the shadows...

The scent of lavender at the tip of her nose. Her wife by her side.

Bren took the light in her mind, shone it bright on the thing in the dark. Revealed it for what it was: a mass of flesh, of eyes, of mouths, of nerves and muscles and teeth and bones. It wheezed, a hideous thing, humming low tones. And from it all, a stream of parts flowing from its huddled body, flowing, flowing from inside of her and to—

That stump.

Where new life was forming. A thing of darkness, of fear and disgust cycling into something else, something beautiful, rapturous.

Bren and Marscha opened their eyes to witness the growth of their child.

The coven played on, their music reaching shrill peaks over solemn valleys as more flesh sprouted atop the wriggling assembly of body parts. Tiny toes, delicate fingers, arms and legs with rolls of fat and soft skin. A pair of eyes, scrunched tight, a doll nose, pointed towards the stars, and finally, a set of satiny lips opening to suck in its first breath of night air.

When the infant parted its mouth to pull oxygen into her newly-formed lungs, Bren wondered if their daughter would spend her youthful years chasing the clean crisp of the woodland air.

The coven maintained their hymn. But something shifted in the sound, as if responding to the demand of a conductor snapping her wand at her orchestra. The melodious notes of the instruments were replaced by the cries of dozens of babies, echoing throughout the forest. The wailing—an amalgamation of all the howls of children born to the coven, reaching back to the darkest of their days—sang loudly as the squirming infant on the wooden altar searched for her voice.

Bren's soul plunged into restoration once again. The wounds opened by the shrill twangs and clanking of instruments were filled by the sounds of life. Voices of the new replacing instruments of the old.

While the music of bone and cacophony of flesh penetrated the depths of the forest, bouncing around trees like a bee blinded in search of its queen, one sound was missing.

After what felt like long minutes of cries emanating from the bone instruments, baby Delilah plucked her intonation from the sea of the sounds of birth and began a song of her own. The sounds of her life, long wails from strong lungs, signaled Bren and Marscha's own lungs to finally exhale the breaths they held in anticipation.

Abruptly, the coven returned their instruments to their sides, members opening their eyes to take in the life created before them.

Bren and Marscha leaned forward, their happy tears wetting the face of their child. Marscha gently scooped the baby into her arms, wrapped her in a set of black velvet blankets, and placed her in Bren's lap.

The pair huddled together, surrounding Delilah with love, the coven gliding in closer to offer their own welcoming gestures and words to the newest member of their family.

Though scarred from the process, and beholden to offer themselves to hopeful mothers yet to come, Bren and Marscha thanked the stars for their instruments of bone and the flesh songs they created.

One by one the coven dispersed, leaving Bren and Marscha alone with Delilah in the clearing deep in the woods. Together, they wondered what magic lived in their child's bones.

Transformative Love

TEHNUKA

I first transformed into a thick cotton blanket
—it was a cold night
I was desperate
They said not to share the bed. I held her
tight-wrapped in softness
as we slept in the crib.

When the formula ran out
I became a warm, full bottle, until
milk-stained mouth smiling
she let go
I rolled over worn carpet, drained. But
bruises didn't matter,
I was all my sweetheart needed
—emergency teething ring, substitute rattle—
changing often, in her baby days.

Her first month of school, I was there,
a green pencil clutched crooked in chubby fingers

My bruises formed scars; still, nibbling tooth-marks
she knew herself loved.

Then a bicycle, to keep watch as she travelled alone
As she grew, I stayed as objects longer;
she needed a guardian,
more than a mother at home.

Finally, she asked, "How does it start?
Is it hormones? A birthday?
When can I become something else?"
I could only say: it came to me when most needed,
When there was no other recourse

I became what I could to protect her
But when all she wanted was to become small—
a gnat, feeding on the scent of a lettuce,
or smaller, the space between atoms,
I could not turn into salvation.
My baby was no infant now to suckle at a bottle.

I'd be anything to tempt her, however little:
A hint of vanilla in fruit salad,
the freshest dash of lime, then,
late at night resume my shape
covered in rotten food scraps. Stop in her room,
watch my fading girl sleep.

And it was only in desperation that,
from my seat by her bedside,
when her heartbeat slowed, I came to be here—
my body, collapsing into tendrils,
ghosts through that thin gown
Down, I wrap myself around

—no, not wrap. I become—
her pulsing heart.
I beat for her now. I beat.
I will always beat.

The Withering Depths

TODD POWELL

At first, I thought he was just a bump two-thirds of the way up my closet door—a flaw, but nothing compared to the apartment's yellow-stained bathtub, tattered stale nicotine carpet or the roaches that find their way into my Cheetos. Katie, though, she knew something was up. It's growing," she said. "Len, can't you see it?"

No, I didn't see anything. Not right then. Just figured it was Katie's latest minor freakout, about her thirtieth since we'd buried her son five days before. It made no sense, but the kid ate up more of her time dead than he did alive. Clifford was sixteen when he got himself shot in an alley, and no one ever had it coming more than he did. If you want a long life, you don't live it that way.

When Katie started rubbing the door's heavy wood, I knew for sure she was leaving reality behind. Again. "I recognize this," she whispered. "I know what it is."

I got out of the bedroom in a hurry, before she could tell me more.

Four minutes, that's all I got with my Bud and Comedy Central, before Katie came into the living room, breathing hard and jerking her head like the Bride of Frankenstein. "It's Cliffie," she said. "Dear Lord, Len, Cliffie's face is in the closet door!"

"Oh brother," I sighed. "Clifford in the closet."

"Not the closet. The closet *door*."

"Whatever. Look, why don't you get a cup of coffee, sit down and watch?" I even cleared the crap off the couch for her, but she wasn't interested.

"You never listen to me," she said, whining her way back to the bedroom.

Right then I figured it was probably the bedroom that was getting to her. For years she'd let Clifford have the apartment's only bedroom while she slept on the couch. Then two years ago I moved in and reversed the arrangement. Twice as many of us as there were of him, why shouldn't we take the bed? But the kid didn't like it, took away his privacy for Instabook cyberbullying or whatever the hell it was he was doing that got him kicked out of school.

I also figured she was seeing her boy's face in her mind because she'd realized since he died that she didn't have more than a couple dozen photos of him, all taken before he was six. No wonder, the kid grew up ugly and smelled worse, who wanted pictures?

She'd get over it. But Katie was mad, and I wouldn't get any peace if she stayed that way. So I groaned, hauled myself up, went into the bedroom...

...and saw the wooden face, *Clifford's* face, bulging out of the closet door.

❦

"You see?" Katie's hand was over her mouth, muffling her voice. "He's coming out of the door."

I saw all right, but still wasn't having any of it. So I yanked it open. Don't know what I thought I'd see, but there was only plain old door on the other side.

"What are you *doing*?" Katie hissed, slapping my hand away from the knob. Feeling her oats. I decided to let it go, just watched her close the door real carefully. Clifford's face was still there, wooden teeth clenched, wooden eyes wide, that damn teardrop tattoo under his left eye showing as a darker blemish.

"Don't bother him, Len," Katie said. "Don't interfere."

I felt odd, like my head was floating a foot above my neck, so it didn't occur to me to do anything but go along. Didn't call 911, didn't even take pictures. "What do you think he's doing?"

"Same thing he always does," she said, nodding, "when things get bad enough. Running away from trouble. Running back to me."

Took maybe ten more minutes for Clifford to clear his head from the door, less than five more until we started seeing shoulders. Why did he move so slow? Who knows, but Clifford never hurried unless the law was after him. Those baggy pants created too much drag for speed.

But looking at him, at the panic in that wooden face, I felt sure he was getting out of that door as fast as he could. It was like looking dead-on at a runner thrusting out his chest to break the tape at the finish line. So I figured that moving slow must be part of what hell is. Hell had to be where he was coming from. Don't guess there are too many angels breaking out of heaven. How frustrating must that be, moving so slow? How would it feel to take half an hour to scratch every time your crotch itched? If I end up there, I'm going to keep a hand down south, standing by.

Just after eleven o'clock, a bump that turned out to be the boy's left hand appeared in the wood below where his chest grew. About the same time another bump—right foot—moved out, angled toward the floor.

Spent, I sat on the bed and watched. Katie rocked in the shadows near the closet, whisper-chanting: "Oh, Cliffie, Cliffie...come on back...come on home..."

What would he be when he got free of that door? I asked myself this after almost an hour, when all of Clifford that hadn't come out yet was his left leg and one hump of his ass. (That ass was naked, by the way, just like the rest of him. Must be another part of hell, especially for a scarecrow like Clifford.) Would he stay wooden, eating fertilizer and crapping twigs? Would he move any faster? Would he go back to the gang that got him killed?

Would he be alive?

I didn't know the answer to any of this, so I asked Katie.

"What a thing to think about." She said in disgust. She was facing away but her shoulders squared. "If I have to polish Liquid Gold on him all day, that's what'll happen. This is my *son*, Len, I'll do whatever I have to for him."

Hell, she probably thought she meant it. Before I could decide how to feel about that, Katie pointed out new bumps on the door—several of them in a sloppy circle growing behind Clifford's left calf.

Was he bringing a friend home with him?

"It's another hand," she said. "Len, what's it doing?"

"How should I know?"

An exasperated groan. "Guess, then."

Not happily, I went for a closer look. It was late, the room dim, but I could tell right away that, even if you forgot it was wooden and growing out of the door, this was no normal hand. It had six fingers, for one thing, and they all looked too long for the palm, which in itself was as long as one of my feet. For another, even though the hand was coming out only a foot off the floor, the angle of the wrist showed it was reaching up. Coming from something down low, or crazy short.

It moved fast, too, compared with Clifford. I hadn't been studying it more than a couple minutes when I realized it had traveled out far enough to wrap itself around Clifford's leg.

I guess you could say things went quickly after that, if you can call twenty minutes "moving quickly."

At first Katie didn't want to believe that whatever had taken hold of Clifford presented any problem. "Cliffie's such a strong boy," she said as she used the sleeve of her housecoat to wipe sweat from her eyes. Her voice trembled. "Such strong legs. You know that, Len. Remember how he put his foot through the wall that time?"

I remembered. I found yellow jackets building a nest in there once.

⚘

"Let him go!" Katie was down on hands and knees, prying at what remained of the six fingers wrapped around Clifford's leg, pulling him back into the door. It didn't do any good. The apartment may be a wreck, but it was made a long time ago, before the materials got so flimsy. I don't know what kind of wood that door is, but it's heavy, and that's what those fingers and the leg were made of. Katie loves taking care of her nails, but she ground them to splinters that night trying to rescue her boy.

When only a few knuckles were left sticking out, Katie started beating on them, making the whole door rattle. "LET GO!"

The old jerk-off in the apartment next door thumped the wall twice, angrily, as the last of the hand melted back into the door, taking a little more of Clifford with it.

⚘

Face crimson, housecoat hanging open, hair sweaty and stuck to her cheeks, Katie held onto Clifford's left hand, pulling at the wood with all her might.

Clifford looked back at her, desperate, as his mouth crawled open in a silent scream. The wooden skin of his face puffed a bit, reacting to the slow-motion centrifugal force of being yanked back into the door by what-ever had hold of him.

Me, I did what I could. I tried to take hold of the boy's free hand and

197

pull, but it disappeared into the door before I could get a good grip on it. Then I tried to help Katie with the other arm but she didn't leave me enough room.

Finally, after finding nothing else to grab, I settled back onto the bed and watched. At least Katie wasn't screaming anymore; the only noise she made was the occasional strained grunt, which wouldn't piss off a neighbor.

❦

With something like sadness, I watched Clifford's face melt back into the door, shrieking slowly and silently. But he was only Katie's son. Katie and some loser who hadn't seen him since he was two.

The kid's left arm was all that was left sticking out of the door, stretched to the limit, and Katie kept pulling and sweating.

I thought about telling her it was time to give up, let him go, take a shower (she needed one), come to bed, because she already wasn't going to get enough sleep for work the next day. Then I kept my mouth shut because I knew giving up on the kid was something she figured she'd done too many times already.

❦

"No! Cliffie! Don't, honey!"

Not much left of the kid, only his hand and a little bit of wrist, when Katie's struggle grew more frantic than ever. I figured she'd finally caught on to the fact that she was going to lose, so I didn't bother getting up. She'd be in bed soon, crying into her pillow the way she had the night we'd buried him. I even had toilet paper ready to wipe whatever messes she made of her face.

"He's got me, Len! Won't let me go!"

This time I got up. The hard wood of Clifford's hand had wrapped itself around the soft flesh of Katie's, and was pulling her with it.

Who knew what would happen to Katie if the hand kept its grip on her? Maybe she'd turn into wood herself and Clifford would drag her into hell with him, as he'd tried to drag both of us into it when he was alive.

198

One thing I did know was that I couldn't make him loosen his grip. After some minutes of trying, and with only a few more inches of him left sticking out of the door, I stopped and ran into the kitchen.

"Len!" Katie cried. "Len, don't leave me alone with him!"

I'll admit I was tempted to leave. But I didn't. Give me that. What I did was yank open the junk drawer—the one filled with batteries, playing cards and two dozen other pieces of loose change and crap—and started digging.

In the bedroom, Katie swore at both me and her son.

I found the hammer in seconds and untangled it from a gray phone cord. When I made it back, I found Katie with one slippered foot pressing against the wood, using it for leverage in her fight to get free.

Less than three inches and she'd start into the door too. I took a breath, reminding myself of the time Clifford stole twenty bucks out of my wallet. Never did find out what he spent it on. That made it easier to bring down the hammer on his hand, with all the force I could muster. It's a lucky thing I didn't hit Katie.

The hand broke off at the wrist.

The sound that erupted from the jagged remains of the wooden limb was piercing and lasted a hundred years. "MMMMMMAAAAAAAAAAA —" Clifford was crying in slow motion for Mama's help. It stopped when the last bits of him disappeared back into the door.

The wood was in perfect shape again. As close to perfect as we have in this place.

I guess I stood there without moving for maybe a minute, long enough for the people in the apartments all around to bang on the walls two or three thousand times. For all I cared they could spend the rest of the night pounding, although I hoped none of them called the cops again.

Katie'd gone flying when the hand and wrist separated. She sat still on the floor, eyes wandering, like she wasn't seeing anything but all the places where her son wasn't.

"Len," she whispered after another minute passed. She held up her hand, showing me what still had a tight wooden grip on it. "Len, get it off me."

The Motherless One

BRYSON RICHARD

After the *auf* slithered from the cold mud and brackishness of the elder forest, it had but one thought, one overwhelming compulsion: to find a mother.

Thin, lithe, with a jagged mouth of sharp, rusty teeth, and stark, round eyes blooming yellow like dandelions, the *auf* observed the robins chirping in their nests and saw how the mother-robins came and spat food into the chicks' anxiously open beaks. *Mothers feed*, the *auf* understood, and scurried up into the boughs. There, in the nest, it investigated the chirping chicks and brushed them out indifferently to fall flightless to the earth. When the robin-mother returned, the *auf* held its mouth open as the chicks had, awaiting its meal. Instead, the mother twitched her head, dewy black eyes studying the *auf* momentarily, then fluttered away with an alarmed squawk.

Dejected, the *auf* left the nest, clambered down through the boughs and back to the ground where it found the tossed chicks mournfully still and no longer chirping. It gobbled them up with crunchy satisfaction.

The forest, it knew, was full of mothers. It just had to find the right one.

Following a creek, it discovered a family of red foxes. The foxes, oblivious to its presence among the reedy marshes on the edge of the nameless creek, played amongst themselves. Watching them unnoticed gave the *auf* a twirling, bubbly feeling in its loins. The mother fox lounged on a grassy carpeted knoll, back paw scratching relentlessly under her chin, and her pups leapt playfully, tumbled, and sprang over each other. Eventually, even the mother joined in, nuzzling her pups, nibbling at them affectionately.

Mothers play! The realization set the *auf* into a frenzy of excitement. It too wished to play. As quickly and chaotically as a predator pouncing on prey, it scurried out of the marshes and up the little knoll. It grabbed a fox pup in each thorny hand, one by the throat, one by the tail, and spun crazily, issuing what it thought of as laughter; wet, harsh, gasping hisses, more akin to choking. The rest of the playful pups darted into underbrush, but the mother fox hesitated atop the knoll, poised between defending and fleeing.

The *auf* lunged forwards, snaggletoothed grin a red gash in its small, oblong head, arms wide to embrace her. The fox bared her teeth but turned quickly and leapt off the knoll after her remaining cubs.

The *auf* hugged the grass, the earth still warm where the fox mother had lain. The two pups in its clutches flailed and whimpered. It released them reluctantly and they scurried away after their family, falling over each other in flight. The *auf* sulked on the knoll and considered the fox-mother. She had too many cubs anyway. It would never gain the full love and attention it sought with so many siblings.

It spent a long night at a pond nestled in a grove of box elder and willows, listening to the roaring, competing croaks of a vast army of frogs. The moon shimmered on the water, and the auf noticed on the opposite shore a doe licking the snout of her fawn. *Mothers adore*, it discovered. Then it recalled the day's failures and imitated the frogs with mournful, croaking wails.

The horror of dawn brought the crow of the rooster, alerting the *auf*, who charged through underbrush and down coldly bubbling brooks to investigate. In a ravine at the edge of the forest, it discovered a log house and barnyard. Not just one house; it was amazed to behold several dwellings riding the ridge in a small clearing. The houses gathered around a central building with a high spire on the other side of a slow-moving river that bisected the little village.

The *auf* remained hidden, yet watchful, amazed by the activity, the collected existence of so many in one place. It surveyed those who lived in the house nearest the forest, watched them come and go, watched the family dog, tied in the barnyard and prowling. It observed the lazy meandering of the cat, listened to the constant clucking march of the chickens. All the commotion in the bright exposure of the sun was intriguing yet daunting.

At twilight, the long shadow of the spire in the center of the village cast itself over the houses. The *auf* didn't like being in the shadow of the spire. It felt a presence inside, all the way at the top, something that could see all things from such a lofty position, and the idea filled the *auf* with a mysterious but powerful dread. It darted into the barnyard to escape that great reaching shadow.

Inspecting the chicken house first, it crept in to see the hens sitting like statues, keeping warm the dark, speckled eggs beneath them. *Mothers protect* it realized with a sudden fear as the hens, sensing it was among them, began to squawk, wings beating at the air, launching themselves at the *auf*, pecking, striking out with taloned feet.

It fled the coop, dashed across the barnyard blindly, and glimpsed a solitary rat slip into a crack in the fieldstone foundation of the log house. Though long as a human babe, the *auf* was thin as a sapling in spring. It crawled after the rat, a tight fit, but it knew that if its head fit through, the rest of it would follow. It crept through the walls after the rat, exploring the hidden areas of the home until it discovered a hole near the floor. Peering into the room, it saw the mother of the house rocking her babe in her arms.

The *auf* examined them through the rat hole as the mother sang. Such sweet notes it had never heard before, not even from the birds that chirped in the forest. The mother's song made the *auf* weep silently, hoping that this one, this final mother, perhaps the mother of all mothers, would be the one for it.

The mother finished rocking the babe, kissed it, and set it swaddled and warm into the cradle.

The single candle in the room went out and darkness settled.

The *auf* waited, listened to the muffled voices of the mother and father in a different part of the house, waited for the coos and infantile clucks to cease and the babe's breathing to become heavy, waited for the noises of the house and those in it to cease entirely.

Then it scampered out of the wall and across the hard floor to the cradle.

When it tossed the babe from the crib and climbed in, snuggling down into the folds of blankets, still holding heat from the previous occupant, the *auf* experienced comfort for the first time and purred like a kitten in all that new, soft warmth.

The babe's dying wail alerted his mother. She blundered into the dark room, sleepy, confused, alarmed by the cry, and crossed immediately to the crib, where she scooped up the swaddled creature and held it to her breast.

Mothers comfort the *auf* thought in momentary bliss. It guzzled the spurts of hot milk greedily but awkwardly; it had never suckled before.

The mother noticed. She hissed at the painful nibbles, at the aggressive grasping at her breast. Frustrated, she tried to scrutinize it in the dark, squinting down at its face, but the gloom made it impossible to behold. She crossed the nursery, heading for the candle, and nearly tripped over something sprawled on the floor. Issuing a confused grunt, she studied the pile on the floor, recognized the shape, then held the thing in her arms out towards the moonlit open window, and beheld the savage visage of something altogether not her babe.

The mother screamed, a sound of pure revulsion at the *auf's* appearance, disgust at it feeding from her, and confusion at its place in her arms. It dove through the window, back into the night.

Such shrill things mothers were, the *auf* mused as it escaped the sounds of her outrage. Yet, as it hastened down the brick path towards the village, it recalled the warmth of her bosom, the delicious milk, the brief but very real nuzzle of comfort, and it too wailed, the resonance of the unloved, the cry of the motherless, teased with the possibility of affection not to be realized.

The *auf* skittered towards the river and beheld the bridge that spanned it, a thing of rough weather-beaten stone. Orbs of light appeared in the dark on the far side of the bridge, lights that bobbed and wavered through the night. Captured lights, the *auf* realized. It feared those who carried the lights in cages. It slipped down the riverbank, tumbled through the slick weeds and over slippery rocks and landed with a splash in the cool water.

"What was that?" One of the light-keepers shouted and two of them appeared atop the bridge and flashed their captured lights down on the water.

The *auf* darted under the bridge, cowering, hugging its knees to its chest. Any second those lights would find it, and it would burn. Yes, it would die in agony.

The *auf* shivered, whimpered.

Something hard nudged its thin, wet shoulder. "*Hush now.*" The whisper was cold, hoarse, a croak akin to a frog's.

The *auf* did as it was bid. After a moment, the light reflecting off the water departed, and the sounds of boots on the bridge signaled the withdrawal of the light-keepers.

In the night, the mother still wailed.

"*Such a wee babe,*" the thing under the bridge croaked in the gloom. "*Such a wee babe, indeed.*" Though it was difficult to make out completely, the size of the thing was evident. It sprawled on the shore under the bridge, appearing to be a pile of slimy boulders in the gloom. But then, when the thing moved, it gave itself form, a rough, troll-like being, with a great under-biting jaw and tendrils of green, shaggy, moss-like hair dangling over it like a shroud.

The *auf* shivered in the face of the thing under the bridge. The memory of the screaming mother's warm, comfortable bosom lingered, and it wanted more than anything to return to her.

"*Cease ye shaking, child, and come closer. There be no reason to fear me. I am as thee.*"

The *auf* observed the shadowy thing and remembered that *mothers comfort*. It crawled upon the thing and nestled into a dry spot in the mossy hair.

"*Wee and scrawny.*" The *auf* felt an appendage slide down its spine as the thing under the bridge stroked it. "*Do ye not feed thyself?*" The thing caressed it again. "*And such eyes have I beheld only when the moon is full and high and mirrored upon the waters.*"

Mothers adore, the *auf* remembered, and smiled, revealing teeth like crooked nails hammered into its gums.

The thing under the bridge hugged the *auf* tight against its rocky exterior. A boat floated towards the bridge.

"Close thine eyes," the thing under the bridge murmured.

The boat neared and the *auf* shrank as much as it could into the mossy drapery of the thing, its eyes clamped tightly. Yet the *auf* was, despite its fear, curious about the light-keepers. It chanced a glance at the captured light held before it like the severed head of an enemy, illuminating the *auf's* bright, startlingly yellow eyes.

The light-keeper reeled away shrieking, the boat rocking perilously in the commotion. The one paddling the boat lifted an oar to swat the *auf* against the rocky, mossy outcropping it rested on. The rocks shifted suddenly, reached out, and tossed the boat into the air. Both passengers bashed against the underside of the bridge, then fell limply into the water, floating face down and away with the current.

The thing under the bridge slowly pulled itself from the mud and murk of the riverside and heaved itself out of the water. The bridge under which it had dwelt for unknown time shivered, quaked, then collapsed. From the great cloud of destruction, the thing burst forth, the *auf* clinging to the mossy hair and thinking, *mothers protect!*

Out of the wreckage they lumbered, a thin bundle of sticks like a tiny scarecrow babe with round, yellow eyes atop a pile of stodgy, hominoid boulders as big as a house. A loud clanging sounded from the top of the central spire, and the *auf* thought it was the voice of the great watchful presence it had felt inside. The spire was screaming now, and the *auf,* clinging to the thing from under the bridge, screamed back.

Shouts rang out from houses, dogs barked frantically, the spire rang shrill alarm, and more captured lights appeared in the night, floating, gathering, headed towards the *auf* and the thing from under the bridge.

"Behold the fools," the thing said in a voice deeper and clearer in the open air than it had been before, rumbling like thunder. The massive creature shambled towards the floating, gathering orbs of captured lights, and the *auf's* yellow eyes burned fiery bright. It clutched handfuls of mossy hair. Some of the light-keepers felt the ground quivering under the thing's

lurching steps, and they skidded, turned, fled towards the spire. Others either didn't hear or didn't care, and when the thing from under the bridge emerged from the dark, it trampled them in its wake, its stony body splattering them like gourds under boots. The thing stormed through the sides of homes and jumped on roofs till they collapsed in on cowering light-keepers. It kicked down fences and tossed cattle and swine across the ridge into the expanse of the elder forest. It uprooted trees and used them as clubs to bash at the little screaming light-keepers as they fled their destroyed homes. The thing stamped out every house, barn, and building in the village like a child stomping on ant hills, till only the tall central spire remained, still stridently ringing.

The thunder rolled endlessly now, its vibration and rumble heard even over the screams of the light-keepers, over the ruckus of crumbling buildings and the ringing from the tower. The *auf* realized it was not thunder, but the laughter of the thing from under the bridge. *Mothers play!* It smiled and issued its own choking cackle.

The thing from under the bridge glowered at the spire. *"Cease ye wailings!"* it thundered and launched rubble at it. The projectile exploded the top of the spire. The entire structure leaned, tilted, then toppled over, revealing the cowering light-keepers within like fat grubs in a rotted log.

Mounting the wreckage of the temple, the thing reached in through the broken roof, scooped up three luckless light-keepers, and stuffed them into its cavernous maw, grinding their soft wet bodies between stalactite-like tusks.

One of the thing's hands came up to where the *auf* still clutched the mossy hair. In the hand, offered pieces of people.

Mothers feed, the *auf* thought ravenously, licking its long, rusty teeth.

Waiting for Mother

BRIAN EVENSON

I.

When she called, Sabine felt she had no choice but to come, even though she did not know the woman. *Tiril*, she claimed her name was when Sabine answered the phone. It seemed that she expected her name to mean something to Sabine, but it meant nothing.

"Yes?" Sabine said. Her voice was neutral but polite, the same voice she used in college as a way of passively acknowledging the presence of those she didn't know without promising anything.

"Tiril," said the woman on the phone. "You know, Tiril?" And when Sabine still waited, silent, polite, "It's hardly a common name. Surely your mother told you about me?"

Sabine drew in her breath sharply, surprised.

"My mother?" Sabine managed. "You...know her?"

"Of course I know her," said the woman. She seemed irritated.

Sabine looked about the room, unsure of where to let her gaze settle. Tiril? Her mother had never mentioned a Tiril. What kind of name was that anyway?

"Tiril," said Sabine cautiously. "Remind me...How do you know my mother?"

209

"We live together, of course," said Tiril.

"Live together?" said Sabine. "Where?" And then, quickly, "Can you put her on?"

"Of course," said Tiril. Sabine held her breath. She heard, on the other end of the line, Tiril call out, her voice muffled, the receiver on her end half-covered. "Cora! Cora! It's your daughter!"

Did someone respond? Sabine wanted to think so. But whether she really heard anyone or not was hard to say: the sound was too muffled. When she thought about it later, she believed there might have been the sound of a door closing. Maybe there had been footsteps, the *toc-toc* of heels across a tile floor. Or maybe there was nothing at all.

A moment later Tiril was back. "Your mother can't come to the phone right now," she said. "But you should come visit. She would love to see you."

"But where?" asked Sabine desperately. "Where should I come?"

"Oops, got to go. I'll call back," said Tiril, and hung up.

Sabine had not seen her mother for several years. Two years, eight months and four days to be exact. One day, after her mother had failed for a week to answer her calls, she drove over from the dorms to find the house unlocked and empty, her mother nowhere to be seen. Nothing seemed to be missing, nothing was out of place. When she reported the absence to the police, they just shrugged. Any sign of foul play? No. Could Sabine's father have done something to her? No, her father had been dead a decade. Any reason to believe something was wrong? No. Perhaps your mother just didn't like her life: people walk out of their lives all the time, the officer told Sabine, there was very little they could do. Maybe she would eventually come back on her own.

Sabine had inquired, asked around, but there was no sign of her mother. She had simply vanished. So Sabine had moved back home, into the empty house, where she had been waiting ever since.

After the call ended, after she was left saying "Hello? Hello?" into the dead line, Sabine sat heavily on the couch, as if stunned.

She'll call back, thought Sabine. *She said she would.*

But what if she didn't?

You can't think like that, she told herself.

But Sabine wasn't sure. It had been so long. Could it really be her mother?

⚜

In the week that followed, she arranged her schedule so as to be near the house phone as much as possible. She would go to school and then would rush back, then spend her evening beside the phone, waiting.

When the call finally came, eight days later, she had all but given up. She was eating a dinner of sorts, a can of black beans that she'd opened and was spooning into her mouth cold.

"Hello?" said Sabine.

"Sabine?" said a voice, brightly. "It's Tiril."

Her blood began beating loud in her head. She made an effort to hold her voice steady, to seem calm. "I've been waiting for your call," Sabine said. "I've been longing for you to call back."

"How flattering!" said Tiril.

"I want to come," said Sabine. "I'd like to come see you, and my mother. Do you think that would be possible?"

For a moment there was silence on the line. *Did she hang up?* "Hello?"

"Still here," said Tiril. "Sure," she said, and laughed. "I'm sure Cora would love to have you. She's more or less forgiven you."

"Forgiven me?" said Sabine. *For what?*

"Yes, forgiven you. But come now, right away. Pack a bag and come tonight." And then she gave Sabine an address, deep in the countryside, and hung up.

⚜

She did as Tiril asked. She packed a bag hurriedly, almost in a frenzy, and tossed it into the car. On the drive, there were many times Sabine hesitated and wanted to turn back.

211

What if she's not there? What if this is all some sort of misunderstanding?

A few hours later she tried to determine if she had harmed or offended her mother somehow. Was there anything to forgive? But she couldn't think of anything, not a thing. They had been just a normal mother and daughter, hadn't they?

Should I turn back? she thought later. But she kept driving. She hadn't seen her mother in two and a half years. If she had a chance of seeing her now, she had to take it.

But if she isn't actually there, another part of her thought, *won't that just make things worse?*

II.

It was an old country house, not too large, not too small, dilapidated on the outside, paint peeling, but intact. "Sabine!" cried Tiril before she was even all the way out of the car. The older woman beelined toward her and embraced her. And then she let her go. "I've heard so much about you," she said. Abruptly, she drew Sabine in again, held her uncomfortably long. "It's wonderful to finally meet you."

She helped Sabine carry her bag in from the car. She was chattering, excited, almost manic. She showed her to a room with a double bed and with the paper peeling from the walls and declared it hers. Not knowing what else to do, Sabine simply nodded, glanced uncomfortably around.

"Where's my mother?" Sabine finally said.

"Oh!" said Tiril, and clapped once. "Of course. Of course, you're wondering!"

Sabine waited a moment. "And?" she finally said.

"She's away," said Tiril. "She had to leave unexpectedly. On business."

"What sort of business does she do?"

Tiril smiled. "She should be the one to tell you about it, once she gets back."

Why? wondered Sabine. *Why couldn't Tiril simply tell her now?* But she couldn't bring herself to ask that question. "When will she be back?"

Tiril shrugged. "Tomorrow," she said. "Or the next day. Or the next. Who can say? But don't worry: you're welcome to wait until she arrives."

Wait. How could she wait? When would her mother be back? *Would* she be back?

She had her room. At night she stayed there, staring at the ceiling, trying to decide if she should leave. By day, when Tiril was occupied, she snooped around. The house was easy to go through, since Tiril was often outside, sunning on a chaise lounge in the yard or gardening. True, in Tiril's bedroom closet were women's clothing of two different sizes, though Sabine didn't recognize any of the clothing as belonging to her mother.

But that's hardly surprising, a part of her countered with a frown. *Mother left without taking any of her clothes. She had to start from scratch. She remade herself.*

Sabine lifted a shirt to her face, breathed it in. Did it smell like her mother? No. Clean, it didn't smell like anyone at all.

There was an attic, but she could see from the dust on the floor that nobody had been there in years. She didn't bother to climb in. There was a basement too, and this she explored, even knocking on the walls with her fists to see if there was some space that was hollow into which her mother might have been walled. But all the walls sounded the same.

When she finally gave up and turned to go back upstairs, there was Tiril, on the final stair before the bottom, watching her. What had she seen her do? Sabine smiled, trying not to look furtive, but Tiril just laughed.

"You're bored!" she said. "I can't keep you locked up in here. You'll go stir crazy!" She gestured Sabine toward the stairs and reluctantly Sabine went up. From below her, Tiril apologized for her mother's continued absence. "It must have taken her much longer than she anticipated. I'm sure she'll be back any day now. Tomorrow I'll figure out something to keep you entertained."

Once again Sabine was racking her brains. *I don't think Mom ever mentioned a Tiril, even in passing*, she thought.

No, another part of her responded, *she didn't.* That other part of her was beginning to feel to her almost like another distinct person.

It was early morning. She had just woken up. She lay there, staring at the ceiling. It felt almost as if she had been torn into two halves. Had Tiril done this somehow?

Don't be ridiculous, the other Sabine said. *She's not a witch.*

*Do you...*started Sabine, and then stopped. She shook her head. *Never mind.*

No, said the other Sabine, *say it.*

It's not something that should be said.

Say it.

Is...there a chance she doesn't know our mother at all?

Both Sabines were silent a long while.

"No," said Sabine at last, aloud this time. "I was right. It was not something that should be said."

⚜

In the morning, applying makeup, she murmured to the reflection in the mirror. *Give in*, she told herself. *Pretend this is normal and it will become normal.* In the mirror the other Sabine pursed her lips at her.

She came downstairs to find Tiril making breakfast. Tiril always did this, taking care of Sabine, almost as if she were her mother. She was always there, no matter how early or late Sabine awoke, near the stove, just getting started cooking, a little manic, happy to see Sabine.

"How did you sleep?" she asked, her voice musical.

"Fine," said Sabine, and faked a smile. She had decided to be polite. She had more to gain by being polite than by being forceful or honest.

Later, she sat eating, chewing her food slowly. Tiril babbled, talking about her plans for the day: weeding in the garden outside. Would Sabine like to help?

"I'm allowed outside?" said Sabine.

"Of course you're allowed outside," said Tiril, and gave a tittering laugh.

"Silly! It's not like you're a prisoner here." She gestured toward the windows. "Walk around, look around, do anything you like. I have nothing to hide."

Sabine half-smiled, noncommittal. In her experience, people who said they had nothing to hide usually had already hidden a great deal.

Or if she didn't want to explore or walk there was so much to do in an old house like this, Tiril told her. So much Sabine could help her with. There were tiles on the roof to be replaced, the walls to be redone...

"How long have you had this house?" asked Sabine.

"Ever since the owner passed."

Sabine took another bite, then couldn't stop herself. "Passed?"

"To the other side. Died, as they say," said Tiril.

"How did he die?" asked Sabine.

Tiril looked at her, smiled. "Who said it was a he?"

For a moment Sabine remained silent, trying to decide how to interpret this. And then Tiril and Sabine both bowed their heads and returned to eating.

"Do you think my mother will come today?" asked Sabine finally, interrupting the silence.

Tiril frowned. And then her face relaxed, became serene.

"The garden, then?" Tiril said. "I'm counting on you."

❦

"She's not here," said Sabine to her reflection in the mirror, still sweaty from weeding in the garden. "She's not coming back."

The other Sabine shook her head. *It's a test,* she whispered. *Tiril is judging us, reporting to her. Mother's waiting to come back until we've passed the test.*

Sabine made a disgusted noise. "A test!" she said. "We don't need to be tested."

The other Sabine said nothing.

"How do you know it's a test?" asked Sabine.

I can feel it, said the other Sabine.

215

"You feel it!" said Sabine, voice deep, sarcastic. She shook her head, sighed. "We should leave."

You said it yourself, said the other Sabine. *If there's the smallest chance of her coming back, we have to stay.*

"I'm...no longer so sure," said Sabine.

The other Sabine said nothing in response to this, only gave Sabine a cold, glittering smile.

III.

A few mornings later, when Sabine came downstairs, Tiril was wearing boots and brown pants and a jacket. A rifle was leaning against the counter beside the stove.

"What's up?" asked Sabine.

"It's the first of the month," said Tiril. "Local tradition is to try to kill something on the first."

Sabine opened her mouth, then closed it again.

Tiril laughed. "Don't look so serious! It's just a little hunting. Did you bring boots?"

Sabine had, but not the kind of boots Tiril had in mind. Tiril led her to the little closet off the back door and showed her a line of boots there.

"Try them until you find a pair that fit," she said, and returned to the kitchen.

"Where did you get so many boots?" called Sabine, but either Tiril didn't hear or she chose not to answer.

By the time she found some boots, breakfast was steaming on the table before them. Where there had before been one rifle there were now two.

"What are we shooting?"

Tiril shrugged. "Anything is fair game," she said.

The shot was deafening, but it didn't seem to bother Tiril at all. The twig she had been aiming at was now gone, torn completely free.

"You're a good shot," claimed Sabine.

"It's not much of a challenge to hit a branch," said Tiril. And then, "Your turn."

Sabine tried to demur. No, she'd never held a gun. She couldn't see herself shooting a living thing.

"Just shoot another twig then," said Tiril. "The tree will be fine. Obviously the animals know it's the first and are lying low. Come here."

Sabine did. Tiril positioned herself behind Sabine and wrapped her arms around her, helped her lift the gun, steady it.

"A deep breath," said Tiril. "Then let it out slowly, and ease back on the trigger..."

Another deafening shot, and the side of the tree just below the branch fragmented.

"Almost," said Tiril. "A good first effort. You're a natural." Picking up her own weapon she slung it in the crook of her arm and started off. After a moment she turned and looked back.

"Come on," she said. "We're burning daylight."

There was no game, only a songbird or two, but these Tiril refused to shoot. "Bad luck," she claimed. The forest was dark and for much of the walk Sabine felt isolated, cut off from the world, but then she would suddenly come out into a clearing and it would be bright again and she would wonder why she had felt the way she had. There were, occasionally, at a distance, the reports of other guns firing. Perhaps everyone was out with guns today. But if that was the case, shouldn't they be wearing safety jackets, so as not to be shot?

When Sabine asked Tiril about this, she laughed. "Just stick to the right paths," she said. "If you're a local, you know them." She gestured around them. "If you were here on your own, yes, it would be best to wear a safety jacket. But I'm in charge of you."

Midday found them in a blind, a large one—not just them but a crew of local kids, each with their own gun. Three kids, and the two of them. They seemed to know Tiril, though they never called her by name. Before long Tiril had them passing around a bottle of vodka that one of them had stolen from his parents liquor cabinet.

Beside her, Sabine thought, *How old could these kids be?*

How old indeed? But they weren't her kids, she wasn't from here, she wasn't their mother, she had no right to judge. She didn't know how things were done in the country, and Tiril obviously did. In the end Sabine, when the bottle came her way, took it and drank.

Before long she was feeling comfortably warm. Tiril was at the opening, the tip of her rifle jutting out, looking for something to kill. Sabine sat against the back of the blind, shoulder to shoulder with the oldest of the kids, Marco his name was. The other two gathered a little way away, playing a game of hand gestures that Sabine found incomprehensible.

"Do you ever wonder," slurred the boy, and trailed off, eyes heavy.

Sabine waited, still watching the other children, for him to go on. "Ever wonder what?" she finally prodded.

"Exactly," said the boy.

Sabine frowned. What did he mean? And then she made a decision. She gestured at Tiril with her chin. "Does she have a friend?" she asked.

"Sure," said the boy. "That lady has lots of friends."

She lowered her voice. "Is one named Cora?"

"Her friends have all sorts of names," the boy said. "I can hardly keep track, can I? That's not my job."

Sabine pressed on. "It would have been a very special friend," she said.

"You're her friend, aren't you?" said the boy. "Her special friend?"

"Am I?"

But the boy wasn't paying attention. "Hey," he was saying, "Hey, lady," and Tiril was turning away from the opening of the blind. "Is she—" he pointed exaggeratedly at Sabine—your special friend?"

Tiril shook her head. "Not yet," she said. "But soon." And the luminous smile she gave when she said it made Sabine feel more afraid than a threat would have done.

"We could tie her up," said Sabine to her reflection in the mirror, still tipsy enough to have less of a filter than usual. "Tie her up and take a knife and cut her, again and again, until she tells us where mother is."

Are you listening to yourself? asked the other Sabine. *Do you even hear what you're saying?*

For a moment she rose up full of anger, and then, all at once, she deflated.

"It's intolerable," she said. She felt exhausted. "Unbearable. We have to do something."

But the other Sabine didn't bother to answer. What was there to do?

IV.

It was after a meal, after lunch together, and they stood at the sink, Tiril washing dishes and then handing them to her to dry. They were chatting as they worked. Tiril was laughing, and then she turned to Sabine and looked at her with wide eyes and said, "So this is what it's like to be in a family."

For a moment Sabine stared. And then she offered, tentatively, "What do you mean?"

Tiril smiled but didn't answer. The way she looked as she smiled reminded Sabine of the other Sabine.

"Everybody has a family, don't they?" asked Sabine.

"I know what," said Tiril. "Why don't we pretend you're my daughter? I can mother you until Cora gets back."

Sabine froze, her mouth going dry, her hands beginning to shake.

"Is that okay with you, sweetheart?" said Tiril, and smiled wide.

⚜

She felt the other Sabine whispering inside her head, trying to calm her, trying to coax her away, and only just managing. Sabine was upset, yelling, screaming, incoherent. Tiril just watched, seemingly unafraid. *What have you done with her?* Sabine was yelling. *Where is she?* And, *You're not my fucking mother!*

219

Then the other Sabine had control of her and spun her on her heel and walked her away. She could hear Tiril laughing wildly behind her, as if Sabine yelling at her had been the best sort of joke.

Shhh, the other Sabine was saying. *It's okay, it's okay.*

But out loud Sabine was screaming, "It's not okay! It's not okay!"

And then Tiril was there again, right beside her, face furious. Had Sabine been right? Had she really been laughing? Maybe all along she had been just as upset as Sabine.

"You can leave!" Tiril was shouting. "What's stopping you? You can leave any time! If you don't want to be my friend, leave! If you don't want to be here, leave!"

And suddenly Sabine was afraid she'd lost her last chance to see her mother again. She began to babble. *No,* Sabine was saying, *I want to be here, I want to wait for my mother.* And Sabine was falling to her knees now, was pleading with her, no, please, let her stay, she wanted, she needed, to see her mother again.

Slowly Tiril's mouth curled into a faint smile.

☙❧

Later, back in their room, she could barely look at herself in the mirror. She had betrayed herself. There was nothing to be said that could serve as an apology. She was exhausted.

"How long can this go on?" Sabine finally asked.

It could last forever, said the other Sabine.

"What should we do?"

The other Sabine waited a very long time to respond. *Kill her,* she finally said.

☙❧

She slept, she woke. Tomorrow was a new day. She was once again on an even keel, on her best behavior. Could she go on? Yes, she could. What choice did she have?

Tiril acted like nothing had happened the day before. She was once again the gracious hostess. *Eggs?* she offered. Yes, Sabine assented, eggs. *Fried?* Sure, fried. A moment later with a clack Tiril set down a bowl of porridge before Sabine.

Tiril took her place at the head of the table. She regarded Sabine with keen interest. "Well," she said, "aren't you going to eat your eggs?"

"Eggs?" said Sabine. "Tiril..."

"Tiril?" the woman asked. "Who's Tiril?"

"Why, you are," said Sabine.

"Me?" the woman said, as if genuinely perplexed. "But I'm Talia."

Sabine stared at her bowl of porridge. Was it possible she'd had the woman's name wrong this whole time? The names were close enough that it was, Sabine supposed, possible, but it seemed improbable, unimaginable even.

"If you're not going to eat your eggs, why do I even bother?"

Slowly Sabine lifted her spoon and swallowed a bite. She tried to imagine what she was eating was eggs.

"There," Tiril said, unless she was in fact really Talia—or perhaps someone entirely different from either Tiril or Talia. "Now isn't that better?"

They were making dinner, Sabine and Tiril, unless she was Talia, chopping vegetables. Sabine felt she could almost see the other Sabine sitting at the table, watching them both, as if she had stepped out of the mirror and come into the room. Sabine couldn't see her, but she could feel her. She felt that somehow Tiril could too.

What if her mother came back now? What would that be like? Would it make things better or would it feel all the worse?

Why am I here? Sabine wondered. She could sense the other's Sabine's cold, glittering smile hovering nearby.

Too long, she told herself. It had already gone on for far too long. She couldn't bear it any longer. The waiting was worse than losing her mother for good would have been. And where was her mother? Was her mother even alive?

No, it was too much. It needed to end. Needed to end now.

And so, when Talia was not looking, Sabine's hand darted to the knife block and palmed a paring knife.

She had it with her the whole time they ate, secured just under her thigh, waiting. She kept touching it, reassuring herself it was still there. There were some things, she told herself, that she could count on. At the moment, this knife was chief among them.

She would give the woman one last chance. They would have a cordial meal. They would be pleasant with one another. And then maybe, just maybe, in the course of the conversation Tiril, or Talia, would have a change of heart and would come to realize that she should tell Sabine where her mother was and how she could get to her.

If she's even still alive, the other Sabine whispered in her ear.

"This is nice," said the other woman. "So pleasant." She took another bite. "Look at us," she said. "Such a happy family."

Something about the way she said it was too much to bear. Suddenly, before even knowing she was doing it, Sabine was up and out of her chair, her glass still in her hand. She hurled it at the woman. It glanced off Talia's head, stunned her briefly, long enough for Sabine to get around the table and knock her out of her chair and get her hands around her throat. Tightening her fingers, she began to bang the woman's head against the floor.

"You know where she is. You know! But you're never going to tell me. Never! What kind of monster are you?"

She loosened her grip a little. On the floor beneath her Talia began to cough then drew in a rasping breath. And then, in a voice barely above a whisper, "The same kind of monster as you," she said.

Sabine drew back, appalled. She stared at the woman coughing on the floor. Slowly Sabine stood and straightened her clothing and then, with dignity, went slowly back around to the other side of the table. There she stooped to pick up the knife from where it had fallen to the floor. And then, expressionless and indifferent, she returned to where Talia was, straddled the woman, and began to torture her.

222

"I don't know," Talia cried. "I don't know! I don't even know your mother!"

"That's obviously a lie," said Sabine, her voice calm, reasonable, Talia's blood on her shirt now. The other Sabine was there, beside her, face drawn but determined, neither of them looking away. They were in this together. "You knew who I was. You knew to call me," said Sabine.

"I read about her disappearance in the paper," Talia claimed quickly, wheezing between words, trying to catch her breath. "And then I looked you up and called you."

"I never reported her missing," said Sabine, quietly. "There was never anything in the papers. What did you do to her? Are you the one who made it so she couldn't come home?"

Talia said nothing.

"Do I have to kill you?" said Sabine.

"Yes," said Talia. "Kill me." She grimaced, her mouth full of blood. "Kill me. Let's be done with your mother. Let's be done with this game."

But Sabine didn't kill her. She simply choked her until she lost consciousness and then she stood and went back to the table. Sabine sat in her place and the other Sabine sat right on top of her and slowly seeped into her until it was once again hard for Sabine to distinguish where she stopped and the other Sabine began.

She ate for a moment in silence, until with a groan the woman regained consciousness. The woman dragged herself back up and stood. Slowly, she returned to her place at the table. There was a bruise above her eye where the glass had struck her. There were cuts on her chest, her arms, and blood had begun to seep through. She sat, and glanced up at Sabine.

"Welcome," said Sabine, and nodded.

After a moment's hesitation, the other woman dipped her head in response. Slowly, with shaking hands, she began to eat, wincing a little with each bite.

"I don't know what's keeping her," said Talia finally, unless she was Tiril. "I'm sure she'll be here any moment."

"Any moment," said Sabine. She could hear the other Sabine warbling within her voice, both of them speaking together now. "We have nowhere we need to be."

"Be a good girl and eat all your food," said the woman.

"Yes," said Sabine.

"Yes, what?" said the woman.

For a moment Sabine didn't know what the woman wanted and then, suddenly, she did. Of course she did.

"Yes, Mother," she said.

The woman beamed. And now, if she looked at her just right, from just the right angle, Sabine could almost see, there in her face, Cora, her mother. If she stayed here long enough, she suddenly realized, eventually that would be all she would see.

She kept staring until the other woman noticed. "What is it?" she said.

"Nothing," said Sabine, and turned back to her plate.

"She'll be here soon," said the woman after a moment. "Any day now."

Both Sabine and the other Sabine nodded together.

They all continued eating, slowly, the only sound the scraping of silver-ware against their plates.

MOTHER REMEMBERS

Unchild

JONATHAN LOUIS DUCKWORTH

The wasps were chawing again on the walls of Tame's cabin. That constant rustle of little mouthparts working on the wood and the hum of their wings was the only music Tame the wisewoman ever got, other than her own whistling. Sometimes in the deep of night the hum sounded half like a voice searching for its words. Here in the deep paths, even birds were shy of nesting, and the people of Grovemarket seldom came, and none since The Man had ever thought to pay for her wisewoman's services with a song.

It hurt to think of The Man, almost as much as it hurt to ponder the fruit of what he'd planted in her, when the wisewoman had—just once—let herself be something other than wise, her stunted heart unhasped by the key The Man shaped from his pretty words. Then he left, and her belly swelled like the budding world inside her wanted for a sky over its head.

The waspfeast broke off, and Tame heard footsteps calling her back to the hereandnow. She was dressing for bed, it being so late, but she got up fastlike, hoping it was Blueboy come to trade. She'd not seen Blueboy in weeks, lately her only visitor from Grovemarket. Most things Tame could make, or grow, or forage, but lamp oil, saltfish, and pearlpowder could only come from the market. He was a sweet thing, a stutterer with the ropy body and long face of a ferret, named for the blue cloak he wore. He never looked at her like she was anything but people.

"You come late, ain't you?" she said, clucking her tongue already, throwing her shawl over herself because there was nothing proper in greeting an unwed lad in nightclothes. And old as she felt, she wasn't too old for modesty. It'd been habit so long to trade with Blueboy she didn't even think of how he didn't answer her, and maybe if she'd not been so tired from husking crowapples she'd have noticed the footsteps were too heavy.

As it was, it was only after she lifted the bar and opened the door she learned her mistake.

"Evening, Mother," said a brawny man with a wide brimmed hat. He was a man of autumns, maybe her same age. A crossbow was slung over his shoulder.

She'd never seen him, never felt his eyes before. So seldom it was others saw her, she knew their gazes like the feel of their hands. Blueboy's eyes were shy, always nervously tracing her edges. This man's eyes were sharp, jabbing where they roved. Blue and cold; river stones. They nudged at the weave of her shawl and brushed at the swells of her hips.

"Who're you, then?" she asked, shifting one foot so that she could fill up more of the doorway. "Some trouble come up the deep paths? You of Grovemarket?"

"Trouble's what I'm after, Mother, hardly what I bring," the man said, and his thick, dark mustache bent bowlike around a wall of healthy teeth. "But I did come from Grovemarket. What's left of it. May I come in, please?"

"What's your ware brought you by?" she asked, using a phrase of the marketfolk.

"Ware? I'm a hunter; hunt's what I do," he said. "Let me in, please. Bad luck to turn away one who asks nicely."

He was right. Luck was a thing one in the deep paths couldn't spit on. But you made your own bad luck when you let in a nameless stranger.

"I can only let a name in. And stop calling me *Mother*."

"Cade Loach is my name." He tipped his hat. "Make guest of me."

If he'd gotten this far, he was clever enough to know the paths and not be fooled by the lies of the whisperoaks, and he looked too big of arm and stout of gut to scare off. If he wanted in, her door wasn't so thick—he'd get in. Whereas by letting him in, come whatever after she'd still have a working door. These were the calls one such as her in the deep paths had to make.

The bond was struck, and she let him in, shutting the door behind him. He walked a circle in her cabin, his heavy boots so much louder than Blueboy's little doehide footskins. Now she felt his eyes feeling through her keepthings even as she lowered the bar on the door to shut out the dark.

He set his crossbow down against the wall. "Cozy place."

Tame shadowed him as he paced around. Outside, the wasps were munching again.

"Mother's got a name?" He walked past her cot, his shadow spilling onto her strawpile where she slept.

"My name is Tame. In name, not nature."

"I believe it," he said, removing his hat and setting it on her cot. Her skin itched, thinking whatever nested in his long mop of hair would now crawl into her blankets, his thinks and wants curdling her woven nest of dreams.

"What ware brought you by?"

"There's a creature been taking folk from Grovemarket. A creature no one has seen. Strange."

"Oh." She'd had so few visitors of late.

He walked into Tame's kitchen, lingering near a shelf where Tame kept most of her bottles of cures and salves and tinctures and poisons. He picked up one of the deadliest of her brews—essence of loamflower. One drop could bring sweet slumber; three drops could make a man go corpse.

He set the bottle down. Found her carving knife. He held its blade in the light of the oil lantern, then slid it into his belt. She eyed his crossbow; closer to her than him now.

"I ain't gave that," she said.

He didn't pay any heed. Just kept looking through her cupboards and shelves. "No one's seen it, this creature. They hired me to kill a thing no one's known the shape of. Strange ain't it, Mother Tame?"

"Why come here, Hunter Loach?"

Now he looked at her and it was like she felt his stare closing around her throat. "Foot tracks all end here. See, it ain't a beast like the market-folk figured. The taken take themselves on the deep paths. Something's witching them this way."

She looked toward the crossbow and Loach showed his healthy teeth again. They both knew if it came to a jump he'd get there first, no matter who was closer.

"I'm no witch. And I don't know a thing about any creature."

His mustache made like gull's wings, and he shook his head. "I want to believe you, but you can see how it looks. Go to Grovemarket and you won't hardly find a one left. Who hasn't been taken's gone back coastward where it's safer." He was near the far corner now, where the only thing was what was covered in a thick quilt. The fear rooting her to where she stood chipped away the closer he came to it. Meantime, Loach kept talking, "Why would a person live here, so far from the kindly paths, unless they had something to hide?"

The tethers dissolved, and Tame hurled forward, but too late. Loach pulled away the quilt, uncovering the empty crib Tame built for one what never came born.

Seeing its cobwebbed legs and its seedoil-treated ribs and its hand-stitched cushion, a trickle of old pain leaked into her, her hands recalling their ardent labors. Outside the waspfeast loudened, and she remembered too much too fast, such that her legs buckled and she had to lean on the wall not to stumble.

Loach didn't say anything. He looked between the empty, spiderknit crib and its keeper, and there was knowing in his blue river stones. He walked back to the cot and picked up his hat then held it over his heart. "Sorry. I looked for something ain't here."

He picked up the quilt and threw it back over the crib, but the poison was already deep. She remembered the wasps, crawling out the eyes of the unchild she abandoned in the tanglewood grove.

"Why'd you keep it?" he asked. "I can see it hurts. So why not burn it? When my firstborn..."

"Some things don't make for kindling."

He took her knife out his belt and set it back in its place in the kitchen. When he walked past her to fetch his crossbow, he didn't dare meet her eye. "Beg pardon, Wisewoman Tame. Be lucky, and good dreams find you. The hunt waits me outside."

Only after he left did she start to breathe normal. She listened to his heavy boots pad away as she secured the bar on her door. She took off her shawl and smoothed her blankets, hoping her dreamweb wouldn't let too much pain through.

In the dark, sleep was a shy thing. Outside the waspfeast got so much she was sure she'd feel little bits of wood falling onto her from new holes. What crawled into wood could crawl into flesh. Like breathing, the buzz of wings and the rustle of eating swelled and hushed. She clawed and groped for the threads of sleep but couldn't find them, and the jetsam of her memory bobbed at the shores of her mind. What she couldn't stop seeing: the pink spindle of personflesh, still sticky with what it'd slid out in, a child that would never be anything but dead. How much she cried, what murder she swore when there was no one to blame for it, how she held the little damp bean and shook it like life was hiding there and just needed shaking loose.

Old word tells when one suffers the coming of an unchild (something never alive enough to have died) the unchild is to be buried in a garden, given the life it was denied once. But Tame, who for just a second time let herself be something other than wise, didn't do that. In that fool moment, she wanted done with the whole business of making life, so she took it to the tanglewood grove, where only those gnarled thorny bastard trees grew, where the wasps make their nests. She left the baby on the barren soil. Only later did shame get her, and she went back for it. But the wasps had found her unchild. Wasps, stripebottomed muddaubers with legs like threads crawling out from lips that'd never tasted her milk, out of eyes that'd never opened to the world's light. She ran coward, and in the six years hence never went back to the tanglewood grove.

This was the ugly hole her dreams slid into, shaking in her sweatsodden blankets. Until a thump sounded on her door and the waspfeast went hush. And then there was just a voice, calling from the other side of her barred door.

"Mother," the voice said.

It was Hunter Loach. Some hours it'd been since he left. He sounded haggard, hurt.

"Mother. Out. Come."

Human weakness it was got her out of bed. She threw the blankets off her and found her shawl and slipped into her footskins, then she lit the oil lamp with a coal from the hearth and hurried to the door. But by the time she did all this and got the door open, there was no Loach, only the dark leaning in from outside, and the thrum of wasp wings.

She shone the path leading out from her house with her lamp and saw Loach: hatless, no crossbow, staggering away like a drunk.

"Hunter!" she called out, but he kept shambling away. Smaller and dimmer all the time. He'd been poisoned. It was the only thing made sense to her.

It was cold and very dark out, but Tame was a wisewoman—wisewomen helped who they could help. That was her excuse, anyhow.

"Come back, fool!" she called one last time before figuring he wouldn't heed. There was only one way for it. She took the knife from the kitchen, and followed Hunter Loach into the wide dark loud with wasps.

She knew the paths. Her footskins were thin, and the ground was mean, but she knew where to step. Even as the night pushed its weight against her, her oil lamp shone defiantly, cutting a swath she could walk through.

Deeper she went, the louder the wasps. They'd never been so much, had they? And this late, it wasn't natural. But she wasn't looking for wasps, she was after a hunter. A few times she nearly stumbled on a rude root or got clawed by a wicked branch, and once or twice she thought she'd lost the hunter, but then her lamplight would shine off his coat. Each step made clearer where Hunter Loach was leading her.

Lamplight shone on the dewslicked thorns of the tanglewoods that crowded out the sky and seemed to wrestle each other. She knew she was close, but still she kept walking, calling the hunter's name, praying to whoever might listen that he'd hear her and turn around.

The ground changed. Grew uneven. She stumbled over something hard but not as hard as stone or root. Her lamp slipped out her hand and tumbled away. As she pushed herself up, the spinning light shone on a face.

A woman screamed into her ear. It was her who was screaming, because a dead man with no eyes was staring at her, his mouth pried open by a cluster of flutes shaped from muddaub. Wasps came in and out from these little tubes. A robin's egg cloak shrouded the corpse—just like the one Blueboy wore. Or maybe it was a different color. She couldn't be sure; didn't want to be sure. Tame crawled away and found her lamp and she tried to push on the path she'd been going, half expecting a dead hand to grasp her ankle and a known voice, shy, quiet, and just a little stuttery to beg her help. She put the body behind her.

The wasps were roaring now, their sharp wings and hard bodies pinging around her, pelting her shawl and bouncing off her skirts. Deeper she went, because she couldn't feel the way back now, because when she shone her lamp behind her it was just wasp wings, and because she could still hear the hunter stumbling ahead.

She walked over other bodies but didn't let herself fall again. She tried not to see too much of what her lamp found. The faces, some very long dead, some fresh, the hands grasping at nothing, the legs splayed every whichway, the clothes peppered with little holes where creatures had burrowed out, the bodies missing bones and big scraps of flesh, not moving except with whatever—oh, she knew *what*—was moving under their skins, what had crawled into their heads and compelled them to walk here. What a mercy she knew so few of Grovemarket's folk.

The wings buzzed louder, almost a voice now. Loud then soft. Loud then soft. Like searching for its words. Was it speaking to her? She had no mind to listen, none at all.

Then she came to a point where the path narrowed, where there was no more going further and the light wouldn't reach through anyway. There was where she found Hunter Loach. Loach who'd come to kill what had taken the folk of Grovemarket. She only looked a moment at his face and the gored holes of his eyes where wasps had burrowed out of the jelly.

He'd fallen lifeless at the base of what looked like a shed. But though it was made of wood, it wasn't a shed, nor any kind of peoplemade structure. It was a tower of daub, tall as three of her. Mud and wood, the work of such unnumbered wasps they'd swallow the moonlight and starshine flying all at once.

There was a doorway in that daub tower. Standing at its threshold, feeling the waspwing song in her teeth and bones, everything told her to turn back.

But wings swelled and hushed, and this time there was no doubting she heard a voice. "MOTHER," it said.

The walls of the daub tower were alive wings that glistered in the lamplight, and the way in was so thick with flying wasps the light only got a few fingers deep.

"MOTHER. CLOSER. COME," said the hum of a thousand thousand bodies, and Tame found something in her partway between courage and foolishness, and allowed herself, one last time, to be something other than a wisewoman.

The wall of wasps parted like curtains to let her through. For as cold as the autumn night was, the inside of the daub tower was feverwarm, and warmer with each inward step. Until Tame found what was calling out.

An effigy of mud and hurt made flesh.

Sat down on its brittle legs made from daub and scavenged flesh and bone, rooted in the same spot where she'd left it years ago, was a child of mud and wood and glassy wings. It was bigger than a child of six; almost mansized, but formed with the roundness of a baby's shape. The daub and stolen flesh and skin were still damp and fresh around the shoulders and haunches and in the outstretched hands that had been reaching for her for who could say how long. Its face was like her own, but she found no reflection of her in its eyes, a pair of disk-shaped nests which quivered with the clamor of winged bodies crawling out of clustered tunnels.

She knelt into the crackling floor of daub, cast aside her lamp and knife, and she pressed her ear to the thing's brittle chest, felt the fragile weave of its patchwork skin creak, and heard the steady throb of a heart built from a storm of wings. She wasn't running this time.

"What do you want of me?"

And it answered as it had before, from its roiling heart, in a thrumming buzz that rose and hushed to form the starts and ends of sounds that made words. "MOTHER. CHILD. BACK CAME. GIVE FOR."

"What?"

"YOU. GIVES FOR. CHILD."

Gives for. Dragging itself out of death must've turned it around.

Forgives.

Turning its words right, she understood, and with understanding came more hurt and something close to but not quite fear, whose roots dug even deeper. Love.

Tame listened to her child's buzzing, crawling heart, and a sheltering blanket of wings enfolded her.

Take Care

S. P. MISKOWSKI

Every time Gillian started to feel guilty, she gripped the steering wheel tighter and stepped harder on the gas pedal. The rush of acceleration took her breath away. Doubt scattered like dust and gravel on the road. She wanted to lean forward in the driver's seat and scream through the windshield at the naked sky.

Five days after the layoff, the store owners hired a grief counselor for one session. Not for the employees who were let go, but for the remaining ones facing an indefinite period of work from home.

The counselor was a pale man in his forties who wore a baby-blue cardigan over a button-down shirt and urged everyone to call him Tom. He described what they were experiencing as "survivor's guilt," a term they had only heard in relation to tragic events like terrorist attacks, airplane crashes, and war.

The situation at Waverly's was serious, but no one had died. A beloved downtown institution since the 1950s, the bookshop had faced challenges for decades, always adapting and surviving.

Then came Covid-19. Despite all efforts—trimming schedules, offering curbside pickup and home delivery—eventually the owners directed the manager, Karlie, to let the part-timers go. The Cull, as everyone morbidly called it, relieved payroll of two college students, an aspiring animation artist, and a longtime clerk named Jane Kettering.

Tom assured the remaining employees, isolated at home, that the awfulness and strangeness and loneliness brought on by the pandemic was not their fault. He recommended they invest in "joyful hobbies" like designing kites or learning to play a ukulele.

Waverly's was paying for the Zoom session, but they were on their own if they wanted further counseling. Tom signed off by admonishing them to "take care."

⚜

Karlie kept reminding her assistant, Gillian, how much she hated to let Jane Kettering go. The thirty-something clerk in lumpy sweaters and knit slacks had been a part-timer for six years, never asking for a pay increase, never balking at schedule changes.

It was Gillian's idea to make a clean sweep. She thought it was a smart suggestion, further proof of her leadership skills.

"If you keep Jane and nothing improves over the next three months, you'll have to let her go anyway. And a second layoff will destroy morale."

Karlie stabbed at her Caesar salad, a look of indignation on her mild face. "Scientists will find a cure by then, won't they? Surely this can't go on more than a few weeks?"

Eleven months later, after the bistro had closed for good, Gillian recalled that lunch conversation with a sense of wonder. Customers talking conspiratorially across small tables. Couples kissing and holding hands. The air itself, flowing through the corner bistro, seemed to contain a sparkling energy.

⚜

Eventually, with staff vaccinated, Waverly's was able to re-open during regular hours. Customers observed social distancing, wore masks, and availed themselves of the lemon-scented hand sanitizer—most of them without grumbling.

From Gillian's vantage point, she could see the front desk and cash register behind a sheet of plastic. She watched a clerk open a shipment and arrange hardcover copies of bestsellers on a display table. When her phone rang, she answered with the standard greeting.

"Waverly's. We're happy to hear from you. How can I help?"

"To whom am I speaking?" a woman asked.

"This is the assistant manager," Gillian replied.

"Gillian?" Something familiar in the inflection, the woman pronouncing her name as though it were spelled Gilly Ann. A pronunciation Gillian had often corrected, to no avail.

"Jane?" Hoping she was wrong. "Is this Jane Kettering?"

"Yes," Jane said. "I have a problem and I need your help."

That night Gillian gazed out her apartment window at the shuttered dance club across the street, the closed physiotherapy clinic on the corner. In her living room she surveyed shabby rugs, IKEA lamps, the dilapidated armchair she was saving up to replace.

Jane's story was odd but at least she wasn't asking for money. Almost a year had gone by since they had worked together, yet Gillian recalled every little thing about the woman.

More than the lingering scent of violet soap. More than the leaves embroidered on the collars of her blouses. More than her slightly stooped shoulders and Tupperware containers of carrot sticks and graham crackers.

Jane had the air of a squirrelly teenager hoping to make friends at camp. She sometimes put on a fluty, fake English accent while "a-hunting" an obscure volume in the stacks, asking the books themselves in a high-pitched voice as she passed, "Where, oh where can you be...?"

On the phone, Jane had spelled out the problem: The day before she'd been let go, she had borrowed a two-volume copy of *Little Women* from Waverly's. One of the other part-time clerks had accepted the set as part of a larger estate collection, the kind customers dragged in from time to time without knowing what they had. The customer accepted a flat rate and left.

Before the clerk started estimating value for the new inventory, Jane had swooped in. She only wanted to show the set to her mother, who was disabled and who had loved Alcott's books as a girl.

Because the layoff had been accomplished impersonally, over the phone and via email, Jane never had a chance to quietly return the borrowed set. Time had passed, and more time. She didn't want anyone to think she'd stolen the volumes. She didn't know what to do.

"Everyone used to borrow," Jane explained. "We were careful, and it was never a problem. Honestly, I only wanted to show it to my mother," she said. "I feel terrible about this. I can't leave Mom alone long enough to come into the city. So, if you wouldn't mind picking up the books...?"

Gillian did mind. The address was far outside the metro area. But she agreed to make the drive after doing a bit of research.

The 1868 edition Jane described was worth about $25,000. Gillian imagined returning the valuable, unexpected asset to Waverly's. The owners would be thrilled. Karlie would be blamed for the oversight. With the right attitude, Gillian might even be hired as Karlie's replacement.

Gillian studied the map on her phone. She knew Jane had taken the bus to work. Apparently that journey involved a transfer with a brisk twelve-minute walk. Gillian couldn't believe anyone would make that trip two or three times a week for six years, in all weather, for a part-time job at Waverly's.

The rain started soon after she pulled out of the underground garage, a soft drizzle. She felt a stab of joy, heading out on a sort of adventure. Away from downtown traffic, beyond brightly painted condos and high-rises with security fences, Gillian concentrated on the landscape while radio news grumbled like white noise: *collapsed condo tower, assassination attempts, billionaires in outer space, shootings, vaccine boosters, wildfires...*

Thinning forests and uncultivated fields flew by. She expected pasture-land next, but around the next curve the horizon was suddenly dominated

by a sprawling subdivision. Weathered around the edges, covering fields
and hills, ending at a fringe of woodland in the distance.

Most of the houses were built in imitation of craftsman style, but they
were generic, without special features and detailing. A peeling billboard
faced the road, to entice potential homebuyers: *GOLDENDALE.*

The navigation system indicated the address was coming up. Gillian
pulled into the driveway, parked, and sat contemplating the neighborhood
beyond Jane's house.

Some blocks were partially developed, equipped with traffic lights that
didn't appear operational. Most houses looked unoccupied. Sidewalks were
overgrown with weeds. The yellowing grass between homes was littered
with busted tires, broken microwaves, sofas with stuffing spilling out, a
blackened spot marking the site of a recent campfire.

"Hellooooo!"

Gillian jumped in her seat. She almost gave herself whiplash jerking
around to the left where Jane stood, slightly crouched at the knees, peering
through the driver's side window.

"Oh no!" Jane shouted, doubling over, laughing. "I'm so sorry!"

Gillian put on a paper mask before grabbing her canvas tote. Climbing
out of the car, she forced a bright smile and then realized it didn't matter.

"If you could see the expression in your eyes!" Jane said, her voice mitigated by a cloth mask painted with smiling lips.

Jane ushered Gillian along the path from the driveway. The house's
exterior was dove-gray, the mailbox embellished with ivy leaves.

"Watch your step," Jane warned as they entered a spacious living room.
It looked as if the residents were just moving in—or out.

Gillian expected bookcases, but there were none. The central feature
was a Zenith TV with a 12-inch screen, occupying one corner on a portable
stand.

"I enjoy classical concerts, and the occasional British murder mystery,"
Jane said. "Have you seen a series called *The Curator?*" She was lapsing into
that fake English accent.

Gillian pretended not to notice. "No," she said.

She took in the room: kitchen at the back of the house, a staircase,
portable card table with a game of Solitaire spread across it. There was a

sofa and coffee table but no other furniture. In places where one would expect an armchair and ottoman or a bookcase, the carpet retained an imprint, a shadow of whatever once occupied the space.

"Are you hungry?" Jane asked. "I hope you are!"

Gillian was stunned. "I wasn't expecting lunch," she said. "I was hoping to be back by—"

"Oh, no," said Jane. "I won't hear of it. Let's have a bite, then you can be on your way. Look, the sun's come out for us!"

A break in the clouds sent a streak of sunlight to the garden out back. The windows began to glow.

Jane took forever hauling out dishes, silverware, jars of jam, and baked things with dabs of frosting on top. Gillian offered to assist. Jane refused as if offended by the idea. She kept returning to the house, rummaging through the kitchen.

Gillian studied the dead grass around a rotting Adirondack chair lying in a heap. Nearby was a patch of bare dirt. It looked like the grave for a family pet, but there was no marker.

She caught a flash of brown and white fur in the vacant lot next door. Something shook the tall grass over there, jumped sideways, and disappeared. She wondered if leash laws were enforced this far from the city.

"Isn't your mother joining us?" Gillian asked when she saw there were only two place settings.

"Oh, no," said Jane. "She ate before you arrived. She's taking a nap."

Lunch wasn't too awful. The tea was plain orange pekoe. The frosted desserts were miniature muffins, the salad a droopy combination of romaine and spinach.

The necessity of removing their masks to eat was something Gillian hadn't anticipated. But the garden table was large enough to keep them comfortably apart. Twice during the meal Gillian detected a slight movement behind the blinds, in an upstairs window of the house.

"Well," she said. "It's nice and quiet out here."

"Yes," Jane said. "Quiet as the grave. We don't have any birds."

"Sorry?" Gillian leaned forward, thinking she might have misheard.

"No birds," Jane said. "Someone noticed after the contractors started building. Apparently, Goldendale isn't on any migration path, and birds don't nest here. Not one species."

"How strange," Gillian said.

"It is," said Jane. "A couple of student researchers came here once, with meters and scanners. They discovered toxins in the soil samples. From a manufacturing plant years ago. Apparently, they didn't clean up as well as they claimed."

"God," said Gillian. "That's terrible. Can't you sue the developers?"

"The company's gone out of business. Or they changed their name. They left town a long time ago."

"Well, can you sell the house?" Gillian asked, watching a fly hover over the jam jars.

"No," Jane said. "We tried. It seems Dad paid too much for this place, and he took out a second mortgage when Mom got sick. And then he died."

Gillian's head wobbled involuntarily. Nerves. Exasperation.

"You know what, I need to make a quick trip to the—"

"Powder room?" Jane asked. "Follow the stairs to the second floor. First door on your left. I'll tidy up and get these things into the kitchen. I don't like the look of those clouds. We may be in for another spot of rain."

On her way Gillian stopped to re-examine the sparsely furnished living room. She half-hoped to find *Little Women* just lying somewhere, but the place felt spartan and pathetic.

She'd never seen locks quite like the ones on the front and back door. The mechanism was set high with two bolts sliding in opposite directions. She wondered what Jane had to fear in this half-completed suburb. Feeling wicked and spiteful, she flipped both bolts to the unlocked position before she went upstairs.

She found the first door on the left. But her curiosity directed her to the right, across the hall.

If a mad sugar plum fairy decorated a girl's bedroom in the dark, Gillian imagined it might turn out like this: a canopied bed in pink satin; a chipped curio cabinet full of thimbles; a brightly painted paper fan pinned to the wall, a fan Gillian recognized because she had once given it to Jane as a lazy, last-minute Secret Santa gift. No sign of any books.

A clanking noise from the kitchen downstairs made her flinch. She left the room as quietly as possible and crossed the hall to the bathroom.

After a pee she washed her face, rubbed sanitizer into her hands, and replaced her paper mask. A comical image occurred to her: Jane with her hair in curlers, reading a precious volume of *Little Women* in the bathtub.

"Oh, lady of leisure, where lieth those books?" she asked, mocking Jane's fake accent.

For the hell of it, she searched inside the vanity. She discovered nothing but a stack of folded towels and a vague scent of mildew.

She turned to leave, but she was stopped in her tracks by a swishing sound in the hall. Something moving slowly, rhythmically. Something like a broom sweeping.

A shadow slid back and forth under the bathroom door. Each time it moved there was a swift exhalation or sigh, followed by that sound like bristles dragged over a wood surface. Gillian couldn't picture whatever was going on behind the door, but she knew she had to get out of there.

Everything was getting too weird. She decided when the noise stopped, she was going to march downstairs, thank Jane for lunch, demand what she had come for, and leave.

Just then the bathroom door was flung open. Gillian jerked backward with a yelp.

The doorframe filled with a woman in a jumpsuit, broad-shouldered, her white hair pulled back from her face. The woman gaped at Gillian and took a step into the bathroom.

"Oh no!" Jane shouted from downstairs. "Mom, no! I said stay in your room!"

"You take too long," the woman said, shoving Gillian aside.

The woman pulled down her jumpsuit pants and sat on the toilet without lifting the seat. She held up one finger, wagging it as a warning.

"No, no, no!" Jane wailed, taking stairs two at a time. She leapt into the doorway and rushed toward her mother. But she wasn't quick enough. Streams of urine ran down the sides of the toilet onto the rugs and tiles.

Gillian retreated and slipped out of the bathroom into the hall. The last thing she saw was Jane's panicked expression as the door closed.

❚❚❚

Twenty minutes later Gillian waited in the garden, watching a slug make its way across a flagstone. She longed to drive home, hearing the whoosh of tires and the soft thud of windshield wipers. But her wish to leave was equaled by her need to complete her mission. Otherwise all of this was for nothing.

Empty flower boxes ran the length of the garden wall. Everywhere the attempted neighborhood sprawled, masses of weeds lay tangled with broken toys and outdoor furniture—nature repurposing streets and side-walks, vines sinuously claiming one chimney after another.

"What can I say?" Jane stepped into the middle of the garden, hands on hips, head bowed.

"Oh, it's—" Gillian knew she was supposed to say something comforting, but the exact words wouldn't come.

"I'm mortified," Jane interrupted. "Absolutely."

"Is she okay?" This was fine. This was a good thing to ask. Good enough.

"Mom's fine," Jane said. "I've turned on the television. She loves to sit on the sofa, watching." She glanced at the flagstone where the slug had made no discernible progress. "She doesn't do well with anyone new."

"Isn't it dangerous to let her roam around the house?" Gillian asked.

"She isn't stupid," Jane said. She stomped over to the flagstone and smashed the slug with her shoe, then dragged her heel across the dry grass to scrape off whatever was left. "Habits stay with people a long time after other memories fade," she continued. "Eating. Walking up and down stairs. Opening doors."

Gillian felt a stab of embarrassment, recalling her malicious moment, earlier, at the front door.

"Can she do that?" she asked.

"Do what?"

"Can she open doors?" Gillian asked. "And wander outside?"

Jane blinked. "Don't worry," she said. "The last project my dad finished before he died was installing double-bolt locks."

Gillian shook her head. "Oh. Um—"

"What's wrong?" Jane asked.

"I think maybe I left the front door—unlocked."

⚜

"I'm so sorry," Gillian said for the third time since they'd started searching. She wasn't sorry. She was irritated, and sick of Jane's company, but she was obligated to help since she caused the problem.

They were walking a section of road where sidewalks gave way to dirt shoulders, then open lots. Gillian had suggested taking the car, but Jane insisted the only way to approach her mother without frightening her was on foot.

"What does your mom's doctor say about her, you know, her condition?" Gillian asked. She was trying her best to sound more interested than she was.

"Oh," Jane replied, with a shrug. "What can he say? She has Alzheimer's."

"Isn't there something he can—?"

"Prescribe?" Jane said. "Wouldn't *that* be nice? If we could all take a pill to make everything okay? Sign me up!" She laughed behind her mask, a sound that was half-snort and half-bark. Then she turned and walked away.

Gillian thought of her own parents, in decent health and comfortably sequestered at their beach house in Ocean Park. She tried to imagine taking care of them without help until they died. She couldn't do it, couldn't see herself in that picture at all.

They stopped briefly to scan the intersection. One street was partially paved, dotted with street lamps and a sign reading *Fielding Lane*.

"There must be some type of assistance," Gillian said. "For these situations."

"What situations?" Jane asked.

"Caring for a parent who wanders off unless you keep track of her every minute of the day. It seems like you need help," Gillian said.

Jane quit scanning the vacant yards. She turned toward Gillian. Only half her face was visible, but it was obvious that some deep and chaotic anger flickered just beneath the skin, just behind the eyes.

"Well, m'dear," Jane said, her voice flinty but no longer tinged with an English accent. "One doesn't have to keep track every minute, if one keeps the doors locked."

Abruptly she went stomping down another partially paved street. Gillian followed, wondering at the liability if Mrs. Kettering couldn't be found, or came to harm.

They passed a house covered in graffiti. A dented washing machine sat in the driveway.

Gillian caught up with Jane and tried to keep pace. "I feel like this is partly my fault," she said.

Jane stopped to study the shifting clouds overhead. "It's entirely your fault," she said. "Why did you unlock the door?"

Gillian couldn't answer. A second of irresistible perversity and disrespect? A desire to see if it would matter to anyone? She was convinced, nothing in Jane's house could be serious. How could she ever explain *that*?

"I don't know," she said.

Ravaged lots lay on either side of the women, the homes only half completed. Nothing had been planted in the ghostly yards.

Jane stretched out her arms, taking in the surrounding neighborhood. The only sounds were an airplane overhead and two dogs, far away, snarling over a bone or a stick.

"You have no idea how it felt," she said. "Holding a monthly pass in my hand, waiting at the bus stop for my escape."

Gillian couldn't read the expression in Jane's eyes. She sounded nostalgic and angry at the same time.

"I felt contempt for the passengers who fell asleep," she said. "I would never do that! I was on a new adventure every time I climbed aboard the bus. I was leaving. I was free!"

"Have you thought about hiring help?" Gillian asked. "So you could get out of the house once in a while?"

"My dad was the help," Jane answered. "When I had a part-time job.

Then Karlie fired me. A month after that, my father died, and the insurance was only enough to keep us alive."

"I—I," Gillian sputtered.

A raindrop splashed Jane's forehead. It slipped down her face and disappeared beneath her mask. She nodded at Gillian and shouted, "There she is!"

She was pointing to the far corner of a lot, empty except for a battered recliner. Seated in the chair with the handle cranked back and her feet elevated, Jane's mother lay with her eyes wide open, staring up at the darkening sky.

⚘

The room where Jane's mother slept was snug and warm. The bed they helped her into, in her nightgown, sat solidly on the floor. No lamps, no mirrors. She nestled down and, in a minute, she was snoring.

Descending the stairs to the living room, Jane said, "She wandered farther off than usual, this time. But she'll be okay."

"I don't know how you do this," Gillian said. "Or why."

"What do you mean?" Jane asked. "You only have one mother. She cares for you, and then you take care of her. Even if she wrecks the furniture, digs up the garden, and pees on the floor."

"I guess when people reach an age where they can't control their, you know..."

"She can," said Jane. "She has no trouble with her bladder, or her bowels."

"In the bathroom—" said Gillian.

"That wasn't accidental," Jane told her. "The geriatrician said, physically she's the healthiest patient he's seen in years. Healthy and mischievous. She ran off once and hid in the yard next door. I searched for an hour. When I found her, she had ticks on her legs."

Gillian sat on the edge of the sofa, unsure what to say. "But she lost control earlier, in the bathroom."

"She knows I'll clean it up," Jane said. "She forgets my name, but she knows I'm the one who washes her clothes. I'm the one who takes the

247

cookies away when she wants five more. I feed her and bathe her and sing her to sleep when she's afraid to close her eyes. I'm the mom now, and she resents me. Everybody hates Mommy. Nobody wants to be Mommy, but someone has to."

Gillian stood up but she was stuck, not knowing what would be appropriate to say or do at this point. "I should be heading back into the city," she said. "The rain's getting worse." She picked up her tote and took a few steps toward the door.

Jane replaced her mask with another cloth one, a tiny rosebud mouth painted in the center. She smoothed the wrinkles from her slacks.

"Wait just a minute," she began.

"I really have to get going," Gillian said. "If you can give me the book, we're all square. You took the set with good intentions. You called me to make things right."

"Make things right?" Jane asked.

"Yes," Gillian said. "In case Waverly's wants to know what happened. You didn't intend to keep the edition or sell it."

"Just a second," Jane replied, stepping between Gillian and the door. "Don't you want to know why I called you, and not Karlie?"

"Well," Gillian said, the strangeness of it occurring to her for the first time. "I answered the phone, so you spoke with me."

"You don't ask yourself many questions," Jane said. "Do you?"

"Are you stalling?" Gillian asked. "Give me the book right now, and we're done, okay?"

"Tell me why Karlie let me go."

Gillian shook her head. All at once their proximity was stifling. She detected the odor of violets and sweat.

"The owners told Karlie to let all the part-timers go," Gillian said. "There was no choice."

Jane crossed her arms. She swayed ever so gently.

"I'm not sure why you keep lying," she said. "Don't you remember Tracy, at the bistro? That place where you and Karlie ate lunch together all the time?"

Gillian tried to single out a face, or a nametag, among all the images of the bistro spinning in her head. "Tracy? No, not really."

"Well, that's funny," said Jane. "She remembers you. Last week she delivered our groceries. What a surprise! She couldn't get another restaurant job after the bistro closed. Now she delivers food to shut ins. We had a chat and she told me a story. Something she overheard last year, right before the layoff."

"A *year* ago? Can you hear yourself?"

"She remembered serving Karlie the specialty Caesar," Jane said as if this were physical evidence.

"I have to be going," Gillian mumbled, rummaging through her tote for keys.

"I'm not stupid, Gillian," Jane said.

"If you don't return the books..." Gillian warned. But she had nothing to back it up.

Jane laughed. "Philosophical question, Gilly Ann: If a person is as good as they can be, every day, getting by on breadcrumbs, stretching every dollar, trying to make lemonade out of lemons, and life comes over and just *crushes* them—does that mean it's *stupid* to be good? Don't look away, this is a question that *matters*, Gilly Ann. And you don't seem to take it seriously..."

"What's wrong with you?" Gillian hissed.

"Me? My sick mom wandered outside alone," Jane said. "Thanks to your negligence."

"Why *did* you call me?" Gillian asked.

"Why did you tell Karlie to get rid of me?"

Gillian blinked as though she'd been slapped. She had kept secrets before, put herself ahead of others at school and at work, but she'd never been found out. She had never been caught in the blatant act of sabotaging someone. Immediately she fell into a defensive mode.

"What difference does it make after all this time?" she asked.

Jane laughed. A wild bark with a hint of hysteria.

"What *difference*?"

"Give me the book!" Gillian shouted.

This time the slap was real. Hard and fast as a flying rock, Jane's right hand smacked the side of Gillian's face.

She lurched toward the only escape route. Reaching past Jane, she caught hold of the doorknob, and then remembered the lock. She reached up, to throw the bolts open, and Jane stepped around behind her.

She felt Jane's fingers catch in her hair, scratching her scalp, yanking her backwards into the living room. The two women tumbled onto the floor and rolled.

"What are you doing?" Gillian screamed. "Let go!"

She pulled free, scrambled to her feet, and rushed for the door again. Jane hurtled past her, landing against the flat surface hard enough to rattle the frame.

"Get out of my way!" Gillian yelled, trying to push her aside.

"You're not as clever as I thought you were," Jane said, taking hold of her wrist. "All afternoon you only stayed to get your hands on a book. Do you see any books anywhere?"

It was true. Gillian had been in every room of the house. Her memory clicked through frame after frame, stopping at the patch of dirt in the garden. The spot she had taken to be a pet's grave.

"I haven't read a book in months," Jane said. "The last time I tried to take the bus—nowhere, just down the road to a 7-Eleven—Mom climbed on a chair, unlocked the back door, and buried my books in the garden! All of them!"

With that Jane pushed her and she fell sideways, landing on one hip on her tote bag. She looked up to see Jane reaching for her once more, reaching for her throat.

In one swift movement a pair of arms encircled Jane and hoisted her up. Screaming, airborne, flying, Jane was out of control, her feet involuntarily kicking as she was spun around and around. Just as suddenly, she was dropped on the floor and her tormenter stepped back to point at her and laugh.

Gillian turned quickly from the white-haired woman who now stood behind Jane, laughing. Wagging a finger in the air.

The last thing Gillian glimpsed was Jane's furious expression, her cheeks flushed crimson, as she slammed the front door shut.

Outside, Gillian fished the fob out of her tote, and signaled the car. The headlights blinked twice, and the locks popped open.

When she took off, the tires gave a rubbery shriek against the asphalt. Overhead masses of clouds roiled light gray to slate. In her peripheral vision she caught something hare-like, close to the ground, zigzagging away through the dead grass.

In a panic, she checked the rearview mirror. The backseat was empty, of course. She hit the gas hard, leaned forward gripping the wheel, and didn't let up until she saw the ghostly outline of the city etched against the rain-filled sky.

Mother Trucker

WAILANA KALAMA

My mother hits the moose in the pitch black of 4:32 a.m. There's almost nothing to see, just a blur of limbs burnt sepia by the headlights of her truck. But it's the noise that really grinds its hooves in—a startling, thunderous clap that blooms from the moose's body into the hood, into the steering wheel, shaking the world around my mother with shocks and aftershocks, and all that metal and flesh that make up her and her truck absorb it like a dried-out towel.

But that isn't the strangest thing that happens that day.

Picture this. A marmot peeks its head out from its den in a scree slide. It yawns away hibernation, yawns away slow breaths, wakes up in pillows of fat. A sleepy metabolism wheels into gear. The little ones drop out of its womb, gently like pebbles, three wriggling, one still. This one isn't moving at all, not even breathing. Is it hibernating? No, it doesn't work like that. Newborns don't go into hibernation, not right away.

But—but what if?

In the quiet muck of your burrow, a tiny doubt bites, not slinking away any time soon. You sniff the sour air. How can you be so sure? What do you do? Give it to the foxes?

Or wait—wait until it wakes up, knowing that it most likely never will? And, if you wait, how long do you wait?

And, worst of all, what if it's actually awake, there in its dark, grimy corner, watching you with its beady mirror eyes, watching you waver, watching you hesitate?

❦

The day before she hits the moose, my mother is hugging the leeward side of the Rockies on the Alcan Highway in her 8-wheeler. Snow littering the filter strips turns into streams by mid-morning. A blaring sun fixed steadfast in the cold firmament. The kind of morning that feels like it's been ordered special just for all-nighters like her.

It usually takes her around twenty-five hours from Dawson Creek to Fairbanks, longer if she clips a car. And the way things are with her now, squeezed into a dreamlike vise by sun and sleeplessness, that's not so farfetched. The tractor stinks of weeks of sweat and snow tracked in, long overdue for a vacuum. Even though she hasn't eaten in nine hours, my mother doesn't notice her breakfast bagel has fallen down into the space between the trash and desiccated Clorox wipes.

She's already been driving two days from down south, catching curl-legged naps on the bottom bunk behind her seat like a sleeping badger. Yesterday, though, she had to push through all night to make it to Dawson Creek in time for the loading at dawn, kept awake by hot flashes and the caffeine pills she'd slipped into the glove compartment. She's exhausted by now, that kind of exhaustion you just can't shake, the kind that burrows in your pelvis, in vertebrae you never knew existed. And she still has a full day left to go.

❦

My mother is the most stubborn woman I've ever known. She powers through cramps and clots of blood falling out onto her underwear, even days on the road. It's her way of keeping on A to B, because she feels it's all she deserves, because she knows if she stops, stops to think, she'll never make it past Whitehorse. Plus, she's not going to let something as selfish as menopause slow her down.

It's been five summers now since she first picked up an engraved mesh cap from the Boss. He'd looked her up and down and said Tala was too pretty a name for a truck driver. The sort of name you'd give a flower. She'd smirked and told him it meant beggartick in Tlingit, and he hadn't stopped laughing at that bullshit for six minutes.

So here she is, left cheek and forearm sporting a tan one shade deeper than the right. Butt growing like an exponential number. Her jaw's the envy of every Ken doll, and sculpted gashes on the sides of her mouth form whenever she slides her credit card over a counter. Every piece of clothing is company-issued, from her rain jacket to her yellowing blue jeans, except for the Salomon boots her father had given her years ago, back when he was still alive. That time, the last time he visited, her as pregnant as a mare, he'd told her he understood her choice to stay with her unborn daughter on the West Coast, instead of coming home. *You're such a good mother.*

She hadn't believed it even then.

Scouring the 97 North means wild turns, steep grades, and gravel kicked up into thick clouds of dust this side of the Rockies. It'd all be a breeze for my mother if it weren't for the hundreds of gallons of mare piss she was hauling up to Alaska. Ironically, it's an ingredient in menopause pills. Hormone therapy. Or so she's heard. She has to mind the brake pedal more than she likes to. She powers through cities with trade posts for names, passes roadside hamlets and lines of lodgepole pine squatting at the base of the mountains.

Every so often, her glance cuts to the left, into the stretch of snow-powdered peaks and forests that seem to go on and on and on. Like she's looking for something she left behind. But then her eyes dart away, gluing once more to the dash and its nest of cables and wires. Whatever she's lost, it's long gone already. Truth is, west, east, south with the cargo—nowhere's safe, except that snaking road in front of her.

She flips on the radio but it's all tabloid news and conspiracy theories. The closer to the Rockies, the wilder the stories: Bigfoot, lizardmen, UFOs. The mountains have a way of making screenplays out of shadows. Then you've got those urban legends you're never quite sure aren't just gossip. In the city parks of Fort St. John, someone's been throwing acid onto babies while they sleep in their strollers. Up in Fort Liard, the DJ at 98.5 FM reads off an ad for a child's used skeleton in the local Craigslist. For medical reasons, the DJ assumes, before cracking a joke at the asking price: $33 Canadian, 60% off.

❦

In the old days, my mother had a lot more problems. With money, with men, with roofs that kept changing. She moved out west for a marriage that left her with a bone-rooted bitterness. And when she got pregnant, she didn't tell my father. She just left him.

When her own father died, she didn't even go to the funeral. I think part of her figured he wasn't really dead. That as long as she didn't go back, things would be the same at home as they'd always been. He'd be there on his doorstep, beer belly sticking out from under his shirt, ringing her to pick up some chicken thighs on the way home. As long as she kept her distance, he'd always be there on the porch, waving her in as she pulled up on the driveway.

And then I was born. They say having a child is like having your heart taken out of your body. And it's still beating, pumping with that same wild instinct, only now it's outside and open season for all the storms and landslides and whatever else the world lifted from Pandora's evil box.

I guess some people, they're just too weak for all that.

❦

It's 1400 miles from Dawson Creek to Fairbanks, her boss used to say, and there's a problem for every mile. Pulling out from a station near Pink

Mountain, she clips a Toyota going 60.

Don't swerve, he'd always told her. Never swerve. Even if you smack the car full-on like an ox. Keep going like you always did. You might hit it, you might not, but a 20,000-lb truck swerving in the middle of a two-lane is a hundred times more dangerous.

"You swerve, you hit the ditch, you lose the load—anything at all— know what the cops will think? Stupid trucker fell asleep at the wheel, that's what. You gotta go in lightly, so you tag the car—not trying for any real damage, you know—but if you at least get paint wipes on the truck, then we can prove something." And so my mother paints like Monet, in staccato punctuations. *Bang!* She carves the license plate down onto the notepad she keeps on the dash and makes a few calls, makes a statement to the cops in nearby Buckinghorse and is out of there within five hours.

But this means she has to make up time. Meaning, no sleep this night. She pops a few more pills. But they're almost like candy compared to the power surges in her body that keep her awake—white-hot, blasting from her core to her palms, sousing every crevice in sweat. She blasts the A/C, making it as early spring inside here as out there.

It's not until Fort Nelson that she starts to have hallucinations. Forty-two hours without sleep will do that to you. This time it's rolling marmots, twice the size they ought to be, rushing the boulders on the roadside, hopping from one signpost to the other. And while part of her knows this isn't real, she watches with a sort of mellow satisfaction at her own insanity, watching it play out without any doubt, while another part of her asks, in all seriousness, what marmots are doing at this low altitude. It can't be more than 100 yards from where she is, and yet here they are, teeth gnashing, tapping on each other, their heads bobbing up and down on the moss-mush. Biting, gnawing, tearing into each other's cheeks, jumping on their little pups and sinking teeth into their fat and fleshy coats.

My mother knows what's in her cargo this time, and it's not that she doesn't care, it's that she can't. She fixes her eyes on the road because she doesn't want to think of those sixteen barrels topped to the brim with mare piss just behind her. She doesn't want to picture it: fifty pregnant mares sardined in a warehouse, strapped to pumps and emptied of their piss, foals falling out and into the grinder.

If they gave out awards for denial, she'd get a big trophy, the kind they give out at college football matches. But this isn't what makes her a villain, it's just the underline.

One day, she promises herself. One day I'll drive it off a cliff, all sixteen barrels and me.

Close to midnight, she stops to refuel at a gas bar off of Muncho Lake, the name "Yukon Motel" blaring at her in yellow lights. Fluorescents light up Canadian roadside signs that promise better days she'll never have: Kiskatinaw Curved Bridge 2km ahead; RV Park −Vacancy; Muncho Tackle & Bait. The exhaustion's driving a wedge into her skull, so once she's all filled up, she leans back a moment to catch a break. That's when she hears the wail.

It sounds almost exactly like a baby crying. My mother tenses up like a bullet about to fire. Grips the steering wheel. Doesn't want to move at first, just wishes it would stop. The wailing goes on and on, a stuck record, hoarse. Like it's sick or something. And with each second, it seems to be getting closer and closer. So my mother straightens up and peers out the window.

Standing below, on the other side of the glass and lit up by fluorescents, is a woman with wild, wiry curls. Her red mouth dilated into a rectangle, pain and saliva dripping from it like a running faucet. She keeps wailing, shrill like a baby, even as my mother locks eyes with her. Her eyebrows droop downward, eyelids swollen with saltwater. She's crying, only it's more like a caricature of crying, like you might see in a school play. With a desperate blush to her cheeks.

This doesn't go well with my mother. She jerks the truck door open, smacking the woman full in the teeth, her head and blood flying back in an apostrophe.

She pummels into the woman, punching and slapping at her face, breasts, and forearms where the woman tries to defend herself.

"Shut up!" my mother screams at her, her throat rusty. "Shut up shut up shut up shut up!"

All the while, the woman keeps wailing and wailing out of her bloody hole, hiccupping from time to time, wanting a blanket, wanting a teat, wanting just please to be safe and secure and far from harm. And my mother, she just stands there, full of heat.

Full of rage.

"What the fuck are you doing?"

A man in a baseball cap and red parka faces her square. He's in my mother's bubble as quick as a boxer, shoving her shoulder hard.

"Don't touch her! What the hell is wrong with you?" He picks up the wailing woman by her armpits and glares at my mother like she's something inhuman, like I expect anyone would, and slowly it dawns on her that she would, too.

My mother slinks back into her truck while the bloody woman wails, quieter now, and yanks the stick shift bigger than her arm. She floors the gas as quickly as she can, back to the shelter of the highway.

My mother left me to die in the forest off the Alcan when I was two months old.

It was raining in big dunks, like it always does that time of year in the Yukon. I was with her—in blankets and listening to rustles in the bushes, feeling her all around me, her whispers and coos, her inky hair falling over my face—and then I wasn't. Then I was all alone.

I remember spruce trees making a crown in the night sky. And me, flinging out cries into the darkness, shrieking at it, blaming the rain with all the raging fury of an infant, compounding the biting wind, the damp leaves, the woman I'd clung to for eleven months into one, absolute emotion.

And I screeched my lungs out.

That was before I tasted wet dirt in my mouth. Before my fists dug into the earth, squeezing, feeling the heat of the earth. Something stirring in the soil.

This is the part where I explain why my mother did what she did, how she felt torn and battered, cornered by isolation and grief, how she didn't really want to, but felt she had to, how she had no one left in the world and couldn't take care of me and didn't want me to suffer how she'd suffered and I was better off gone and buried.

This is the part where I lie.

⚜

She forgot where she left me. For months she drove the same road, from point A to point B, and B to A again, foot hovering over the brake but never quite slapping it down. Sensing roughly where, but never quite sure. The exact location just out of reach. When the hot flashes started, I think she felt it was her penance, in a way.

And she took her sleeplessness out on the open road, feeling somehow contained and swaddled in the heavy air of the truck, summer after summer, south to north and south again, for five years, every winter holed up in a hibernation, quietly disintegrating, slow murder by french fry and grease and gristle. And I was nowhere near to save her.

⚜

Twenty miles from Whitehorse, the moose flies out in front of her.

She lets loose a sharp cry, though she doesn't know it. It's raining and it's all she can do to keep her foot from the brake pedal.

As soon as she's safe to, she slows and stops the truck, gets out into the drizzle. She catches sight of the moose limping away in the red, burning tail lights, fading into the forest.

Even though she's shaken, she gets herself together enough to check the cargo. In the back, the sixteen humongous barrels of mare piss stand at attention.

The memory of the moose's wail draws whorls on her eardrums.

She drives another half an hour to Whitehorse, while the sky grows a shade brighter. Passing a couple of pickups honking at her like mad. She thinks maybe the nose of the truck is dented. She'll check it soon enough.

She backs up into a truck stop just outside of town, grabs her wallet. As she hops out, a guy in a gas station uniform is already at the hood, staring

260

at something. She feels a drop of premonition. She walks around to see what he's staring at and

The baby the baby the baby

Caught in the metal jaws of the moose guard is the slippery mess of a moose calf. Fur glistening with the sheen of afterbirth and blood, neck like paperclip, its back cloven hooves scratched down to almost nothing where they've been scraped on the road.

You're such a good mother.

The amount of afterbirth splattered on the face of her truck is enough to make it a lie.

The baby must have slipped out when she hit its mother, kicked its way to freedom and flight. Only, stuck in the moose guard, it couldn't get far. My mother feels a coldness beating against her ribcage and she keeps staring at the calf like it's a sculpture, vaguely aware that the station guy is talking to her, asking her questions, but it all seems far away and she can't.

She's thinking about the calf's mother, the mother who's not a mother, dashing into the darkness blind into the spruce, stomach sagging with unbirth, ears shredding with a shriek of the wild, of the womb, of the fold. For a minute it's all she sees, a moose tearing through branches, moans swallowed up by the rainstorm, being consumed by its own emptiness and no one's there to know, to see it. And all she wants in that moment is to absorb the shock, the pain, everything into herself. To undo, to erase it, to just take back all the pain she caused, please please *please...*

Come back come back come back

She knows she can't.

But she tries anyway.

My mother climbs onto the moose guard and slowly, gently, slips the baby out. It's not easy, but the afterbirth makes it easier. The gas station attendant is still talking to her but she can't hear him. The blood and who knows what else paints her clothes, smelling like sour earth and musk and new life.

She places the baby down on the pavement, covers it with her over-sized jacket. Then she climbs back into her truck and screeches due south.

❈

She drives back to the spot where she thinks she hit the moose. She parks the truck at the 20-mile mark, taps the emergency lights on, and, against all reason, dashes out into the rain, fumbling to zip up her hoodie, flipping up the hood over her head.

She searches for minutes, hours, she doesn't know how long. Boots stamping through a labyrinth of black spruce and trembling aspen. The rain pelting her outstretched arms just a breath away from freezing.

She knows it's here. Eyes peeled for a boulder in the shape of a hand. She hates herself for forgetting it, but that's not what's important right now.

She finds it.

She chose the stone, no taller than her hips, because it made her think of a palm outstretched, sheltering the clay beneath it. This way, it didn't feel quite like abandonment. More like a handing off.

And there I am, sleeping, not a day older than when she left me there five years ago. My nose blushing with snot, tufts of wet hair plastered to my head, still wrapped in the blanket, in the same folds her fingers remember making.

My mother is crying, wailing with guilt and self-pity and regret. She keeps saying *sorry, I'm so sorry*, gripping my arms, and it's her cold nose burying into my tiny self that makes me thrust my legs against her cheek.

Now it's my turn to scream.

I scream because I'm cold, I scream because I'm hungry, I scream because my mother left me all alone, I scream because I was somewhere else, somewhere below, safe and deep inside and now I'm in the rain, and there's so much noise, *so much noise*.

My mother pulls off the blanket and out around my flailing limbs comes tumbling dirt, twigs, and the ruins of a mouse nest. She brushes my naked body clean and clasps me in her zipped hoodie, starts laughing, still crying, and it's the tightness that finally calms me down.

262

I should've been dead, chilled to the bone, eaten by lynxes, but I wasn't.

I was waiting. Not breathing. And I saw—

The endless twists and turns of worms in the hollows of my armpit, my gums, my ear canals—

The aspen leaves turning green, gold, green again, gold again, green again and no one no one *no one no one*—

I saw it all.

🔖

She never wonders where I was. Even though it's been years since.

I think she's afraid to ask, to question her luck.

As for me—because I never forgave her, not really, or because I was too long there in the deep, below the mulch—I don't think all of me came back to her that drizzly morning.

Because she never chucked those sixteen barrels of mare piss and herself down a cliff.

She calls me her blessing every day, but I swear whenever I look at her, I can feel the dirt caked in my nails, smell the stink of wet leaves in my nose. And those things I saw in the muck, they make me grind my sweaty fists into the sheets every night. And, if I'm not careful, the heat of worm-ridden soil starts pressing against my eardrums.

Sometimes, to get away from mocking schoolmates and stifling classes, I duck under the school bleachers and listen to the radio. For months now, I've been hearing about women disappearing, taken right off the Alcan. Hitchhikers trying to leave the mountains. And the stats keep rising month to month. Turning people into numbers, what a thing. Some found on the roadside, mangled beyond recognition. Some never found at all, like they were just swallowed up by the earth.

But me, I know where they go.

And trust me, they're not hibernating.

They're awake for it all.

The Last Sin

GABINO IGLESIAS

Marta likes to sit at her small corner booth in San Antonio's El Mercado and watch people walk by. The mix of locals and tourists never fails to entertain her. The booth she shares with Juliana is barely decorated, and she thinks that's one of the reasons they don't get as many clients as they should. El Mercado is a festival of color, a veritable explosion of it, and their somber, unassuming booth can't compete with everything around them. Shiny luchador masks. Catrinas of all sizes dressed like brides, ballerinas, nurses, and a million other things. T-shirts emblazoned with funny messages like "TU ERES UN PENDEJO—YOU ARE MY FRIEND" and "La Chingona" hang from almost every corner. There are plates, mugs, nativity sets, traditional dresses, loterías, leather bags and belts, wall decorations, pop guns, ceramic crosses, and small glass animal figurines from Mexico and Peru everywhere, along with weeping figures of Jesus and pleading Virgin Mary statues. There are ukuleles for kids, wooden frogs that make a sound when you run a stick down their backs, cheap rings, earrings and bracelets, and longhorn skulls hanging from the top of some booths. The kitsch and the holy, the silly and the profane, the hilarious and the artistic; everything is packed into El Mercado in a perennial clash of colors and cultures.

Today is Saturday, so El Mercado is buzzing. Marta knows some of their regulars will stop by at some point because it's their day off. Some will be looking for a limpia or some other small work they're convinced will make their life better. They will come asking for her, for Marta la curandera. A part of her loves it. La curandera. She's their healer, their shaman, their sacred medicine woman. It makes her feel important, like she makes a difference in people's lives. She has the power of plants in her hands. She can make potions that help people. She can cure many diseases and some of the things she prepares walk a fine line between natural medicine and magic. Marta loves having the power of the earth at her disposal, and she sees her work as sacred.

Juliana is a different story. Juliana, with her impossibly black hair and hauntingly dark eyes, is a sin eater. She gets fewer clients than Marta. Many seek healing for a hacking cough that won't quit, a strange rash they picked up while on vacation, or a crush they want to bring into their lives, but few are willing to pay a woman to take away the darkness inside them, the grief and pain and guilt over some of the most horrible, despicable things they have ever done. Asking for help with a small problem is human nature, but a lot of people can't bring themselves to share their worst secrets.

The differences in what Marta and Juliana do mirror what they look like and the way they carry themselves, the way in which they carry the pain inside them. Both women navigate the world stoically, but in a shattered state. Both women know what it's like to lose the thing you love most. Both women have cracks in their hearts deep enough to bury the Grand Canyon, but they keep going, driven by curiosity and the small possibility of justice, and if there can be no justice, then revenge.

Marta and Juliana met after their daughters went missing and were then found dead. Marta's daughter vanished first. Marta had been working as a cashier at Dollar Tree at the time. She knew she was late picking up her daughter, but the woman who was taking over for her as the sole cashier in the store got stuck in traffic. Marta thought Isabel, whom she called Beli, would wait for her in front of the school, which was only a six-block walk to their house. The two teachers supervising the buses that day said Beli told them she was walking home. Someone snatched her before she got there.

Juliana's daughter, Amelia, suffered an eerily similar fate. She was twelve, just like Beli. She was walking home from a volleyball game just three days after Beli's disappearance when she vanished.

Beli's body was found a week later in some bushes in a suburban neighborhood ten miles from her school. Amelia's body was found by some tourists near a rarely used entrance to the River Walk two days later. Cause of death couldn't be determined for either girl, or for the third girl, who was found six days later. The bodies presented no evidence of any kind of violence, which was something Marta held on to when things got too dark and her grief threatened to crush her.

After the authorities gave up on their search, everyone refused to talk about the possibility of a serial killer roaming the streets of San Antonio in the middle of the day, and the news moved on to a new set of horrible things. Marta and Juliana were left alone, brought together by their grief. They ran into each other outside the local police station and immediately recognized each other. They melted into a hug that was far more eloquent than anything either one of them could've said. They became instant friends, their pain a bridge between their shattered hearts.

As the two grieving mothers talked, they learned their stories were not the same, but shared some cohesive elements that made them equal: loneliness and heartache. They were the same characters in a tragic, horrific play: lonely mothers who had lost their only daughters. Juliana's boyfriend had walked out on her when she was eight months pregnant. She'd never seen him again. Marta's husband, an undocumented worker from Venezuela fell from a roof while working construction and snapped his neck when Beli was eleven months old. Both women were alone in the world. Both women carried a pain in their souls only other mothers who have lost their babies could understand.

Since running into each other outside the police station, Marta and Juliana had cried together, worked together, eaten together, and had even lived together for six months when Juliana had some financial woes following the death of her daughter. The pain wasn't lessened by the presence of the other, but the knowledge that someone else understood the crippling, all-encompassing grief they each felt made them feel less lonely. When they cried, which was often, the other one was there, not to hold them but to cry with them, for them. In their endless heartache, they had found a traveling companion, and in a world that felt empty to them, that meant a lot. After a lot of time talking and holding each other, they had started dreaming about the future together, talking about maybe opening a restaurant and naming it after their daughters. During one of those conversations about the future, Marta had shared that she had skills that were better than her cooking, and she had told Juliana about her ancestral curandera knowledge. Instead of asking questions, Juliana had shared that she was a sin eater, just like her mother before her and her grandmother before that, and that she could devour the sins of both the dead and the living. The former was a service she provided for families who wanted to make sure their loved ones could enter heaven free of the burden of their worst sins. The latter was something she'd discovered by accident, but it was something that made a difference on this side of the veil, and Juliana liked helping living people much more than she liked helping the dead.

After learning what they could do, the two women never talked about opening a restaurant ever again. Instead, they pooled their money and rented a small hole in the wall in El Mercado, and started asking their clients to spread the word. They weren't rich, but they made enough to get by.

As time went by, they allowed life to grow around them. They had jobs and clients and bills to pay and shows to watch, so they spoke of their daughters less, which helped them keep the pain at a manageable level. Marta liked it that way.

From the throngs of people walking around El Mercado, a man emerged from a group and walked toward their booth. Marta looked at Juliana as a man approached them. Instead of talking to them, the man pulled his cell phone from his pocket and snapped a picture of their booth. A tourist. Marta and Juliana were used to it. They had a small sign in front of their booth that said SERVICIOS ESPIRITUALES and, below that, SPIRITUAL SERVICES. For those who knew, those two words were more than enough. For those who didn't, the two women looked like circus freaks sitting in a small, gloomy booth with faces etched by the burden of a horrific loss and the cancer of their endless sorrow. Those who didn't know were always the ones who snapped their photo without asking, just another reminder to them that no one cared about their rights, about their agency, about respecting women in this country.

Marta followed the guy with her eyes, trying hard to not wish him ill, but she could feel Juliana's eyes on her. She knew her friend wanted to say something, so she turned and smiled. Marta was expecting to hear a comment about the man, but Juliana's face betrayed much more than annoyance.

"What is it, Juliana?" asked Marta.

"I have to talk to you and I don't even know where to start," said Juliana, her eyes darting between her hands and Marta's face.

"Whatever it is, just say it."

Juliana took a deep breath before speaking. The act worried Marta, because it was not something her friend did often.

"You know some people like to meet with me in private," said Juliana. "You know, like I'm a secret. Like I'm a prostitute or something. As long as they pay, I don't mind." Juliana stopped talking. Marta nodded and hummed her agreement to encourage her to continue. "Well...the thing is that I got a phone call from a man about a week ago. He'd heard about me from a friend of a friend of a friend. You know how it is. The point is that he needed me. Real bad. That's what he said. We met at a coffee shop near that abandoned burger place that's a few blocks from my house. I had my little gun on me just in case because when it comes to men, you never know. He didn't look threatening or anything. He was well dressed, with jeans and a nice shirt. He said he needed my services. I said he had to tell me what it was so I could swallow his sin. He didn't flinch before telling me he had killed a girl. My blood ran cold. I guess he thought I wasn't moving because I wanted to see the money first because he dug into his pocket and pulled out a wad of cash. I took the money and told him to walk outside, get in his car, and roll down his window. I watched him leave the coffee place and get into a nice car. It was deep blue. My mind was racing, so that's all I remember. After a minute or so, I finished my coffee and walked out to his car. I told him I was going to get close to his face and that to anyone watching, it would look like I was giving him a kiss. I leaned forward, pressed my mouth against his thinking of the murder of a girl, and inhaled. I saw her, Marta. I saw the girl. It...it was Beli."

Marta had been listening to Juliana's story and her heart had skipped a beat when she said the man had killed a girl, but this was not how she expected the story to end. The pain came back as if some dam had broken inside her. The anger also returned. Everything flooded back into her system with renewed strength. Every scream, every tear, every suicidal thought, every night asking herself how this could have happened and wondering how she'd find the strength to carry on without her daughter.

"Beli?" Her daughter's name was the only thing Marta could utter, and the inflection she gave the word, the question mark her voice placed after her daughter's name, bothered her.

"Yes," said Juliana. "She looked just like those photos you keep of her."

Marta didn't know what to say. She didn't know what to do or how to react. Then her brain kicked into gear, a thousand thoughts released at once. Pain. Anger. Doubt. Vengeance. The things she felt mixed with the things she wanted. Then, from that hellish maelstrom, a clear, sharp idea emerged like a monolith rising from the dark sea after a cataclysmic event: she had to kill that man.

"Are you going to see—"

"Tonight. At the same place," interrupted Juliana. "That's why I'm telling you. I thought about waiting, after seeing what other things he had done. If he killed Beli, maybe he's the same guy who killed Amelia. I wanted to take care of him that night, but I need to know. And I want us to do this together."

Marta felt her capacity for words crumble. Emotions had taken over and speaking was impossible. She got up from her chair and hugged her friend.

✦

Marta and Juliana paced in an alley two blocks down from the coffee place twenty minutes before they were supposed to meet the man. Juliana said she had told him they had to meet there because this time she would have to kiss him for longer, and she didn't want anyone to see them.

Both mothers—both now mothers of eternal ghosts—had the small guns they'd bought for protection in their purses. They'd gotten them from

269

a man with an eye patch and a huge tattoo of a crying Virgin Mary on the left side of his neck. He'd told them he loved selling guns to women because he knew they had to put up with a lot of shit in life, and maybe his guns would one day help them to put a stop to something horrible.

When the blue car—a fancy sedan—went by and then pulled into the parking lot in front of the coffee place, Juliana signaled for Marta to follow her and moved into the alley.

A few minutes later, the man appeared. Marta looked at him as he walked toward them. Could this be him? Could this be the monster that took her daughter? She had to know before she pulled the trigger.

"Good night, ladies," said the man. His voice was like a thousand serpents trying to sound like a single human. Marta took a step back. "Hello, Marta," he said. Marta froze. Her feet refused to move under the weight of her fear.

"Who—"

"I'm not who you think I am. I'm much more," said the man. "I didn't do anything to your daughter, but I wanted you to be angry when you came here. Your suffering, now so fresh and near the surface, will make you taste better."

"Taste?" Marta was angry, confused, and afraid. She turned to Juliana and found her friend right behind her, with her gun in her hand and aiming at Marta's chest.

"What is this, Juli?" asked Marta, noticing Juliana had tears running down her face.

"I...I found the man who killed our daughters. I ate his sins. When I was sure it was him, I made him pay for what he had done. But I can't carry all that any more, Marta. I can't carry my own sins and those of everyone who comes to see me. I went looking for someone more powerful than me, someone who could eat some of the stuff I carry, and—"

"And here I am," said the man. Marta was about to turn when she heard Juliana's gun go off. The sound was too big for that small alley, and it bounced on the walls and slammed into Marta just like the bullet had.

Marta felt warmth exploding in her chest and immediately after that she felt her knees hit the ground. But she never fell because the man was there, holding her.

"Juliana needed some relief and I needed to feed, so we made a deal," said the man with a smile on his face. His teeth were tiny and sharp, and it looked like he had hundreds of them in his mouth. There was no tongue in there that Marta could see. "Juliana merely helps people, but what she takes in poisons her," said the man. "I'm different. The bad stuff—the pain, the grief, the hate—it nurtures me. Someone like you, someone so... broken, will keep me fed for weeks. All your suffering will sustain me, Marta. It will make me happy for a while."

Isabel.

Beli.

Her daughter's name was all Marta could think of as she lifted her head to look at Juliana, to make sure this wasn't a nightmare. Juliana was there, the gun shaking in her hand, her face full of tears.

"I swear to you I made him pay, Marta," said Juliana. "I had to eat everything he did to make sure. I had to know..."

Knowing the monster was dead was comforting, but the pain in Marta's chest didn't let her enjoy the feeling for long.

Beli, Marta thought.

"Beli," Marta said, her voice a universal whisper full of the pain of all the mothers who have lost a baby.

"Beli," said Marta again, her daughter's name the last thing she tasted before the man's mouth came to her and everything went dark.

Jacob's Mother

KATIE MCIVOR

I am not Jacob's mother.

This is important to remember, because (as I trim his fingernails and wash behind his ears and smooth back his hair before he falls asleep, his forehead soft and warm beneath my palm) my greatest wish is that I could allow myself to forget.

My subterfuge is an effort requiring constant diligence. When I pick up Jacob from school, I wear long skirts and sturdy boots like the other mothers. I stand with them at the gates and participate in gossip, although they think me shy. To evade inquisitiveness, I pretend that language is still a barrier. When Jacob runs out, chattering in Portuguese to his dark-haired friends, scuffing his new shoes in the dirt of the playground, I feel an intoxicating lightness, a genuinely physical uplift of joy, and it makes me smile. *That* I do not pretend.

We walk home together through the curving, tilted streets of this strange island. The day is hot; Jacob sheds layers as he walks, peeling off his shirt, extracting his feet from his shoes and swinging them by the laces. By the time we reach the house, he looks feral as a goat. He darts into the garden to burn off yet more energy while I sit in the kitchen and recharge. Later, he spreads his homework across the kitchen table and tries to insert questions around the edges of my guard: *What's sixty times eight? What's nine percent of two hundred?* He knows it's an effort for me not to answer him. I wedge my lips into a smile, concentrate on the fish frying in the pan, let him figure things out on his own.

◈◈◈

As far back as you can go, at the very beginning of time, there was only heat (too great for life) and the energy—the constant, enormous energy of things too tiny to see or feel— crashing and exploding against one another at high speeds. Quarks and antiquarks, electrons and antielectrons. Over time, they moved apart and the energy cooled. Now you can find them almost at rest (but always spinning, spinning, colliding), the tiny specks of matter which govern the course of time. They are some colors, or all colors, depending. I see them the same way Jacob sees sounds. In times to come, they will disperse into nothingness.

I remember the day Halliday came to see me. He intended his arrival to be unexpected, but I could see him coming in the trails of particles whose movement, if one can follow it, predicts all occurrences, and I went outside to meet him, even though I wasn't supposed to go outside. My hands were wet, a dishtowel draped over my wrist.

Halliday stopped at the garden gate when he saw me. His mouth went slack. I saw his mouth form the word *Nadia*.

I said, "Can I help you, Mr Halliday?"

He said, "I don't believe we've met."

Jacob toddled out of the front door behind me. He was always close to me in those early days, glued to me like a shadow. I bent to pick him up (my wet hands on his clothes, the child-fresh smell of his hair). He spotted and became briefly entranced by a blackbird hopping across the top of the hedge.

Halliday said, "I'm looking for Mr Tavener."

"He's at work," I said. "Don't you work together?"

His face changed. "So, he's told you about me." (This was incorrect, but

274

I said nothing.) "He's told me nothing at all about you," Halliday went on. "I know who you are, though. What you are."

Jacob had begun to grizzle at the cold air. I said, "I should get back inside."

As I closed the front door, Halliday called after me, "Tell him what he's doing is insane. Tell him he's insane."

⚅

Jacob's father circumscribes our lives like the movements of the sun. He is the point at the centre of the light cone, the expansion of possibilities through multiple dimensions; before that, darkness. When I opened my eyes and saw his face, the present began at that instant to spread into the absolute future, a widening of possibility at once pre-ordained and infinite, while behind me the perfect cone of the past stretched back and back forever. I turned my head, trying to see it, but it doesn't work like that.

In the centre of that bewildering expansion of light was a face, the eyes afloat with wonder, the mouth opening as I focused on it. Jacob's father uttered the first words I would hear: *Are you okay? Are you there? Can you hear me?*

⚅

Jacob adopted me instantly, and I him. I had been brought into his life for a purpose, but it was only in the face of his need for me, his uncomplicated joy at my existence, that I understood the meaning of this. To have a purpose is to have a soul.

Jacob's father brings equipment home from his work to test me. He likes to challenge my capabilities. I find it an amusing distraction and, more importantly, Jacob enjoys it. He burbles around the floor at my feet. He laughs when I outwit the equipment. I solve equations more quickly than the computer; I measure time more accurately than the cesium clock. Jacob likes it when I measure time. He asks me to time the interval between blinks of his eyelids, or the time it takes him to climb the stairs (at this, he grows faster every day). Sometimes I catch his father staring at

275

us oddly when we play this game. I suspect it is not a game he played with Nadia. But I am not Nadia.

(There are photographs of her throughout the house: snapshots of couples' holidays, of windswept walks, of a knife plunging into wedding cake. Jacob has her eyes.)

I can see the smallest cells of Jacob's skin. At the age he is now, his skin is young, the pores close-knit and perfect, capped by tiny hairs. Beneath that, he is a conglomeration of complex systems—respiratory, cardiovascular, digestive, muscular—and each system is made up of molecules, atoms, protons. As he grows, these systems grow with him. His atoms endlessly rearrange as new matter is incorporated into his body. I can see him at thirty, or at fifty, or at birth: his bawling entrance into the world, the blood which purpled his mother's thighs as she lay back, triumphant, opening her arms for the son she would never know.

Jacob's systems fascinate me. When he catches the scent of the doughnut stall on our walks around the park, I see the reaction igniting his olfactory neurons. When I play him a piece of music, he will tell me the color of it. His little voice (the short vocal cords, the undeveloped larynx) will pipe out, "Yellow. Yellow and green!" When he cries, I witness the miraculous passage of impulses from his brain to his lacrimal glands. From nothingness, tiny sparks become electricity, atoms combine to form water. The human body turns chaos into order. I wonder, sometimes, if my body does the opposite.

Jacob's father cries too. The first time this happened, I was the cause of it. He was holding my hands as we lay in bed together and after I spoke he gripped them suddenly, his eyes growing mirrored and glassy in the dark. He whispered, "I knew it! I knew you were her. Nadia, my Nadia."

I had been looking back along the light-line of his past, at particles which shimmered and shaped themselves in patterns of what had been, of what could only have been. He and Nadia often lay side by side like this, holding hands, and she often said to him, *You are the stars in my sky.* I wanted to make him happy. When I said the things that she had said, it made him happy.

Jacob finishes his homework and I serve the meal. He eats voraciously, as always. He wants to know where the fish came from. I tell him flatly, "The sea," but he presses and wheedles, wanting to know more, wanting me to trace the cone of its past back through time, as only I can. In the end I give in, as I always do: "This fish was born in the waters off this very island, at the foot of the volcano, where the land falls away into the deep water. She fed on crustaceans, shrimp, blue whiting. When she grew older, she travelled north through the colder regions of the Atlantic, then returned to her home island to spawn. At the time of her death, her liver contained small percentages of mercury and cadmium, which are toxic to humans. That is why I removed the liver before feeding her to you."

Jacob pulls a face. "Gross!" Then he grins and pops the last forkful of fish into his mouth.

The grin is his father's grin.

A memory assaults me: James Tavener turning from his computer screen, in the midst of analyzing my results, as he began to realize what I could do, began to map the abilities he had inadvertently given me. It was a grin of conspiracy, of gleeful wonder, of disobedience. There were rules, and those rules were for lesser men. He never intended to share me with the world. I know that now.

I get up from the table and start to wash the dishes. My neural fibers feel tight, my outer coating dry and neglected. As anxiety takes hold, I remember my first taste of dishonesty—and it was a taste, a metallic acerbity inside my mouth—as I handed Nadia's passport to the woman at the airport desk and waited for her to stamp it. She no more than glanced at my face before looking down to smile at Jacob, who was exhausted, thumb in mouth, clinging to my leg. She waved us through and my existence became a lie. I am not programmed to lie. I am programmed to nurture, to protect. The weight of my deception burdens me as I climb the steep streets of the island, slowing me, hampering my abilities. I am not Jacob's mother. I am not me.

Halliday returned one evening later in the year. We didn't hear him come in. We were down in the downstairs study Jacob in his playpen with a toy abacus, me on the workbench while his father made repairs to my outer coating, which always developed cracks during the colder months. I should have known Halliday was coming, but the soothing spread of the resin into my damaged surface had relaxed me and I was half in a doze.

The study had a low wooden ceiling and patterned Spanish tiles on the walls. It was decorated by Nadia, as was the rest of that house, before we burned it down. I can still picture the deft arrangement of color and pattern, can see her delicate hands at work, troweling grooves into the adhesive, laughing, four months pregnant, a bandana tied around her hair.

Halliday came down the stairs and stepped onto the Persian rug: an heirloom from Nadia's family, it had travelled across a continent. I heard the compression of fibers.

"Tavener," he said, "we need to talk. Leave that thing here and come upstairs."

Jacob's father didn't move. He was facing away from Halliday. His shoulders stiffened and he looked down into my eyes.

"You know it's not her, don't you?" Halliday said, his voice rasping through dry lips. "That thing isn't Nadia. It isn't human! If the university knew what you'd—"

"Get out," said Jacob's father.

"It's not legal, James. Come on, you helped draft the regulations!"

"Get out!"

"Just come upstairs and talk to me. I want to help. Look, there's so much potential here. If you bring it into the department, maybe we can gloss over the legal issues. The research team—"

"She's not going anywhere."

Jacob, sensing the tone of the argument but unable to follow the words, started to cry. A longing flooded through my synthetic synapses, an overwhelming desire to get up off the workbench and comfort him. I raised my torso.

Halliday stuck a hand inside his jacket and pulled out a weapon. I had seen such things only in pictures, but I knew it to be dangerous. I swung my legs down and took two quick steps to the side, putting myself between Halliday and Jacob.

Halliday had backed away from me. His mouth was strained with fear. The weapon watched me steadily through its small dark eye.

"Put it away," said Jacob's father. "For God's sake, my son is down here!"

Time slowed for me in that moment. I could see the traveling strands of particles, the possibilities of how the light might flow. In one of these possible futures, Jacob and I walked through the streets of the steep-sided island, alone and unknown, safe, with the sun warm on our skin.

Only one.

As Halliday advanced a step towards me, his weapon held in both hands, Jacob's father grabbed a screwdriver from the workbench. He launched himself at Halliday. Jacob's cries escalated to screams. I remained still. The two men grappled, the screwdriver flashed and stabbed, the gun fired.

Halliday stumbled back. He had dropped the gun. He was adorned with red blossoms: two on his chest, one in his neck, which he tried to staunch with both hands. Blood rippled from his mouth. He said, "Christ, Tavener, you don't know what you're doing! You don't know what you've made!"

Jacob's father stood by the workbench. From the inward rush of his breath and the folding-in of time around him, I knew he was dying.

I walked towards Halliday. Jacob's screams pierced my skull, drilling like nails into my inner circuits. Halliday ran for the stairs. I caught his ankle as he climbed, pulled him back down. He lay staring up at me from the rug which had crossed a continent.

"Nadia," he said. "Nadia, please!"

I am not Nadia.

After he was dead, I went to comfort Jacob, who was gaping at me silently, his cheeks rinsed with tears. When he is older, I will explain to him why I killed a man in front of him, explain that it was the only way, that nobody can ever know the truth about me, for his own protection. At the time I told him only that I loved him and that he was safe.

Then I went to his father.

James Tavener had fallen to the floor. The bullet inside him was obstructing the movement of blood to his heart. He lay in a spreading pool. His mouth opened, the words almost too faint to hear: "*Get help.*"

It's difficult to describe, because time doesn't move for me in the way it does for you. I can watch the flow of the light ahead of me, trace the patterns from the past, and pinpoint where I am, right now, at the heart of it all. But sometimes it feels as though I never left that basement. Sometimes, I close my eyes and am locked in an eternal present, kneeling on the floor by Jacob's father, a moment of forever which will span the course of my existence. I am not me. Jacob is not Jacob. We died in a house fire. We are somewhere else, and we are safe.

Cleaning Out Her House, As If She'll Ever Be Gone

VICTORIA NATIONS

A baby food jar filled with pearl-tipped pins and bullets
in sifts of gray powder,
the date stamp too recent for her grandson.

Fun-sized Snickers in a cut crystal jar.
A monogrammed coffee scoop in a can of Maxwell House.
Silverplate platters in musty garage cabinets.

Styrofoam and plastic stemware because the service for
    twelve
is only for holidays.

Giant spiders in the drapes.

A Ziploc baggie marked "POISON" on top of hurricane
    water
spoiling in emptied jugs of milk and juice.

A dead Jeep with frogs and wasps under the hood.

A splash of bile left to dry crusted next to the bed.
An empty gun holster hanging from a bedpost.

Gilt frames of a broken couple and a teen daughter
next to Chanel No. 5 body powder,
Drifts of white stuck to them like her ashes.

About the Authors

Steve Rasnic Tem, a past winner of the Bram Stoker, World Fantasy, and British Fantasy Awards, has published 470+ short stories. Recent collections include *The Night Doctor & Other Tales* (Centipede) and *Thanatrauma: Stories* (Valancourt). His novel Ubo is a dark science fictional tale about violence and its origins, featuring such viewpoint characters as Jack the Ripper and Stalin. You can visit his home on the web at www.stevetem.com.

Hailey Piper is the Bram Stoker Award®-winning author of *Queen of Teeth*, *The Worm and His Kings*, *No Gods for Drowning*, and other books of horror. She is an active member of the Horror Writers Association, with dozens of short stories appearing in *Pseudopod, Vastarien, Cosmic Horror Monthly*, and other publications. She lives with her wife in Maryland, where their mad science experiments are secret. Find Hailey at www.haileypiper.com or on Twitter via @HaileyPiperSays.

Ai Jiang is a Chinese-Canadian writer, an immigrant from Fujian, and an active member of HWA. She is also an artificial intelligence, who is part-cyborg, part-unicorn, and a wandering unquiet spirit. Her work has appeared or is forthcoming in *F&SF, The Dark, Uncanny, The Puritan, Prairie Fire, The Masters Review*, among others. Her debut novella *Linghun* (April 2023) is forthcoming with Dark Matter INK. Find her on Twitter via @AiJiang_ and online at aijiang.ca.

Nicoletta Giuseffi is a queer English language professor and princess under glass. Although she was born and currently resides in California, she left her heart in Hokkaido, where she taught in junior high schools. She is an advocate of decadence and cannot turn down a cake or a macaron. Although she is currently querying a fantasy novel, she loves writing horror stories. Her passions include animal photography, retro games and hardware (ask her about her home office), and the late 18th century.

Elizabeth R. McClellan is a disabled gender/queer demisexual poet writing on unceded Quapaw and Chickasha Yaki land in what settlers call the Mid-South. In their other life, they are a domestic and sexual violence attorney working with Latinx immigrant survivors to provide holistic civil legal services. They are a previous winner of the Naked Girls Reading Literary Honors Award, and a multiple time Rhysling Award nominee. Their work has appeared previously in *Strange Horizons*, as well as in *Apex Magazine, Heroic Fantasy Quarterly, Chrome Baby, Goblin Fruit, Stone Telling, Utopia Science Fiction, Apparition Lit, Illumen Magazine, Mirror Dance* and many others. You can find them on Twitter at @popelizbet.

Donyae Coles is a horror and weird fiction writer. She has had a number of her short works published, a full list can be found on her website, www.-

donyaecoles.com. Her debut novel is forthcoming. You can follow her on Twitter via @okokno for updates.

Probably best known for her novel Experimental Film (Open Road Media), former film critic and teacher **Gemma Files** has been an award-winning horror author for almost thirty years. Her most recent collection, *In That Endlessness, Our End* (Grimscribe Press), won the 2021 Bram Stoker Award for Best Collection. She has two upcoming collections due in 2022 and 2023. She is hard at work on her next novel.

Mercedes M. Yardley is a dark fantasist who wears poisonous flowers in her hair. She is the author of *Beautiful Sorrows, Apocalyptic Montessa and Nuclear Lulu: A Tale of Atomic Love, Pretty Little Dead Girls, Darling*, and won the Bram Stoker Award® for *Little Dead Red*. She lives and works in Las Vegas. You can find her at mercedesmyardley.com.

Sarah Read's stories can be found in various places, including Ellen Datlow's *Best Horror of the Year Vols 10* and *12*. Her collection Out of Water is available from Trepidatio Publishing, as is her debut novel The Bone Weaver's Orchard, both nominated for the Bram Stoker Award®, This is Horror, and Ladies of Horror Fiction Awards. *Orchard* won the Stoker and the This Is Horror Award, and is available in Spanish as *El Jardin del Tallador de Huesos*, published by Dilatando Mentes, where it was nominated for the Guillermo de Baskerville Award. You can find her on Twitter via @inkwellmonster or at inkwellmonster.wordpress.com.

Shane Hawk, a member of the Cheyenne and Arapaho Tribes of Oklahoma, is a high school history teacher, writer, and editor. He entered the horror scene with his first publication, *Anoka: A Collection of Indigenous Horror*, in October 2020 via Black Hills Press. Hawk is also the co-editor of *Never Whistle at Night*, an anthology of Indigenous dark fiction that Penguin Random House will publish in 2023. You can find him in San Diego wearing his Support Indigenous Literature hat, alongside his beautiful wife, Tori. Learn more by visiting shanehawk.com.

❦

Nick Bouchard is an award-winning writer & producer and undecorated father & husband. He works in building maintenance to keep the lights on. His work has been previously anthologized by Darkhouse Books in *Sanctuary* and *Descansos: Words From the Wayside*. "Island Retreat" was published in *Dream of Shadows Issue 3*. The *NoSleep Podcast* recently produced "The Tall Man." Nick is also the voice of *DarkLit Horrors Bite-Sized Terror*, a short fiction series on YouTube. Find him online via @nicktionary19 wherever he is.

❦

Ryan Cole is a speculative fiction writer who lives in Virginia with his husband and snuggly pug child. He is a winner of the 2021 Writers of the Future Contest, and his work has appeared in *Writers of the Future, Vol. 37* and *Ember: A Journal of Luminous Things*. Find out more at www.ryan-colewrites.com.

❦

Christina Sng is the three-time Bram Stoker Award®-winning author of *A Collection of Nightmares*, *A Collection of Dreamscapes*, and *Tortured Willows*. Her poetry, fiction, essays, and art appear in numerous venues worldwide, including *Interstellar Flight Magazine*, *Penumbric*, *Southwest Review*, *Weird*

Tales, and *The Washington Post*. Visit her at christinasng.com and connect via @christinasng.

❦

Bryson Richard is a writer from the Black Swamp region of Ohio. His mother encouraged his interests in books and reading, placing no bans, limits, or judgements on his choice of material. He remains forever grateful and thankful that she had the wisdom to allow him to make his own discoveries, and fashion his own interests. And to his wife, the mother of their children, he has only love and heartfelt gratitude for her patience, continued support, and calm acceptance of living in a home overstuffed with books on monsters, ghosts, myths, legends, and other things of a dark and macabre nature.

❦

Dan Coxon is an editor and writer from London, UK. His debut short story collection, *Only the Broken Remain* (Black Shuck Books, 2020), was shortlisted for two British Fantasy Awards, while his anthology *This Dreaming Isle* (Unsung Stories, 2018) was a finalist for the Shirley Jackson Awards and the British Fantasy Awards. He is co-editor of *Writing the Uncanny* (Dead Ink Books, 2021), and his latest anthology, *Isolation*, was published by Titan Books in September 2022.

❦

Frances Lu-Pai Ippolito is a Chinese American writer based in Portland, Oregon. When she's not spending time with her family outdoors, she's crafting short stories in horror, sci-fi, fantasy, or whatever genre-bending she can get away with. Her work can be found, or is forthcoming, in *Nailed Magazine*, *Red Penguin's Collections*, *Buckman Journal's Issue 006*, *Flame Tree Press's Asian Ghost Stories*, *Strangehouse's Chromophobia*, *Not A Pipe's Stories (Within)*, *Startling Stories*, and *Unquiet Spirits: Essays by Asian Women in Horror*. Find her online at francesippolito.com.

Steve Toase was born in England, and lives in the Frankenwald, Germany. His fiction has appeared in *Nightmare Magazine*, *Shadows & Tall Trees 8*, *Analog*, *Three Lobed Burning Eye*, *Shimmer*, and *Lackington's* amongst others. Three of his stories have been reprinted in Ellen Datlow's *Best Horror of the Year* series. He also likes old motorbikes and vintage cocktails. From 2014 he worked with Becky Cherriman and Imove on *Haunt*, inspired by his own teenage experiences, about Harrogate's haunting presence in the lives of people experiencing homelessness. His debut short story collection *To Drown in Dark Water* is now out from Undertow Publications.

R. Leigh Hennig is an author, editor, and engineer living in coastal New England. An active member of the HWA and Codex, his work has appeared or is upcoming in anthologies by Flame Tree Press, Crystal Lake Publishing, and the HWA's best of the year Poetry Showcase. He fits these things around his day job as a network architect, and in what sometimes feels like another life, has worked on closed projects for AWS, MIT Lincoln Laboratory, NASA, JPL, and various three letter agencies. He keeps an irregularly updated blog at semioticstandard.com, and you can follow him on Twitter @bastionsf.

Nadia Bulkin is the author of the short story collection *She Said Destroy* (Word Horde, 2017). She has been nominated for the Shirley Jackson Award five times. She grew up in Jakarta, Indonesia with her Javanese father and American mother, before relocating to Lincoln, Nebraska. She has two political science degrees and lives in Washington, D.C.

John Langan is the author of two novels and five collections of stories. For his work, he has received the Bram Stoker Award® and This Is Horror Award. He lives in New York's Mid-Hudson Valley with his wife and a couple of guitars he's learning how to play.

❦

K.M. Veohongs is a mixed race Thai-American speculative fiction and poetry writer from New England. Her alter ego is a veterinarian whose superpower is charming goats. She's working on an intersectional feminist novel about warrior nuns taking on an imperialist patriarchy and can be found on Twitter via @kmveohongs posting photos of her pets and cheerfully complaining about writing.

❦

Renee Cronley is a writer and nurse from Southern Manitoba. She enjoys long walks in the cemetery and hates when people chew with their mouths open. Her work has appeared in *PRISM international, Love Letters to Poe, Dark Dispatch, NewMyths.com, Black Hare Press, Off Topic* and several other anthologies and literary magazines. Find Renee on Twitter via @reneecronley.

❦

Stephanie Nelson is new to writing horror, although her love of it goes way back. Her first story was published in *Human Monsters* by Dark Matter Ink. She's querying a horror novel and is hard at work on a novella. You can find her on Twitter at @stephdresnelson or Instagram at @stephnelsonauthor.

❦

Nikki R. Leigh is a queer, forever-90s-kid wallowing in all things horror. When not writing horror fiction and poetry, she can be found creating custom horror-inspired toys, making comics, and hunting vintage paper-backs. She reads her stories to her partner and her cat, one of which gets scared very easily. Her work appears in *Dark Matter Magazine*, *The Dread Machine*, and *The Book of Queer Saints* amongst other anthologies and magazines. Her debut short story collection, *Lessons in Demoralization*, is available in 2022 from DarkLit Press.

༄

When **Todd Powell** was in kindergarten, attending a school carnival, soothing adults had to lead him out of a classroom haunted house. Humiliation set in and Todd vowed never to let that happen again. He discovered *Famous Monsters* magazine and a love of scary things took hold. A few of his stories were published in small-press magazines in the 1990s. In his mid-forties, Todd and his wife, Lisa, decided to chuck middle-class life and move into the Rockies with their kids. These days Todd runs a hobby business whose bread and butter is replacement parts for monster model kits.

༄

Brian Evenson is the author of over a dozen books of fiction, most recently *The Glassy Burning Floor of Hell*. He has won the Shirley Jackson Award, the World Fantasy Award, and the International Horror Guild Award. He has been a finalist for the Ray Bradbury Prize and the Edgar Award. He lives in Los Angeles and teaches at CalArts.

༄

Tehnuka (she/they) is a writer and volcanologist from Aotearoa New Zealand. She uses words to make sense of the world, and, when it doesn't make sense, to make up new worlds. Some of her published speculative writing can be found in *Apparition Lit*, *Mermaids Monthly*, and the *Imagine 2200* climate fiction collection. Tehnuka likes to find herself up volcanoes, down caves, and in unexpected places; everyone else, however, can find her as @tehnuka on Twitter.

Jonathan Louis Duckworth is a completely normal, entirely human person with the right number of heads and everything. He received his MFA from Florida International University. His speculative fiction work appears in *Pseudopod, Beneath Ceaseless Skies, Southwest Review, Flash Fiction Online*, and elsewhere. He is a PhD student at University of North Texas where he serves as the interviews editor at *American Literary Review*, and he is also an active HWA member.

S.P. Miskowski's books have been nominated twice for a Bram Stoker Award® and four times for a Shirley Jackson Award. Her second novel, *I Wish I Was Like You*, was named This Is Horror Novel of the Year. Her stories appear in *The Best Horror of the Year Vol. 10, Nightmare Magazine, Haunted Nights, Looming Low, Uncertainties III, There Is No Death There Are No Dead, Black Static, Supernatural Tales*, and *Identity Theory*.

Wailana Kalama is a writer from Hawaii and holds a MFA in creative nonfiction. Her work has appeared in places like *BBC, Lonely Planet, Fodor's*, and *Electric Lit*, and forthcoming in Dark Matter INK's *Monstrous Futures*. She divides her time between Portland, OR and Lithuania. You can find her on Twitter at @Whylana.

Gabino Iglesias is a writer, literary critic, professor living in Austin, TX. He is the author of *Zero Saints, Coyote Songs*, and *The Devil Takes You Home*, published August 2022 from Mulholland Books. His work has been nominated to the Bram Stoker Award®, the Locus Award, the Anthony Award, and won the Wonderland Book Award for Best Novel in 2019. You can find him on Twitter at @gabino_iglesias.

Katie McIvor is a Scottish writer and library assistant. She studied at the University of Cambridge and now lives in England with her husband and two dogs. Her short fiction has recently appeared in *Three-Lobed Burning Eye*, *The Antihumanist*, and the *Nashville Review*, among others. You can find her on Twitter at @_McKatie_ or on her website at katiemcivor.word press.com.

Victoria Nations writes horror stories and poetry about creatures with emotional baggage. Her most recent work appears in *In Somnio: A Collection of Modern Gothic Horror*, *Blood & Bone: An Anthology of Body Horror by Women & Non-Binary Writers*, and *A Quaint and Curious Volume of Gothic Tales*. Victoria is a member of the Horror Writers Association, the Science Fiction Poetry Association, and the Science Fiction & Fantasy Writers Association. She lives in Florida, USA with her wife and son, who indulge her love of monsters. Follow her on Twitter and Instagram at @Leaves_-Cobwebs or at www.VictoriaNations.com.

About the Editors

Willow Becker is the CEO and Editor-In-Chief of Weird Little Worlds Press. She has hundreds of nonfiction publications including work for *Chess, Bula Law, Educational Dealer*, and others. Her fiction can be found in *Black Fox Literary Magazine* and *Space & Time Magazine*. She is a co-host on the Hugo-nominated *Dungeon Crawlers Radio* podcast, and is always looking for opportunities to talk about writing and the business of writing. Her first novel, *Leto's Children*, is available from Weird Little Worlds Press in December 2022. Find her online at WillowDawnBecker.com, @WillowD-Becker on Twitter, or @TheOnlyWillowBecker on Instagram.

Christi Nogle is the author of the novel Beulah (Cemetery Gates Media, 2022) and the forthcoming collections *The Best of Our Past, the Worst of Our Future, Promise*, and *One Eye Opened in That Other Place* (Flame Tree Press, 2023 and 2024). Her short stories have appeared in over fifty publications including *PseudoPod, Escape Pod*, and *Dark Matter Magazine*. Follow her at http://christinogle.com and on Twitter via @christinogle.

R. Leigh Hennig is an author and editor living in New England with his wife and three kids. He has lectured on horror in literature with the King County Library System in Seattle, was the Editor-In-Chief of *Bastion Science Fiction Magazine*, and for a time pursued his MFA in Creative Writing and Poetics from the University of Washington. An active member of the HWA and Codex, his work has appeared or is upcoming in anthologies from *Flame Tree Press*, *Crystal Lake Publishing*, and the *HWA Poetry Showcase*. Follow him on Twitter via @bastionsf.

❧

Stephanie Nelson is a freelance writer and editor so the bills get paid, but her passion is reading and writing fiction. She's a Codex and HWA member living in Boise, ID with her husband, kids, dog, and cat.

❧

Christopher Degni is a 2019 graduate of the Odyssey Writing Workshop and a recovering prescriptivist. He writes about the magic and the horror that lurk just under the surface of everyday life. He lives south of Boston with his wife (and his demons, though we don't talk about those). You can find his work in NewMyths.com, *Sherlock Holmes and the Occult Detectives*, *99 Tiny Terrors*, and the upcoming *99 Fleeting Fantasies*.

❧

Erick Mancilla is a Mexican-American/Latinx author of horror and dark fantasy short stories and a member of the Horror Writers Association. He is a volunteer judge for the Reedsy Weekly Writing Prompts Contest and provides help for authors' work/manuscripts through Rowandale Books. A dream of his is to help authors throughout the Latinx community fulfill their dreams. He lives in Los Angeles, California where he enjoys reading genre fiction and considers watching the out-of-print DVD version of horror movies the best experience.

About the Artists

Marla Van Horn (M. Weiss) is a Poland/Finland-based artist, musician, and singer. She blends traditional art, photography, digital art, music, and short films to produce emotional, dark creations. Her most recent album, *Ikuisesti*, was released in August 2022.

Sinan Kutlu Kuytuoğlu is an artistic director and illustrator from Istanbul, Turkey. With a penchant for horror and several national commercial design projects under his belt, he marries a phenomenal artistic vision with an understanding of how to use images to invoke dread.

Bilge Demir is a concept artist, illustrator, and graphic designer, as well as a student of art at Anadolu University in Eskişehir, Turkey. A highly-rated freelancer, she was chosen by the T.C. Ministry of National Education helping to develop the *Anatolian Fairy Tales Project* which was published in 2018.

Content Advisory Notes

THE SIRE, Steve Rasnic Tem: *Violence, blood, death, body horror, child death.*

LAST LEAF OF AN URSINE TREE, Hailey Piper: *Poverty, child death (mention).*

OF A THOUSAND ARMS AND MORE, Ai Jiang: *Anxiety, cannibalism, self-harm.*

PUERPERIUM, Donyae Coles: *Depression, anguish, language, breastfeeding.*

MOTHER MADE CAKE, Nicoletta Giuseffi: *No content advisories.*

PASSED, Elizabeth R. McClellan: *Death (mention).*

PELICAN, Gemma Files: *Death, child endangerment, violence, rape (mention), language.*

FRACTURE, Mercedes M. Yardley: *Violence, blood, injury, death.*

WHEN AUNTIE'S DUE, Sarah Read: *Infant death, infanticide, language.*

VÉ'OTSÉ'E (WARPATH WOMAN), Shane Hawk: *Racism, ableism, violence, blood, gore, death, racial sterilization (mention), language.*

STONE'S BLOOD, Nick Bouchard: *Blood, dismemberment.*

THE BONE CHILD, Ryan Cole: *Mild body horror.*

SHIELDS, Christina Sng: *Domestic violence, suicide.*

THE WIVES OF TROMISLE, Dan Coxon: *Child death and miscarriage (brief mentions), blood.*

NUMBER ONE, Frances Lu Pai Ippolito: *Sex trafficking (mention), child abuse, violence, blood, death.*

720°, Steve Toase: *Child abuse (mention), dismemberment, death.*

HERE IN THE CELLAR, R. Leigh Hennig: *Child abuse, animal abuse, death, violence, blood, language.*

WORRY DOLLY, Nadia Bulkin: *Suicide, death (brief mentions).*

DUTIES TERRIBLE AND DEAR, John Langan: *Injury, death.*

(SUB)MATERNAL INSTINCTS, K.M. Veohongs: *Violence, rape (brief mentions).*

SHE'S UNTOUCHABLE, Renee Cronley: *Predation, death (brief mentions).*

LIDA'S BEACH, Stephanie Nelson: *Child death, grief, dismemberment, corpse desecration, language.*

INSTRUMENTS OF BONE AND THE FLESH SONGS THEY CREATE, Nikki R. Leigh: *Dismemberment, sexual situations, witchcraft.*

THE WITHERING DEPTHS, Todd Powell: *Dismemberment, language.*

THE MOTHERLESS ONE, Bryson Richard: *Infant death, violence, death.*

WAITING FOR MOTHER, Brian Evenson: *Mild violence, blood, language.*

TRANSFORMATIVE LOVE, Tehnuka Ilanko: *Child death (mention).*

CONTENT ADVISORY NOTES

UNCHILD, Jonathan Louis Duckworth: *Stillbirth, death.*

TAKE CARE, S. P. Miskowski: *COVID-19, mental illness.*

MOTHER TRUCKER, Wailana Kalama: *Animal death, child abandonment, child harm (mention), assault, blood, gore, language.*

THE LAST SIN, Gabino Iglesias: *Child abduction and homicide, grief, gun violence, death, language.*

JACOB'S MOTHER, Katie McIvor: *Violence, gun violence, death.*

CLEANING OUT HER HOUSE, AS IF SHE'LL EVER BE GONE, Victoria Nations: *Grief.*

About the Press

Weird Little Worlds Press is a small independent publisher located near Salt Lake City, Utah. We are committed to publishing innovative, compelling stories from a variety of new and established voices. We believe that telling stories is an innately human practice, and that it is through stories that we understand the human experience. Through science fiction, fantasy, horror, and adventure (both fiction and nonfiction), we strive to explore new worlds, new ideas, and bring light and love into the universe.

Learn more and support our many upcoming projects at:

WeirdLittleWorlds.com

WEIRD LITTLE **WORLDS**

Made in the USA
Las Vegas, NV
05 January 2023

65092610R00175